D1565343

TAKEOVER

It took a few minutes for Mac's mind to believe his eyes. It was the stuff of nightmares. In the moonlight he could see small groups of people being prodded along by masked men with snub-nosed machine guns. There wasn't much question. A terrorist group had taken over the Molokai-Surf resort. And things were going to get a lot worse . . .

Books by Ralph Glendinning
from Jove

THE ULTIMATE GAME
DEATH MATCH

DEATH MATCH

RALPH GLENDINNING

A JOVE BOOK

DEATH MATCH

A Jove Book / published by arrangement with
the author

PRINTING HISTORY
Jove edition / July 1985

All rights reserved.
Copyright © 1985 by Ralph O. Glendinning
This book may not be reproduced in whole or in part,
by mimeograph or any other means, without permission.
For information address: The Berkley Publishing Group,
200 Madison Avenue, New York, N.Y. 10016.

ISBN: 0-515-08225-2

Jove books are published by The Berkley Publishing Group,
200 Madison Avenue, New York, N.Y. 10016.
The words "A JOVE BOOK" and the "J" with sunburst
are trademarks belonging to Jove Publications, Inc.

PRINTED IN THE UNITED STATES OF AMERICA

DEATH
MATCH

PROLOGUE

Kepuhi Beach, Molokai—1970

The young girl stood motionless on the emerald cliff high above the crashing surf. To the west, the vast Pacific stretched almost to the setting sun. The shimmering rays glistened on her golden body. Flecks of fire sparkled in her dark red hair. With eyes focused on the foamy wake surging among the rocks, she ticked off the seconds in her mind. The timing had to be perfect. Her leg muscles tensed.

From the beach, the old Hawaiian with the wrinkled face watched, idly drawing circles in the sand with a gnarled walking stick. He shook his head slowly. His only grandchild. That wahine was wild . . . daring . . . with more courage than all the young men in the village put together. He remembered only one other who had ever jumped from that cliff. But that had been long ago,

1

in the days of the high chiefs, the *niaupio*. He closed his
eyes when he saw her dive.

As she knifed through the air, the girl's heart was
singing. Down below, she'd enter the secret grotto
under the rocks where the ancient chiefs once gathered
to discuss secret matters, then follow the old lava tube
and come out in the forest just over the hill, close to her
home. The old man who'd been watching from the
beach would wait until dark for her to reappear. He'd
think she'd drowned.

PART ONE

ALOHA

CHAPTER ONE

Molokai-Surf Resort—1985

Fire flexed her shoulders, fluffed up her pillow, and reached to turn off her reading light. She inhaled deeply on her cigarette, then snuffed it out in the ashtray on the bedside table. The moonlight shining through the soft night clouds made spidery patterns on the wall.

The tall, naked girl lay back on the bed and closed her eyes, the sounds of the surf a rhythmic background for her thoughts. The plan was diabolical. Its strength was its daring and simplicity. In just a few days, she'd capture the attention of the entire world and perhaps change the course of history. Taking the hostages would be easy. No one expected it. They'd huddle together, like lambs at slaughter. Her lips curled into a smile. Then the fun would begin.

Fire felt a thrill of excitement mixed with apprehension. It had been her plan, all the way. She ran through it quickly in her mind. So far, their cover had been perfect. The takeover of the resort would be routine. Their demands shocking. One for one. She smiled again. An offer that couldn't be ignored. An end to the nuclear arms race. Public pressure would demand that the government give in. They'd have to . . . or face the consequences.

The dancing moonlight moved from the wall and played on the girl's body. She adjusted her position slightly so her eyes could see her reflection in the mirror on the wall. A tiny shadow of doubt came into her mind. The team itself. They were all professionals. Cold-blooded killers. A *Who's Who* of terrorists from around the world. Damn, if only she could have selected them herself. She'd argued, but they'd been assigned. It was a wild group, but they were all willing to die and she was in charge. What more could she ask? Her mind pushed the doubt aside.

What if the plan failed? She breathed deeply to calm herself. She didn't plan to die. Her escape plan was perfect. It couldn't fail. Her body quivered at the thought of the danger, excitement stirring her desire. A tongue of silvery light licked at her lower body. She parted her legs slightly to accommodate it. Her fingers moved slowly downward, tracing the course of the dancing moonbeam. Her excitement built, her body tensed and trembled, until finally sleep quieted her breathing.

Hours later, Fire tossed violently, face contorted. Her dream was one of vivid color and raw violence. A river of bright yellow-orange molten lava flowed toward the ocean, with Pele, Goddess of Fire, riding on the foremost billow.

The tall girl could smell the sulphur. The earth shook with harmonic tremors, then cracked and opened into giant fire fountains shooting geysers of boiling orange magma high into the air. The molten lava slowly engulfed the Molokai-Surf. The hostages huddled together on the cliff, and as the sea of incandescent magma approached, one by one they jumped screaming into the ocean below, into water whipped white by the frenzied thrashing of a pack of killer whales, supremely efficient predators, stripping away flesh, piece by piece . . . The piercing screams of the hostages died slowly.

The river of fire reached the cliff line. On the horizon the sun was setting, the sky a blaze of orange fire. The tall girl was sleeping now, her face lit up like a child's.

High above the Pacific, United's Flight One droned on toward Hawaii. In seat 17A, Mac McGregor stirred briefly, then settled back as if to sleep. His black eye mask hid the fact that his eyes were wide open.

It had been a two-minute meeting. The new president had been direct. "All I can say, McGregor, is that the sales force has not responded to your direction. We've decided the company needs . . ."

The young executive had hesitated, so Mac had stood and said, "Thank you, sir." He'd put extra emphasis on the *sir*. "It's been a pleasure."

Now thinking about his career—a forced retirement —Mac swallowed hard. It wasn't his work. He was good. Everyone had always said so. More importantly, as a vice president they'd paid him well. But he'd earned every cent. The old-fashioned way. He'd outperformed everyone else.

No, it was his damn age. No one had mentioned it, but it had been no coincidence that the meeting had occurred just two days after he'd turned sixty. The computer kids were taking over, with their mechanized thinking—Mac sighed—and their new brooms. Physically, he was still in great shape. It was the daily jogging and the squash. He could still beat anyone in the club. Mentally, he was still running on a full tank. Thirty

years of hard work and then in two minutes it was all
over. Not even a gold watch. He smiled bitterly. All that
experience down the drain. Hell, he wasn't ready for
retirement. A gun should be empty before it's hung on
the wall. Marge was right. He'd have to forget about the
past, get involved in some positive projects. His eyes
closed.

A crease of worry crossed Marge McGregor's face as
she watched her husband's momentary grimace. The
sleep would do him good. The vacation in Hawaii had
been her idea. A week of golf and total relaxation at a
new resort on the very tip of Molokai. The travel agent
had described it as remote, beautiful, and exclusive. Out
of this world, but not out of the country. Few people
even knew it existed. Just what they both needed, the
chance to unwind in seclusion, bask in the sun and sort
out how they'd handle life after retirement. Old age was
a matter of mind. If you didn't mind, age didn't matter.
The retirement had come as a real blow to Mac. His
pride had been hurt and there had been two weeks of
self-pity. Time would make it bearable, but the turnaround had to start deep inside. This vacation was the
first step.

"You'll love it," she'd said. "I doubt it," had been
his immediate reply.

Marge had been secretly pleased by the company's
decision. It would have been better had they planned for
retirement, but then Mac would never have accepted the
decision. The office had become a paper prison. Now
they could travel, entertain, and enjoy one another.
With what they had saved and the company's golden
parachute indexed against inflation, their future would
be comfortable. Hopefully, by the time they went home
they'd be totally relaxed, measuring time like the
Hawaiians, by the tides and the passage of the sun.

The crease of worry on her face had been replaced by a smile. Mac was still handsome. Well . . . at least to her. Once he could have posed for those Arrow shirt ads. No longer. The years had taken their toll. Now it was tough to tell where his weathered face stopped and his head began. He was getting very thin on top. Marge smiled more broadly. A perfect couple, she was getting fat on the bottom.

Her hand reached over and touched Mac's as she whispered, "Did you sleep well?"

"Hell, no!" he grumbled. "I dreamt I was awake."

The rectangular service room in the basement under the kitchen in the main building was small, with little ventilation. In the late morning the heat was almost unbearable. The one small window near the ceiling was streaked with mist. The tall girl's T-shirt clung to her body.

The cobalt blue eyes of the young man across the table watched the jiggling motion the T-shirt made as the girl slit open the large carton and checked the contents, making notes on a small pad of paper. Sweat beaded on his forehead. When she was finished, he closed the carton, lifted it from the table, and placed it on the growing stack of cartons against the wall on his side of the table. Each carton was stenciled plainly in large block letters: SAVE THE WHALES—MOLOKAI-SURF. There was no other printing on the carton. He did his work quickly, watching the girl turn, bend over, and pick up the last carton. The cheeks of her worn denim jeans strained against the machine stitching of the thigh seams. The tight jeans fit like a second skin.

The man licked his lips and wiped the perspiration from his forehead with the back of his arm, crazy thoughts running through his head. Christ, this girl Fire was driving him wild. He closed his eyes trying to regain his composure. This was an all-important mission, for which he'd traveled halfway around the world in a roundabout fashion. It was vital to the whole cause. Yet all he could think of was her beautiful breasts and her perfect ass.

"That does it," she said, a look of relief on her face. "Here, Marco, you double check the list." She handed the small pad to him, lifted the last carton off the table, and sat down on it.

Marco glanced at the list, checking it against his memory of what he'd seen loaded onto the plane in Havana. Twenty-six AK-47 assault rifles, two per person; four rocket launchers; two flame throwers; six cartons of grenades; two hundred pounds of C-4 explosive compound in plastic packages; two SAM antiaircraft missile launchers; twenty missiles; two cartons of rockets; six thousand rounds of 7.62mm bullets, half hollow nosed, half regular. He grinned to himself. The slim bullets were designed to heel over as they struck the target to crash through the body sideways. The hollow nosed ones inflicted horrible wounds. They were being used by the Russians in Afghanistan with devastating effect.

Suddenly Marco frowned, glanced up at the tall redhead, and said, "Oh, shit. The camouflage outfits. They're not here."

Fire nodded. "I unpacked them earlier. They're in my room. I'll distribute them tonight, after we check the food supplies. Feeding these rich tourists is going to be a major problem."

"No problem at all." Marco grinned. "Let the fat pricks starve."

Fire smiled. She'd thought of that. Rising, she said, "Let's get out of this sauna. You can only do so much planning . . . then . . ." Her voice trailed off.

"A little nervous?" Marco's voice carried a hint of sarcasm.

Fire stared coldly at the handsome Cuban and said nothing.

"You'll feel better once we make our move."

The girl's face brightened, her eyes sparkled. "In two days, Marco, the whole world will know about us and Operation One for One."

"Do you really think they'll buy it?" Marco asked, with a questioning voice.

"They should. It's one way to save the world from a nuclear nightmare," Fire answered.

"Yeah. They should, but will they?" Marco's blue eyes searched the girl's face.

Fire threw back her head and laughed. Then, looking straight at Marco, she replied, "No. You know fucking well they won't. We'll probably have to kill the hostages."

Marco grinned and slapped his hands together.

They double locked the room with padlocks and walked down a dark corridor, emerging from the service entrance at the side of the main building.

"Follow me. I'll show you a shortcut," Fire said, ducking behind the bougainvillea lining the side of the lanai. Marco's eyes widened. At the end of a narrow passageway totally shielded by the flowering bushes, he could see the sparkling waves. They came out on the top of the cliff, walked up the steps to the lanai, selected a table, and ordered two glasses of chilled chablis. The sun was bright, small wisps of clouds flecked the blue sky, the breeze was balmy and refreshing.

Two small, bright yellow birds lit on the table, looking for bread crumbs. "Japanese white eyes," Fire said, watching the birds hopping about. Marco shooed them away.

Under the table, Marco's leg moved against the jeans

that had been tormenting his genes. Feeling the pressure, Fire pulled her leg away, sighed deeply, put down her drink, and spoke sharply.

"Marco, for the last hour I've felt your eyes crawling all over my body. You're looking for a playmate. It's not me." Her green eyes flashed. Seeing the look on his face, she added, "Not now, anyhow. Maybe, when this is over. If we're still . . ." Her voice trailed off.

"Alive." Marco completed her thought, then added, "Not a chance." Eyes glistening, he moistened his lips and reached out to touch her hand. They sat in silence for a few moments, then Marco spoke again.

"You're very beautiful. I'd like the memory to take with me."

"Thanks, Marco." The tall girl suddenly smiled, a negative smile. "But no thanks. You're just not my type." She laughed aloud. "I make it a rule never to sleep with anyone crazier than I am."

The McGregors settled into the Molokai-Surf quickly. Rock Resorts had carved out a five-star oasis from a windswept desert. It was remote, isolated, and peaceful, nestled on the edge of a cliff overlooking beautiful Kepuhi Beach on Molokai's western coast.

An attractive wahine with an orchid in her hair showed them to ocean suite seven. It had two king-size beds, one of which they knew they wouldn't use, and a small kitchenette, with stove, sink, and refrigerator. Marge quickly noticed it had no pots or pans. She laughed. She wasn't planning to cook anyhow.

Marge stood in the center of their suite, face beaming, eyes sweeping through the attractive dining and sitting areas, out to their private lanai and the ocean beyond.

"Mac, this is fantastic. No television. No telephones. No traffic. No newspapers. We unpack once and that's it. We're at the end of the road. All the lines are cut. It's total seclusion."

Moving close to Mac, she put her hands on his shoulders, drew his face to hers, and kissed him warmly.

"Just the two of us."

In the late afternoon, they tried nine holes of the resort's eighteen-hole championship golf course. They agreed it compared favorably with anything they'd ever played. But Mac had left his game on the mainland, mind elsewhere, concentration lacking. For seven holes they played even. Then on the eighth hole, Marge chipped a short iron from the frogs' hair to within three inches of the flag for a gimmee, and on the undulating ninth green boldly stroked home a thirty-five-foot no-brainer. Without benefit of handicap, she'd beaten Mac two up in nine holes. It was the first victory for her bright orange ball. Grudgingly, Mac congratulated his wife, saying, "There's a first time for everything." Deep down he thought it was a lousy way to start a vacation. His wife was now beating him at his own game. It was never easy to lose.

After a quiet but elegant dinner in the Koa Lounge, they'd sat on their lanai watching the strange shadows cast by the flickering outdoor oil lamps and listening to the rustling of the palm fronds. The smell of salt in the air was regenerative.

"Close your eyes and listen to the sounds," Marge suggested. "It's so relaxing."

"I hear better with my eyes open," Mac replied.

Now in bed, Marge was asleep, Mac awake. Still in a bad mood, he felt older than dirt. Clearly, he had to open his eyes, open his mind, and let the sunshine in. Marge had been right, this was the place to do it. An environment of total tranquility. The light breeze swept through the open windows, carrying with it sounds from

the suite next door. A young couple had just arrived.
Obviously newlyweds, they were doing what newlyweds
do best. They'd been at it all evening, bouncing on and
off the bed and one another. It might not be a Guinness
record, Mac thought, but they were setting a damn good
average. Now the bride was screeching her desires
aloud. It was obvious that while the groom was finished, she wasn't. Mac hoped he would soon find the
bride's volume-control button and turn her off. As he
tried to go to sleep, Mac was tempted to go next door
and show the guy where it was located.

The fourteen-foot, light gray Zodiac inflatable was
skimming the water at a speed of almost twenty knots.
A pair of sleek, spotted dolphins was streaking before
the bow wave. One after the other they leapt jubilantly
into the air, crisscrossing in front of the boat.

A tall girl with long black hair and golden skin knelt
in the bow, head cocked as she listened, a look of rapture on her face. She gestured to the broad-shouldered
young man in the stern.

"Michael, listen! Hear what they're saying? They like
you."

"It sounds like a creaky pair of rusty hinges,"
Michael replied.

Kona nodded. "To you maybe, but you never listen.
They're telling us they want to be friends. Look at the
smile on the face of that one. He's laughing at what you
said."

Kona made several quick gestures with her hands and
abruptly as they had come, the dolphins were gone.

"Can you really understand them?" Michael asked,
staring at the back of the tall girl.

Kona turned and sat on the bottom of the small rubber boat facing Michael. Adjusting her white bikini, she

smiled, then spoke slowly, as if choosing the words carefully.

"In Kaneohe Bay, NOSC has a big lab, they've been studying the behavior of dolphins for years. Can dolphins talk? The scientists disagree, but most of them don't listen, either."

"Their swimming is incredible, like a water ballet." The young blond shrugged his large shoulders. "How can they do that?"

"With bionic sonar," Kona explained. "Those staccato clicks you hear are the sounds of echolation. Dolphins emit clicks through their foreheads like a sonic laser beam. This beam focuses, strikes a target, and returns. The dolphin instantly computes the object's distance, direction, speed, size, and configuration."

The young man wiped his tanned face with his hand and said nothing.

"They could pinpoint this hairpin if I dropped it near them. A dolphin's complex brain weighs more than yours, Michael." Kona laughed and added softly, "or mine."

"But can they talk?" Michael persisted.

"They whistle, chirp, squeak, click, groan, and—they talk." Kona emphasized the word *talk*.

"Really talk?"

"With an elaborate language."

"Look. They're coming back," Michael said, pointing.

"I asked them to check something out for me," Kona said, rising on one knee and facing forward. Both dolphins started chattering at once.

Kona called out several times. In close formation, the dolphins surfed on a swell, dove, then thrusting forward with powerful flukes, leapt directly over the Zodiac, clearing it by at least six feet.

"The dolphins say there are humpback whales about six miles due north. We can still catch them if we hurry," Kona reported.

Michael stared at Kona, a look of amazement on his face. Saying nothing, the blond shook his head in disbelief, then headed the Zodiac on a northerly course.

They spotted three whales at a distance of about two miles. The whales were spouting water and coming directly toward them. Beating their tail flukes up and down for forward thrust and steering with stubby foreflippers, they were cruising at a steady four knots an hour.

Kona shook her head sadly, then spoke in a low voice, as much to herself as to Michael.

"Poor things have to breathe. They're mammals just like we are. But those spouts of air filled with moisture from their lungs are a dead giveaway. Whalers spot them easily. As smart as they are, the whales don't have a chance."

When they had closed to within a quarter mile, Kona signaled Michael to slow the Zodiac and then cut the outboard engine. Michael gave her a questioning glance, then did as the tall girl had suggested, placing the small inflatable directly in the path of the oncoming whales. After all, he thought, anyone who could talk to dolphins . . . Next she'd be out there walking on the water among the whales. But he looked again and gulped. These creatures were gigantic, each thirty to forty feet long.

Suddenly, the largest whale breached. As tall as a four-story building, the whale rocketed into the air, turning its massive black and white body slowly before falling back with a tremendous splash. The Zodiac rocked from the waves, as a plume of water shot fifty feet into the air and sprayed down on them.

"Holy Mother of God!" exclaimed Michael. "He'll swallow the boat!"

Kona laughed. "Don't worry. That's just a medium-sized humpback saying aloha, with a forty-ton belly flop. He's glad to be back."

Michael remembered the story of Jonah that his grandmother had told him. He still wasn't sure that the monster wouldn't swallow the boat, but Kona seemed sure, and she should know.

"Back from where?" he asked, using his bravest voice.

"All the way from the Arctic . . . six thousand miles."

"How do you know where they've been?" Michael asked.

"The dolphins told me," Kona answered, green eyes sparkling.

"Holy Mother of God!" he repeated.

"Michael, I'm kidding." The girl laughed. "Humpbacks don't have teeth. Their mouths have curtains of bony plates, called baleens, with which they strain their food from the water. They eat krill—tiny shrimplike creatures that grow in the Arctic. Every year the whales migrate up to the Arctic and eat for four or five months. Before it freezes they come back here, to give birth or to mate. It's obvious. They're coming back from their feeding grounds—the Arctic."

The blond looked puzzled. "What do they eat here?"

"They don't," Kona replied. "It's the ultimate diet. Once they leave the Arctic, the whales fast for almost eight months, living off their internal fat."

"They don't eat anything?" Michael asked, suddenly feeling hunger pangs.

"Nothing. They'll stay here all winter and start back in the spring. The trip back will take two or three months. Look, Michael, look!''

The smallest humpback, a thirty-foot male, moving slowly and deliberately, glided under the Zodiac, his huge bulk dwarfing the rubber inflatable.

"He'll flip us over," Michael shouted, reaching for the starter cord of the outboard.

"Sit still," Kona commanded. "He won't attack unless he feels threatened."

Rising on her knees, Kona reached over the side, arm extended toward the whale. Slowly, the whale made a gentle turn and rose to within inches of her outstretched hand. With huge eyes he watched the golden-skinned girl, hesitated, and then pressed softly against Kona's fingers. Slowly, gently, Kona stroked the giant mammal's head and lips. The whale slid his nose under the rubber inflatable, gently lifted the boat and turned it around. Then, taking a long look at Kona, he dove to follow the other two humpbacks.

"Fantastic!'' What a sight!'' Michael shouted.

"A very gentle creature. It wants to be friends," Kona said quietly. "And men slaughter them with such ruthless cruelty." There was bitterness in her voice.

Michael started the outboard and turned the Zodiac toward Molokai. Kona undid her bikini straps and leaned back against the cushion in the bow, thinking. The sun glistened on her face and body as she closed her eyes.

A female and two males. The usual *ménage-à-trois*. The whales would start courtship and love play now. It was always quite a ritual. The two males would chase the female, but only one would prevail, normally the larger male. In lovemaking, the couple would swim close to the surface in intricate synchronous patterns, two heads emerging periodically above the water, side by side.

Kona opened her eyes. Michael was staring at her body, sweat glistening on his face. Sitting up, she retied her bikini straps and laughed to herself. It didn't make any difference what the species, the damned males were all the same.

Mac McGregor drained the mai-tai and beckoned for another. The smiling young wahine in a flowered sarong saw his motion and brought the tray of drinks over to him.

"*Mahalo*," he said, taking two. Watching the hula motions of her hips as she moved away, he grinned. It was tough to keep the eyes on the hands.

Mac was finally enjoying the taste of the tropics. The drinks, compliments of the Molokai-Surf, made him lighthearted. The sunset cocktail party, on the terrace overlooking the sea, was another free offering from the hotel.

"A chance to meet the other guests," Marge had said, bubbling with enthusiasm. Trivia time, Mac had thought. The same old questions. "Isn't it beautiful?" "Isn't the weather perfect?" "Where do you live?" "What do you do?" Mac swallowed hard. Now he didn't do anything. He'd never enjoyed meeting new people. They were always someone you didn't know.

Mac inhaled deeply. The air was salty. He looked around, then admitted to himself, it hadn't been a bad day. They'd taken the rental car and had spent eight hours sightseeing Molokai, a delightfully lonely experience. It was a small, rather stark island, shaped like a shoe, with few people and spectacular scenery. They'd seen sheer cliffs that hung from the clouds to the crashing sea below, incredible rain forests, taro patches, valleys filled with delicate ferns, and misty waterfalls too numerous to count. They'd explored ancient fish-

ponds built for royalty from coral and rocks half a ton
in size; burial grounds as big as football fields built over
six centuries ago; a sandalwood pit, a gigantic hole the
size of a ship's hold dug in the early 1800s. When the
natives had filled this pit with sandalwood, they knew
they'd cut enough for a shipload.

After a light lunch, they'd driven to the top of Ka-
laupapa lookout on the Pali coastline. The lookout
provided an incredible view of the isolated, yet beautiful peninsula. Where Father Damien had founded his
famous church in a living graveyard, bringing hope to
the outcast, the mutilated, and the forsaken, until he,
too, had contracted leprosy and died taking care of his
people. Marge insisted that they visit the colony. They'd
made arrangements with the local rent-a-mule company
to ride down and back up a two-thousand-foot rocky
cliff to visit the patients. Fortunately that trip was
several days off; maybe he could talk Marge out of it.
With his current run of luck, he'd probably catch the
damn disease.

During the drive they had passed miles of swaying
palm trees, pineapple fields, sugar plantations, maca-
damia nut groves, flowering bougainvillea, scented pine
forests, tangled bamboo thickets, and trackless beaches.
They'd stopped at the phallic rock and both had
laughed while admiring the six-foot high natural rock
formation. Marge had said, "It's another big Mac."
Her eyes had sparkled and then she'd laughed. "But
mine's better. I never wanted the biggest, only the
best."

On the way back to the remote end of the island
where the Molokai-Surf was located, their last stop had
been at Papohaku Beach. They'd both wanted to find
an unspoiled beach and put some footprints on it, and
this was the most spectacular beach this side of the

South Pacific. Walking hand in hand, they'd collected a beautiful cowrie and almost enough puka shells for Marge to contemplate making a necklace. Then they'd walked past a nudie group, several young couples sunning their buns with nothing on but the radio, recharging themselves with solar energy. Molokai was truly a magic land of endless wonders.

Mac had found four heart-shaped lucky beans that had floated in from some faraway place. According to local legend, the four beans could bring him four days of good luck. He sighed. It was about time. If there were any truth to the legend, he'd spend the rest of his vacation on the beach looking for lucky beans. Now, on the terrace, Mac gazed out at the sea, thinking upon what they'd seen, sights so spectacular he knew they'd go back for more. The blazing red sun was edging toward the horizon.

A tall girl in a strapless off-white ankle length dress, a white orchid in her dark hair, extended her hand to Mac.

"Welcome to the Molokai-Surf. I'm Kona, the manager."

He'd replied automatically, taking the warm hand and squeezing it too hard, momentarily taken aback by the startling beauty of her face. "You've got a magnificent hideaway here."

"Thank you, Mr. McGregor, anything we can do for you or your wife . . . just ask." Kona gave Mac a dazzling white smile and moved off to greet the other guests.

Mac's gaze followed Kona, eyes moving slowly from the top of her head all the way down, then back up again. He swallowed. All of her had been sculpted perfectly and she moved lightly with rhythm and grace. The white dress showed off her golden skin and her perfect figure. He guessed her age at twenty-six.

Mac looked back toward the ocean, then moved to the rock wall at the edge of the terrace. A white tern was hovering in the wind with slow, effortless wingbeats. A flight of wedge-tailed shearwaters was returning from the sea, soaring gracefully one minute, dipping close to the water the next, heading for their nests in crevices in the cliff. Marge was talking with three attractive looking young women, their clothes sunbelt simple. As he passed the group, he heard one of them say, "This trip was the prize. We're the leading Avon sales . . ." Three top Avon salesladies. They'd probably sell Marge another trunkload of cosmetics. Just what she didn't need. Someday, maybe she'd realize she was already beautiful and leave well enough alone.

The sun was now sinking fast in a fiery sky directly behind Diamond Head across Kaiwi Channel. It was a red ball touching the horizon line, then half a ball, a sliver of red and then gone. As the light faded, the high cirrus clouds glowed red, then quickly dimmed. Mac joined the applause. The sunset had been some sight. He caught Marge's glance, and they exchanged eye messages.

Now there was a slight suggestion of chill in the air. Two men with dark complexions next to Mac were talking in low, confidential tones.

"Soon it will be nothing but condominiums owned by rich haoles. Hawaiians can't afford decent homes. Hawaii should be for Hawaiians. The damn haoles have to go . . ."

Mac nodded. That sounded right. He turned to join in the conversation and the two Hawaiians moved off. A heavyset, matronly type in a brightly patterned muumuu peeled off from another group and headed directly toward him. It was too late for escape, so he smiled a welcome. After the introductions, the trivia questions began. The third one jolted Mac. Brusquely the lady had asked, "What are you planning to do, now that you're retired?"

Mac swallowed back his first answer, drowned it with the rest of his drink, then turned and looked at the woman more closely. Age had shrunk the skin on her face so that it didn't fit anymore. She looked like a fat carp. Somehow that pleased Mac, so he answered slowly.

"I'm planning to float out to sea in a rowboat with some fishing lines, a case of white wine, and that young lady over there." Gesturing toward Marge, he'd put special emphasis on the word *young*. A few more questions and briefer answers, and the lady in her new Andrade dress excused herself and walked away. Mac gestured for another drink and took two. The question about retirement had left a sour taste. Damn, he hadn't needed to be reminded.

A slink of white matte jersey appeared close to his shoulder. The white jersey spoke softly. "Very few people ever see a place like this," the voice purred. "A place to get away. A place to be alone. To do what you've always wanted to do."

Mac answered without even looking in the young girl's direction. "A place to get away from all the people who are trying to get away from it all."

The white jersey moved even closer. "It's paradise," she purred, even smoother. "But it's expensive to live in paradise."

In the gathering dusk, the white jersey was now touching Mac, body softness molding into his side.

"And your hobby," Mac paused, then suggested, "could it possibly be . . . collecting money?"

"I'm very reasonable . . . and very good." The girl's

.voice was pure honey. "What's your pleasure?" The heat from her body seared through his clothes.

Mac sighed, contemplating an appropriate answer. Hawaii was known for the warmth of its people. Now he knew why. The girl was pretty, pleasant, and undoubtedly a good buy. Molokai was the friendly isle. He grinned inwardly. Maybe he should ask for a lei. Fortunately, an answer wasn't necessary. A young man in a blue flowery shirt appeared at the blonde's elbow. Mac heard him say, "Cool it, hot pants, you'll keep." As the young girl unglued her body from his, Mac looked into the newcomer's swarthy face and knew instantly. The little boy smile hid a wide mean streak.

Mac watched the couple walk away. The blonde was well put together, but her dress was a size too tight, showing everything, all of her body lines. Mac swallowed, watching her hips move, and thinking. Underneath everything, gentlemen prefer nothing. Sometimes women could be too damn friendly. He inhaled deeply, chest swelling. Retired or not, he still had some sex appeal.

Marge came rushing up, face beaming, and took hold of his arm. "Dear, I want you to meet some new friends."

"Friends?" Mac questioned.

"There are no strangers here on Molokai, only friends we've yet to meet," Marge replied.

Oh shit, thought Mac. He'd already met enough new friends for one night. He didn't need any more.

Marge sensed the hesitation, read his mind, and pulled Mac along, saying softly, "The time to make friends is before you need them."

After dinner, Mac and Marge wandered into the recrea-

tion room. A short movie about whales was just starting. They sat down, and within minutes they were
fascinated. A whale mother was playing with her calf.
She submerged under the calf and blew a terrific blast of
bubbles underneath the baby, delightedly spinning it
about in the boiling water. Then the mother slid her
nose under the calf and gently bounced and rolled it
about in the surge of the waves.

Just as suddenly, the mood of the movie changed.
Two fast, modern whalers, armed with cannons, depth
charges, and explosive-tipped harpoons were fast closing in on a small herd of blue whales, the largest creatures the world has ever seen. Overhead, a helicopter
followed the whale's telltale spouts and directed the
killer ships. Wallowing miles behind, the whaling fac-
tory ship was shown efficiently processing the previous
day's catch. The bloated corpses of fifteen blue whales
trailed alongside.

"Jonah's been avenged," Mac whispered. "The ship
now swallows the whale."

"Dreadful," Marge answered quietly.

On the screen, a seventy-foot-long blue whale surfaced. The closest killer ship aimed, using the most
modern electronic techniques, and fired its harpoon.
The one-hundred-and-seventy-pound missile flew in an
arc for almost half a mile, striking the whale high on its
back. The harpoon penetrated and exploded. Wounded
mortally, the huge whale dove to escape. The sea was
channeled with a river of blood. All of a sudden, the
whale rose straight out of the bloody froth. Huge eyes
looked straight into the camera. The leviathan hovered
in midair, then slid slowly back into the water.

Marge grasped Mac's arm, saying, "Let's go. I've
seen enough." Her stomach was churning. "That's bar-

baric to kill those poor defenseless things. That whale was looking right at us, pleading with his eyes . . . all the time he was dying.''

In the hall outside the recreation room, a young, tall, darkly tanned girl with luminous green eyes and short, curly dark auburn hair sat behind a table passing out pamphlets entitled *Save the Whale*. She was wearing a white T-shirt. On the right sleeve was a small blue whale, on the left one a small blue hula dancer. Mac took a pamphlet and slipped a ten dollar bill into the jar on the table.

"That's a bloody scene in there . . . not too great for after dinner,'' Mac commented, staring at the girl's pretty face.

"It makes the point,'' the tall redhead said in a surprisingly hard voice. "If they killed elephants, or pet poodles, or anything else with explosive harpoons . . . can you imagine the outcry?'' Not waiting for an answer, she went on, eyes flashing in anger.

"The whale is the greatest creature ever born. When a work of creation is gone, there is no way to bring it back. Extinction is the ultimate crime. It is forever. What a loss if the whale disappears.''

Mac nodded and turned to leave as the young man with the blue flowery shirt and the little boy smile approached the girl behind the table. He touched her shoulder and whispered something in her ear. Mac couldn't hear the conversation, but did hear the man call the girl "Fire.'' Some name, he thought, the redhead must be hot stuff! Yet he was certain that if Fire were involved with Little Boy Blue, she'd be the one to get burned. In just two hours, Mac noted, the same fellow had turned up at the side of two red-hot numbers. If the guy wasn't careful, he was going to be the victim of early burnout.

CHAPTER TWO

By midafternoon of their third day on Molokai, the McGregors were finding the Kalua Koi golf course challenging, the weather pleasantly balmy, and the views spectacular. On the tenth green, Marge curled a long putt toward the hole. It lipped the cup and spun out.

"Damn," she muttered. "That ball's afraid of the dark. That would have given me a par."

Her husband grinned. "Remember what the pro said . . . *makai*. Everything breaks toward the sea. Look out there." Mac pointed out over the cliffs.

The surf was up! The fast moving swells came out of deep water, hit the shallow coral reefs, then moved into Kepuhi Bay, resulting in explosive waves filled with enormous power. The long, hollow, peeling rollers were perfect for surfing, and there were at least a dozen boards and riders in the huge swells below.

Mac parked the golf cart on the side of the eleventh tee. He and Marge sat on a rock shelf watching the surfers trading wave for wave, pulling off insane snapbacks, going for devil-may-care maneuvers. The boards rode just in front of the falling lip of the waves, scribing

diagonal, frothy white courses as they moved toward
the shore, peeling off into calm water before the waves
crashed against the rocks at the base of the cliff with a
noise like sonic booms. Then the surfers paddled out,
riding the rips through the channels to do it over again.

It was at least twenty minutes before Marge broke
their silence. "Graceful, aren't they?" she asked.

"Unbelievable," Mac replied, his face suddenly alive.
"That's a solid two-meter surf out there. Watch that
tall waterbaby in the white bikini on the *olo*. She's on a
takeoff."

Marge saw the golden body hurtling forward on the
crest of a huge wave. Suddenly, the surfboard whipped
around in a forty-five-degree angle, and the golden girl
was riding a different diagonal. Marge shook her head
in disbelief.

"Bravo. A perfect cutback," Mac shouted in ap-
proval, clapping his hands. "She's on the critical now.
That's the steepest part of the wave. In the green room.
The place to be."

Marge looked at Mac in wonder. How did he know so
much about surfing? Obviously, after seven years of
marriage there were still some things she didn't know
about her husband. A lot of details had been hidden in
his first marriage, and she'd always felt it was better not
to pry. She knew the essentials.

Far out, a rushing wave curled its lip.

"Watch that big fellow on the yellow boogie board.
He's a goofy foot . . . he's caught a close-out." Mac
laughed. "In the soup, a wipeout."

He turned and Marge could see the flush of enthusiasm on his face as he spoke. "Come on, kid. Let's
finish our golf game. A dollar a hole."

As Marge rose, Mac patted her gently on the bottom

of her paisley slacks. Things were looking up, she thought.

Dinner was over, but the night was still young. The McGregors sat alone at a corner table in the Koa dining room, with a view of the ocean and sky outside, as well as most of the other tables.

Mac watched the lights of a small freighter in the channel that was heading for Honolulu. Finally, he broke the silence.

"Good dinner."

Marge nodded. "That *mahimahi* was the best I've ever eaten. Delicious." She leaned forward, her eyes catching Mac's eyes.

"You know, eating out is half the fun of a vacation."

"What's the other half?" Mac asked, half-guessing the answer.

"*Okole maluna.*" Marge spoke the words slowly, raising her wineglass in toast.

A puzzled look crossed Mac's face.

Marge smiled broadly. "*Okole maluna* . . . Hawaiian for bottoms up."

They drained the last of their wine. Mac leaned forward and whispered, "If I haven't told you, Mrs. McGregor, you're very beautiful tonight."

Marge glowed at the compliment. "Give me a sunset, candlelight, a few glasses of chablis, a compliment . . ." She reached across the table and touched Mac's hand. "And I'm yours."

"You're an incurable romantic."

"Look at the stars out there. This is a fantasy world," she said, squeezing his hand.

"Nothing but blue skies and velvet nights—ready to call it an evening?" As he asked the question, Mac leaned back in his chair and reached in his coat pocket for his cigarettes and lighter, looking as if he knew the answer.

"Mac, let's sit here for a few minutes more. It's so beautiful." The candlelight flickered on her face. "Moments like this are special . . . they're for sharing."

The two sat in silence. Mac's eyes scanned the room.

"There's the honeymoon couple." He gestured. "Take a look, the bride's got a big hickie on her neck."

"Mac . . . remember our honeymoon? You were covered with them."

"We're still on it, you vampire." He grinned. "Hey, maybe later . . ." His eyes flashed at her.

Marge laughed. "Promises, promises. You do something to me." She leaned forward and whispered, "Just not often enough."

Four tables away, the honeymooners were talking quietly, the bride speaking.

"Another three-minute cowboy ride. It's supposed to be great." She shrugged. "It wasn't even good."

"Jenny, I'm doing my best. Sometimes, it's just not there. Besides, you're . . ." The young groom searched for the right phrase. "Well, insatiable."

"I am not," she said, voice rising. "But I'd like to feel something, too, Tommy."

His face clouded and he said nothing.

Hesitating, she touched his face gently. "Sweetheart . . . tonight . . . let's try it my way." He looked at her face and could see the sudden sparkle in her eyes, and wondered what she had in mind.

At the table next to the McGregors, a lanky blonde in a white silk pants suit was seated across from a chunky man in a white dinner jacket whose wavy hair had turned an even paler shade of white. Their conversation was terse. It was obvious that in their family both wore the pants, but as Mac had noticed earlier, hers fit better. They were both drinking vodka, clear and straight over ice.

The blonde's nose was delicately upturned, her mouth pouted slightly, eyes empty and bored, the sparkle gone. Apparently, when they'd first met he'd tried everything, flowers, candy, jewelry, and furs, and they'd all worked. Now it was lover burnout. Mac could hear her say, "I could live within your income, but what would you live on?" The voice was crisp and smoky.

His reply was blurry.

"You're drunk again," she said flatly.

He laughed loudly, his mind rejecting the truth.

The lanky blonde shrugged her shoulders. She should have known better. Boredom tears apart more marriages than pressure. The trip was a bad idea. A relationship that isn't working doesn't change just because the scenery changes. The marriage was cold, the fizz gone. She turned her head, looked at Mac, and winked.

Mac never noticed the wink. He and Marge were laughing, enjoying one another's company. Mac had described his experiences the night before on the terrace. Now they were discussing another couple seated nearby.

"That biddy. On a scale of one to ten, she's a thundering three, maybe a three and a half." He frowned. "The last time I saw a mouth like that, it had a hook in it."

"Mac, be kind," Marge scolded, knowing Mac's sense of humor. Then she asked, "The young man with her . . . think it's her son?"

"Are you kidding?" Mac asked, grinning widely. "That's her way of keeping her youth. Probably has two of them."

"The group in the other corner, the tall redhead . . ." Marge gestured with her head. "Isn't she the surfer? Your golden girl?"

Mac turned to look and stared hard. He recognized the girl called Fire and the ever-present Little Boy Blue, but didn't know the other two. Finally Mac turned back, saying softly, "It could be. I thought the surfer was Kona—the manager. From a distance she and Fire look very much alike."

"Those are two pretty wahines," Marge said enviously. "Their skin is extraordinary, almost caramel in color. Pretty hair, too."

"T-shirts aren't bad either," Mac said, a look of delight crossing his face, pleased by the thought that had struck him. "On that one it looks like a V-shirt. Some cleavage. Nature at its best."

"That girl looks the way every woman wants to look," Marge replied.

"The parts look genuine and they all fit," Mac said, pouring some more coffee from the carafe on the table. "I liked young girls at eighteen and I still do."

"I'd give anything to have that figure. Once upon a time . . ." Marge said wistfully. "But, the years take their toll. The sands of time shift slowly to the bottom." Her eyes dropped.

"Honey, I love your bottom just the way it is. Not perfect, but damn . . ." Mac looked into his wife's face and smiled. "It sure turns me on."

Marge smiled outwardly, knowing she had to go on a serious diet . . . again . . . just as soon as they got home.

At the corner table, Fire, Marco, Michael, and a man called Carlos were seated together talking quietly over coffee.

"Does your sister suspect anything?" Marco asked Fire.

"No. Kona's so wrapped up in her whales and dolphins. She's in for a real shock."

Marco leaned forward and spoke in a low voice. "This Save the Whale idea of yours . . . a perfect cover. Really brilliant."

"Thanks, Marco. I appreciate that." Fire looked warmly at the young handsome man, then smiled.

Marco smiled back, looked around the room, and said, "She does run a good hotel, though."

"She's a bigger sham than anyone knows," Fire snapped.

Michael leaned forward, put down his coffee cup, and told the others how Kona had talked to the dolphins and scratched the whale's head. "It was absolutely unbelievable. I did as you told me. I played dumb . . ."

Carlos spoke for the first time. "Probably wasn't too hard for you."

Fire's green eyes glistened. "The world changes. You've got to move with it." Her voice hardened. "My sister will find out. She fucked up. She trusted me."

The others laughed their agreement. Fire checked her watch and said, "It's time to start the damn whale movie again. One last time." She pushed back her chair, rose, and started toward the exit. Mac watched her progress. On the way she stopped at two tables that had been pushed close together, leaned over, and whispered something at each table. One of the men put down his coffee cup, pushed back his chair, rose, and followed Fire into the hall.

Mac noticed that he was wearing the same type of white T-shirt that Fire was wearing. On the right sleeve, a small blue whale, on the left one, a small blue hula dancer.

"Penny," Marge said softly.

Mac turned back, a troubled look on his face.

"Sorry, hon, I was just watching that weird looking group." His head gestured in the direction of the two tables that had been pushed together.

Her eyes sparkled. "I thought you were mentally disrobing the tall gorgeous one with the perfect figure."

Mac laughed lightly. "No such luck. I'm puzzled, though . . . it's beauty and the beasts. She stands out like a peacock among roosters." Mac frowned as his head turned back toward the other table. "Look at that big ugly guy sitting across from the Puerto Rican, and the huge black . . ."

Her eyes took in the men at the far table. "Mac, Hawaii's the melting pot, a rainbow of people . . . mixed races . . . mixed marriages . . . mixed cultures."

"They've got it all at that table." He looked back at Marge as he put out his cigarette. "Strangers in Paradise. That's a crazy-quilt macho zoo."

"Hawaiian culture has many roots," she replied. "Maybe they're shooting another film about whales."

Mac laughed, then whispered softly, "Maybe, but if they're making a movie, I doubt if it's about whales. With that cast, it's probably a porno flick."

Marge leaned closer and said, "The way you look at that tall waterbaby, I think you're jealous."

At one of the two tables the huge black was talking in a low voice to the man on his right.

"Dig in, Milo. This may be our last supper." He laughed aloud and slapped the one he'd called Milo on the back.

Milo fingered the scar on his swarthy face. "This is some mess hall. Right, Angel?"

The tall, thin, light-complexioned man on the other side of Milo took a long swallow of his Seven-Up and grenadine, grinned broadly and said, "It's poverty deluxe. If I die it don't matter, Little Man. Not now, I've already been to heaven."

The huge black swiveled his head around. Slapping his meaty hand on the table, he said quietly, "It's not a bad place to die."

Across the table, the fat Hawaiian called Anahu swallowed hard. The group was talking too loudly. He could feel the rich haoles staring at them, giving them the stink eye.

Jorge, the big, rugged man seated next to Anahu, turned to face him, then spoke softly. "It's almost time. We'll unleash the spirit . . . give 'em the white eye." He rolled his iris so that it was totally obscured by the upper lid, leaving only the white of the eye showing.

Anahu's face paled and he turned away. He checked his watch and felt uneasy. Rising from the table, he headed toward the lanai for some fresh air.

It was later. The pungent scent of orchids and hibiscus filled ocean suite seven. Music from the hotel drifted faintly along the beach. In his pajamas, Mac was seated in a comfortable chair, skimming a light novel.

Marge emerged from the bathtub, toweled herself dry, powdered herself with a light scent, and slipped into a sheer nothing gown. She did her exercises in front of a mirror, in front of Mac, feeling free and feminine. Slowly, deliberately, the lace swirled. It was slightly sinful, definitely exciting. Fascinated, Mac put down his novel. He could see all of her through the sheerness. The most beautiful thing, next to nothing. An elegant silhouette, sensuously revealed. It was mirror magic, for adults only. As he watched, interest grew into desire.

Marge glided close. Mac's eyes told her she was beautiful. She spun away whispering, "Stare too hard and your eyes go funny.'' Mac could smell her orchid scent. Molokai was a place you could go to heaven on your nose. It was like dancing through a rainbow. He laughed. They were both getting high on orchids. Maybe orchids were the ultimate aphrodisiac. As he rose from his chair, she pushed him playfully onto the bed. The same motion untied his pajama bottoms and pulled them off. Marge smiled and whispered, ''Dessert time.''

Mac could hear the newlyweds. Marge must have heard them also. Her white teeth flashed a dazzling smile. ''Sweetheart, they're rank amateurs. Let's show them how it's really done.''

''*Okole maluna*,'' Mac suggested.

''*Okole maluna*. My favorite position,'' she said, laughing while turning out the lights.

Climbing into bed, she whispered, ''Energize me.'' He reached for the gentle lace. It was almost too elegant to take off. Almost, but not quite.

Their loving was easy and uninhibited. Once was not enough, for either of them.

The tall girl shivered, took a last drag on her Marlboro, then snubbed it out, putting the butt in the pocket of her khaki coveralls. Adjusting her lightweight mask, she checked her watch. Three minutes to go. The time was dragging now. Her heart was beating loudly. She glanced around, but the others didn't seem to notice.

Marco broke the silence. ''Move fast, but not in haste. No mistakes. If need be . . . kill.'' Marco spat out the word icily. ''This is what we've trained for. It's what we do best.''

Fire interrupted. ''Kill only if necessary. Don't forget that, Marco. And don't let your group forget it, either. At times you're too *pupule* . . . crazy wild.''

Marco looked at Fire and smiled. "I'm hot blooded, not hotheaded." His arm encircled Fire's waist.

"Keep your hands to yourself." Fire's voice was sharp. "You're here for one purpose only. Keep your mind on that."

Marco's smile, which had left his face momentarily, now returned. "Fire, One for One will succeed. Hula won't fail. The Whale is all powerful."

Fire nodded, bent down, and picked up her assault rifle. The others did the same. Checking her watch again, she said quietly, "Aloha."

Twelve other voices repeated, "Aloha."

The group moved out, underneath their masks a look of grim determination on every face.

PART TWO

THE TAKEOVER

CHAPTER THREE

First Day—Midnight to Dawn

It was after midnight and Mac McGregor was still awake. It was the noise of the giant combers crashing against the cliff. Ocean suite seven not only had a view, it had wraparound stereophonics. He'd noticed that tonight the newlyweds had finished their trampoline exercises early and had gone to sleep. Either the groom had found the bride's responsive chord or she'd given up. Glancing at Marge, who was sound asleep, mouth curled in a little girl smile, he grinned. She had really been turned on by the moonlight and orchids. Or maybe it had been the chablis. Whatever it was, their sex had been multidimensional and fun. It had always been good, like no other feeling in the world, but tonight had been special. He was beginning to relax. It had been a good day. Tomorrow promised to be even better.

Through the lanai doors he could see the huge swells

far out on the ocean. It was a velvet night, and every ripple reflected moonlight. Mac's eyes closed and his mind
sought sleep. Suddenly his body tensed, sensing trouble.
At first it was a whisper on the night wind. Then the
sound of low voices, threatening voices. Now fully alert,
he rose and padded to the windows facing the courtyard
and the other guest rooms.

It took a few moments for his mind to believe his
eyes. It was the stuff of nightmares. In the moonlight he
could see small groups of people being prodded along
by masked men with snub-nosed machine guns. A heavy
man, wearing only undershorts, turned to argue and
was knocked to the ground. One of the masked men
ordered two of the other men to grab the fat man's legs
and drag him along the path. Before they could do so,
he staggered to his feet and moved along quietly.

Mac stared hard, then moved away from the window,
mind racing. What the hell was going on? The resort's
guests were being rounded up, room by room, and
herded toward the main building. They were either in
the process of being robbed, or worse yet, were being
captured to be held hostage.

Checking the window again, Mac heard the quick
knock on the door of the newlywed suite next door, saw
the lights go on, heard muttered exclamations, sharp
commands, and moments later saw the young couple in
their nightclothes being pushed along the path.

The pattern was now obvious. The gunmen had di-
vided up the buildings housing the guests. One approached each room, captured the occupants, took
them to the main building, then returned to the next
room. Christ, he and Marge were next. A quick glance
told him Marge was still asleep, mouth moving in
cadence with her soft snores.

Half the buildings were now lit, half still dark. Suddenly it hit Mac. The gunmen had left the lights on and doors open where they'd already captured the occupants, indicating which apartments had been covered.

Mac reached for the switch and clicked on the lights. Maybe he could fool them. The involuntary groan from Marge was audible. He could hear her turn first her face, then her body, away from the light; then seconds later, he heard the renewed sounds of sleep. Unlocking the door, he swung it partially open and stepped behind it. Glancing about for a weapon, he saw none and swore softly. Oh, for his old Marine Corps .45, a grenade, or a bazooka, nothing fancy. This would teach him to travel light! The head of his driver prodded into his back. He'd forgotten that he'd removed the #1 club from his golf bag and put it in the corner. For accuracy he always drove with a 3-wood. The damn driver sliced. Slipping off the headcover, he could hear two of the gunmen returning. Under his breath, Mac muttered, "What a weapon. I can't hit anything with a driver."

Through the crack of the door, Mac could see two shadows hesitate in front of their room. The tall, thin shadow spoke sharply to the big, wide shadow. "Jorge, no killing. Unless . . ." The voice trailed off as the thin shadow moved past. The big, wide shadow stood for a moment, apparently confused by the lights in suite seven. He took a few steps toward the next darkened building, stopped, then turned back. Holding his Kalashnikov assault weapon in front of him, the shadow pushed the door open wider and stepped cautiously into ocean suite seven. The shadow took form, a huge man in khaki camouflage, moving slowly toward the bed.

With a choked grip, Mac swung his driver in a downward arc. The head of the club hit the head of the big man with a resounding crack. He fell at right angles to the floor. "Aloha, Big George," Mac whispered.

Old habits die hard, Mac thought, as he kicked the
door partially closed, picked up the automatic weapon
and placed it on the empty bed. Then grasping the gun-
man's feet, he crossed his legs, twisted and turned him
face up. The big man groaned as his lightweight mask
was pulled off.

Mac let out a low whistle when he saw the face of Big
George. It was the ugly creep they'd seen in the dining
room with the Puerto Rican, the huge black, the as-
sorted macho types, and the beautiful Hawaiian girl
called Fire. The dirty movie group in the white T-shirts
who were going to save the whales! Mac shook his head.
It didn't make sense. This guy didn't look like a whale
lover. He looked like a fucking terrorist.

The ugly one groaned again. With golf club in hand,
Mac moved quickly toward the bathroom, grabbing
towels and a small roll of adhesive tape from his shaving
kit. He'd gag the bastard and tie him up. Emerging
from the bathroom, Mac saw Big George rise up on one
knee and pull a long straight razor from a sheath on his
belt.

In one fluid motion Mac dropped the towels and
adhesive, stepped toward Big George and swung his
driver, hitting the ugly one an awesome blow behind his
right ear. The huge body crumpled to the floor.

Mac exhaled audibly. He could feel his stomach
churning. It had been years since he'd killed a man.
Kaleidoscopic images flashed through his mind. Every
time, he'd had the same reaction. He could feel the bile
rising. He had to focus his thoughts on something else.
Damn, his pro was right. With a loose grip and a slower
swing, he'd get more accuracy and power from his
driver. A golf club should be held like a soft lady. He'd
been holding the damn club too tight and swinging too
fast.

Stomach settling, Mac knelt and checked the big man's pulse, then dropped the arm to the floor. There was no question about it. Hawaii was going to be an even more beautiful place. One real ugly son-of-a-bitch had just checked out, permanently.

Mac picked up the Russian AK-47 from the bed and checked the banana-shaped magazine. It had thirty long, slim 7.62mm bullets ready to fire. He whistled noiselessly, knowing that around the world terrorists were now using AK-47s the way cowboys once used six-shooters. There wasn't much question. A terrorist group had taken over the Molokai-Surf resort. Marge had slept through everything. It was time to wake her and get moving. There was a lot to be done and things would probably get worse.

Mac dressed quickly, then sitting on the edge of the bed, woke his wife gently, explaining what had happened.

Marge sat bolt upright, eyes wide as saucers, mouth sputtering.

"Shh . . . Shh . . . Don't look at the guy unless you've got a strong stomach," Mac cautioned in a whisper.

Marge's eyes sought out the body on the floor.

"Mac, he's dead . . . You killed him!" The anguished voice shattered the stillness of the room.

Mac moved with instantaneous reflexes, cupping his hand firmly over his wife's mouth and holding her tightly to him, praying that no one had heard. He waited for a few moments, then whispered, "The guy is dead . . . that can't be changed. It was either him or me. It was an easy choice."

Marge gave a shudder. He could hear her stomach churning, feel her gag. Afraid she was going to be ill, he kissed her lightly on the cheek, then spoke quietly but firmly.

"We must be absolutely quiet. No noise at all. Get dressed, jeans and shirt, tennis shoes. If you must use the john, don't flush it. Don't touch the lights. No noise. None!"

Taking a deep breath, he loosened the pressure of his hand over her mouth. Marge swallowed nervously, tears welling in her eyes. Mac kissed them gently, removed his hand, saying softly, "I love you. Remember that."

Marge nodded her head slowly, then spoke almost inaudibly, "I'll be okay . . . it was the shock."

Mac gave her a weak smile and signaled for her to dress. She rose, moving slowly toward the bathroom, as if lost in a nightmare, senseless thoughts running through her mind.

Looking through the partially open door, Mac confirmed that the lights were now on in almost all of the rooms. As soon as they had rounded up all of the guests, the terrorists would probably recheck the rooms, turning out the lights as they went. If so, they'd be back in fifteen or twenty minutes. Possibly sooner, if they started looking for Big George.

Kneeling next to the big man on the floor, he checked again for a heartbeat. There was none. The color had drained from the face, now a hideous gray. Odd, the eyes were open wide, but only the whites were showing. Mac grimaced to himself, remembering something he'd heard. Beauty is skin deep but ugly goes clear to the bone. Big George had certainly had a lifetime of ugly. Being big and ugly hadn't saved the dinosaur either. Bowing his head, Mac closed his eyes and silently spoke a few words, knowing that sometimes it is better to ask forgiveness than permission.

Now staring at the motionless body, realization slowly permeated his mind. He'd just killed a man in cold blood. Murder? It had been self-defense. The

police would understand. The police. Of course. Call
the police and tell them about the terrorists. Damn!
There were no phones in the rooms. The only phones
were in the main lobby. He rose, mind still churning.
No. The terrorists had control of the resort. The switchboard would have been one of the first things seized
There was no way to call. He and Marge had to get out
of the resort as quickly as possible and reach the police.

Their rental car was in the parking lot about sixty
yards away. If they moved fast . . . with a little luck . . .
He turned and picked up the lucky beans from the top
of his dresser, stuffing them into his pants pocket.

Marge was now dressed in jeans, dark pullover
sweater, tennis shoes, and a kerchief tied over her salt
and pepper hair. Mac took the small cosmetic case out
of her hand, and set it back in the bathroom. Grabbing
a blanket from the closet shelf, he tossed it to Marge,
whispering, "You look great, hon. This might be more
useful."

Quickly he outlined his plan to Marge, picked up the
Kalashnikov automatic weapon, crouched low and signaled his wife to do the same, then slid open the screen
door to the lanai facing the ocean. It was darker on this
side of their room, which was shielded from the main
building. Skirting their unit, staying close to the bushes,
in less than two minutes they had reached their car. Mac
gasped at the sight. The terrorists had slashed all four of
the tires. Glancing about, he saw that all of the cars in
the parking area were resting on their rims. It was obvious they'd taken no chances on anyone escaping.
Without even looking, Mac knew the terrorists had also
cut the ignition wires. This was a well-planned operation.

Opening the door to the Toyota, he pushed the front
seat forward and signaled for Marge to slide into the

back seat, whispering, "Make yourself comfortable, hon. Cover up with the blanket. The bastards won't recheck the cars. They're useless. Lie low and don't move. I'll be back soon."

Crawling into the car and lying down on the back seat, Marge wanted to protest, to shout, "Don't leave me. For God's sake, Mac, don't leave me." But she knew her husband well enough to know that he had good reasons. She whispered instead, "Be careful, sweetheart . . . don't try anything spectacular. I love you."

Mac knew that their car was well protected from view by the other cars parked alongside. The area was shielded from general view by a screen of heavy bougainvillea bushes. Marge would be scared, but safe. Moving rapidly but cautiously, he quickly retraced his steps to their ocean suite. Everything was as they'd left it . . . Big George and all. The plan of escape he'd sketched out mentally would have to be discarded. The Molokai-Surf was in the remotest section of the island, with nothing else around for miles. Not knowing where the terrorists had set up outposts or roadblocks, or how many were involved . . . it would be foolhardy to attempt to walk out. They wouldn't get far. There was only one road. Moving around the resort, the cliffs would be especially dangerous.

If they couldn't escape, maybe they could lie low, at least until daylight. They'd know more by then. Odds were that the terrorists didn't know that he and Marge hadn't been captured. With a little luck—he touched the bulge of the lucky beans in his pocket—maybe they'd never know. Deep down, he doubted that.

A fire. He could start a fire. It would be seen for miles, create chaos among the terrorists, give the hostages a chance to escape. But, with the wind off the ocean the fire could get out of control. It would probably burn down the whole resort. Many or all of the hostages might be killed. A fire was too risky!

Walking around the room, he almost tripped over Big George. The corpse was becoming a fixture. One that had to be eliminated. If the terrorists found the body they would know that someone had killed George. It wouldn't take long for them to realize that they hadn't taken all of the guests hostage. Drop the body over the cliff into the sea. The corpse would wash up and they'd spot it in the morning. The sea always returns what it takes. Maybe they'd think George had fallen over the cliff. Never be able to prove otherwise. No . . . long before they found the body, they'd miss Big George and start to search for him. They might find Mac and Marge instead. That wouldn't do.

Mac knelt again over the body. The corpse was about his size, extra large. No question, Big George had been a heavy-duty guy, a hammer. Picking up the lightweight ski mask, Mac started to pull it over his head. He gagged, a queazy feeling in the pit of his stomach. He wasn't sure which upset him the most, wearing the mask of a dead man or the mask of one as ugly as Big George. He took a deep breath and pulled it all the way over his head. A perfect fit. It covered the entire head, with narrow eye slits and a flap over the mouth opening. He took several more deep breaths. The cap fit also. Mac checked his reflection in the mirror. It could be anyone . . . even Big George . . . looking back at him. A new plan was slowly forming in a remote corner of Mac's mind. Unzipping George's camouflage shirt and trousers, Mac pulled them off the terrorist and put them on over his own clothes.

Big George had huge feet. He'd crept into their room on size thirteen tennis shoes. Thank God, thought Mac,

the guy hadn't worn combat boots. I haven't worn mine
for years. He slipped off his Bally loafers and put on his
own Nikes. If anyone got close enough to notice the difference in foot size, he'd be in deep shit.

He studied George's white T-shirt closely. The blue
whale, the blue hula dancer. An advertisement for
Hawaii? For the Save the Whale group? Or . . . Mac's
heart skipped. Could these symbols be the clue to the
identity of the terrorists?

Mac slumped down on the edge of the bed, thinking.
He couldn't make a move until he knew the layout of
the hotel. The pretty wahine with the orchid in her hair
who'd showed them to their suite had described it. Why
the hell hadn't he listened? Shit, he remembered her
every curve, all her important parts, virtually every
move her little round ass had made. But he couldn't
recall anything she'd said. Maybe it was the first stage
of senility. The brochure! Of course, she'd left a
brochure describing the Molokai-Surf.

Mac fairly leapt from the bed. Moments later he
found the brochure in the top drawer of the built-in
dresser, where Marge had put it. Thank God she was
organized. The centerfold of the brochure was a map of
the Molokai-Surf. Mac's breathing eased as he studied
the map. The main building, which contained the Koa
Lounge and all of the basic hotel services, sat on the
edge of the cliff. The rest of the resort's buildings were
arranged in a campus-type layout, forming a semicircle
around the main building. Most of the guests had been
accommodated in large, two-story, motel-like struc-
tures, spaced out among lush lawns and tropical flower
gardens, all within short walking distance of the main
building. There were twelve separate ocean cottages,
each containing two luxurious suites, facing directly on
the ocean. Mac pinpointed ocean suite seven, then tore

out the map, folded it, and put it in his pocket.

Time was becoming precious. Picking up Big George in a fireman's carry, he slung him over his right shoulder and almost collapsed. At least two hundred and ten pounds. Dead weight. "Christ!" he muttered to himself. "I'm getting weak in my . . ." The words *old age* stuck in his throat. With his left hand he picked up the Russian AK-47. He'd decided that George's clothes were important to his plan. It wouldn't do to have Big George's body float up on the beach dressed only in his underwear. Mac chuckled to himself. It might ruin the image of the Molokai-Surf. The body had to be stashed someplace and he'd thought of just the place.

The terrorists had established their command post in the hotel lobby. Fire was seated crosslegged on a high stoollike chair behind the reception counter. The plaque on the counter read, WELCOME TO THE MOLOKAI-SURF. The terrorist called Carlos leaned his machine gun against the counter and pulled off his mask, muttering, "Damn thing itches."

"They'll recognize you," Fire said.

"I doubt it." Carlos's face twisted into a crooked grin.

Fire's eyes widened. Carlos's eyes set deep in the sockets were a constant, but the rest of his face changed as she watched. Deep lines appeared in his cheeks and forehead. As he moved his mouth, the lines shifted, forming two or three distinctly different faces. No wonder this terrorist had never been caught. Carlos had the face of a chameleon.

With a springy gait, Marco walked quickly into the lobby from the lounge area and reported to Fire. "We've got thirty hotel employees and 185 guests."

"One hundred-eighty-six, with this guy here." With

his foot, Carlos prodded an elderly man who was lying
on the lobby floor. The man groaned.

"What's wrong with him?" Marco asked.

"Too much excitement for a weak heart. Drag him in
with the others!" Fire commanded.

Marco waved his arm, and a tall, thin terrorist appeared, lifted the old man's arms, and dragged him
along the floor.

The old man groaned louder.

"Shut up!" commanded the terrorist.

The groans grew fainter as the old man's limp body
disappeared into the lounge.

"Any other casualties?" Fire asked.

"Couple of bruises, nothing serious." Carlos's
crooked grin returned.

Fire turned to Marco, green eyes shining through the
slits in her mask.

"One hundred-eighty-six. That's two short by my
count."

"We got all the guests. I'm positive."

"As soon as they settle down, we'll check them off
against the guest list." Fire tapped the book on the
counter with her index finger. Then she laughed. "What
difference would it make? We've got more than
enough."

Carlos picked up his AK-47 and his mask. His eyes
focused on Marco as he spoke.

"My men are ready to set up the outposts on the
southern perimeter." There was a hint of challenge in
his voice.

"My team's ready, too," Marco replied to the challenge. "No one will get in or out."

Both men strode out of the lobby, each headed in a
different direction. As Marco reached the lounge, the

tall, thin terrorist met him. "Have you seen Jorge?" he asked.

Cramped in the back seat, Marge was counting the stars through the car window to keep her mind from dwelling on what had happened. The night had been so beautiful, so precious—a fantasy world—and then terrorists had changed everything. She closed her eyes. It had to be a dream. No. Mac had killed one of them . . . and he was such a gentle man. Now, feeling like a fish flopping in the sand, she was worried. Maybe she was going crazy. Sane people slept in beds.

The low whisper startled her.

"Marge . . . it's me, Mac."

Lifting her head, she turned to see a huge shadow with a black mask and slits for eyes on the other side of the window less than a foot away. The shadow was carrying a large bundle on one shoulder.

"Don't scream," Mac's voice was saying.

"Don't scream," she told herself, cupping hand over mouth and muffling the scream which had already started.

The dark shadow gave her a thumbs-up sign with the left hand and disappeared. She heard the trunk of the Toyota open, then a heavy thud. The rear of the car sagged. The lid closed. Then silence.

Marge went back to counting the stars. There were millions of them, clustered together in tight little families. The moon had come into view now. It was alone. Maybe the moon was an orphan.

CHAPTER FOUR

Mac swallowed hard, then took a deep breath. It was time to roll the dice. He had to find out what was happening, and Big George had to make an appearance. Almost casually, he sauntered up the path toward the main building, cradling the AK-47 in his right arm, finger lightly touching the trigger housing. On the terrace he saw the tall, thin shadow silhouetted against the light from the doorway. Merging with the bougainvillea, moving as lightly as a butterfly with sore feet, he crept up behind the thin shadow, almost close enough to touch him, inhaled deeply and said, "Boo!"

The shadow spun around, Kalashnikov pointed at Mac's chest.

"Jorge, you shithead! You scared me. Where the hell you been?" There was a tone of relief in the voice of the tall, thin shadow.

Mac grunted, waved his left arm, mumbled something through his mask that even he couldn't understand.

"You're on guard here. Take over. I'm inside." The thin shadow laughed lightly, turned and pointed through the glass doors with his weapon. "Look!" he said.

Mac's eyes followed the pointing barrel and widened. It was almost like a scene from *Caligula*. Dressed in just about nothing, the hostages were milling about the room.

"Jeez-us!" He exploded in the best imitation of what he thought Big George would have said.

The thin shadow laughed again, opened the door, and stepped inside, sliding the door closed behind him.

Mac expelled a lungful of air. So far, so good. He was guarding the lanai door to the main lounge. In the dark shadows, he couldn't be seen. Between the lanai and the ocean was a steep cliff. Across the channel, on the distant horizon, where earlier they'd watched the sun set in blood, was now the faint glow of Honolulu at night. Just another balmy night in paradise. The people there had no way of knowing that at the Molokai-Surf, paradise had turned into hell. They wouldn't know for hours yet. The terrorists were still one step ahead of the headlines.

The lights inside the main building were blazing. Mac could see the terrorists moving about in an organized pattern, tying the male hostages' hands behind them and then seating them in rows on the floor. Most of the women hostages were still standing.

Mac counted eight terrorists in the room. He didn't know how many there were in total. Wait a minute, if the whole white T-shirt group were involved . . . there had been a corner table of four, including the girl called Fire, and nine at the other two tables, where Big George had been sitting. That made a total of thirteen. If so, with eight inside, there were five elsewhere. Four, excluding him. One would be guarding the front entrance, one probably in the lobby, near the switchboard, and two on patrol. That would mean no roadblocks, or other perimeter strongpoints. Put one or two on roadblocks or at set emplacements, then there was no patrol. But then, he was guessing. Maybe there were more than thirteen terrorists. Unless there were more, the terrorists could only set up an interior defense. They couldn't guard all of the buildings. The Molokai-Surf layout was too extensive, spread out over five or six acres, not including the golf course. Mac was trying hard to remember what he'd read in the brochure. There were over thirty wooden buildings. Most were two story, except for the ocean suites and the main building. In the morning, police would be able to move into the outer buildings and gain the advantage of height. But the terrorists held the hostages.

Mac looked again and made a quick estimate. There had to be over one hundred and fifty hostages. Good thing it was the slack tourist season and few people knew about the Molokai-Surf. The resort had almost three hundred rooms.

He'd been able to sneak up behind the tall, thin shadow because of the guy's total absorption in the lady hostages. Mac could see why. He was having a hard time not staring himself. At his age, a peeping Mac. What was it Marge had said, "Stare too hard and your eyes go funny." He grinned inside the mask, remembering the old song, "Cockeyed Mayor of Kaunakakai." Maybe that's what had happened to the mayor. Mac turned away and glanced out toward the ocean. Knowing that Big George was supposed to be watching the hostages, he turned back.

Most of the women, especially the younger ones, were wearing underthings designed to invite overtures. Lacy, filmy sheers and gossamer fluffs. He recognized the bride from the suite next door. The plunging neckline of her see-through peignoir seemed perilously close to merging with the shrinking hemline. He could tell she was a real brunette. Near the door, the Avon ladies were bravely standing together in a back-to-back triangle. Mac noticed that they'd looked a lot younger with their clothes on. The scene was dramatic proof that women are not all alike. There were all sizes, shapes, and forms. His eyes scanned the group rapidly.

One young thing had only a minishift to cover her naked bottom. It didn't reach. She sat on the floor crosslegged and gathered the shift around her. Another was wearing only a teeny bikini bottom, her arms crossed over her breasts. Mac nodded his head when one of the male hostages handed her his shirt. In one corner prowled a tigress in a leopard print bikini. Provocative and proud of it. Nothing tame there. She looked as if she'd had her hair done in a pet shop. A lanky blonde was covered in a full-length white satin gown. She'd planned her wardrobe from the inside out. One terry-clad teenager was tastefully undressed in a towel. The warm body for hire, who'd been so friendly to him at the cocktail party, was wrapped in a sheet. Probably had been working when the terrorists knocked. Somehow, Mac felt relieved to know she wasn't one of their group. He had to do something quickly to help the hostages, especially these women. But what?

Mac heard a soft noise behind him and spun around to face the muzzle of another Kalashnikov.

"Jorge!" There was disgust in the voice. "You're no better than the Scorpion out here. You're both useless. Check the rooms and turn out the lights. And bring back some blankets and robes. If we don't cover up the girls . . ." The rest of the thought went unspoken.

Mumbling to himself, Mac moved quickly away. He'd recognized the voice and shape of the girl called Fire. Even in camouflage outfit and mask, she had a subtle elegance, and a strong haunting fragrance of white ginger.

He'd almost spoken her name, thinking that Big George might have, but stopped himself just in time. Fire still had her machine gun pointed at him, finger on the trigger. She might have taken him literally. How stupid could he get—a real dingdong. The girl terrorist had zipped up behind him on little cat's feet, while he was watching a tits and ass show. From now on he had to be more careful, head on a swivel. If he weren't, his own ass would get shot off.

The girl with the warm body for sale gathered the sheet tightly around herself and moved over to where a fat, middle-aged man in undershorts was sitting on the floor. She hunched down next to him and lightly touched the massive purple bruise on his face.

"Thanks," she said.

The man forced a semismile. "Just my luck. At least I didn't pay in advance." He laughed, wincing at the effort.

"For what you said back on the path, when that big prick knocked you down . . ." She paused, then smiled warmly at him. "You've got a lifetime warranty. Anytime."

"It wasn't much." The man gestured. "I didn't like him calling you a whore."

"It took guts."

"I got plenty of those." The man put his hand on his fat stomach and laughed again.

The young blonde girl leaned forward and gently

kissed the bruise on his face, then started to rise, holding the sheet tightly with both hands.

"Stay here, next to me," the man said. "You look
good and you smell good."

The girl sat back down. She liked men who liked her.

"Funny, I don't even know your name."

"It's Candy," she said.

"Like in good enough to eat?" The fat man laughed
again.

She nodded.

"I'm Dan," he said. "I'm a bachelor. Never been
married. Bet most men tell you that." He looked at her
face.

Candy nodded again.

"It's true. Came close a couple of times. I've got a
cauliflower heart."

"So have I," Candy said softly.

"What got you started . . . ?"

She'd been asked the same question, in different
ways, it seemed at least a thousand times. Usually,
the question started out, "How come a nice girl like
you . . ." She'd never answered the question truthfully.
Usually joked it off with, "I'm a lemon and just love to
be squeezed." Or, if she were on a trick, "I was born
with a fire between my legs. I've been looking for someone man enough to put it out." That usually built the
man's ego and most replied something like, "Tonight's
the night, baby . . . let me at it . . . look out, here I
come!"

Maybe it was the situation, the fear, or Dan's standing up for her long-lost honor. Whatever it was, she
decided to tell him the truth.

"My family was poor, dirt poor. We lived on a sheep
farm in Australia. I was twelve years old and I used to

sleep in the same room with my brother." The blonde
paused, then continued. "Paul was fifteen, big for his
age. Really handsome and muscular. We used to
wrestle. He was stronger . . . could pin me easy . . . and
knew what he was doing. I didn't . . . but I got so I loved
it. Couldn't wait 'til it was nighttime and we were in bed
together. I adored him. He was really my first . . . and
my only love."

Candy stopped and looked at Dan. His eyes told her
to go on with the story.

"I was fourteen when two girls at school told me I
was secondhand . . . adopted. It was a shock. But then I
realized that Paul and I weren't related, weren't really
brother and sister. We could get married. I ran all the
way home to tell him. He just laughed and laughed, said
he'd never marry a nobody like me . . ." Candy was
silent for a while, then added, "Do you know what it's
like to feel like a nonperson?"

The fat man shook his head, reached out and covered
her hand with his.

"That night he attacked me. Really raped me . . .
every which way . . ." She shuddered. "The next morning I just left home—ran away with only the clothes on
my back and the pain and ache in my heart. Didn't wake
the family. It was easier that way. I couldn't explain.
Never have, to anyone. Never been back. Went from
Adelaide to Melbourne to Sydney. Came up from down
under the hard way."

Candy brushed her eye with the back of her finger.

"I'm really sorry," the man said, as if somehow he
were responsible.

"I guess now I'm a jet-set hooker, with horizontal
recall." The girl smiled, looking directly at the fat man
for the first time. "It may be odd, but I don't resent it. I

work hard and I'm very good at what I do. When it comes to making love, I don't have many inhibitions . . . and now instead of men, I love money." Candy blinked her eyes quickly.

The fat man squeezed her hand. "You were very good." Then he added, laughingly, "As far as we got."

"Thanks," Candy said. "Oh, and I'm clean. I learned that early. When you're poor, you have to be clean. It's the only thing you've got."

The fat man put his arm around her shoulders and gave Candy a gentle hug.

Mac grinned to himself. The assignment Fire had given him was perfect. It was a chance to go room to room and check the layout of the resort carefully, and to find out how many terrorists were involved and where they were located.

Passing through the lobby, he noticed the lights had been dimmed. The terrorist at the switchboard waved and beckoned to him. "Hey, Jorge, watch this for a few minutes." Mac nodded, not recognizing the voice, and watched the terrorist disappear into the men's room. Standing next to the switchboard, Mac's eyes surveyed the area. The guest book was on the counter. He turned the page. "Mr. and Mrs. Mac McGregor, ocean suite seven" popped out at him. The guest book went under his camouflage jacket. No need to make it easy for the terrorists to have roll call.

Four minutes later the terrorist came out of the men's room. Mac was on his way before the man could thank him, skirting another terrorist behind the gun emplacement at the front door. Just about what he'd expected, a terrorist in the lobby, one at the main entrance. Now he moved toward the buildings in the front, those farthest from the ocean, on the northeast side of the resort. It seemed like every window in every building was ablaze with light.

From each of the rooms in the first two-story building, he picked up several blankets and an assortment of robes and clothes. He piled these at the end of the building. Mac dropped the resort's guest book into the water tank behind the toilet in the first vacant room. After all the lights had been turned off in the first building, Mac started carrying the blankets and clothes back to the main building, piling them in the lobby. On his second trip, the terrorist at the switchboard told him that they now had enough blankets and sheets. Kona had opened the supply closet. Now Mac concentrated on turning out the lights and finding out where the rest of the terrorist outposts were located.

He found one in the suite on the second floor at the end of the fourth building. The main lights had already been turned off. A dim night light had been plugged into the baseboard. As Mac entered the room, the terrorist swung his swivel chair from the window to face him. He couldn't recognize the face in the dim light, even though the terrorist had his mask off.

"Hey, Jorge, got a cigarette?" Clearly, the man guarding the outpost had recognized him. Mac put down his AK-47, fumbled in the pocket of his camouflage suit and handed over the almost full pack of Winstons and a book of matches. Behind the swivel chair Mac could see two AK-47s, a grenade launcher, and a carton of grenades.

The terrorist tapped out a cigarette, lit it, then put the pack in his own pocket.

Mac hesitated, wondering what Big George would do. Picking up the AK-47 in his right hand, he aimed it menacingly at the other terrorist, holding out the left hand and snapping his fingers.

The other man laughed, hesitated for a moment, then handed over the pack, saying, "Jorge, you always were a cheap shit."

Mac took the pack, flipped out two more cigarettes and tossed them in the terrorist's lap.

"Hey, Jorge, thanks. If you get any beer . . ." The man laughed again.

Mac laughed back, turned, and moved quickly out of the room.

Now he knew. This outpost guarded the outside perimeter of the buildings overlooking the golf course to the northeast. The other window of the room would also cover the main driveway leading to the front entrance, as well as the front entrance itself. It was strategically well placed.

Outside the building, Mac glanced up at the corresponding suite on the building across the main driveway. It was the only room on the south side of the complex with the lights out. That would be the outpost overlooking the golf course to the southeast. Moving on, turning out the lights room by room, building by building, he covered the twelve two-story buildings on the northern side of the resort. Spotting another room with the lights already out at the northwest corner of the hotel, he guessed that would be another outpost. Presumably there would be a corresponding one on the southwest corner as well. Four second-floor outposts would be adequate to provide a good field of fire covering the entire perimeter of the complex. Additional gun positions could be set up quickly in any of the rooms as needed.

Mac approached the outpost carefully, fearing that

sooner or later someone would ask him a direct question that would have to be answered in George's voice. The air escaped through his teeth. He didn't even know what George's voice sounded like. Fortunately, when Mac reached the outpost there was no one manning it. Fire had probably reasoned that no one was going to attack them through the woods and across the golf course the first night, since no one yet knew that terrorists had taken over the Molokai-Surf.

Mac checked the equipment carefully. Stacked in the room were two AK-47's, a box containing 1,000 rounds of ammo; a grenade launcher, a carton of grenades; a pair of 100-power binoculars, and a Litton M-845 nightscope. Peering quickly through the nightscope, the golf course lit up like day. He watched a mongoose scamper across the thirteenth green, and shook his head. Even the mongoose was confused, he wasn't supposed to be nocturnal. Mac took two grenades from the lower layer in the carton and put them in the pocket of his camouflage suit, carefully replacing the packing and the upper layer of grenades. He figured that if enough grenades were fired to get that low in the box, everyone would be too busy to notice that two were missing.

Moving rapidly now, he searched for supplies. In one of the guest rooms he found a ten-inch sheath knife, razor sharp, which he slipped onto his belt under his suit. From another room he appropriated an underwater spear sling, three spears in a carrying case, and a pair of thin latex black scuba gloves. From various rooms he picked up three darts in a sheath, a ball of strong twine, a thin cylinder of mace, a box of Hefty garbage bags, a quartz-Halogen flashlight with 12,000 candlepower, a large box of Snickers, four packs of cigarettes, and a six-pack of Coke. He placed most of the items into a garbage bag which he threw over his shoulder. The cylinder of mace he put in his pocket. The Snickers weren't the best thing for Marge's diet, but at least she wouldn't go hungry. Snickers were a hell of a lot better than *poi*, that Hawaiian wallpaper paste. Mac also pocketed the keys to three rooms in widely spaced strategic locations.

Passing the parking lot, moving up quietly on the rear of the Toyota and listening, he could hear Marge's soft snores. Thank God, she'd fallen asleep. It was a great ability of hers. She could fall asleep anyplace and sleep through most anything. Mac checked his watch. It was now three-fifty A.M.

Reaching the ocean cottages, he could see that the lights were now being turned out in the buildings of the southern side of the resort as well. At ocean suite seven, he put the garbage bag, the speargun, and the grenades in the closet. In ocean suite four he found a fully stocked refrigerator and drank a glass of orange juice. Most of the refrigerators in the other ocean cottages were like the one in the McGregors' suite, empty.

Mac finished turning out the lights and walked quickly back to the main building. The hostages had settled down, now covered with blankets, and most were dozing. Three terrorists sat on perimeter guard duty in the lounge. Fire and Marco were nowhere to be seen. Kona, in blue jeans and a plain yellow T-shirt, was passing out pillows and blankets and attempting to make the hostages comfortable. Mac moved close enough to see her face. It was tear-streaked.

The tall thin terrorist he'd replaced earlier on guard duty on the lanai, whom Fire had called the Scorpion, approached Mac as soon as he saw him.

"Jorge . . . Fire said to get some rest. See you back here at seven."

"Aloha," Mac muttered.

"A good night to stay alive," the Scorpion answered. Mac nodded his agreement.

It was well after four in the morning when Mac arrived back at the Toyota, checked the trunk area, lifted Marge up, and carried her to ocean suite seven.

Her arms tight around her husband's neck, Marge was not fully conscious. Placed on the soft bed in their room, she could feel Mac's hands rubbing her neck and shoulders, and heard his reassuring whisper, "You've been dreaming. Go back to sleep." She was sound asleep within thirty seconds.

Mac had a theory that had always worked well for him. When in doubt, sleep. The best ideas always come from the subconscious. Taking off his mask and camouflage outfit, he doused his face with cold water in the darkened bathroom, toweled his face and hands dry, then lay down on the bed next to Marge, exhaling forcefully. If lucky, he'd get two hours' sleep.

Arms crossed behind his head, eyes open wide, Mac went back through the events of the night. His best guess still was that there had been thirteen terrorists. Without Big George there were now twelve. The terrorists looked and acted like trained killers. A dark frown crossed his face. Tomorrow would probably tell. At least, he'd pinpointed their outposts. Manned, they'd make it difficult, if not impossible to escape. Damn, he hadn't expected the nightscopes. They'd have to wait until help from outside was close at hand. Marge and he would just have to remain invisible . . . play for time . . . sit it out . . . improvise.

He reached for a cigarette. It would taste good, calm him down. No way. Too risky. He put his hands back behind his head. While waiting for rescue, maybe he could help free the hostages. There was one big problem: He couldn't kill any of the terrorists, even given an opportunity. If he did, Fire and her group of cutthroats would know he existed. Worse yet, they might take reprisals against the hostages and start killing them. Whatever happened, he couldn't risk Marge's life or the lives of any of the hostages. That much was certain.

There was one possibility. Just suppose he could pick off a terrorist or two and make it look like an accident. That might lower the odds, help the hostages. But how? By God, there could be no question. It would have to look like the victims had killed themselves. A tempting thought, but not likely.

Ticking off his thoughts, he shoved them into the far reaches of his mind. Time to switch off and let his unconscious take over. Eyes closed, his mind raced, body pumping adrenaline. It seemed like the old days . . . Tarawa, Okinawa, Korea. God, that was long ago. Still excited. Mac was bone weary, but not mentally tired. If only one could see around the bend in the river of time. Not only couldn't he do that . . . the damn current was running against him. They'd have to take tomorrow as it came.

The sky was growing lighter now. An almost imperceptible change, but in the sharp light of day, it was going to be difficult, damn near impossible, to continue to masquerade as Big George. The odds were stacked against him—long and final. He exhaled audibly.

Marge was dreaming. Two pure white humpback whales shot up from the depths, expelling air and water through their blowholes with a loud whooshing sound, a steamy sigh. One whale was singing to the other in melodious fashion, each breath a burst of pearly bubbles. The other listened. She couldn't make out the tune. The larger whale started to lobtail, raising his twenty-foot-wide tail flukes high in the air and smashing

them on the water with tremendous force, creating a
sound and a splash that could be heard and seen for
over a mile. The smaller whale raised its white head high
above the water to see what was on the surface. Suddenly, a wave appeared that was too big even for the
whales to swim, a rogue wave rising high above an enormous trough. The creatures were caught up and swept
along, rolling over and over in the frothy curl of the
mountainous wave. The magnificent creatures were
drowning . . . drowning . . .

In her sleep, Marge stirred and cried out. Mac's hand
touched her shoulder and Marge quieted. His arm
curled protectively around her. Unaware of Marge's
dream, Mac was thinking that trouble never came in a
trickle, it always came in a flood. If they weren't careful, they were all going to drown in an ocean of it.

As he lay there, daylight dawned along the golden
beach.

CHAPTER FIVE

First Day—Morning

The first rays of sun were brushing the top of Diamond Head. As the sun lit up the far horizon, a bright band of dawn streaked through the window, and leapt across Marge's face. The first burst of sunrise forced both eyes open. She stirred, face waking up slowly, fuzzy thoughts in her mind. Hawaii. Today was going to be another gorgeous day for golf. Maybe later they could . . . Her eyes took in Mac's clothes tossed over the chair, the camouflage suit, the mask. Memories of the night before flooded back and Marge shuddered violently, sitting bolt upright in the bed, suddenly realizing she was fully dressed in jeans, dark pullover sweater, tennis shoes, and kerchief.

It had been a long night crammed into a few hours. Mac hadn't slept, but neither had he been totally conscious. Awake now, his arms reached out for Marge and pulled her close to him. "Damn, but I love you," he said.

"What happened last night?" she asked, eyes searching his face.

"A group of armed nuts took over the hotel," he explained. "All the guests, except the two of us, are up in the lounge."

Marge's heart sank. That's what she remembered.

"Anybody hurt?" she asked.

"Not yet . . . but," Mac exhaled sharply, "the men are all tied up."

An image of the dead terrorist on their floor floated through her mind. She discarded the image, bit her lower lip, waited a moment, then asked, "Why? What do they want?"

"No one knows." Mac swung his legs over the bed and looked at his watch. "Probably find out this morning."

"Did they see you?"

Mac nodded, turned, and smiled. "They think I'm Big George."

Marge's mouth opened, then closed when Mac leaned back and kissed her.

"What do we do now?"

"You stay here," he answered. "Keep a low profile."

Marge looked at her husband questioningly. She started to object, then caught a glimpse of his eyes.

"You can't go up there," Mac said. "We're playing for time." He stood up and turned to face the bed. "You've got to stay invisible, until we find a way out of here."

Her eyes narrowed. "They might come back."

Mac looked straight into her eyes, then nodded his head, speaking slowly. "They might, hon. But I don't think so. There's no reason. They've checked all the rooms twice now." He turned, walked to the chair, picked up the camouflage suit, and started to put it on. "They'll be too busy."

"But, if they do?" Marge got up from the bed.

Mac smiled. "You were asleep. They must have missed our room."

Marge looked at her husband. Jesus, she thought. He's serious. She moved closer, hand gripping his arm. "But what about you?"

"Tell them Tom picked me up last night right after dinner." Mac sat on the edge of the bed and pulled on his Nikes. He could see the questioning look on her face. "The fellow we met who lives near here and works for Del Monte. We've gone boar hunting on the eastern end of the island."

She nodded silently, eyes misting.

He stood up and kissed her eyes.

"Think it'll work?" she asked.

Mac smiled. "It's survival time. We improvise." He slid the lanai door open slightly and looked out. "I'll be right back," he said.

He was back in six minutes, having borrowed a loaf of bread, a stick of butter, six eggs, a papaya, half pound of Kona coffee, a package of corn flakes, a carton of milk, a small package of cheese, a six-pack of Primo beer, and several pots and pans, all from ocean suite four.

Marge had to laugh when she saw what he'd brought back. Watching him put the items in the refrigerator, she said, "A six-pack. I was hoping for Dom Perignon, Moet Chandon, or even Piper Hiedsick."

"Don't touch the beer," Mac admonished, moving two cans to the small freezing compartment. "That's for later."

Mac ate a bowl of cereal in silence. Marge watched him. He had almost finished when she asked, "You're not going up there now? In the daylight?" Her tone of voice asked him not to. "It's too risky," she added.

"I have to. Risk is part of life." In that instant she saw his warm eyes turn to steel.

"Be careful," she said. "You're my very favorite husband." Their kiss was warm, sweet, and passionate. He pulled on his camouflage mask.

At six fifty-five A.M., Big George was headed toward the main building. He passed the royal poinciana tree at the junction of two paths, the left one leading to the front entrance, the other to the lanai. His eyes drank in the beauty of the huge, scarlet umbrella as he took the path to the right. Mac knew he had to keep going. If he stopped, he'd have to face reality. One thing caught his attention. The morning was exceptionally quiet. No birds sang.

Big George took a deep breath, slid open the lanai door, and clumped into the Koa Lounge. Through the slits in the mask, Mac's eyes quickly surveyed the scene. There were three other terrorists in the room, all with their masks on. He recognized the walk and build of the one Fire had called Scorpion. He couldn't place the other two. It was still early morning cool, but beads of perspiration ran down his back under his clothes as he walked toward them.

"Jorge, find any beer yet?" That had to be the terrorist who'd tried to steal his cigarettes.

"Not yet," Mac muttered, pulling out George's pack of Winstons and offering the man one.

"Gracias, amigo." The man moved his AK-47 to his left hand and took two. He put one in his pocket, then lit the other one.

Mac moved on toward the tall terrorist and nodded a greeting.

"That Angelo, a wild man when he drinks. El Diablo. Don't give him any beer," the Scorpion cautioned.

Mac nodded. So the light-fingered terrorist's name was Angel.

"Have a cup of coffee." The Scorpion gestured toward a pot and some cups on the corner table. "Then give me a hand. We're guarding the hostages this morning."

While pouring his coffee, Mac noticed that Kona, the manager, had taken over and was organizing her staff, who were also being held as hostages, to help care for the resort's guests. A simple breakfast of juice, coffee, sweetrolls, and mixed fruit was being set up on the long buffet table.

Mac sipped his coffee slowly. He watched the third terrorist walk over and say something to the Scorpion. At one point they both glanced in his direction and he felt the skin crawl along the back of his neck. Coffee finished, he picked up his assault rifle and saw the third terrorist turn, signal Angel to follow, and walk out the doorway into the lobby.

The Scorpion beckoned and Mac joined him. Together they moved down the rows of hostages, the tall Puerto Rican holding both AK-47s, one in each hand, like a western gunslinger, while Mac untied the captives. Several of the knots were too tight to undo, so Mac cut them with his knife.

"Kona convinced her sister to untie the hostages," the Scorpion said matter-of-factly. "Said it would be easier to take care of them." Shrugging his shoulders, he added, "Probably have to tie them back up later."

Mac stored away the information. So Kona and Fire were sisters. Of course. That accounted for the dazzling facial resemblance. A pair of heavenly bodies. Two eye-catching, long-stemmed beauties as uniquely Hawaiian in form and color as the exotic bird of paradise flowers. Except for the difference in their hair styles and color, they looked exactly the same.

The Scorpion watched each pair of men as they were untied and allowed to head to the men's room. The women had been free to use the ladies' room throughout the night. Most of the hostages took advantage of the opportunity to wash their hands and faces. Mac smiled as he looked around at them. The sexual connotations of the night before were gone. Most of the women didn't look as good in the bright light of day. Mascara had run. Makeup had faded, caked, cracked, and flaked. Hairdos were disheveled. Faces and eyes looked puffy. Mac glanced around again. Most of the hostages were sitting there staring at one another and wondering if they could possibly look that bad.

"Don't I know you from someplace?" the thin wiry man in the elegant pair of blue silk pajamas asked the man tied behind him, in a voice little louder than a whisper.

"I've been waiting for the right opportunity," the heavyset man in white boxer shorts and T-shirt replied softly. "Your name, by chance, wouldn't be Harrison?"

"It has been," answered the wiry man, the voice mildly British.

"Reginald?"

"I have been called that, yes." The British accent was stronger now.

"Two . . . three years ago, in Rome?"

"I'm still trying to place you."

"I'm Max Parker." The heavyset man lowered his

voice to a whisper. "The Moro kidnapping. Red Brigades. Our paths crossed."

"You looked familiar. But what happened to your moustache and your hair?"

"They were fake. This is the real me. Chrome-dome Parker." The heavyset man chuckled softly.

"Small world."

"Seems smaller every year. What is British Intelligence doing on Molokai?" Parker's eyes roamed the room checking the location of the terrorists.

"It's complicated," the wiry man answered.

"I'm afraid we've got a lot of time."

"Yes, unless they find out who we are." The man's lips turned down momentarily. "By the way, my name is now James Mason."

"Very original." Parker chuckled again. And very British, he thought to himself. "Keep your voice down. At least tied back to back no one can surprise us."

"For the last nine months I've been tracking Carlos, that fellow in the lobby." Mason nodded in the general direction, forgetting that Parker couldn't see his head.

Parker turned to look, picking out Carlos instantly. "He's got some reputation."

"About the worst. I've followed him from Libya to Germany to Italy to Lebanon to Libya and now here."

"Strong Libyan connection?"

"No doubt Qadhafi's behind this. He's a power-hungry madman, volatile and unpredictable. Libyan oil money finances most of the world's terrorism. They're training hundreds, possibly thousands of terrorists," Mason took a deep breath, "placing small units all over the western world. Hit teams of fanatics. Three or more terrorists per cell. Suicide squads, armed to the teeth."

"It's either going to be a big explosion . . ." Parker

paused, face expressionless.

"Or a lot of little ones like this." Mason completed the thought.

"This seems well organized. Very professional."

"What's Virginia's interest?" the Englishman asked.

"Very similar to yours. The young handsome playboy out there with your man. Until now we had nothing concrete. Agent in the Cuban DGI. Commutes between Cuba and Libya. In the U.S. he's got strong connections with the black revolutionaries and the Weather Underground."

Mason's eyes caught a glimpse of Marco through the lobby doorway. The young terrorist with the swarthy face had his mask off.

"Looks like a handsome hunk of macho man."

"Crazy, wild—a tiger. Loves young women. When you get close, look at his eyes. You'll see the real Marco. They're hard, cruel, pitiless." Parker spit out the words, hesitated, then said, "Already you can smell the fear in this room."

The thin wiry man moved his arms, pushing them against his lower back, forcing Parker to move with him. "Sorry, old chap," he said. "I'm afraid that's not fear you smell. But at my age, when you're plumbing gets old . . . I do hope they untie us soon."

Parker smiled in spite of himself. "I hope so. They're halfway through the line now. It shouldn't be too long."

Mason settled back, sighed, then asked, "Don't you find it odd that neither your man nor my man is running this show?"

"Yes. The girl called Fire seems to be in command. I've never heard of her before. Have you?" Parker asked.

"No. But she's got expert help from all over the world."

"A truly international terrorist group."

"Getting together as one."

"Think of it. If the PLO—FALN—IRA—Red Brigades—Weather Underground—Black Liberation Army—African movements—the Red Flag Group all started planning and working together."

"Backed by Libya's money and unlimited arms."

"A world in chaos!" exclaimed Parker.

"Exactly! A death match, from one bloody sea to the next." Mason shook his white head sadly.

Parker could feel the color leaving his face.

"And you think this is their first operation?"

"Yes . . . possibly the start of a worldwide explosion of terrorism."

"Why Hawaii?" Parker asked, not really expecting an answer.

"I don't know, but I think we'll find out soon enough. Maybe just because it's paradise—the most un-likely place of all. Terrorists are totally unpredictable."

"And behind it all the KGB and the Marxist fanatics. The revolutionaries are all playing right into Russia's hands . . ."

Parker stopped in midthought and nudged Mason. Both men lapsed into silence while the terrorist known as Jorge walked past.

"Something odd about that one," Parker remarked flatly.

"Cuban, isn't he?" Mason asked.

"By name, possibly Puerto Rican. Don't know for sure. Haven't heard him say anything. I saw him last night and was impressed by the size of his feet."

"You always were one for details."

"Yeah, but the oddest thing. This morning his feet have shrunk."

"That's not so odd, so have my kidneys," Mason said, groaning.

Parker laughed softly, but there was little mirth to it.

Free to move about, the hostages ate breakfast and gathered together in small groupings. Some sat at tables, but most sat or lay down on the floor. Kona had produced about a dozen decks of cards, four backgammon games, and two chess sets. Most of these were now in use. A pile of paperbacks was stacked on one table. Like an angel of mercy, the tall golden-skin girl with the long black hair was everywhere.

"Stay patient and don't panic," she whispered to an older man, half-frozen with fear. "Have faith," to a white-haired lady producing a Bible for her to read. To an upset young couple, she spoke reassuringly, in a voice surprisingly soft, almost gentle. "I'm sure Rock-Resorts will refund your money, but I hope you'll come back here. It's really a perfect place." Smiling warmly at them, she moved on.

A young couple tried to blend into the woodwork. The harder they tried the more obvious they became.

"I told you, Carol, this was a bad idea," the man said, his voice low, face downcast, eyes examining the room furtively.

"Will you relax, Jerry? No one here knows you," she said, her eyelids trembling in anger. "That damn wife of yours . . ." Her voice trailed off, the thought unfinished.

"We'll probably make all the front pages." There was real concern in his voice.

"I hope they do a television special on us," she said,

spitefully. " 'Doctor and nurse caught together in hostage drama.' It's probably been done before on 'General Hospital.' "

An attractive, middle-aged couple from Colorado, Rick and Joan Waltz, couldn't help but overhear. They glanced knowingly at one another.

"Thank God those days are behind us," Rick spoke softly.

Joan nodded, then laughed. "You looked too good to be true. I had to be sure."

Rick looked at the couple carefully. The man she'd called Jerry was about six feet tall, 180 pounds, uncommonly handsome, in his early forties and obviously rich. His white pajamas and lounging robe were pure silk, his watch a Piaget Polo, 18-carat gold, hand-carved link by link. His face had *guilty* written all over it. A honey blonde, the girl was stunning in a slinky slip of a blue gown. Elegant, yet provocative. Her skin had a healthy glow and Rick sensed a strong inner radiance.

Joan was thinking similar thoughts. The girl, Carol, had a pretty face. Her makeup was understated, giving her a soft look. She was probably the doctor's assistant, lover, companion, secretary. His everything, except wife. She probably helped with his business, ran errands, made phone calls. Whatever he wanted, she gave. In return, he probably gave little—a few dinners here and there, an occasional trip. He'd probably changed everything about her, except her name. The girl was maybe ten years younger than the doctor. Young would become used and used would become old. Joan's heart went out to the girl. As for the handsome doctor, she suspected he could hide behind a corkscrew.

Rick nudged his wife. "Smith or Jones, for five bucks."

"Jones, but make it ten."

"You're on," Rick replied. Then turning to the young couple, he extended his hand, saying, "Hello, I'm Rick Waltz; this is my wife Joan."

The doctor's face flushed momentarily. Shaking Rick's hand, he answered, "I'm Jerry this is . . . ah . . . Carol."

Rick smiled. It was no bet.

The girl shook her head sadly, then flashed a pretty smile. "It's Jerry Anderson and Carol Terry," she said, emphasizing the last names.

"Terrible situation, isn't it?" asked Rick.

"A damn circus," Jerry replied. "The world is going down the drain."

"It sure looks that way, but I'm a born optimist," Rick said. "If you keep your face to the sun, you can't see the shadows."

"Unfortunately, I'm a fatalist," the doctor replied. "Yesterday we were all children laughing in the sun. Today . . ."

"We've been locked in our room," Rick finished the thought.

"Let's try to make the best of it," Carol said.

Rick nodded. "You can't fight the people who have all the guns."

"Do you play bridge?" Joan asked.

Jerry nodded. It would pass the time.

"I'd love to learn," Carol said. "It would be something that Jerry and I could do together." Under her breath she added, "That we could talk about." She knew Jerry was a superb bridge player. It was one game that didn't require balls.

On the other side of the young couple, a heavyset woman wearing a wrinkled muu-muu gestured and said,

"Do you mind if I watch?"

"Not at all," Joan said.

Jerry gulped. The lady had the face of a carp.

Carol smiled broadly. It would serve Jerry right. He couldn't stand the sight of ugly women.

Patroling around the room, all senses alert, Mac watched Kona disappear into the kitchen area, and wondered how two sisters who looked so much alike could act so differently. The hostages were talking more freely now. Most of what Mac overheard he immediately discarded, but a few comments were pushed onto a shelf in the back of his mind. Repeating them occasionally, he hoped to remember one or two to tell Marge.

"A mob doesn't run across town to do a good deed . . . goddamn alimony, it's like pumping gas in another guy's car . . . I don't have stress, but I think I'm a carrier . . . You can tell the bald men. They're the ones wearing hats . . ."

Mac smiled behind his mask. He agreed with all of those, especially the one about the bald men. He reached up and touched the cap on top of his mask. His smile broadened. He was wearing two hats. The hostages still had their sense of humor. He could feel a wave of optimism building in the room.

Joan Waltz shuffled the cards, riffling the edges of the deck expertly, and dealt. She opened the bidding with a short club, and Rick responded with a heart. At her mention of a spade, her husband jumped to four hearts, closing out the bidding.

"About time I got to play one," he said.

His wife laid out the dummy's hand and sat back.

The fat lady who was slumped on the chair alongside

the cardplayers looked at Joan, and in a low voice commented wistfully, "You have such a nice figure."

Joan smiled at the compliment, turning to talk to the lady. "I didn't always. Three years ago I was thirty pounds overweight."

"What's your secret?"

"I call it my Fat in the Can plan."

The lady's face looked puzzled.

"Most people who want to lose weight set themselves impossible goals, twenty or thirty pounds. They go on a crash diet and expect it to melt away overnight. It doesn't. They give up and out of frustration go on an eating binge."

The fat lady nodded, her jowls flapping. That was her problem.

Joan checked the table; the hand was half-finished. She turned back to the lady. "Anyone who goes on a diet has to set a realistic goal. Regardless of the diet, you should be able to lose a pound a week. Be conservative —three pounds a month."

"That doesn't sound like much."

"Do you know what three pounds of fat looks like?" Joan's brown eyes flashed. "It's a three-pound can of shortening. That's a lot of lard."

The lady smiled, visualizing the amount of lard in the can.

"My secret plan," Joan leaned close to the woman and whispered, "was that every time I lost three pounds, I'd buy a can of shortening and set it on my kitchen counter. It meant three pounds less I was carrying around. I could actually see the fat I'd lost. A real incentive to take it off and keep it off. Those ten cans are still there. When I'm home, I look at them every day and think of all that fat spread over my body."

"Made it," Rick announced. "We're vulnerable, dear."

Joan turned back to the game.

The fat lady sat back, wondering if she lost some weight what she'd look like. Her mind flashed to her dressing table covered with cosmetic jars. All her life she'd been searching for a miracle cream, the one beauty secret that would change her appearance overnight. She'd never found it. She shook her head sadly at the thought. Maybe, just maybe . . . if she were thinner . . . But she'd have to lose sixty pounds. Twenty three-pound cans of shortening. Her mind piled them into a mountain. She couldn't possibly carry all of that around. She blinked her eyes, when realization hit her. She was doing it every day.

Mac felt eyes on his back and glanced around. The fat lady with the strong facial resemblance to the Japanese carp, hovering behind the bridge table, was watching him, blinking her eyes. She was still wearing a muumuu. Must have been sleeping in it, Mac thought. Avoiding her eyes, Mac moved slowly away, remembering a similar look on her face at that cocktail party. He knew that she knew he looked familiar and was doing her best to identify him. That would teach him to make nasty remarks. It would be his luck. The carp would wind up hooking him.

"Jorge!" The Scorpion's shout from the lobby doorway startled him. Mac started running toward the Scorpion, seeing the urgent wave of his arm.

"Police," the Scorpion said in a voice low enough that none of the hostages could hear. "Three patrol cars." The Scorpion turned and ran through the lobby door.

Big George turned and walked back into the main

room. "Okay. Everyone down. Put your head on your knees and sit tight." He gestured menacingly with the Kalashnikov.

The hostages moved quickly. In thirty seconds all of them were sitting on the floor. Mac sighed to himself. Gloom had returned to the room. The optimism of the early morning had evaporated.

CHAPTER SIX

The phone call had come into police headquarters in Kaunakakai at seven-thirty A.M.

Sergeant Yamato yawned as he reached for the phone. "Police," he said.

"This is unit one of HULA."

"Who?" Yamato asked.

"Shut up and listen!" The command was cold and deliberate. "HULA—the Hawaiian Underground Liberation Army. We've captured the Molokai-Surf."

"What?"

"We have 216 hostages. We'll kill them all—unless we get what we want."

"You're kidding. This is a joke," Yamato suggested hopefully.

"We're not kidding." The coldness of the voice left little doubt.

"What do you want?" Yamato asked.

"You'll find out soon enough."

The phone clicked dead.

Yamato touched the hook on the receiver twice, then dialed 522-3000. At the Molokai-Surf switchboard the same cold voice answered, "Unit one—HULA."

Yamato hung up the phone and pulled out the center
draw of his desk, rummaging quickly through the
papers, confusion overwhelming his mind. There had
been a recent bulletin from Honolulu. Instructions to all
Headquarters . . . Hostages . . . What to Do . . . He
hadn't read it. No one had. They'd all laughed. Damn
bureaucrats wasting money again. Terrorists? Hostages? On Molokai? Not bloody likely.

He went through the papers again. Where else could
he have put it? He sat back to think, mind and stomach
both churning. He had to find it. The commissioner
would have his ass. He'd be back working in the pineapple fields. About to close the drawer, he glanced in
again. The bulletin was staring at him from the top of
the pile. Taking a deep breath, he read through it
quickly. Now following the instructions, he made a
number of phone calls.

Forty-five minutes later, three police cars, sirens wail-
ing, lights flashing, roared up the road toward the
Molokai-Surf. In the cars were Yamato and five other
policemen, one-half of the entire Molokai police force.
Each one of the policemen was armed with an S&W .38
and a riot shotgun. Each was wearing a combat flak
jacket and helmet. Five miles from the resort the police
turned off the sirens and flashing lights.

The only road to the Molokai-Surf approaches the
resort in a long downhill straightaway. The terrorists
saw the police cars when they were still over two miles
away. Marco signaled to Carlos and together they took
up positions on opposite sides of the road behind large
stone boulders about fifty yards from the front entrance, weapons in place.

Yamato stopped the lead police car about a half-mile
from the resort entrance. With powerful binoculars he
scanned the buildings. Then slowly the police cars

moved toward the front entrance. At 100 yards, the three cars pulled into a V formation, blocking the road and preventing escape for the terrorists. The six policemen took up positions behind their vehicles. Yamato pulled his radio microphone extension cord to its full length. From behind the center vehicle he called in a report to headquarters, then gave the others a circular sign with his thumb and forefinger. They'd followed instructions. Now it was up to the rest of the force and the Marines. It was eight thirty-two A.M.

The police on Molokai wear dark blue fatigues, but their helmets and the markings on their white police cars are baby blue. They made easy targets. Marco and Carlos sighted through the scopes of their Russian-made bazookas. At eight thirty-three A.M. Marco shouted, "Fire." The first rocket pierced the front of the center car and blew the back away. All three police cars disappeared in one giant fireball. Clouds of acrid black smoke drifted across the golf course. There were no survivors.

The thump of the bazookas and the explosions of the police cars shattered the silence that had descended on the Koa Lounge. Six or seven of the hostages screamed. In a few minutes the terror quieted, except for one elderly woman who sat bent over her knees rocking back and forth on the floor, screaming hysterically. Many of the hostages wept openly. As the sound of the explosions faded, the hostages could hear the cheers of the terrorists and then their loud laughter as they came back into the lobby.

Standing inside the lounge, close to the lobby doorway, Mac had seen everything and gritted his teeth in frustration. He could hear Fire's voice as she came into view.

"Great shot, Carlos."

Turning to Marco, she patted the side of his face.

"Marco, I knew you were more than just a pretty boy."

The Scorpion came into the lounge, laughing, followed closely by Fire and Carlos. Like Marco, Fire had also taken off her mask and was shaking out her bouquet of dark, curly red hair. Her face had the color of coffee with a rich dab of cream mixed in. Carlos wasn't wearing his mask either. His face was grizzled and scarred and his teeth were crooked. Mac gulped hard, hoping that mask removal wasn't either compulsory or contagious.

Fire heard the repeated screams of the elderly woman and quickly walked over to her. Kneeling in front of the woman, she slapped her hard across the face. The white-haired woman stopped screaming and sat mouth open with a dazed expression on her face. Slowly she drew into herself. Fire stood up and walked over to Mac.

"Sorry you missed the show, Jorge." Fire stared at the big terrorist.

Big George's mask nodded back. Fate had Mac by the throat. Afraid to speak, afraid she'd hear the loud thumping of his heart.

Fire continued to stare, then suddenly threw back her head and laughed. "Behind that mask," her fingers reached out and patted the side of the mask, "lies a real chatterbox." Removing her hand, Fire turned abruptly and walked into the kitchen.

Mac inhaled deeply. The girl had left a strong scent of white ginger. Still breathing heavily, Mac walked over to the coffeepot, poured himself a full cup, then slumped down on the nearest chair. The coffee burned his lips. It didn't matter. He needed another shot of caffeine, right now. He felt like a pigeon in a room full of cats. Sitting there, he couldn't help overhear voices from the kitchen. It sounded as if the two sisters were arguing.

"You don't have any feelings at all," a low voice said bitterly.

"You're just a dreamer, playing with whales." It was the hard voice that Mac knew to be Fire's. "While I'm doing something important for the whole world."

"Holding my guests hostage . . . you're trying to humiliate me. The voice of Kona trembled and trailed off. Mac had difficulty hearing her.

"Sister, dear, the strong always rule." Fire's voice was hard and cold. "It's time you realize you're a hostage, too. Get your ass in there and help."

Moments later, Mac watched Kona emerge from the kitchen and walk out among the hostages, a deeply troubled look on her face. Maybe, just maybe, if he could talk to Kona alone, she could help.

The explosions had shattered Marge. Alone with her thoughts, seated on a chair in the corner of ocean suite seven, she was terrified. Not for her own safety. But suddenly the realization hit her of what life would be like if something happened to Mac. He was her everything. His love was her pillow; she went to sleep on it every night.

Her first husband had died tragically. An airplane accident on a business trip. Here one moment, gone the next. It had been six months of shock and grief. Then for four years life had been lonely. After meeting Mac her whole life had changed overnight, opening like a rose coming out of a tight, tiny bud. Their marriage had brought real happiness, true contentment. He'd set her spirit free and it had soared.

She jumped at a harsh, rasping scream close by.

Glancing out the window, she could see a large, white-tailed tropical bird gliding along the cliff line. It screamed again, and dove after a squid in the sea below.

Marge looked forward eagerly to the rest of her life with Mac. They had common interests and still found each other fresh, interesting, and exciting. Their hearts beat in rhythm. With his retirement, they'd have more time together. Next Sunday would be her birthday. A biggie. One she'd like to forget. She wondered if Mac would remember. They were getting along in age. Marge wasn't afraid of growing older. There was no acceptable alternative. But she had made up her mind she was never going to grow old. It was all a matter of staying interested and interesting. Her mother had taught her that.

But, she couldn't imagine a future without Mac. And right now he was flirting with death, trying to help some people he didn't even know. Mac was acting strangely. It was almost like he was enjoying . . . No. That wasn't fair.

Emotions churning, nerve ends frayed, Marge started to cry, not wanting to, but unable to help it. She walked to the bathroom and sat on the toilet, with a towel in her hands. Ten minutes later she washed her face. Emerging from the bathroom, somehow feeling better, Marge had made a decision. Whatever Mac decided he had to do would be all right with her. She'd put her trust in God. Only God was immortal.

The stillness of the morning was suddenly shattered by the sudden steady thumping of a helicopter overhead. Moving closer to the sliding glass lanai doors, her heart leapt when she saw the helicopter and read the word MARINES in bold block letters on the fuselage. "Thank you, God," she whispered. Help was on the way.

• • •

The rotors clacked, sunlight reflecting off the spinning blades. The dark green whirlybird made one pass directly over the main building, banked steeply around the smoldering remains of the charred police cars, then began a gradual circle of the perimeter of the resort.

The pilot, First Lieutenant Tuckey Fenton, glanced at his copilot, Lieutenant Grizz Risley, who pushed the button of his microphone and reported to base headquarters on Oahu. "The three police cars are still burning. No one survived. It's a terrible mess."

Outside, near the front entrance, Fire and Marco watched the chopper. Fire spoke first. "Things will start heating up now."

"I thought they'd send in the Marines. We deserve the very best." Marco grinned and signaled to Carlos.

Carlos ducked inside the lobby area. A moment later he emerged carrying a long tubelike apparatus. Maneuvering in the shadow of the roof overhang, eyes intently watching the helicopter, he mentally timed the flight pattern. Now the chopper was out over the water flying parallel to the cliffs at rooftop altitude. Carlos lined up the cross hairs and pushed the red switch on the SAM-7 portable antiaircraft missile launcher.

The Marine helicopter exploded in a giant fireball, pieces falling into the sea. An oily ball of smoke hung low over the water, then dissipated in the morning breeze. For the second time in one morning there were no survivors.

From inside the Koa Lounge, Mac had heard the sound of the helicopter, seen the terrorist activity in the lobby area, and heard the explosion. Through the lanai doors, all of the hostages could see the pall of oily smoke rising from the sea.

Mac breathed deeply to control his emotions. The morning was one to be forgotten. Things were looking down. Everything had turned to worms. This was as sadistic a group of cold-blooded killers put together anyplace, since man first dropped out of a tree. They shot first and talked second.

The hostages sat mute on the floor. In their eyes, Mac could see terror.

It was close to ten when the fat Hawaiian called Anahu and another terrorist unknown to Mac came into the lounge carrying a spool of wirelike cord and several large containers. The Scorpion signaled to Jorge to cover the three of them. Unrolling the cord, they wound it down among the hostages, crisscrossing the entire floor. From the containers, they removed small packages of a plastic substance, placing them at intervals along the cord and connecting them to it. Mac's eyes followed the wire to where Anahu was inserting several leads into a small box placed next to a chair near the lobby entrance.

Mac bit his lip, feeling lightheaded, stomach muscles tightening in revulsion. Even the most ghastly scenes of his past paled in memory. His eyes took photographic images, like a Nikon, impersonally and without passion. It was important to know the exact location of every one of those detonating cords, and every one of those packages of plastic.

Walking slowly among the hostages, he heard a voice with a British accent saying softly, "A person without fear is a damn fool."

"Let me tell you about that stuff," said another man. "I'm scared shitless myself."

Mac had to agree with both of them. Then the full impact of their words registered deeper in his mind. Those two men knew what that plastic stuff was. They obviously knew it was C-4, one of the most powerful explosives available. He glanced quickly in their direction and filed their descriptions away in his head. One was a tall, wiry man in an elegant pair of blue silk pajamas and a matching dressing gown. Mac guessed he was the one with the accent. The heavyset bald man was pure American, dressed in white boxer shorts and a T-shirt.

It was less than ten minutes later that Big George and the Scorpion were replaced by two other terrorists. They had a two-hour break. Mac walked slowly past the small box to which Anahu had connected the wires, studied it as carefully as he could without appearing to be interested, and then headed for the lanai door. Thank God, he thought, at least it wasn't a timing device. The hostages were sitting on a live volcano about to erupt. All it would take was a simple push of a button.

Lloyd Reynolds pulled his pickup truck into a parking spot in front of the Golden Eagle Diner on the outskirts of Honolulu and turned off the engine. He glanced into the mirror, pleased with what he saw. The skin on his baby face was tanned like fine leather, his teeth were even and white, his hair was blond and wavy. He took a comb from his pocket and ran it through his hair twice. From a small paper sack on the seat, he took out a small pill, popped it into his mouth, and swallowed it. He slid out of the truck, slammed the door, and walked into the diner.

The pleasant brunette behind the counter smiled and said "Aloha" as he mounted the stool at the end.

Lloyd grinned. "The usual," he said, eyes riveted on the movements of her hips under her tight-fitting jeans as she poured him a cup of coffee and turned to place the rest of his order. His tongue wet his lips at his thoughts.

The phone on the wall near the end of the counter rang and she answered it. Reynolds couldn't help but overhear the one-sided conversation.

"Golden Eagle. Oh, hi, Tom."

"What!" The brunette's voice registered astonishment.

"Oh, damn, it's Jonnie's birthday."

Twenty seconds of silence, then . . . "We'll manage. Be careful, darling. I love you."

The waitress hung up the phone and stood quietly, head down, her back to Lloyd. The bell from the pass-through window startled her out of her thoughts and she picked up Lloyd's ham, eggs, and toast and placed it in front of him. Her face, normally radiant, was a pale white.

"Trouble?" Lloyd asked.

"Can you imagine?" She spoke in a low voice. "Some terrorists have taken over the Molokai-Surf. Tom's unit is going over to rescue the guests."

"Jesus!" Lloyd said. "The world is full of crazies. But why Molokai?"

Biting her lip, the brunette didn't answer. She didn't know why. Shaking her head, she picked up some dishes from a spot down the counter and walked slowly into the kitchen.

With one eye on the round wall clock, Lloyd wolfed down his ham and eggs, swallowed the rest of his coffee and pushed two dollars under the empty plate. With two pieces of toast in hand, he walked quickly out of the diner.

Arriving at the airport less than twenty minutes later, still wearing his yellow Adidas T-shirt, white Levi's and sandals, he half-ran, half-slid to the Air Molokai counter.

"Your ten-thirty plane to Molokai. Can I still make

it?'' Lloyd's hand held out an American Express credit
card.

The pleasant-looking Hawaiian girl behind the
counter, wearing a pink orchid in her hair, turned and
checked the board behind her. Turning back, she
smiled, showing large white teeth. "You have time."
She filled out his ticket, while Reynolds fidgeted.

"Return?" she asked.

"Open."

"Baggage?"

He held up his carryall. It contained a windbreaker,
toilet kit, cap with a press badge, press credentials, Nikon camera, and film. Three months before he'd pur-
chased the entire kit at a secondhand store. The press
kit rode with him in his truck.

"Gate One." She smiled again.

During the twenty-three-minute flight, the blonde's
mind was churning. His friends didn't call him Crazy
Lloyd for nothing. Crazy like a sly fox. At age thirty-
four, Reynolds lived by his wits. When you live by your
wits, your wits get sharp. He grinned. His room in his
mother's house was filled with racing forms and tout
sheets. Most gamblers were creatures of habit. Not
Lloyd Reynolds. For years he'd hopped around like a
psychotic flea looking for his golden goose. So far
they'd all laid scrambled eggs. He'd walked the tight
line where hope and frustration meet. No longer. There
was nothing but big money ahead. He touched the
heavy gold chain on his neck. From now on they'd call
him Lucky Lloyd.

Terrorists taking over the biggest hotel on Molokai.
The Marines involved in a rescue mission. It would
become a media circus. Intensive coverage. It was time
for guts, for daring. A show of his character. He'd be
the first reporter on the scene. Free-lance. Get the inside

story, firsthand. Grab the headlines . . . a samurai without a code. Results were what counted. Closing his eyes, he visualized the remote Molokai-Surf, out beyond reality, out where there were no rules, no regulations, no inhibitions. Out where he'd function at his best.

By the time the plane landed at Hoolehua airport, Lloyd Reynolds was almost hyperventilating. He sat for a moment to catch his breath, then ran for the Tropical Rent-A-Car counter.

Driving on the lonely seven-mile road to the Molokai-Surf, Lloyd Reynolds roared with laughter. Laughing aloud was one of his real pleasures. He was hell-bent for glory. He laughed again. Just one hit of coke and he'd feel like a new man. Then the new man would want another hit. Shit, there wasn't any coke. Reaching for his small paper bag, he fingered a pill, checked its color, then popped it into his mouth. He laughed. Gold to make him bold.

Before noon, Lucky Lloyd, gambler, thief, and self-appointed free-lance reporter, was in position up the road, on the high ground above the Molokai-Surf, waiting for the Marines to arrive.

CHAPTER SEVEN

The Scorpion waited for Jorge outside the main building. Mac saw him at the lanai door and tried to leave through the lobby. The Scorpion intercepted him.

"Jorge, *ven*." The tall thin man spoke in Spanish, then turned.

Mac followed closely, watching carefully, sensing trouble. He spotted the hypodermic needle in the sheath on the Scorpion's belt. It was probably his trademark, the lethal sting that backed up his nickname. Mac swallowed. An apt nickname sticks on the mind like flypaper. It never goes away. Right now he felt like Chicken Mac.

They passed six buildings. Mac knew they were going to turn into the next one. He'd guessed where they were headed. The temptation to shoot the Scorpion in the back as they walked gnawed at him. But that would mean a shoot-out and instant death—for a lot of people.

As they turned into the entrance of the next building, the Scorpion stepped aside and waited for Jorge to lead the way.

"*Nuestro cuarto,*" the terrorist said.

Mac knew he was playing a game of Russian roulette with five loaded chambers, but he had to take a chance. While turning out the lights in the buildings in the early hours of the morning, he had located the strip of rooms that had been occupied by the terrorists. They were in this building, second floor, overlooking the golf course. He took the stairway to the second floor. The Scorpion followed.

He remembered that the dirtiest room was the one opposite the stairway. It was a long shot and Mac knew he was squeezing the trigger on the Russian roulette pistol pointed right at his head. Without hesitation he walked straight to that door and threw it open, stepping aside to let the Scorpion enter first.

Bingo, Mac thought with a sense of elation. He'd fired the empty chamber. So far, so good.

"Something smells wrong, Jorge," the man said, taking off his mask and revealing a long scar down the side of an otherwise ugly face.

Mac gestured with his hands, the momentary sense of elation gone.

"It's you, Jorge, *el zorrillo*. You don't act right. You don't sound right. And you don't smell right . . ." His assault rifle was pointed at Mac's chest. "Drop your gun, amigo."

Mac's AK-47 clattered to the floor.

"*Dice algo en espanol!*" the Scorpion commanded.

Mac stood there, mind whirling. Someone had just slipped a deadly dum-dum bullet into the sixth chamber of the Russian roulette pistol. There was no way to win. He knew the Scorpion wanted him to say something in Spanish. The problem was that he didn't know any words or even how to speak Spanish.

The Scorpion waited, tightening his grip on his assault rifle. From the look on the terrorist's face, Mac knew he was going to use it.

Mac pointed to his throat, indicating a sore throat, and coughed.

"*Dice!*" the terrorist hissed.

"*Uno, dos, tres . . .*" Mac spoke hopefully, mind searching for any scrap of Spanish.

"*Mas!*" the Scorpion spoke excitedly.

Mac could think of only one phrase. It came from early childhood.

"*El ganso esta suelto,*" Mac blurted out.

"What!" the Scorpion snarled, prodding Mac's chest with his weapon.

"The goose is loose, you stupid ass," Mac snarled back, adding, "Don't you Cubans know any real Spanish?"

"Not Cuban . . . Puerto Rican . . . FALN . . . take off your mask!" the Scorpion commanded.

With a heavy sigh, Mac reached up and pulled off his mask.

"Jesus Christ," the Scorpion said, eyes wide open.

"Just call me Mac, it'll be a lot easier," McGregor answered, smiling broadly, left hand reaching for the thin pressurized container in his pocket, palming it.

"Funny man!" the Puerto Rican snarled.

"Smile . . . it no break your face . . . it's better to go out laughing," Mac said calmly. "By the way, what's '*un zorrillo*'?"

"A skunk," the Scorpion answered, concerned by the other's calmness, wondering who the hell he could be.

"Before you kill me, I think you'd better ask Fire," Mac said.

The Scorpion's lips curled into a gap-toothed smile.

"I don't think that's necessary . . . Fire's the one who thought you smelled too good."

"She might want to know about the mole in your group." Mac was throwing up a prayer, hoping for a miracle.

The Scorpion's eyebrows arched and his scar deepened in color. "Hands up high, gringo, and turn around."

He turned, but out of the corner of his eyes Mac saw the Scorpion's right hand reach down for the hypodermic needle in its sheath. The thought raced through Mac's mind that this guy was about to become a genuine pain in the ass. The Scorpion was now holding the AK-47 with only his left hand, and had just touched the sheath with his right when Mac spun back, pressing the valve on the top of the thin container in his left hand. The mace sprayed directly into the terrorist's face from a foot away. With his right hand, Mac chopped down on the barrel of the assault rifle, knocking it to the floor. The chemical continued to spray into the Scorpion's eyes, nose, and open mouth.

Both hands flew up to cover his face. Retching, he doubled in pain as Mac's knee caught him in the groin. Dropping the mace container, Mac's right hand chopped down expertly on the back of the Scorpion's neck and he crumpled to the floor.

Mac was coughing, his eyes watering from the chemical in the air. Crouching low, he retreated from the room and sat near an open window breathing deeply. Now he lit a cigarette, waiting for the fumes to dissipate.

Finished with the cigarette, Mac returned to the room and withdrew the hypodermic needle from the sheath. He looked at the thin plastic vial wondering what it contained. The picture of the police cars blowing up at the entrance to the Molokai-Surf flashed through his mind—and the Scorpion laughing as the bodies of the

policemen burned. Mac jabbed the needle full length
into the terrorist's thin buttocks. Finished, he replaced
the hypodermic needle back in the sheath. "It goes with
the nickname," Mac said to the body on the floor.
"Scorpions often get so frustrated they sting themselves
to death."

Moving rapidly, he dragged the body into the closet,
tossed the Scorpion's mask in behind it and closed the
door. The Scorpion had told him that Fire suspected
him. Mac's cover was all but blown. Now he had to
dispose of two bodies immediately. It had to look genuine. It had to look like an accident. Most of all, Fire
had to be convinced that he really was Jorge. Mac
picked up the big militant's mask and pulled it back
over his head.

The sound of a large flight of helicopters sent Mac
running.

As Mac emerged from the building, he glanced up
into the clear blue sky. For a few moments he stood
blinking in the bright sunshine, his shadow black
against the light gray of the pavement. He couldn't see
the helicopters. They had to be coming in low on the
other side of the golf course. Mac knew he was taking a
chance, but there was little time to waste. He raced for
the parking area. Reaching it and seeing no terrorists, he
opened the trunk of the Toyota. Hefting Big George's
body to his right shoulder, he wrinkled his nose, muttering to himself, "The Scorpion was right, the guy does
smell like a skunk."

Closing the trunk, Mac moved laboriously, staying
close to the hibiscus and bougainvillea bushes along the
path, knowing that the terrorists' attention would be
focused on the flight of helicopters now circling wide
around the resort complex.

Feeling as if the veins in his neck were about to pop,

his heart thumping wildly, and his breath coming in painful gasps, Mac reached the room on the second floor where less than twenty minutes before he'd killed the Scorpion. Dumping Big George's body on the floor, Mac closed the door, took a number of deep breaths to steady himself, then crouching low moved to the window and looked out. Waves of Marine Huey helicopters, staying low and out of range of the terrorist missiles, were touching down at the far side of the golf course, raising clouds of thin red dust. The dark green helicopters were disgorging hundreds of battle-equipped Marines, personnel carriers, and heavy weapons. Forming into small combat units, the Marines were moving slowly on a line toward the buildings, establishing a perimeter circle around the complex. Geronimo, Mac thought. Flat-bellies. Men at their best, in rock-hard, top physical condition, who knew how to handle tough situations.

Mac removed his camouflage suit, cap, and mask, and with difficulty dressed the big terrorist. Finished, he moved Big George to the nearest window, propping the corpse over the sill. Next, he dragged the Scorpion's body out of the closet, pulled the terrorist's mask back over his head, leaned him against the other open window, and wedged his Kalashnikov between his arms.

Out the window Mac could see a ribbon of Marines crouching, moving across the fourteenth fairway. From his vantage point, Mac realized that they were only thirty yards from a line where the sod had been recently disturbed. My God, thought Mac. Sometime during the night the terrorists had planted land mines. Quickly Mac sighted and fired a burst from his AK-47 along the freshly dug shallow trench. Two mines exploded with loud thumps as the closest Marines dove for cover.

Staff Sergeant Doug Harris threw himself to the

ground, dirt and debris showering down around him. Antipersonnel mines! They hadn't expected that. He shouted to Corporal Thomas to bring up the detectors.

The automatic weapon's fire had come from the upper window in the center building. Through the telescopic sight on his M-16 he could see the two terrorists in the windows in firing position. The Marines were under strict orders not to fire unless lives were in danger. His whole platoon was exposed. Squeezing the trigger, the head of one terrorist disappeared. He swung his rifle to the other terrorist and fired.

Crouched on the floor, Mac saw the bullets splatter Big George's brains, then saw a bullet dissolve the back of the Scorpion's head. He slid crabwise along the floor, opened the door, then ran quickly down the stairs, heading for ocean suite seven.

Marco's eyes were bright and nervous, flicking like automatic beacons from side to side. Crouching low, Kalashnikov in hand, he moved with deceptive speed, quickly covering the ground between the resort lobby area and the second-floor rooms the terrorists had occupied. He had heard the rapid fire from the AK-47s and the answering burst from the Marines.

Damn, it had to be the Scorpion who'd shot first. No, most likely it had been Jorge. That guy was trigger-happy and had been acting strangely. Fire had asked the Scorpion to find out what the hell was wrong with him. He personally had given explicit orders not to open up first against the Marine ground forces. It was not his intention to get into a fire fight with the Marines. Even he had to face reality. That would be a no-win situation. Their strategy of forward defense involved sucking the Marines in close, then forcing them to retreat in total embarrassment.

The hostages were the key to success. They were the key to everything. If HULA held to their demands, they had to win. The government of the United States would never sacrifice the lives of 216 innocent people. There was no doubt about that. Killing the hostages would be the easy part. That would be fun. A fool's grin covered his boyish face.

Marco climbed the stairs cautiously; the silence heavy and ominous. The door to the room opposite the stairs was open. The young terrorist stepped into the room, eyes quickly surveying the bloody scene. With eyes averted from the bodies of the two dead terrorists, he picked up Jorge's automatic rifle, gagged once as his hand touched a bit of flesh, and retreated from the room, closing the door. Taking a deep breath, he descended the stairs, having decided to send Anahu up to take care of the remains. The big Hawaiian disposed of corpses for the Yakusa, the local branch of the Mafia. He'd seen his share of headless bodies.

Lips clamped tightly, Marco checked Jorge's AK-47. A blind guy could tell that Jorge had been the one who'd fired. Shit. That big Cuban wouldn't miss his head, it had no brains in it anyhow. Damn. HULA needed all the men they had. Now two had been blown away. It would make it tougher to control their destiny. Dying was hard, but sometimes it made it even harder for the living. The Scorpion would be a real loss. That creep had venom in his blood. A born terrorist.

He was walking briskly now, back toward the lobby. Maybe they'd kill a couple of hostages in retaliation. Never forgive and forget, let bygones be bygones. Hell no. At the right time he'd stick it in their ear and blow their brains out. Give the tourists some pineapples they'd never forget. His mouth twisted into an evil, crazy grin. But timing was important. It was too early to start killing the hostages. Right now they were more valuable alive. HULA hadn't even made its demands known yet. It was just about time.

Marco neared the lobby, mind still churning. The rewards were worth the risk. The purpose of terrorism was to terrorize. The grin broadened on his handsome face. They'd do that, but they had a much broader goal. Their success would unleash the armies of hate around the globe. All over the world, suicide squads were poised on the brink, set to follow HULA's example. They'd jumped the gun by almost a week. Hell, someone had to be first, seize the lead. He and Fire had worked it out and Carlos had gone along. Now all the other cells would be followers. He laughed aloud. It was heady stuff. In every country doubters would become believers. The terrorists would all unite and the WHALE would become all powerful. The Worldwide Humanitarian and Liberation Effort. He laughed again. Throughout the world small groups of trained terrorists would seize large groups of hostages and offer to exchange them. The demand in each case would be exactly the same. "One for One." Soon the world would know what One for One meant. The United States would have to give in. The alternative was that thousands of hostages would be executed. Public opinion wouldn't stand for that.

Marco entered the lobby, almost high on the intensity of his thoughts. Damn, he could use a night with a female animal. Fire had turned him down. He'd get her yet. In the meantime maybe he'd approach Kona. In appearance, the two sisters were almost twins. The only difference was the color of their hair. He sucked on his teeth. What a pair of bodies. Just one time he'd like to

see them together to make a part-by-part comparison.
Odd, he never had. Hell, there wasn't time to persuade
either one to make love. This was no time for courting.
Tonight he'd just take his pick of the hostages and rape
her.

CHAPTER EIGHT

First Day—Afternoon

In ocean suite seven, Marge sat near the window, the balmy early-afternoon breeze rustling the louvered blinds, her eyes searching the path in both directions, checking for any movement of terrorists. In the last hour she'd spotted two. Mac had identified them quickly as Jumbo, the huge black, and Angel, a Cuban. Together they'd watched them carefully until they were out of sight.

Mac was sitting at the round *koa* table in the dining area, where he could view anyone approaching the room from the ocean side. On the table in front of him he'd unfolded and smoothed out the map from the brochure centerfold showing the layout of the resort. Now with a black felt pen he circled those rooms where the terrorists had set up gun positions, listing the weapons he remembered seeing at each location.

Moving from her chair, Marge leaned over Mac's shoulder, checking his progress and rubbing the back of his neck with her fingers. "You're something," she whispered in his ear, then returned to guard duty near the window.

"The Marines have probably already spotted the terrorist positions." Mac was talking softly, half to Marge, half to himself. "But then, maybe not."

Mac rose quickly, rummaging in the drawers, looking for a piece of writing paper. Finding none, he pulled the cardboard out of the middle of a freshly laundered blue shirt. Thank God, he thought, Marge didn't like to iron. Now, reseated at the table, he sketched out a diagram of the Koa Lounge on the cardboard, showing the general location of the hostages and the placement of the network of explosive charges he'd help set that morning. His mind replayed the photographic images he'd stored there. His hand traced them on the grid before him, marking an X for each package of C-4 plastic compound. Glancing at Marge, he sighed deeply. She didn't know that the hostages were one giant bomb, just waiting to go off. For the last few hours he'd been battling with himself, trying to decide whether to tell her. He still wasn't sure he had enough courage. He added a caution in the margin of his hand-drawn diagram. At a whim the terrorists could change everything.

On the other side of the shirt cardboard Mac listed the terrorists he'd seen, giving a brief description of each one, with particular emphasis on Carlos, Marco, and Fire. Next to Jorge and the Scorpion he put large crosses. Underneath, he wrote a brief note addressed to the C.O., Marine Assault Team, Molokai-Surf.

Finished, he signed the note with a flourish: Mac McGregor, USMCR-025841, astonished that he'd remembered his old service number. He grinned to himself. Once a Marine, always a Marine. With a piece of tape he attached the brochure map onto the shirt cardboard. Then he carefully slid the cardboard back into the blue shirt, replaced it in his drawer, and walked to the lanai door overlooking the ocean.

Near the shore the sea was unusually calm. The gentle swells of clear blue water sparkled like sapphires in the early afternoon sun. There was a large sailboat in the channel beating upwind, and beyond, the dark shape of Oahu. Nothing registered. Mac's mind was looking beyond the visual, almost into another dimension, all in an indigo haze. Suddenly he imagined a giant explosion—a fireball—and out of his blue shirt floated through the air out to the Marines. They were crowded into a small group, studying his sketch. When they looked up, the main building was leveled and all the hostages were stacked like cordwood, dead. With a shudder, Mac snapped back to reality. He shook his head, then turned and smiled weakly at Marge.

"Hey, hon," he said. "Let's figure how to check out of this place."

In the Koa Lounge, some of the hostages napped, others read, still others chatted in small groups, occasionally rising and walking in the prescribed areas, using care to avoid the wires and the small packages of plastic compound. The three Avon ladies were still huddled together like calabash cousins at a luau. They'd agreed that the more they talked, the less they'd worry. Connie, the short blonde from Costa Mesa, lit another Vantage, sipped at her plastic cup of coffee, leaned back, elbow on the floor, and started talking again.

"When I was in high school, I was an unhappy girl

with plump thighs." Her right hand automatically patted the outside of her right leg.

Betty Jane, the willowy brunette from Mesa, Arizona, smiled. She liked Connie, the girl had a self-deprecating way of talking about herself and her accomplishments. It was disarming, and Connie had enough talent and self-confidence to make it work for her.

"I still have the plump thighs." Connie grimaced. "But I'm glad I'm not a teenager today."

"So am I," Evelyn, the tall blonde from Boulder, Colorado, added. "It's a lot tougher. Sex—permissive sex—it's on TV, in movies, magazines, in advertisements. It's everywhere."

"Back home, when I was in school," the brunette looked around as if afraid someone might overhear, "if you weren't a virgin, you had to say you were."

Both of the others nodded, remembering their own teenage years. Connie laughed to herself. That hadn't been her problem. The damn plump thighs had kept the boys away.

"Now my daughter tells me that to be popular, if you're still a virgin, you have to say you're not." The brunette shook her head sadly, her eyes looking at the other two.

Evelyn didn't comment. She remembered her mother's lectures. Once gone, you can't get it back, you'll be sorry. Her mother had been wrong, she thought to herself. It had been worth it. Good girls did it, too. She'd been very good until she was eighteen, then she'd gotten better. It hadn't hurt her popularity.

Life was one moral challenge after another, Connie thought as she took another sip of coffee and looked at Betty Jane. The tall brunette was attractive in a strong and sexy way that didn't need cosmetics. She was drawn to her. Maybe too much. She was beginning to fantasize about the two of them together.

Evelyn studied the blonde from California, so short that people felt a compulsion to protect her. She had the strongest urge to hug Connie to herself. It wasn't necessary, she thought. The short blonde had proven she was big enough to overcome her shortness.

Betty Jane glanced around the room, then leaned forward and whispered to the other two in a confidential tone. "That couple we met at the cocktail party . . ."

"You mean the McGregors, Marge and Mac, the golfers?" Connie asked.

"Yes, I thought she was awfully nice."

"He wasn't bad, either, if you like bald men," said Connie, knowing that the brunette had mentioned Mac several times since.

"Well, I haven't seen them around."

The other two looked carefully around the room. Evelyn used the opportunity to go to the ladies' room. When she returned, she said, "They're not here. Where could they be? Don't you think we should ask about them?"

By midafternoon the advance units of the Marines had moved to within a hundred and fifty yards of the outermost resort buildings, tightening their perimeter circle.

Close to this front line, four Marine officers were hunkered down behind a monkeypod tree on the edge of the fourteenth green. A big rawboned man with a square jaw and a major's leaf on his helmet spoke first.

"We're set to move in whenever you're ready, Colonel."

The colonel nodded his head and glanced at the second major, the glance a request for the other's opinion.

"I say wait until it's dark. We'll infiltrate from all

sides, overpower them.'' The second major spoke with assurance, his confidence backed by innumerable combat decorations.

Colonel Donahue took off his helmet and ran his hand over his close-cropped, graying hair, then he crouched lower, shaded his light blue eyes and squinted around the monkeypod tree at the buildings. He sat down, back to the tree, putting his helmet on the ground. Slowly, almost deliberately, he removed a battered cigarette case with a Marine Corps insignia, inscribed with the words ARTHUR DONAHUE, 2ND LIEUTENANT USMC. He tapped out a cigarette and lit it, not bothering to offer any to the others. It annoyed him that they didn't smoke.

The others waited half a cigarette for him to speak.

''This isn't Korea. It isn't 'Nam. We're dealing with terrorists. Totally unpredictable . . . irrational. Crazies! They've got hostages. We don't know how many. We sit tight. We don't do anything until we know more, until we know what those bastards want.'' The colonel took a last drag on his cigarette and snuffed it out.

''Make your men comfortable. It could be a long wait.''

Donahue's fingers worked automatically, tearing the paper on the butt, crumpling it into a tiny ball and scattering it and the remaining grains of tobacco to the winds. Checking his watch, the colonel slipped on his helmet and stood up. Then, mouth set in a hard line, he glanced down at the other three officers.

''Men, if anyone gets tempted to charge in there,'' the colonel nodded his head at the resort, ''just think of your wife—or your daughter—as one of the hostages.''

The colonel turned and walked back toward his command vehicle. It was time to report into headquarters.

It was three P.M. when they heard the recorded sound

of taps coming over the loudspeaker. It was beamed directly to the Marines. It was loud and clear. It lasted twenty seconds and was followed by an announcement. The voice was clear. The voice was cold. The voice was Fire's.

> "Marines of the imperialist United States. This is unit one of HULA. Listen and listen carefully. If any one of you moves one foot closer, three hostages will die.

> "If you make any rescue attempt, all the hostages will die. Powerful explosive charges have been set among them and they will be blown sky-high.

> "You have exactly thirty minutes to move back out of our sight. If you don't, three hostages will be executed.

> "So that there is no mistake, the time is now one minute after three."

The front door of the resort opened and in plain sight of the Marines three hostages, hands tied behind their backs and linked together by a light nylon line, were led out to the flagpole in the center of the turnaround driveway. Carlos quickly tied them securely to the base of the flagpole. Leaving, he spoke reassuringly to the three. "Behave yourselves. You'll be perfectly safe here."

Once again the three Avon ladies were bravely standing together in a back-to-back triangle. They were fully clothed, wearing jeans and light sweaters.

It was not yet three-ten when Colonel Donahue made his decision. "Move the men back. I want every one of them out of sight by three-thirty."

The pullback began immediately. By three-thirty not a single Marine could be seen from any of the resort buildings.

Lieutenant Colonel Red McKenna shifted his briefcase between his feet, turned his head slightly, and glanced at the other two passengers in the small helicopter. There was a look of obvious pride on his face. There was no doubt in his mind. This was the best hostage negotiation team in the entire Corps. After the fiasco in Teheran, he had personally recommended that the Marines train a number of small, select units to be available to negotiate the release of hostages, civilian as well as military, whenever and wherever necessary. General Clark had supported this recommendation. After approval by the commandant, McKenna had been appointed to hand-pick his own team for eight months of intensive training at the War College in Newport. McKenna's team was now one of six such units located at strategic locations around the world.

McKenna knew what it meant to be a prisoner, having spent fourteen long months as a guest of the Vietcong. He rubbed his knee, an unconscious habit, whenever he thought of the past. There were so many screws holding his knee together he couldn't pass through the metal detectors at the airport. He winced. Damn knee had kept him from combat command. Now he was staff. So far his hostage negotiation team had achieved nothing. His idea looked great in theory, but this was the first major test. The moment of truth was approaching fast and hard.

He'd picked his team carefully and well. His eyes settled on Jim Corwin, a quiet, deliberate man with short black hair hugging his head. A superb tactician with the mind of a computer, Corwin's thinking was precise and

organized. McKenna grinned to himself. Even the
major's cat was potty trained. Corwin was an academi-
cian who'd always been at the top of his class.

The colonel's eyes slid over to Bill Bailey, a heavyset,
gregarious, fun loving captain. His face was the first
thing anyone noticed. He was a dead ringer for Buddy
Hackett, but the captain's head was pure gray, and
McKenna knew that each hair stood for a colorful
adventure. Bailey had seen death often and had few illu-
sions. Needing excitement, all he had to do was go back
through the paths of his memory. Bailey was a superb
negotiator, fast on his feet, with sound judgment, yet
innovative and articulate. His soft voice never rose
above a buttery drawl.

McKenna glanced through the windshield of the helicopter. They were approaching Molokai. In the distance
he could make out the Molokai-Surf where the terrorists' early morning message had been written in blood.
The pilot turned, staying out of range of terrorist missiles, heading now for the far edge of the golf course
where large Hueys were still disgorging their combat
cargoes.

He shifted his position again. Colonel Donahue was
in command of the total operation. One of the best—
tough, brave, smart, a pleasure to work with. It had
been fortunate that McKenna's team was still in Hawaii.
They'd been scheduled to leave that afternoon for
Tokyo, where they were going to put on a seminar of
current antiterrorist techniques and strategies for advance units of the Pacific Fleet. But that would have to
wait. This was precisely what they'd been set up to do
with all their training. Their assignment was simple
—convince the terrorists to release the hostages un-
harmed. Just persuade a wild-eyed group of fanatics to
change their minds, turn their backs on their cause, and

release their prisoners. The problem was obvious. The hostages were the only thing keeping the terrorists from instant attack, sure capture, and, more probable, death.

McKenna swallowed. His group had done well in practice, at tactics, consistently winning their little cat-and-mouse games. But now they were going up against a group who didn't play games, and all the hostages' lives were at stake. This was for real.

The McGregors were standing close to one another in their kitchenette sharing a Coke and a Snickers bar when they heard taps being played over the loud-speaker. Mac automatically checked his watch. It was three o'clock. His arm reached around Marge's shoulder and together they listened to Fire's announcement. He could feel his wife's body tremble when Fire said that "powerful explosive charges have been set among the hostages and they will be blown sky-high." Her face looked up and sought his, eyes begging for reassurance. Not getting any, Marge asked hopefully, "She's bluffing, isn't she?"

"No," Mac answered tonelessly. "This is a group of brutal killers. They're animals. I've seen them in action." His arm tightened around Marge's shoulder as he talked. "This morning they killed six policemen . . . in cold blood. God only knows how many were on that chopper they blew out of the sky." Mac hesitated and glanced out of the window. Seeing nothing, he continued, "They've planted explosive charges all over the Koa Lounge. I was there," his voice trembled, "when they did it." Biting his tongue, he stopped it from saying, "Big George helped."

Marge glanced quickly at his face. Their eyes met. Instantly, he knew she knew and understood. Suddenly Mac felt better.

"There are over two hundred hostages in there, sitting in the middle of . . . they're just one big bomb."

"The terrorists wouldn't blow up themselves, would they?" Marge asked.

Mac closed his eyes and nodded his head up and down slowly. "They're fanatics. It's a suicide squad."

Face aghast, Marge stared at her husband. She saw the tear form and roll down his cheek. And then it was gone.

"I've got to get you out of here," he said, squeezing her tightly with his arm.

"What do you mean me?" she asked. "We've both got to get out of here."

Mac didn't answer. From the moment Big George had helped set the explosive charges, he'd known he had to stay. He was in this now all the way. To the very end.

Tied to the flagpole with the other two Avon ladies, the tall brunette started weeping softly. "I never really thought about death until . . ." her voice broke ". . . today."

"For Christ's sake, cut it out, Bee Jay," Connie said. "I'm so scared, I'm afraid I'm going to . . ."

Evelyn, the tall blonde, laughed a mirthless laugh. "You must have read my mind."

Both noticed that Betty Jane had stopped crying. Now her body was straining at the ropes.

"Have you noticed the sky?" Betty Jane said, looking up. "It's magnificent."

The other two looked and noticed that the sky had turned a gorgeous shade of amber and copper. Red banners of sunset flew over the flagpole.

"Maybe it's the Lord's way of telling us . . ." she added, taking a deep breath ". . . tomorrow will be better."

"A glowing promise of things to come?" asked Evelyn.

"Yes. Red sky at night . . ."

"Prisoner's delight," Connie said lightly.

"Let's the three of us," Evelyn said, "make a pact."

"That we'll never travel again," Connie said, a touch of humor in her voice.

"No. That we don't lose hope," the tall blonde said seriously. "We keep our faith."

"Amen," said the brunette.

Connie added an amen under her breath. "Think positive the Avon way." She smiled to herself. It was the pep talk she always gave to her salesgirls.

"Right!"

"I've got the four-day trembles, myself," Evelyn said. "Wouldn't you know . . . PMT."

"You, too!" Betty Jean exclaimed. "I thought I was the only one . . . my psychiatrist told me . . ."

"You, seeing a psychiatrist?" Evelyn's surprise was genuine. "What on earth for?"

"She's training him," Connie interjected. "He's got a lot of problems." Connie had decided not to mention her monthly tensions. They usually only lasted thirty days.

"No, I'm being serious," Betty Jane said. "I went to him for some therapy. I'm no sex kitten, never have been. I got tired of the constant fights with Tom."

"Did it work?" Evelyn asked.

"The guy convinced me that Tom should be married to a sexually aggressive, uninhibited woman . . ."

The other two listened in silence.

"I told him I didn't want to lose Tom, so he suggested that I learn to be more . . . ." Betty Jane hesitated ". . . adventuresome."

"And?" Evelyn asked, clearly interested.

"He showed me a few pictures of things to do . . . then . . . he made a pass at me . . . nothing serious." Her lie sounded false before she'd spoken it. "It was when he said, 'Happiness is being single,' " she glanced sideways at the other two and spoke sadly, "that I knew he was married."

"Bee Jay, at least half of today's married women are having affairs," Evelyn said, thinking that at least she'd been smart enough not to tell anyone.

"It wasn't all his fault," Betty Jane said, anxious to share her guilt with others. "It was his idea, but I went along. It wasn't love . . . but it wasn't bad." That was another convenient lie. She's resented him, because of her lost self-respect.

The other two girls remained silent, each with her own thoughts.

"I got a mink out of it," Betty Jane added.

Mink had changed her own life, thought Evelyn. Anything that gave so much pleasure had to be practical.

Connie laughed to herself. Girls usually got minks the same way minks got minks. It was always the warm girls, not the cold ones, who wound up with the mink coats. Confession may be good for the soul, thought the petite blonde. But hard on the reputation. The rumor mop swishes through every life. No need to add the bubble bath and make foam. Even out here, tied to the stake, she was not about to let it all hang out. Who knew, they might get rescued. She laughed again, this time out loud.

"What's so funny?" Evelyn asked.

"It's something we all learn—before you meet the handsome prince, you have to kiss a lot of toads."

Both of the others smiled. Connie had a way of joking about things to remove the tension. Their attention was diverted by a flock of seabirds returning for the day. They were dipping, weaving, and cawing above them. At the top of the flagpole, the American flag hung limp.

Connie noticed Carlos walking toward them holding a knife in his hand. Either he was going to cut them loose or . . .

"Don't forget our pact," Evelyn said bravely. " 'Til death do us part."

Oh, damn, thought Connie. Why did she have to say that?

Evelyn saw the knife, sucked in her breath and released it in a terrifying scream. Connie felt a trickle of fear. Now she knew she'd never make it to the ladies' room.

Mac peeked through the crack in the door, and saw no terrorists. He swallowed the dryness in his throat. Close by there were at least eleven of them who would just love to kill him. It had probably been a mistake to give up Big George's clothes. It limited his mobility. All afternoon he and Marge had been confined to hiding out, staying invisible. It was becoming increasingly difficult to operate. He needed to know what was happening. Somewhere he had to find another khaki camouflage outfit. Unfortunately, there were only two other suits and masks big enough. Anahu, the fat Hawaiian, and Jumbo, the huge black, each had one. The problem was that they were wearing them.

Anahu never left the front lobby. Mac gulped. It had to be Jumbo, and he just knew that big son-of-a-bitch was a one-on-one killer. Negative and positive thoughts slammed together in his mind as he touched the lucky beans in his pocket. Maybe he'd get lucky. Maybe Jumbo had brittle bones.

Mac outlined his plan to Marge. "Jumbo comes by here every so often." Her mouth flew open and she said, "You must be going crazy in your old age." Marge almost bit her tongue when she saw the hurt look on Mac's face, knowing the comment on his age had hurt.

The sun was moving toward the horizon, and there was probably an hour left to sunset when they saw the huge black moving cautiously down the path, Kalashnikov in hand. Passing by ocean suite seven, he saw the door swing partially open. Jumbo stopped, crouching, assault rifle aimed. His eyes blinked behind the mask. A woman in a pink see-through nightgown was twirling in the doorway, beckoning to him. The big man moved toward ocean suite seven, all senses totally alert.

Behind the door, driver in hand, Mac waited. Marge had now moved to the far side of the room and had ducked down behind the bed. Through the crack in the door Mac assessed the huge black. Over six feet two inches in height, 220 pounds at least, probably heavier, massive thighs, ox neck, broad shoulders, muscular arms, thirty-two-inch waist—a perfect upper body V. The guy certainly had size and strength, built for heavy-duty. Oh shit, Mac thought, this was going to be tough. Marge had been right. He was going crazy. He'd forgotten that he was sixty.

Eyes searching for the swirling nightgown, the huge black moved through the door quickly, pushing it hard against Mac as he did so. As a result, Mac's swing was short, vicious, and off line. The driver hit the Kalashnikov, bending the gun barrel and sending the gun skittering across the floor of the room. The shaft of the driver snapped in half and Mac tossed it aside.

He stepped quickly from behind the door, pushing it shut with his arm. The huge black spun to face him, pulling off his mask and dropping it to the floor. Jumbo was grinning from ear to ear. His head was an ebony battering ram. There was scar tissue under the eyes and cauliflower ears. Oh, shit, a professional, Mac thought, as his heart lurched.

"Hello, mudderfucker," Jumbo said.

They circled one another grim faced, like strange dogs. It was a classic encounter of the experienced versus the inexperienced. Mac remembered the first rule of boxing, always box a puncher. He'd use his smarts and quick hands. Instead, he led with his face.

Jolted backward, Mac ducked and felt a stab of pain high in the back above the rib cage. He moved again. The pain lashed back. This time on the other side. Jumbo's hands were sledgehammers. His knuckles were the size of walnuts. The guy clearly had a high tolerance for someone else's pain. Out of the corner of his eye, Mac could see Marge, standing in the corner, white faced, trembling, eyes wild with terror. Now she was moving. Whatever happened, he had to stay between . . .

The next blow numbed his left shoulder. His mind told him to stay out of the reach of Jumbo's power. Hopefully, the guy was too big for his brain. It was his only hope. He slipped two lunging punches and countered with a quick left hook. Jumbo's stomach was solid muscle.

Realization crashed through that on this level of hand-to-hand combat his reflexes were gone. No longer was he what he used to be. But he still had a toughness honed by fear—the fear of what would happen to Marge if he lost. Jumbo was now toying with him, tormenting him. It promised to be a slow-motion death, being beaten to a pulp with bare fists. Mac felt a solid blow to the head. He could see two Jumbos now. Remembering that the eyes are linked straight to the brain, he blinked three or four times in succession. The two Jumbos merged back together. Maybe the big guy would punch himself out, have a coronary. Jumbo slammed Mac against the wall and aimed a lethal blow at his face. Mac jerked his head sideways and felt the blow graze his cheek and smash into the wall, hearing the crack of bones and seeing the instant pain in the ebony face. The big black had broken his right hand on a solid wall joist.

Mac took a deep breath. Damn lucky beans were working. The huge black did have brittle bones. That could even things considerably. He could see Marge more clearly now. She had picked up the assault rifle and was aiming it at Jumbo's back. If she pulled the trigger, they'd both be killed. More likely, with the bent barrel, the AK-47 would blow up in her face. He waved his free left hand at Marge and took a hard left on the side of his head that rattled his senses. His teeth felt numb. Mac's survival instincts spun wildly in his brain, then surfaced. The juices began to flow and his memory went to work.

Mac worked free and aimed a vicious kick at Jumbo's knee. Nothing happened. The big man was stone tough. Spinning completely around, his foot built up torque, like the head of a rotating club, then smashed against Jumbo's groin. The black man doubled over. A vicious kick arched from Mac's hip level to Jumbo's head. The kicks were not haphazard. They were calculated. It was full-contact karate. In the old days when he'd been a Marine karate instructor, his nickname had been "Superfoot." That, he now realized, had been long ago.

Jumbo lunged with a roundhouse left. Mac dodged and countered with a stabbing kick to Jumbo's chin. The big black saw red, eyes jolted in their sockets. Mac spun and lifted a backward heel kick. It missed Jumbo's testicles, but slammed into his kidneys. Jumbo reeled backward, just as Marge charged forward with the broken shaft of Mac's driver held in front of her like a lance. It entered the big terrorist's neck on the left side and emerged on the right. He staggered and fell to the floor, making the strange gurgling sounds that go with strangulation as life rapidly flowed out of him.

Weeping, Marge turned and ran into the bathroom. Breathing heavily, Mac knelt to make sure Jumbo was dead. There was no pulse. Jumbo's eyes were windows into nothing. It was not a nice way to go. It was written all over his face.

Dizzy and nauseous, Mac slumped on the floor next to Jumbo's body, his head on his knees. He hurt all over. His hand felt his left shoulder, then his rib cage. He winced at the touch. Hopefully, there was nothing broken. But he needed some time to heal. His face grimaced. At his age, it would probably take months. Shit, there was no time. He had to keep moving to stay alive. Slowly, he pushed his body erect. He could hear Marge retching in the bathroom.

Mac's eyes took in the small pool of blood on the floor. He checked carefully but none had spattered onto any of the throw rugs. He moved the rugs farther away. Eyes averted, lips clamped tightly, he pulled the shaft of the golf club out of Jumbo's neck and put it into a garbage bag. Slipping the head and shoulders of the big black into a large trash bag, he wrapped it securely with twine.

Checking carefully to make sure that no one saw him, Mac carried Jumbo's body into the newlyweds' suite and lowered it carefully into the bathtub. "Aloha, Jumbo," Mac said. "God put us here and God tells us when to go." As he was returning to his own suite, he thought, I'm safe. The good Lord won't let me die. He's going to keep me here and make me suffer.

With a mop and pail from the kitchen, Mac cleaned up the mess on the tile floor, dumping the residue down the kitchen sink, finally washing the sink, his shoulder talking to him every time he moved. Returning to the living area, touching up the floor, he moved the rugs back into position. Finished, he walked into the bathroom to console Marge and to thank her for saving his life.

There was no question now, he had to get Marge out of the resort as quickly as possible. Her safety was the most important thing. If he could get her through the terrorist line of fire to the Marines, she'd be safe. Mac checked his teeth. They were still all there. His body felt like a dish of crushed pineapple. Muscles that he'd retired thirty years ago shouted in protest. He breathed slowly and carefully. Fortunately, his ribs only hurt when he inhaled. It was mind over pain. No longer was it survival of the fittest. It was survival of the luckiest. Suddenly, Mac felt old.

Marge was close to hysteria. "I've murdered a man," she repeated over and over, between deep, racking sobs.

"It wasn't murder," Mac kept saying.

"Murder is forever," Marge said, tears welling in her eyes and rolling down her cheeks.

Mac grabbed Marge forcefully by the shoulders and held her face closely in front of his, speaking quietly. "You saved my life. Would you rather he'd killed me?"

The question jolted her. Marge shook her head from side to side.

"He was a terrorist. He'd have killed others," Mac added, feeling his wife's pain in his heart.

For the next half hour, holding a cold washcloth to

her forehead, Mac talked soothingly to his wife, gradually leading the conversation to talk of their escape. Slowly, but steadily, she regained her composure. Mac sighed deeply. He had butterflies in his *opu*. He needed a banana cow. Death was one thing. He was used to that and could deal with it. But he couldn't bear to see Marge cry.

He watched Marge's face, the movement of her head, the pulse in her throat; he touched her hand and shoulder, kissed her eyes and lips. The physical contact seemed to connote a deeper, more significant bond. Friendship as well as passion.

Calmer now, Marge noticed the bruises on Mac's face.

"Hey, you're banged up pretty bad."

"I'll survive," Mac grinned. "It's not half as bad as dying."

Marge smiled. "Let me take care of you," she said.

Mac's deep sigh sounded like the soft breeze whispering through the palm trees.

CHAPTER NINE

It was shortly after five o'clock when the resort phone rang at the switchboard.

"HULA One."

"This is Colonel Donahue, United States Marine Corps. May I speak to the person in charge, please."

"I'll do," a female voice said.

"What's your name?" Donahue asked.

"Cut the shit, Colonel."

There was a long pause on the other end of the line. Then Donahue said, "We've done what you asked."

There was no answer from Fire.

"What do you want?" Donahue asked.

"The liberation of all oppressed peoples."

Marxist crazies, thought Donahue. Oh, no, not again, thought the three men of the hostage negotiation team sitting in the command vehicle with Donahue, listening to the conversation.

Donahue took a deep breath, then asked, "Could you be more specific?"

"As a first step," the voice was precise, "the liberation of Hawaii from the imperialist United States."

Donahue rubbed his eyes with his fingers and waited. Lieutenant Colonel Red McKenna slipped him a note. He glanced at it briefly, then asked, "What do you want to free the hostages?"

"The destruction of all the nuclear warheads stored in Hawaii."

Donahue glanced at the other men. All of them knew that was an impossible demand. Hawaii was the main storage base for the U.S. Pacific Fleet. Most of their nuclear warheads were stored in revetments dug deep in the volcanic rock of Oahu. McKenna gestured to Donahue, suggesting he narrow down the demands. The female terrorist was still talking in broad ideological terms. Surely the terrorists wanted something very specific. They always did.

"Could you give us a more limited objective?" Donahue asked hopefully. The other three leaned forward waiting for the answer.

"We have 216 hostages, 186 guests and 30 employees." Fire paused to let the numbers sink in.

The air escaping from Donahue sounded like a low whistle. Suddenly the colonel had a vivid mental image of 216 body bags laid out in a row, a scene witnessed too many times before in combat. He swallowed.

"We'll release one hostage for each nuclear warhead that you destroy." The voice was crisp. "One for one."

"It will take time," Donahue said slowly over the phone, trying to stall, thinking, looking at the others for help.

"No it won't." The girl's voice was flat and positive. "You can start first thing in the morning."

Narrow it down further, Major Corwin gestured.

"Could you narrow . . . ?"

"Colonel," the voice said sharply, "we've been pussyfooting around. Now we've told you what we want. We're not kidding. That's it." The voice was hard now. "You get back one hostage for each nuclear warhead you destroy. It's very simple. We'll match you, one for one. Otherwise, we'll really show you an explosion."

The phone clicked dead in Colonel Donahue's ear. He put down the phone and shook his head. "Doesn't sound too hopeful. Two hundred and sixteen hostages in there . . ." His shudder was involuntary, his mind having trouble comprehending a mass killing of that dimension.

"At least we've got them talking," McKenna said, a flush of optimism on his face. "That's the first step. They've made a demand. Now we set up a face-to-face meeting, establish a dialogue, then negotiate."

Colonel Donahue stared at the sky and said nothing.

"One for one. A hostage for a nuclear warhead. A death match." Captain Bailey grimaced. "That's going to be an explosive issue in Washington."

"Not a chance, and the three of you know it," Donahue said flatly.

"We know, but somehow . . ." Red McKenna's eyes rolled upward as if searching for help. "We've got to make the terrorists think there's some chance." He paused and looked questioningly at Donahue. "Any way to fake it?"

"You mean . . . announce we're destroying nuclear warheads and not do it?"

McKenna nodded.

"Washington won't do that."

"Why not?"

"The principle," Donahue said. "It would be a lie."

"You mean it's more important not to lie than to save the lives of the hostages?"

"I'm afraid so . . ." Donahue sighed. "You can't be

false in the pursuit of truth. George Washington set the standards and John Wayne perfected them."

McKenna laughed lightly. "Don't forget, Colonel, in war the first casualty is truth."

Mac slipped on Jumbo's camouflage suit and mask. It wasn't as good a fit as Big George's had been, but it would have to do. He'd at least heard Jumbo talk. The guy spoke American—real basic, ghetto American. Mac knew he could handle gutter talk. In the Corps, profanity had been their common language. He practiced a few words, ending with a rhythmic "mudder."

Marge looked him over critically, then asked simply, "Aren't you forgetting something?"

Mac stopped, puzzled, thinking. "I don't think so," he replied.

"What color is a *popolo*?" Marge asked, then after a short silence, watching Mac's frown, she added, "I've never seen one, big or small, with white hands."

Mac stared at his hands hanging out of the sleeves of Jumbo's camouflage suit and started to laugh. The hands would have been a dead giveaway. Marge had saved his ass again.

"No problem, mudder," he said, still laughing. Opening the closet, Mac rummaged quickly through his garbage bag of supplies, pulling out the pair of thin latex black scuba gloves.

"You can't be serious," Marge said, a look of alarm on her face.

Mac didn't answer. An idea was forming in the deep reaches of his mind.

Marge turned and disappeared into the bathroom. She was back in a few moments, carrying her cosmetic case, thinking that some dark eye shadow around his eyes might just cover the white spots peeking through the eye slits in Jumbo's mask.

Sitting on the couch the McGregors sipped cold beers, watching the red sun spread over the sea. They could see their reflection in the lanai glass doors, faces orange in the sunset, backs in violet shadow. Marge picked up Mac's hand as the sun splashed into the Pacific. Another time it would have been a very special hour at a very special place. Not tonight.

"I'm not going without you," she said, a touch of finality in her voice.

"You have to," Mac said. "It's important. We might be able to save a lot of lives."

The darkness of the evening deepened. Marge's mood darkened with it. "I'll stay with you," she said flatly.

"The information I wrote down—the Marines need it," Mac said, voice rising. "You can deliver it. They also need to know that they have someone in here. Someone who can help them."

Marge turned to face Mac, pulling away her hand. Even in the darkness, he could tell that her face had hardened and lost its friendliness.

"You want to stay, don't you?" she asked.

"Marge, you've got to understand. The Marines need someone inside." His voice was harder now. "You heard Fire. They'll have a tough time getting anyone inside without risking the lives of the hostages. I'm already here."

Marge turned back and bent over the edge of the couch, hands covering her face. Mac's arm slid around her shoulders.

"With luck, they might get one or two men in the outer buildings. They'd never get near the Koa Lounge. I've been there. I can go back."

"Oh, my God," she sobbed, body shivering with a chill of apprehension.

"I know their pattern. I'll adapt, move, keep them off balance. Capitalize on their mistakes. When I see an opportunity—hit them."

Mac didn't see Marge slide her thumbs into her ears, shutting out the rest of what he said.

"They'll have to wonder every minute what I'll do next, who I am. They'll have to change their plans. They won't be able to ignore me. I'm versatile. They're not. I can move in a dozen different ways. That's got to affect them. Maybe, just maybe, I can save a few lives."

Marge lifted her head, took a few deep breaths, turned and asked, "You're enjoying this, aren't you?"

"No," Mac said. "But I'm good at it. It's the way I grew up. It's part of me. When I was a kid, we'd play cowboys and Indians." His face wrinkled in the darkness. "I always wanted to be the Indian."

They sat for a long time in a deepening silence, both with their own thoughts. It took a while for the silence to subside.

"How are you going to do all this?" Marge asked.

"I don't know," Mac answered truthfully. "Right now it's only a sketch in my head. I'll play it as it comes."

"Jesus, that's reassuring!" Marge stared at her husband in disbelief. "I don't know whether you've lost your mind, or just misplaced it."

"I've seen the elephant and heard the owl."

"What the hell does that mean?" Marge turned and grabbed his arm. "That you don't want to live anymore?"

Mac didn't answer, his eyes hardened. He couldn't explain.

"You're not being reasonable," she said.

"Nothing important was ever accomplished by a reasonable man."

"Or a rational one. You're on a kamikaze mission."

"I hope not. I'll be careful." Mac stood up and walked to the window. Moths batted softly at the screens. He peered out along the path, then came back and stood by the couch. "Sometimes you can't wait around for things to happen. You've got to make them happen. I'm sorry, Marge, but I have to do this."

"It wasn't supposed to be like this," she said softly.

"Next time we'll book passage on the Love Boat." Suddenly Mac laughed. "With my luck, the damn boat would sink."

Marge looked up at Mac. Her whole life was standing there. He was trying to help. Without him, a lot of people were going to die. Maybe she was being selfish, thinking of herself. In that instant, she made up her mind. The dark moments had passed. It was no time for bitterness. It was time to help him. Standing, she walked to the lanai door and breathed the ocean air. The lights of Oahu were winking at her from across the channel. Calmer now, she walked back and put her arms around Mac's neck.

"I'm ready," she whispered.

The terrorist "one for one" demand was quickly passed through channels. At six P.M. Honolulu time, Brigadier General Clark, commandant of the Pacific Division, called General Wolfe, commandant of the Marine Corps at his home in Arlington, Virginia. It was almost eleven-thirty P.M. EST when Wolfe caught up to General Porter, head of the Joint Chiefs of Staff at the Center for the Performing Arts. Porter, who was attending a benefit performance of the Leningrad Ballet Company, called his contact on the White House staff from a public phone outside the men's room. The President had already gone to bed and was not awakened, since it was not an urgent matter of national security. Porter was assured that the President would be told first thing in the morning.

Along the line the reactions were predictable.

"Impossible."

"One for one. They're crazy."

"We can't destroy any nuclear weapons. We need more."

"The United States will not be held hostage."

"Give in once and there'll be no end to terrorism."

"No! Tell them to stick it up their jumper."

The message that came back through channels to Donahue was exactly what he'd expected.

"Stall. Bluff. Wait them out. Don't do anything rash. Don't risk the lives of the hostages."

First Day—Nighttime

It was dark when a big man slipped out of ocean suite seven, wearing a slightly oversized camouflage suit, mask, hat, and a pair of thin, black scuba gloves. He was followed closely by a short female shape in jeans, dark pullover sweater, and tennis shoes with a kerchief tied over her head. Together they moved through the shadows toward the building on the northwest corner of the resort.

Cautiously, Mac mounted the stairs and approached the terrorist outpost on the second floor. The dim night light was on. The swivel chair was by the window; there were weapons alongside. The room was empty. He was right. This had to be the nest, where Jumbo had been headed when he'd been distracted by a swirling see-through nightgown. Mac exhaled with relief, then winced as he reached to pick up the spare AK-47. The pain was bound to linger.

Marge waited below, out of sight, around the corner of the building in the shadow of a large, bushy flame tree. The sound of the surf was in her ears. There was a warm, soft breeze blowing in from the ocean. The stars were bright. The moon had not yet risen. She sat perfectly still on a flat rock, staring in wonder at the magnificent yellow blossoms of a night-blooming cereus plant. The flowers had a unique, haunting beauty. Their fragrance mixed with the salty tang of the ocean air. She inhaled deeply. It was the smell of heaven's gate. Mac had warned her that it might be a long wait. "Waiting is never easy, but sometimes it's the only way." Damn, she was getting hungry. She poked her stomach and thought of the box of Snickers back in the refrigerator.

Seated in the swivel chair in the corner room above, Mac also waited, not quite sure what to expect. He checked his watch again. Two minutes after ten. His palms itched under the gloves. If one of the terrorists was going to check the outposts, he was overdue. Maybe no one would. That didn't make sense. Mac knew the terrorists were a well-trained military unit; he'd felt that from the first moment of the takeover. Today's action had confirmed it.

Mac sat facing the window, head low over the M-845 nightscope. He sensed the presence of the man in the room before he heard his light footstep.

"Jumbo?"

"Yeah." Jumbo's mask raised slowly. The big man stretched his shoulders and upper arms and slowly the chair swiveled around.

"Brought you some coffee." It was the voice of Little
Boy Blue, Marco.

"Thanks." Jumbo's hands stayed in his lap, head
gesturing toward a small table. Marco set the cardboard
container down on it.

"Seen anything?" Marco asked.

Jumbo shook his head negatively. "Nuthin . . .
wanna look?" He started to get up.

"No," Marco said quickly. "Anything wiggles, hit it.
I've got to run. See you around three." Marco turned
and started out of the room. At the door he stopped.
"If you need any help," Marco laughed, "you know
how to reach us."

Jumbo's hand waved good-bye. The chair swiveled
around and his head bent down over the nightscope. He
wondered how Jumbo was supposed to contact the
others. It didn't make any difference. Mac didn't have
the slightest intention of asking the terrorists for any
help. Marco had already helped. Mac now knew that he
had almost five hours in which to operate.

Marco shook his head as he walked down the path
heading for the outposts on the other side of the complex. That big black had an empty head. He spoke in
monosyllables. Probably didn't know how to use the
walkie-talkie. His mind was in a different area code,
anyhow. Dumb or not, he was weird enough to be scary.
It sure looked like the big bastard was wearing rubber
gloves. Most of the HULA team was weird. But what
can you expect, when you recruit volunteers for a
suicide squad? He laughed to himself. He'd make his
next rounds before three, then spend some time with
that good looking young hostage, the bride in the see-
through peignoir . . . leave some hickies . . . he licked his
lips . . . in the right places. She was a real honeytrap . . .

and best of all, she had hungry eyes.

Marge heard the low whistle from above and stood up, muscles stiff from sitting. Quickly, she entered the building and with surprising speed moved up the stairs and found the corner room.

"Over here," Mac said, without raising his eyes from the scope which he was adjusting for azimuth and elevation on its tripod. Satisfied, he moved aside and gestured toward the chair.

"It's like day," she whispered, amazed at the clarity of the view through the nightscope. She could see a sand trap to the front left and below a raised green, the pin still in the cup, the number "12" on the gently waving flag.

"You go straight from the corner of this building to the left of that sand trap, go close around it and up and over the twelfth green, be sure to walk across it—that's important—then follow the cart path to the thirteenth tee and walk up the middle of the fairway." Mac spoke in a low voice, moving the scope slowly so his wife could see and remember the terrain he was describing. "The ocean will be out to your left. The Marines will see you coming."

He repeated the directions, then had her repeat them twice. Finished, she swiveled the chair, stood up and grabbed his arm with both her hands, a look of terror on her face.

"You don't really expect me to walk alone out there in the dark!"

"It will be lighter," Mac explained. "The moon will be up."

"No way!" Marge tossed her head defiantly. "I might step on a snake."

"There are no snakes in Hawaii."

"Why can't I drive?"

"With what?" he asked, a tone of exasperation in his voice.

"Why not a golf cart?"

There was a moment of silence, then Mac began to laugh softly. His arms reached out for his wife and hugged her to him.

"Mrs. McGregor, you're much more than a sex symbol. You're a damn genius."

The bright cobalt-blue eyes surveyed the room. Marco had removed his mask, and standing next to Anahu, he was enjoying himself thoroughly, carefully making his choice. He chuckled. Some young lady was going to get an excursion into the realm of ecstasy. Most of the tourists were golden oldies with too many wrinkles, pouches, and sagging parts. The tall brunette in the brown blanket. If she were the only horse in the race, she'd have to come from behind. The thin blonde with the knobby knees. Her pilot light had probably gone out. A hippy young hippie. No, she had an ass like a forty-dollar cow. He shook his head sadly, and shuddered. The short girl with the long face who looked as if she'd been weaned on a pickle. Not even for rape.

His eyes now skimmed a few nubile young sun-kissed beauties. Desire quickened into a primitive growl. The young thing in a sleek satin tricot lavished with lace, her mouth a dark shade of pink. A sheer delight that could light up the night. A strong contender. But wait a minute, it looked like she was wearing a bra underneath. Why for bedtime, unless it hid a beauty secret? The girl dropped a few notches on his mental list.

Candy was dandy, but this was amateur night. The young hooker was probably the prettiest girl in the room and he knew she was really good at what she did. That was the problem, she was too good. He wouldn't be able to control the situation. His eyes moved on, lusting from one body to the next.

There was an attractive girl with long hair, with large breasts, in a lettered sweatshirt that read, TAKE ME. He grimaced. There were sweat circles under the arms.

Seated on the floor next to her was a pushover in a snowy white pullover. She seemed lost in the soothing shallows of herself. An animal in a striped leotard. She'd go from a roar to a purr. But she looked used. Another sun baby, dark complexioned, flashing brown eyes, and jet black hair. A mindless, jiggly thing. Too damn young, or he'd give her a pineapple split. He grinned and adjusted his left pants leg. If he didn't make his choice soon, it might be too late. The bride . . . his eyes kept coming back to the bride. Attractive, with a nice body, she seemed receptive, in the mood, too. Married women were always easier. He'd show the bride what a honeymoon should be like. He'd keep her stroked. Maybe the groom would like to watch. The little boy smile was back on Marco's face.

Then he saw the pair of tight designer jeans, molded onto a perfect rear end. Marco believed in astral projection. Maybe he'd have an out-of-the-body experience with her. But first the real thing. The action-stretch lycra had shrunk to fit, and what a fit. Eyes glued to them, his whole body responded, all senses alive. What was under those jeans? The bottom line? Even without them, he knew she'd have that Jordache look.

The tall blonde turned around. Very attractive, but older. Experience wouldn't hurt. She'd certainly kept her figure. He recognized the body now. It was one of the ladies they'd tied to the flagpole. Damn, there were three of them. They stuck together. Maybe he'd try all three. Avon calling . . . mix or match time. Marco's eyes went back to the jeans. He stared at the crotch and wet his lips again, a bad habit. He could see her body lines through the cloth. He smiled again. There was no question, he'd picked a groovy thing. His mind videoraped her.

Excited now, he turned and whispered something to Anahu, then crossed the room, approaching the body in the tight designer jeans. The Avon ladies saw him coming and tightened their back-to-back triangle, butts to butts, shoulders touching, feeling uneasy. He circled them, staring at their jeans, but almost past them into another dimension. As they saw his eyes close up, their embarrassment turned to fear, then to fright. The cobalt eyes focused on Evelyn, and she looked away. Marco cursed silently, then suddenly grabbed the tall blonde's arm and pulled her away from the other two. Evelyn opened her mouth wide and the primordial scream that emerged startled the hostages, but Marco clamped his hand tightly over Evelyn's mouth and hustled her toward the door.

With his AK-47 pointed at the other Avon ladies and a leer on his wide, dark face, Anahu stepped in front of Connie and Betty Jane, forcing them to move back with the other hostages. There was a general undercurrent of protest from the male hostages, but no one moved to help.

Candy had been watching Marco closely. She knew him well. Having him guard the hostages was like putting Dracula in charge of the blood bank. Now she sprang to her feet, telling Dan to stay where he was. As Marco and Evelyn reached the lobby, she intercepted them. "Sweetheart," she purred to Marco. "I thought this was my territory." Her hand touched the bulge in his trousers.

"This is my plaything for tonight." Marco grinned and patted Evelyn's bottom. She cringed, staring at him with wide and terrified eyes.

"Besides, she's free," the terrorist added, eyes flashing at Candy.

"I don't like competition," Candy said, expert fingers gently rubbing, with a woman's touch, right where it did the most good. "And with you, sweetheart, it's pleasure before business, always . . . Satisfaction guaranteed." She leaned closer and whispered something in his ear. Marco felt the hot flame of her breath and released his hold on Evelyn. With her free hand, Candy pushed Evelyn back toward the Koa Lounge. With the other she tightened her grip and allowed Marco to lead her to the nearest guest room.

Connie and Betty Jane breathed big sighs of relief when they saw Evelyn come back into the room and quickly rejoin them, tears of joy glistening in her eyes. In a charged voice, she said, "Can you imagine . . . that blonde in the sheet . . . what type of woman would want to make love to . . . that animal!" The tall blonde shuddered.

Connie spoke in a quiet voice. "Help comes from unexpected places. That blonde in the sheet may be a saint in disguise. Certainly, she's the bravest person here."

The other two stared at the short girl in wonderment.

"Do you realize what she did?" Connie asked. "While the rest of us were cowering and sniveling that girl gave up herself. To save you."

It was later, when Candy was back sitting with the fat man, that Evelyn walked over and thanked her.

"It was really nothing," Candy said, touching her hand to her eye. "I thought it might make it easier on you." She laughed lightly. "You might have guessed, I've done it before." Her voice trailed off. "Just another motel memory."

After Evelyn had left, Dan put his arm around Candy. "You're a pretty fantastic woman. That was a brave thing to do." He gave her shoulder a squeeze.

The moon was just coming into view when the McGregors found a golf cart. It was right where Marge had suggested they'd find one, in the shed attached to the laundry room, behind the screen of hibiscus and bougainvillea bordering the parking lot. She'd seen the maids using the cart, picking up and delivering laundry to the ocean suites.

Mac checked the cart over carefully as best he could in the darkened shed. It was a standard four-wheeled, battery-powered golf cart, without a top, one that had obviously seen a lot of hard use. The key had rusted in the ignition. Mac's fingers traced the raised imprint of the manufacturer, E-Z-GO. A smile flicked across his face. E-Z-GO. It had to be a good sign. He whispered the name to Marge, while his hands felt the wheels. The four tires were good. The battery was fully charged. It was still plugged into the battery charger, where the maids had left it when they'd finished work the night before.

Mac gave his wife a thumbs-up signal, glanced quickly outside, then pushed the shed door open wide, unplugged the battery charger, and slid into the driver's seat. He turned the key, moved the gear setting to forward, held his breath and pressed down on the accelerator. The cart moved noiselessly forward and out of the shed. Marge closed the door to the shed and slipped into the passenger's seat.

"Easy go," she whispered.

Less than ten minutes later the cart had negotiated the path to and around their ocean cottage and up a six-inch step to the lanai, with the help of a simple, temporary ramp that Mac had made out of two closet shelves. It was now parked in the center of the newlyweds' suite. The moonlight shining through the lanai doors revealed an eerie scene.

On the floor alongside the cart, Mac had laid out a spare blanket from the closet shelf. Placing the body of a big man with a black garbage bag over his head on one edge of the blanket, he rolled him up in it. With strong twine he circled both ends and the center and tied it securely. The big six-foot-tall bundle was then strapped tightly onto the rack behind the cart, where the driver's golf clubs normally would be. Surveying his work, he tied the top of the bundle to the cart with extra twine, pulling and tugging on the body from all sides. It was secure. It wouldn't bounce off.

"Jumbo's riding shotgun," Mac said simply.

"But?" It was a question, not an objection.

"Don't forget, mudder dear," Mac answered, "I'm Jumbo. It will be easier if there aren't two of us in here."

Marge didn't answer. She bit her lip instead.

CHAPTER TEN

Second Day—Midnight to Dawn

It was a few minutes before midnight, and the McGregors were back in their own suite. From his clothes drawer Mac pulled out his blue shirt and handed it to his wife. "Put this under your sweater. Tuck it into your belt. Special laundry service for the Marines."

From his garbage bag of supplies, Mac took out two items and put them in his pocket. Rummaging through the kitchen drawers, he selected a flat table knife and a wide spatula. From the freezer unit he took out the two frozen cans of beer. These items all went into the large pockets in his camouflage suit. From the trash can Mac rescued the four empty beer cans and put them in a small plastic bag.

Marge had been watching the big shadow move about the suite. "What are you doing?" she asked in a low voice.

"Sweetheart . . ."

Her heart thumped. Mac rarely called her sweetheart, unless he had bad news. She braced herself.

"I've got a brief errand . . . it's important."

"I'll go with you."

"No. This one will be easier," Mac paused, "alone."

He touched the luminous dial of her watch, turning it so she could read it.

"This should take about an hour. If I'm not back by one," he'd given himself an extra five minutes, "take the golf cart and go. Follow the route I showed you. If you hear any explosions, any weapons firing, don't wait the hour. Go! Don't look back. Go!"

He took her face in his hands. "Promise?"

She nodded. The tone of his voice jangled all of her alarm bells. Marge's heart begged her to try and stop him. Her mind said help him. Seeing his assault rifle by the couch, her calm voice said, "Don't forget your gun."

In the dim light he smiled broadly. "I'm traveling light tonight." He picked up the small plastic bag with the four empty beer cans and chuckled to himself. "My Hawaiian Punch. Keep the gun close to you 'til I get back."

At the door he hugged her tightly against him.

"I love you," he said simply, and was gone.

Marge wanted to ask where and why, but knew it would be easier if she didn't know. She settled back on the couch to wait, watching the moonbeams dancing far out on the black swells of the ocean, inhaling the aroma of the salt water mingled with the perfumelike fragrance of the ginger plants and . . . worrying.

Mac stopped briefly in the suite next door and retrieved the broken shaft of his driver, still wrapped in plastic, then walked with long strides to the outpost where Jumbo should have been. It was important that he check one more time. Through the nightscope he studied the strip of sod where the terrorists had planted land mines. Probably plastic beauties, thought Mac. Marge didn't know she'd be driving through a mine-field. She might have exploded. From the other outpost, Angel's field of fire would cover most of the route Marge was going to drive. He hadn't bothered to tell her that, either. Angel was probably a hell of a good shot. No need to upset her any more than necessary.

Mac lined up the nightscope. A straight line staying close to, but on the left of that big sand trap. Angel wouldn't be able to spot the golf cart until it popped up on the twelfth green. Good Christ! He'd told Marge to walk across the green. But now she was driving a golf cart. There was no way that woman would drive across any green. A dedicated golfer who played by the rules . . . she'd drive around it . . . by at least thirty feet. Then . . . he swallowed hard, not completing the thought.

He could see the strip of newly planted sod plainly. The terrorists had done a helluva lot of work in a short period of time. They knew what they were doing. Thank God, his memory was still good. The strip ran straight across, about six feet in front of the green. He could work in the shelter of the raised green and that bunker, out of Angel's sight.

Rising from the swivel chair, he started down the stairs on the way toward the twelfth green. His mind flashed vivid images of exploding mines, vignettes of horror from the past, wondering whether the terrorists had used magnetic mines or the fiendish type that, once set, exploded at the slightest touch or movement. His tongue wiped some of the dryness from his lips. The taste of fear was like a thin coating of rust. Without any sophisticated equipment, there was only one way to find out.

Flat on his stomach, Mac crawled forward using his arms and elbows for propulsion, inching the last few feet toward the strip of disturbed sod. Scuba gloves in his pocket, his fingers gently felt for the line where the sod had been replanted and touched it. A tiny shadow of doubt came into his mind. He pushed it aside. For a brief second he closed his eyes and prayed. Now his fingers were lifting the sod and exploring underneath. He touched something solid and, expecting the worst, his heart stopped. Nothing happened and the beats returned. He could hear the irregular thumps. Clearing the dirt around the plastic disk, the flat table knife slid under and gently, ever so gently, pried the disk loose. Up on his knees, he lifted the disk. Crouching, he moved toward the sand trap and set the disk down behind the lip of the bunker. Then he was back on his stomach, feeling for the next one.

Working faster now, deftly, and with growing confidence, a long-dormant skill returned. In the next fifteen minutes he cleared the sod strip of mines for almost twenty feet, finding four and nestling them snugly behind the lip of the sand trap. He replaced the sod, confident that all had been found. Unwrapping the black plastic from the end of the broken handle of his driver, he jabbed the shaft into the ground. The area between that marker and the bunker was free of mines. It was Marge's safe corridor through the minefield. He laughed to himself. He'd have to revise his opinion. Damn driver. It had sure proven useful on this trip.

Mac checked his watch. It was twelve twenty-five. There was still thirty-five minutes left until one A.M. Marge could now safely reach the twelfth green. Now he had to make sure she could cover the rest of the route. The thin black scuba gloves back on his hands, Jumbo was headed for the building on the northeast corner of the Molokai-Surf complex. The big man was looking for Angel.

As he moved, Mac's mind was racing. The timetable was tight, probably too tight. It was the way to get things done. That had always been his method. Now that he had more time . . . with nothing to do . . . that new president, the son-of-a-bitch who'd fired him. Someday he'd learn. His mind pushed that youngster aside; that seemed so unimportant now; it focused on Angel and a deadline.

In a regular war, killing Angel without risk would be easy. A grenade lobbed into the room, a burst of fire from the Kalashnikov. There were many ways, all noisy and obvious. Anything like that and all hell would break loose and the hostages would all die. No, whatever he did had to be quiet, and the terrorists couldn't know it had happened. Preferably, Angel would just disappear. "Hocus pocus, Abracadabra," Mac muttered softly.

Mac slowed his pace as he neared the building. He entered noisily and stomped up the stairs, already deciding that Angel was not the type who surprised easily. Mac wanted Angel to know that Jumbo was coming.

"Angelo, you mudderfucker," he shouted partway down the hall, mustering his best Harlem accent.

"Hey, Elefante," the Cuban answered.

Mac stood in the doorway, eyes squinting like a mole at midnight. Angel had swiveled his chair, and leaning back, was facing the door, assault rifle held loosely, aimed at the doorway an inch or two over Jumbo's head.

"Fire will kill you, Negro," Angel began.

"Found beer." Jumbo belched loudly, hands held high in front slightly to the side, showing Angel two cans of Primo. "Good cold beer."

Angel sat up, mouth watering, guard slightly relaxed.

"Catch!" Jumbo's left hand lobbed a frozen can of Primo in a high arc toward Angel.

"Jesus!" His automatic reflexes took over, and both of Angel's hands went up to catch the can of beer. His eyes swiveled upward, searching in the dim light for the can coming down at him.

Mac took three rapid strides forward, cocking his right arm, then threw the other still-frozen can of beer from a six-foot range full force into Angel's uplifted face. Stunned, nose and teeth shattered, Angel fell backward as Mac leapt upon him, arms working furiously, fists pounding downward, left hand reaching for the jugular, finding it and squeezing it with his thumb and fingers. Mac's right hand reached in his pocket and removed a dart from its sheath. The dart poised menacingly over Angel's chest. Moments later the dart went back into its sheath, unused. He'd decided he wanted Angel alive. It was all over within three minutes.

Rising, Mac righted the chair, glanced out of both windows and listened for any sounds at the top of the stairs. He heard nothing. Apparently, no one had noticed the dull thump Angel had made falling backward. Wasting little time or motion, Mac pulled a plastic garbage bag from his pocket, unwrapped it, punched a few air holes near the bottom, and tied it over the unconscious Angel's head, shoulders, and arms. From the closet he removed the spare blanket and rolled Angel up in it, tossing in the Cuban's camouflage mask and cap and the smashed can of beer, tying the outside securely with three circles of twine. The sludge from the broken beer can was scattered around the room. Mac pulled the tab on the other can and sloshed the contents around, setting the can next to the swivel chair. From his bag he took out the four empty cans of beer, tossing them on the floor. When he was done, the room smelled like a brewery.

On the way back to ocean suite seven, carrying a bundle that looked like a bedroll over his shoulder, Mac reflected that at the moment, with both Jumbo and Angel out of the way, the terrorists had no one guarding the outside northern section of the Molokai-Surf complex. Of course, they didn't know it yet. He wasn't sure that he wanted the Marines to know it either. They might decide to move in, and that would be tragic. They might not appreciate the depth of the terrorists' inner defenses. It was C-4 plastic explosive. The hostages were sitting ass-deep in the stuff. It was a dynamite defense.

Reaching their ocean cottage, Mac dumped his bundle behind the bushes. It was twelve fifty-six A.M. when Marge saw his shadow on the lanai and heard his whisper, "Marge, it's me." She was in his arms before he'd slid the door closed.

"Where have you been?" she asked. "I've been so worried."

"Me, too!" he said honestly. "The last twenty-four hours have been a helluva week."

The newlyweds sat on the floor in silence. The honeymoon fever had cooled. Having difficulty communicating, they now had their doubts in common.

"Love is more than physical, more than just making love," Tom said softly to Jenny. "It's a whole person kind of thing, a lot of little bits and pieces that add up to caring. The core of love is interest in one another. Over time, lovers become partners."

Jenny sighed audibly and turned away. It was no longer important whether their marriage went down the chute or not. This bride knew what she wanted and it was obvious that Tommy didn't have it. The nerve endings in her skin tingled. From across the room she could feel the cobalt-blue eyes probing her body. Stretching, she moved her body sensuously, emphasizing the strong points. Inexorably her eyes sought out the handsome terrorist, fascinated by the baby face, the little boy smile, and his macho magnetism. He had the style of a buccaneer and the face of an altar boy. She could tell by the bulge in his trousers that he was all man.

A wave of heat swept through her body. She wondered if the color showed as her cheeks began to burn. Marco's smile broadened and she could see his white, even teeth. With an effort, Jenny kept her eyes unwavering on his. Her inner warmth increased and she could feel herself responding to his strong masculinity. The excitement and fear of the situation had increased her sexual desire, now at a fever pitch.

Pulling her sheet around her like a toga over her peignoir, Jenny rose and walked across the room slowly and deliberately, body flowing like a melody. As she passed the young terrorist, heart beating rapidly, she could feel his strong eyes staring at her breasts. Inhaling deeply, she could feel them swell and her nipples harden.

Marco watched the young bride enter the ladies' room. He had put out strong mental waves and felt the answering vibrations. Some will, some won't. He knew she would, and eagerly. Emotional quicksilver. He smiled smugly. His first choice, the pick of the litter. She looked calico. He guessed part Irish, Spanish, some Oriental and Hawaiian bloodlines. Quickly, he signaled to Michael to take over his guard post.

Marco was standing near the door when she came out of the ladies' room. With a slight smile, he touched her arm and beckoned with his head. "Forbidden fruit is sweet," he whispered. Her eyes, open wide, showed no fear. Breathing unevenly, heart palpitating, Jenny turned and followed the young terrorist.

Candy and the fat man watched the scenario. Dan's eyes looked questioningly at the pretty blonde and she shook her head negatively and laughed lightly. "He's a woman chaser and she wants to be caught. That one's got her desire up. She'll come out scratching." Candy moved closer to the fat man and whispered, "Maybe I should have warned her, he bites." Dan laughed when she rubbed her rear end.

Marco steered the young bride into the nearest guest room, closing and locking the door behind them. She moved into his arms. Their kiss was long and passionate, his hands feeling the curves of her body and then her moistness. Eagerly, her hands reached for him. He was right. She wanted it all.

"Now I lay me down to cheat," she whispered, slipping out of her sheet as he undressed. Their bodies meshed together and Jenny loved him like she meant it. Theirs was a ride on the wild side, and she met him more than halfway.

Forty minutes later, Jenny returned alone to the Koa Lounge, walking dreamily, a look of rapture on her face. She'd known it could be perfect. It had been. Wicked sensations and strong sexual currents still running through her body, she couldn't keep her face from glowing. Her whole body tingled. Under the sheet there were dark purple hickies on the most sensitive parts of her body, which she planned to enjoy for days. Inwardly, ecstasy was a reality, having given as much as she'd taken. Marco had one giant hickie which would keep him throbbing for some time. Her lips had driven him wild and she'd been well rewarded, the taste a step above cognac. It was only fair, one great taste deserved another.

The fat man chuckled and touched Candy's arm. "Baby, you were right. You're a better psychic than any I've ever known. When we get back to California . . ." Candy shifted her eyes to glance at him. Dan's face was all smiles. Her heart bumped. What did he mean, "When we got back to California?"

The groom was aware of everything that had happened. Self-pity clashed with a strong feeling of relief. Her beauty had blinded him. He had fallen in love down a chute of passion. Tonight he hated Jenny for the same reason he used to love her. The girl could be turned on in a microsecond and then become insatiable. He'd thought it was his animal magnetism. It obviously wasn't. It was anybody's, even a fucking terrorist. She was a no-good nympho bitch, and this was a good time to find it out. It would be easy to get the marriage annulled. He smiled, a bittersweet smile. Some things you learn by losing. He'd given her the ring and she'd given him the finger.

Lloyd Reynolds, free-lance reporter, put his hand over his mouth to keep from laughing aloud. He was a fucking *Menehune*. He had to be. No one had ever seen the ancient Hawaiian elves. But Reynolds believed in them. He was now pretty sure that he was a direct descendant.

First, he'd flashed his press credentials and interviewed a few noncommissioned officers. Then by standing around next to the Marines, mingling and talking with them, he'd gradually become inconspicuous, almost accepted as one of them. The press badge was now pinned to a Marine camouflage jacket that he wore over his yellow Adidas shirt, Marine pants covered his white jeans, and his baby face looked out from under a Marine combat helmet.

As darkness descended and the stars slowly drilled holes in the sky, Reynolds edged closer and closer to Donahue's command tent. For several hours now he'd been in position, crouched between two large boulders in the dark shadows of a sandalwood tree, to see and hear everything involving the marine command.

It was time for Marge to leave. Quickly Mac retrieved Angel from behind the bushes and strapped the thin terrorist into the passenger's seat, tying the tall bundle top and bottom securely against the back of the seat. "Your Guardian Angel," Mac grinned.

Marge grimaced.

"Got the shirt?" Mac asked.

Marge patted her stomach.

"Give it to the C.O."

"You've told me that at least half a dozen times."

"Tell me your route once more."

"For God's sake, Mac, I drive between the stake and the trap and up over the green, gouging deep ruts in it."

"Don't get angry." Mac slid the lanai door open. "I just want to be sure."

"Remember, Mac, vengeance belongs to God."

He didn't reply, thinking that God had never refused his help before.

Mac drove the golf cart out of the newlyweds' suite across and off the lanai and onto the path, then got out of the cart. Marge closed the lanai door and took the driver's seat. She drove slowly with the big figure of Jumbo walking first alongside, then behind, cradling his AK-47. Reaching the corner building, Mac signaled her to stop.

"Good luck, hon, see you in a day or two." He kissed her. "I wouldn't miss your birthday."

Marge flushed, turning warm inside. Despite everything else, he'd remembered.

"A kiss for each year."

"We'll do better than that," she promised.

"Be careful! I'm too old to start playing the field again."

Marge looked up and wrinkled her nose at him.

"Besides, compared to you," Mac kissed her nose, "it's all crabgrass."

"You're tough, Mac McGregor." She smiled at him with admiration.

"You're something else, Marge McGregor." He smiled back with love.

Marge nodded, and driving slowly, headed in a direct line for the sand trap at the corner of the twelfth green. Mac took the stairs two at a time, and running to the corner room, he slumped into the swivel chair, eyes glued to the nightscope.

The golf cart approached the sand trap and swung between the stake and the bunker. Mac closed his eyes and heard nothing. Marge was through the minefield. He breathed easier. The cart slowed going up the hill, then onto the green, straight across, narrowly missing the pin in the cup. She did it on purpose, he thought. Off the green and onto the cart path headed toward the thirteenth tee. Mac smiled at the silence. No one was firing from the other outpost. If anyone did, he'd roast them like a luau pig.

Marge was picking up speed. "E-Z-Go," Mac reminded her under his breath. The cart was moving at top speed now, straight down the middle of the thirteenth fairway. "Slow down," he almost shouted, watching the bundle containing Angel squirming in the passenger's seat. "I should have killed the Cuban son-of-a-bitch," he muttered to himself. The cart was bouncing wildly as it went over a series of bumps in the fairway, almost out of control, careening on two wheels, back down on four and then over a rise and out of sight.

Mac let out an explosive sigh, feeling exhausted, drained of emotion. Good Christ! It would have been safer to have let Jumbo drive. He sighed again. By now Marge would have reached the Marines. If she remembered how to stop the damn cart.

In slow motion his mind went back over Marge's escape. The cart was almost out of control, careening on two wheels. The hospital scene came back to Mac in a blurry montage of noise and people. A North Korean rocket had hit his jeep and blown him thirty feet in the air. They had to put tubes everywhere. He was breathing and then wasn't. He heard the word "coma." Ten days later he regained consciousness. In a month and a half he was back at the front lines.

Fingering the scar at the back of his scalp, he shuddered at the memory. It was better to forget the terror hidden in the past. Thirty-two years ago. It couldn't be, but it was. Damn, he was getting old. He shook his head, clearing unwanted thoughts. Marge had been great. It had been almost six years since the old girl had stood on the back fender of his Harley-Davidson. She still had guts. Damn, he missed her already. Someday he'd take the time to tell her that she was always on his mind.

Marine PFC Juan Gonzales swept his eyes from bush to bush, tree to tree, his range of vision limited by the luxuriant undergrowth. Assigned to sentry duty, on his first combat mission, all of his senses were alert. In the inner recesses of Juan's mind was a hope that given an opportunity he would be brave. From boyhood, when he'd heard about the Marine Corps from his uncle, his fondest hope was to be a Marine hero.

The trees waving in the wind cast eerie, dancing shadows on the ground. Moonlight reflected off the sheen on rocks that had been created by innumerable flat threads of volcanic glass—Pele's hair. Gonzales removed his helmet and wiped his forehead. Nightmares could come true out here. Suddenly his eyes opened wide. Over the top of a knoll he could see a four-wheeled vehicle lurching from side to side, bouncing toward him at top speed. Juan closed his eyes for a brief second, then snapped them open. The place was spooked. Like an apparition, the vehicle materialized, then vanished. Then there it was again. But it couldn't be a vision. It was a golf cart and it had moved closer. Eyes narrowing, he sighted carefully through the scope on his M-16 automatic rifle. His finger snuggled into position against the trigger and, heart beating faster, the Marine sentry took a deep breath.

Suddenly his eyes popped open wide again. A woman was driving the golf cart. A woman with two large bundles, one of which seemed to be moving. Holy Mother of Christ! He couldn't shoot a woman. But maybe it was a terrorist trick. Terrorists would do anything. They'd even been known to put bombs in baby carriages. They maimed children. Holy Mother, he'd better do something, fast. A warning shot? Shoot out the tires? Sound an alarm? For a woman in a golf cart? His first combat assignment, the safety of the whole Marine detachment in his hands, and he was frozen. Instinctively, he sensed another presence. Out of the corner of his eye Juan saw his sergeant watching the golf

cart through binoculars. One nod of the sergeant's head
and Juan was crouching, moving forward, rifle in hand
to intercept the vehicle.

As the cart came closer, slowed, and stopped, Juan
noticed that two other sergeants had appeared almost
miraculously, then three or four officers, and finally the
colonel himself. No one had sounded an alarm. No one
had said anything. Damn. He thought he was the only
sentry on duty. It must be what they meant by defense in
depth. His sergeant touched his shoulder. "Good job,
Gonzales," he said quietly. Juan's chest swelled. Maria
would be proud.

Marge sat in the golf cart with a defiant smile on her
face, oblivious to the deep scratch over her eye and the
blood oozng down her cheek. The Marines gathered
around the golf cart, helped Marge out, then removed
the corpse of Jorge and the screaming, squirming body
of Angel. Major Baldwin signaled for a medical corpsman. The corpsman swabbed the cut over Marge's eye,
noticing the fragile sort of candlelight in her eyes, the
lostness in her face, the lips clamped tightly together.
The frown on his forehead told the colonel that Marge
was close to shock.

Donahue stepped forward and introduced himself.
Marge liked him instantly. He reminded her of Mac,
with the quiet confidence of a man in charge. They
moved into Donahue's command tent. She was silent
for a moment, then began talking in a calm voice. "I
was really shaking out there . . . when Angel came to
and started to scream . . ." She shook her head. "It was
like a ride on a rollercoaster . . ." She laughed lightly.
"Exciting."

The colonel asked questions to which he really didn't
expect answers. But Marge answered every question,
hesitantly at first, then expansively with detail. She sat

in the middle of the group and talked, looking straight ahead, recalling the terrorist takeover, Mac's actions, describing the terrorists as best she could and their locations, as well as the position of the hostages. The longer she talked the more her eyes glistened, thoughts coming from deep inside.

"Even the terrorists," she said. "They have to be people first. Guided by their own conscience . . . and a conscience doesn't forgive or forget."

There was a look of genuine awe on Donahue's face. This was a class lady. He asked her about Mac.

"He'll outsmart them," she answered simply, her eyes sparkling proudly. "God has his arms wrapped around that man. I just know he'll be all right."

Donahue nodded his close-cropped head. Faith is the evidence of things unseen, he thought. The colonel liked Marge. She had a lot of guts. She'd put her ass on the line for all of them.

Suddenly a sob escaped from her throat. In a quiet voice she whispered, "I don't know how much longer I can keep going. There's not much of me left."

The colonel looked at her face closely. It was serene. He signaled for the corpsman, lips mouthing the words, "Sedate her."

Suddenly Marge reached under her sweater and pulled out Mac's blue shirt. "Oh, he sent this out to you. You know husbands. He thought I might forget something." The defiant smile was back on her face.

It was almost two in the morning when Mac saw a red flare fired in the distance out over the cliff, flaming up in an arc, then dying out as it fell into the sea. That was the signal. Marge was safe. They had his messages. He flicked his shielded SabreLite flashlight twice in the direction of the Marines. Then he settled back to wait.

An unearthly silence slowly descended on the resort.

• • •

In the dark shadows of a sandalwood tree, crouched between two large boulders very close to Donahue's command tent, Lloyd Reynolds licked his lips, then smiled. What a scoop! The Marines had someone inside the Molokai-Surf. A Mac McGregor—ex-Marine—impersonating a terrorist. His wife had already escaped in a golf cart and brought out two terrorists—one dead, one barely alive. Now the Marines were planning to infiltrate the terrorists.

That information was worth real money. It wasn't filler. Reynolds had a front-page headline grabber and he knew it. No other reporter knew what he knew. All he had to do was get that story on television, with a byline, and his reputation was made. He moved and almost groaned aloud. Wedged between two rocks, all of his muscles were cramped tight. Maybe he'd finally found his niche in life. He grinned and popped the last pill into his mouth, crumpled the bag, and threw it into the brush. All those pink footballs, black beauties, and yellow jackets were gone. No matter now. There'd be money for the real thing, coke. His nostrils twitched involuntarily.

Struggling, Lloyd freed himself, removed the Marine jacket, pants, and helmet that he'd appropriated and placed them inside his carryall. He moved out of his hiding place unchallenged, and had almost reached his parked car, when he heard the sharp command.

"Halt, who goes there? Advance and be recognized."

Lloyd flashed his press credentials.

"Where are you coming from?" the sentry asked.

"Colonel Donahue's command post," Reynolds answered honestly. "I'm going out to phone in my story."

"At two-thirty in the morning?" the sentry asked.

"I've already missed the morning papers on the East

Coast," Reynolds snapped. "If I don't hurry, I'll miss the network news shows."

The sentry squinted at Reynolds. This reporter sounded bigtime. Goddamned reporters were everywhere. They'd been flying into Molokai all afternoon and evening. It wouldn't be long before they outnumbered the Marines around the Molokai-Surf. He glanced out at the tents that had been thrown up just outside the Marine perimeter line. The Marines would soon be under siege from the media. They were swarming in laden with bedrolls, duffel bags, cameras, and note pads. Soon they'd clutter up the roads, infiltrate their lines. Someone would get hurt. His job was to keep them from interfering with military activities. Keep the fuckers out. At least this guy was moving in the right direction.

"Okay, but no one gets past here tomorrow—coming or going—without an authorized pass." The sentry's mouth was grim.

Reynolds grinned, knowing he'd get by. The damn Marine was too uptight. He reached in his pocket and fished out a card, and handing it to the sentry, said, "Give this guy a call. He's done wonders for me."

The Marine glanced at the card and turned it over. In the moonlight he could read, "T. Thomasa, M.D., Psychiatric Practice." The sentry glanced up, but the reporter was gone. The damn flake had given him a card for a shrink.

It was almost three in the morning when Marco found that Angel was missing. After storming around the room for a few minutes, Marco sat in the swivel chair by the window, thinking.

Five empty Primo cans and the strong smell of beer. That damn Angelo had found a six-pack. His clenched teeth forced repeated curses into explosive hisses. Angelo had crawled away to sleep it off . . . No, not five beers, that alcoholic . . . once he'd started drinking . . . He hissed again. No telling what he'd do.

Marco picked up the beer cans and put them in the trash can. This information was better kept to himself. Angelo was his man. Shit! He'd brought him along from Havana. No need to get Fire and Carlos excited, they were asleep anyway. He'd take care of Angelo himself. That hophead would owe him one. For the next couple of hours he'd cover for Angel. There was only one other outpost to check. He reached for his walkie-talkie.

Mac rubbed his eyes. The night was wrapped in a quiet so complete that even the slight breeze seemed an intruder. Shifting his heavy body, he leaned forward and yawned again, thinking of one of Marge's "good night specials" from the bottom to the top.

Mac jumped as if shot. The muffled voice came from somewhere close by, someplace in the room. The closet. Cautiously approaching the closet, he threw the door open and his body sideways, assault rifle covering the empty space. The muffled voice was louder now. "Aloha twelve, this is Aloha two. Come in. You big black . . ." The last word was garbled. It was coming from the pocket of the heavy denim jacket on the shelf. Mac picked up the walkie-talkie. So that's how. Of course.

"Hey, big shee-eet." Mac pushed the button and spoke in a loud voice. "Lookin' fa me?"

"Jumbo. Marco here. For the next few hours I'm taking over for Angelo. He's not feeling too well."

Mac grinned broadly. That was certainly true. But why was Marco covering . . .

"Come dawn," Marco's voice was clear now, "sleep

in for four or five hours. I'll get you if we need you. Over and out.''

Mac set the walkie-talkie next to the swivel chair and chuckled to himself. Standard GI issue. The Marines would be monitoring every channel. Now he had a way to communicate with them. But it had to be subtle. Very subtle indeed.

Colonel Donahue, his three senior field officers, and his personal aide were sitting around a folding metal table in the center of a lean-to tent attached to and folded down from the colonel's command vehicle. With the canvas sides and insect netting rolled up, the tent was open to the soft night breeze. The flickering oil lamps cast eerie shadows which danced grotesquely on the dark red earth.

The colonel adjusted his bathrobe, moved his canvas chair closer to the table, and grinned broadly at the other three. ''McGregor's in there . . . Mac McGregor.'' Donahue spoke the name as if in awe. ''That S.O.B.'s a legend. I was just out of Quantico when I first met him in Korea. He was a major . . .'' The colonel paused, caught up in memories of the past. It was a story he'd told so often he'd almost forgotten the facts. ''Someday, when you've got three or four hours, I'll tell you about Mac McGregor. He was some Marine. The master had no mold. We couldn't have picked a better man. He walks in nobody's tracks. He makes his own. Goddamn, Big Mac is back.'' Donahue slapped the table with the palm of his hand.

''I've heard about some of the things he's supposed to have done,'' the big rawboned major with the square jaw said. ''Tarawa, Okinawa, Korea. I thought he'd died years ago. He must be ancient—over sixty by now.''

Donahue nodded, then swiveled his head, glancing around to make sure that Marge McGregor was out of hearing. Major Baldwin had all the charm of an earthquake. But then, he'd thought McGregor was dead, too. He should have known, old legends die hard. Flipping out a cigarette, the colonel tapped it twice on the table, then lit it. Inhaling, he spoke in a husky voice, his words intermingled with the vapors of smoke. "We need absolute secrecy. No publicity. None. If the media boys learned that we had two terrorists out here and a man inside . . ." The colonel shook his head slowly. "Lord knows what they'd do with that information. It might jeopardize McGregor and all the hostages. Put Jumbo's body on ice and Angel in the deep freeze."

Turning and flipping the ashes from his cigarette into the coffee can on the table, he beckoned to his aide, Captain Alexander. "Bill, Marge McGregor is your responsibility. Take good care of her. She's to be seen by no one until this is all over. She needs some rest. Understand?" His eyes met Alexander's.

Donahue's aide nodded, his glasses glittering in the flickering light. Rising, he left the tent, mumbling to himself. Combat action—the first since 'Nam—and he was assigned to nursemaid a sixty-year-old woman.

"Colonel, we've gone over McGregor's notes." Major Fleming's prematurely white hair and heavy eyebrows were dominant features in the dim light. "We think we should move in now, in force. No one fired at the golf cart when Mrs. McGregor escaped. According to McGregor's map, there are two terrorist outposts with fields of fire covering her route." He pushed the sketch across the table. "We know McGregor's in Jumbo's outpost. Since no one fired, the other outpost must have been Angel's."

Donahue listened attentively. He'd assumed as much.

"McGregor has opened up the entire northern side for us," Fleming continued.

"As well as a clear path through the mines," added Baldwin.

Fleming nodded, his shock of white hair adding weight to his words. "We could occupy all of the northern perimeter buildings without the terrorists knowing what had happened. Then our men would be in position to pick off the remaining terrorists and rush the main lounge."

The other two majors nodded their agreement.

Donahue sat in silence for a few minutes weighing the argument. It was a sound military maneuver. But . . . "No, we'll play it Mac's way. There are 216 hostages in the lounge sitting in the middle of a giant bomb. They're up to their asses in explosives." He sighed deeply. "One mistake and . . ." His eyes closed, then snapped open. "We just can't risk it."

Major Murray spoke for the first time. "We could get one man in there tonight. McGregor asked us to send in a kid with guts to impersonate Angel."

"Yes," Donahue said. "But not until tomorrow night."

"That's the point," Murray argued. "McGregor's picked off four of the terrorists, but they don't know he's done it, nor even that he's in there. Apparently the two that Sergeant Harris shot in the window were already corpses, but the terrorists think the Marines did it. McGregor's wife delivered Angel and Jumbo special delivery. He's impersonating Jumbo and Angel hasn't been missed yet." Murray paused to catch his breath. "Now, my point is that the sooner Angel gets back in there, the less chance he'll be missed."

Donahue raised his forefinger. "We don't know how Mac plans to cover."

"McGregor probably thought we needed more time to get our man," Murray continued. "There's a young corporal, Mike Garcia, tall, skinny build. Tough and smart."

"Speaks Spanish fluently." Baldwin leaned forward, eyes staring into Donahue's. "McGregor asked for a kid with guts. That's Garcia. Angel's camouflage outfit fits him like a glove. He's primed and ready."

"McGregor really did a job on that Angel," Fleming said, a touch of awe in his voice. "He's not a pretty sight. The medics have him now. The tooth fairy owes him a fortune."

Donahue glanced at the mountains rising high above them. Even in the moonlight he could see the rows of pineapple plants marching up the hills. Then he glanced back at the three majors, eyes focusing on Murray seated to his left.

"I say send him back tonight. Hesitation kills. The path through the minefield is clear," answered Murray to the unasked question.

The colonel's eyes flicked to Major Fleming.

"If we wait until tomorrow night, as McGregor suggests, we waste a whole day. We're wallowing out here," said Fleming, eyes returning the colonel's gaze. "This is the moment. Who the hell knows what's going to happen tomorrow?"

The colonel's eyes flicked to the third major.

"Get the point of the wedge in and go from there. You taught us that, sir." Baldwin's jaw jutted forward. "McGregor needs help. I say the sooner the better. Nobody can go on forever. A halo only has to slip a few inches to become a noose. The hostages are all going to die, Colonel, unless we rescue them."

"Get Garcia in here and let's talk." Colonel Donahue had made his decision. He turned and stared out at the nearby hill, knowing the dark mass of the Molokai-Surf complex was just over the rise out of sight, and felt uneasy.

Mac sat at the window in darkness, motionless, narrow slits for eyes, body relaxed, partially sleeping. Suddenly his nose twitched, eyes popped open, sensing a slight movement in the distance behind the rise at the end of the thirteenth fairway. Seconds later the top of a golf cart appeared. Then the whole cart. Marge's cart coming back toward the resort. Blood pumping through him now, senses totally alert, Mac sighted through the M-845 scope. "Oh, shit!" he murmured to himself. Angel was driving the cart.

There was no way it could be Angel. It had to be a Marine dressed as Angel. "Dammit," Mac muttered, anger burning in his throat. The shitheads weren't following his instructions. They were supposed to wait. He couldn't let the poor bastard get any closer. By now Marco would have him in his sights. Mac aimed the Kalashnikov well in front of the golf cart and squeezed the trigger. The Marine kept coming. Damn Marine pride. It would live forever—but that kid wouldn't. It was white knuckle time. Mac fired again, this time closer, then watched, overwhelmed with a sense of helplessness.

Angel! What in the hell . . . ? Marco sighted through his nightscope, emotions churning. That fuckin' traitor . . . the slime had sold out. He'd fry his ass. Marco aimed his grenade launcher. No, Jumbo! That goddamned stupid black was firing. He'd missed. How could anyone shoot wearing rubber gloves? And Angel was still out of range. The cart was dodging now, moving faster, coming closer. Marco's little boy smile widened second by second into a broad grin. He fired once. The golf cart disintegrated.

Lips clamped tightly, Mac's eyes closed behind
Jumbo's mask. He breathed deeply to control the emotions rising deep inside. Some poor kid . . . another no-
frills funeral. He'd died alone and for nothing. The
damn gung-ho legacy. The payoff was zip. Mac opened
his eyes and watched the smouldering wreckage.

The flames were flickering now. Mac tore his gaze
away and stared into a darkened corner of the room, no
expression on his face, mind sorting thoughts. Death is
the price of life, a ticket to heaven. From earth to glory,
forever and ever. The young man would now visit the
Lord and dwell in the house of tomorrow. An en-
chanted paradise. A place to do nothing at all and enjoy
it as never before. Mac pictured the Marine he'd never
met and talked to him. And sooner or later, all your
friends will join you. Your soul is restored. Your future
lies where it began. Get close to God, son, and he'll let
you in on some of his secrets. Besides, no one dies, they
just get recycled. With God, all things are possible.

Mac shook his head and rose from the swivel chair. It
was close to dawn. His body ached. I'm not a winner, he
thought, just a survivor. The sun rises, the sun sets. Life
goes on. It was no time to start doubting his invincibil-
ity. Morning is the time for optimism. Marco. That evil
. . . Mac didn't even complete the thought. Way back
he'd learned, don't get mad, get even. He had an idea
for Marco. It would blow his mind.

Mac dragged himself slowly to the nearest bed, fell
into it, and was asleep.

CHAPTER ELEVEN

Second Day—Morning

The first light of dawn swept away the night, revealing Lloyd Reynolds sitting in the front seat of his rental car, which was parked outside a phone booth on the main street of the sleepy town of Kaunakakai. Eyes closed, head resting on the back seat, his mind was detached, drifting, visiting a subsystem of his senses, the twilight zone.

Lloyd's thoughts were vivid images. The interview on "Good Morning America" had just ended; David Hartman reached for Lloyd's hand. "How did you do it?" he asked, over and over, shaking his head in wonder.

"You should get the Pulitzer," Joan Lundon said, matter-of-factly, her pretty eyes sparkling with admiration.

Lloyd smiled his good-byes quickly. Jane Pauley was waiting to interview him on the "Today Show." The

image faded, he shifted his weight on the seat, arm
dangling almost to the floor. With the money flowing
in, he could afford a regular supply of cocaine, maybe
move up to speedballing or freebasing. His unconscious
grinned. Snow in Hawaii. From now on, Lucky Lloyd
would be wired permanently, the center of the universe,
every nerve alive.

It was almost eight o'clock when the morning street
noises shook him out of his mental imaging. Momentarily disoriented, he glanced at the reflection in the
rearview mirror. The eyes that stared back were angular
from lack of sleep. His mouth was dry, and he ran his
tongue over teeth that were heavy with donkey dust.
Part of him felt like it didn't exist.

Fully awake now, he moved to the phone booth, heart
beating rapidly. It was time to sell his story. Time to
move into the fast lane, into network television, into
prime time.

Twenty minutes later, Lloyd Reynolds emerged from
the booth, a broad grin on his baby face. He walked
down Ala Malama Street looking for a diner. This
morning he could afford steak and eggs.

Mac woke with a start, in a cold sweat. He'd been
dreaming that a man in a camouflage mask, mouth slit
twisted into an evil, boyish grin, was chasing him with a
noisy chain saw—and gaining. He rolled over and
turned off the alarm on his wristwatch. Nine thirty-eight
A.M. It had been buzzing for almost ten minutes.

He rose with an effort, joints aching, muscles pro-
testing, mind groping. The chance to dream was always
followed by the need to wake up. This morning he
didn't know which was worse. It would be so easy to lie
back down and let the crazies win. Hell, they were going
to win anyhow. If not today, then tomorrow, next

week, or next year. What difference did it make? The
world was in intensive care and nobody gave a shit. The
terrorists, the sadists, the scum with twisted minds were
all multiplying like roaches in dark corners of sleazy,
filthy sewers all over the world, oozing out of every
crack and crevice. They were hidden behind camouflage
masks, and armed with assault rifles, grenades, and
rockets. They were trained by the KGB and financed by
Libyan oil money. And they had an almost unlimited
number of unarmed and unprotected targets—the decent people trying to live normal, happy lives. Mac
shook his head sadly. Their victory was inevitable. It
was only a matter of time.

Closing and locking the door to the room from the inside, he walked into the bathroom, moving easier now.
Taking off Jumbo's mask and scuba gloves, he stared
into the mirror above the sink. An old man with a worn
face that had more lines than a road map stared back
out of red-rimmed eyes. Opening his mouth, he looked
in vain for the big brown bear who'd slept there, then
ran his tongue over the coating on his teeth, forced a
grimace, and spat into the toilet. Running his hand over
the stubble on his chin, he sighed. Even the damn
whiskers on his face were mostly white. He was getting
old. Turning on both faucets, Mac splashed water over
his face and swished some through his mouth. Damn
Jumbo, the cheap bastard. No razor, no toothpaste, no
deodorant, not even soap. Nothing. His face wrinkled
into a semismile. Fire wouldn't notice him this time. If
he were going to act like a terrorist, he'd just have to
smell like one, too.

Putting his mask and gloves back on, he picked up the
Kalashnikov, pocketed two extra thirty-round clips,
took a deep breath, unlocked and opened the door, and
stepped out heading for the Koa Lounge. There was a

distinct aroma in the air. At first Mac sensed it intui-
tively, then smelled it plainly, instantly recognizing the
odor for what it was—the unmistakable haunting fragrance of trouble.

Halfway down the stairs, Mac stopped. The skin on
the back of his neck was moving, his nerve endings close
to the surface. Something was wrong. He didn't know
what. Maybe he was moving too fast, not taking enough
time to regroup, think things through, sort them out
and plan his actions. Quickly he turned, climbed the
stairs and went back into Jumbo's nest. Seated back in
the swivel chair, Mac picked up the binoculars and
sighted out the window. The shattered and burned
frame of the golf cart was still sitting in the middle of
the thirteenth fairway, but the charred lump that had
been a brave Marine was gone. Sometime in the early
light of day the Marines had reclaimed one of theirs. He
nodded approval. They were taking no chances that the
terrorists would find out the corpse wasn't Angel's.
Easy enough, thought Mac, behind the shelter of an armored vehicle. And Marco had virtually announced
over the air that come dawn the terrorists guarding the
outposts were going to sleep in.

Slowly he moved the binoculars, reversing the path
Marge had traveled. On the twelfth green he could see
the indentations the wheels of the golf cart had made.
Farther along, he saw the shaft of his broken golf club
still sticking out of the ground, a marker showing
plainly where the mines had been removed, the safe
path. The raised green was between Marco and that
spot, but as soon as that sadist awoke, he'd think it
through. Angel would have had to remove some mines
to drive a golf cart out there. Marco would send out a
team to repair the gap in their lines. They'd find the
four mines nestled in the sand trap and the broken golf

shaft. Jesus, it probably still had his name sticker on the neck that the golf bag attendant at his club had affixed.

He reached for Jumbo's walkie-talkie, and for the first time this morning grinned to himself. If he were up and working, he was going to make sure that pretty boy, son-of-a-bitch Marco wasn't going to sleep. His mind went back over Marco's call the night before, then swallowing his nervous saliva, pushed the button on the walkie-talkie, knowing the Marines would be listening also.

"Aloha two, this is aloha twelve . . . do ya read?"

Mac waited, then repeated the call. After the third attempt an answer crackled back.

"Aloha two here, go ahead, Jumbo." It was a voice blurry with sleep.

"Covah me, willya? Hasta be a hole in our fence. Gonna go fix." Mac slurred the words, Jumbo style.

Marco was awake now, mind quickly remembering the events of the night before. That big black was a lot smarter than he sounded. Of course, Angel couldn't have driven through the strip of mines without clearing some first. But then, Angel was an expert with mines. He'd planted the strip. Marco didn't know whether Jumbo knew anything about mines.

"Need any help?" Marco asked, knowing he should offer, hoping for a negative answer.

"No. Ratha have ya covah me."

"Good boy," Marco said, then grimaced, wishing he could somehow recover his words.

Mac looked at the walkie-talkie, anger rising, then just as quickly subsiding, replaced by a sadistic smirk. That snot-nosed killer was speaking to Jumbo like he was a dog.

"Arf." Mac signed off, swearing to himself that at the first opportunity the big black dog was going to take a vicious bite out of Marco's ass.

Assault rifle in hand, he moved quickly now, cutting diagonally from his building toward the thirteenth tee until he reached the line of sod that had been disturbed and replaced. He moved along that line toward the twelfth green, knowing he was in plain sight of Marco, wanting the terrorist to see him searching for cart tracks. Seeing the twelfth green clearly, he turned and signaled Marco with his arms and hands, indicating cart tracks across the green. The binoculars of the terrorist followed his pointed signals.

Moving behind the raised green, out of sight of Marco, Mac pulled up the broken shaft of his golf club, peeled off his name sticker, then planted the shaft in a slight indentation in the bunker, covering it with sand. Moving carefully, he scooped out a shallow, short trench in the corner of the trap and moved the four mines sitting alongside on the surface gently into the trench, covering them with a thick layer of sand and raking the rest of the trap so that it looked uniformly smooth. Standing back and surveying his work, he was satisfied and confident. The evidence was buried. No one was going to poke around and check his work. It was too risky. Even if they did, it was worth the chance to know that there was still one way out.

Mac took the shortcut back to Jumbo's room. It was important that he let the Marines know the path was still open, but it had to be so subtle that Marco and the other terrorists wouldn't suspect.

"Aloha two, this is aloha twelve."

"Come in, Jumbo," Marco said.

"Found the spot. Everything's exactly like it was."

"Thanks, Jumbo. Good work. You may want to get some coffee at the lounge."

"Rogah and out," Mac said, smiling. The Marines should understand that message. Nothing was changed.

The three Marine majors sat dejectedly across from the colonel, avoiding his blue eyes, knowing from past experience that his angry stare could freeze-dry them.

"We should have followed McGregor's instructions," Colonel Donahue said flatly.

No one wanted to argue the point. Two Marines in an armored personnel carrier had just brought back the charred remains of Mike Garcia.

Major Murray leaned forward, voice matter-of-fact. "We just picked up a message from McGregor, Colonel."

"I heard," Donahue said. "Everything's exactly like it was. I assume he means the path through the land mines. But after what's happened, the terrorists will probably post another sharpshooter in Angel's outpost."

"I don't think so," Major Murray said, holding up both of his hands, palms outstretched. "But then, I suggested we send Garcia in there last night."

Donahue nodded. His memory was long and exact. This wasn't the time to place blame. It had been a command decision. He held out his cup. "Pour me some coffee, Bob, will you please, before it hardens?"

Major Fleming reached for the pyrex coffeepot on the small Coleman burner and poured some into the colonel's cup. The silence in the tent deepened as the others watched the colonel swallow his coffee and light yet another cigarette. Baldwin suspected that Donahue was smoking just to blow clouds of acrid smoke at the three of them. He coughed and saw a wisp of a smile cross the colonel's mouth, then disappear.

"Sometimes the best action is no action." Donahue's eyes were dark and intent, his mouth now a thin line. "We certainly blew that opportunity. Angel can't go back in there again."

The others stirred in their chairs. The colonel was right. They'd have to sit back on their heels. Hang tight. Keep their poise and wait—wait for another opportunity.

Major Murray rubbed his face with the palm of his hand, then spoke in a soft, gentle voice with just enough accent to guarantee attention. "Do you know the last thing that kid Garcia said before he took off in the golf cart?"

The others nodded negatively.

"I asked about his next of kin. He said he didn't have any . . . said his family tree was artificial. Then he laughed."

"He was a good, hard-nosed Marine," the colonel said. "Sometimes patience is the best weapon. It's tough to learn." The colonel looked at each of the other officers, then stood, the meeting was over.

"Gentlemen, we'll give our hostage negotiation team a chance."

Mac walked slowly toward the Koa Lounge, noticing beds of delicate *koali* morning glories and starbursts of the *iliau* plant reaching heavenward for the morning sun. A few clouds had appeared in the sky, little white pufferbellies drifting with the wind. The play of sunlight through the openings presented an assortment of images. Another day he and Marge would have sat fascinated, pointing out to each other the shapes of huge castles, faces, animals, and special visions. This morning Mac ignored the clouds and the mental imagery they stimulated, all of his attention concentrated on playing the role of Jumbo in broad daylight. It had to be a perfect performance or the curtains would come down quickly and the show would close on the spot. He pulled up the thin black scuba gloves, adjusted his mask, said a short prayer, walked across the lanai, slid open the door, and stepped into the lounge.

Momentarily, the huge bulk of Jumbo stood inside the door surveying the room. The hostages had finished coffee and rolls. Free to move about, they were seated in small groupings, as subdued as children at a party they didn't want to attend. The air seemed unusually quiet, with a low undercurrent of conversation. Mac rubbed the mask under his nose. The odor given off by the large group of hostages was unmistakably stronger than it had been the previous day. Kona and several of her staff were moving about among the hostages. He was relieved to see that neither Fire nor Carlos was in the room. He knew Marco wouldn't be there! Two terrorist guards, both wearing masks, were standing together. One he recognized from his build as Anahu, the fat Hawaiian. He didn't know the other tall, thin one, but from the hands dangling from beneath his camouflage jacket he could tell he was a black. Mac swallowed nervously and glanced at his own black gloves. If it hadn't been for Marge . . .

He moved toward the coffeepot, set down his assault rifle, and poured himself a cup of coffee. He picked up a sweetroll and was holding it in his gloved left hand trying to figure out how to get it through the slit in his mask, when the black terrorist he didn't know approached him. Mac's right hand slowly set down his coffee cup, fingers encircling and lifting his rifle slightly off the floor.

"Jumbo, hey man." Mac didn't recognize the jivey voice. "What's happenin'?"

Jumbo stuffed the sweetroll through the mouth slit in his mask and bit it in half. Slowly he munched the roll, the cloth flap over the mouth covering the movement of his lips.

"Starvin'," he sputtered through the roll, pushing the other half into his mouth. The thin terrorist stood and watched.

"Hey, watcha doin' with the gloves?" The question was as light as the voice. Mac had known that it was inevitable, and he'd decided the situation required an innovative, wild idea. He set down his rifle, picked up his coffee and washed down the rest of the roll, then leaned close to the black and whispered confidentially.

"Brother, rubber gloves . . . they're the answer."

Mac could see the puzzled expression in the other's eyes, one obviously bloodshot.

"Molokai. The home of lep-ro-sy." Mac spoke the dreaded word slowly.

"Leprosy!" Fright made the other voice louder. Several of the hostages, hearing the word, turned their heads toward the two terrorists.

"Shhh." Jumbo's mask glanced around. "Brother," Mac whispered, close to the other's ear, "this is just between us, man. Understand?"

The wiry terrorist nodded his agreement.

"Right over the hill . . . the big leper colony."

The other nodded. He'd heard about Father Damien.

"It's the damn red dust," Mac said, pointing at the other's pants.

The thin black brushed some of the dust off his camouflage outfit.

"The red dust. It's all over." Mac hesitated, speaking slowly. "It carries leprosy."

"You're shittin' me!" The tall, thin black moved back, staring at Jumbo.

"Man, why would I do that?" Jumbo's shoulders shrugged and the big hands covered with the black rubber gloves flashed in front of the tall terrorist's face mask. "Why?"

The thin black shook his head. He didn't know. Mac moved close again, speaking very softly. "Whitey. Didn't tell me. Did he tell you?" The other shook his head again.

"They don't tell me nothin'."

"Blacks have sensitive skin, very fragile. We catch leprosy easy." Mac could see the worried expression in the other's eyes and pressed on. "Man, it's all happenin'. Nobody cares. Look! The first sign . . . around the eyes." He pointed to the slits in his mask.

"Holy shee . . . eet!" Through the slits the other could see the vivid bluish-purple ring around Jumbo's eyes and he backed away. "Leprosy . . . you got . . ."

"Shhh," Mac said. "Don't tell anyone. I've been saved. Just in time. Rubber gloves. Makes you immune."

The tall thin terrorist turned and scurried away. Mac grinned to himself, reached for the coffeepot and poured himself another cup of coffee.

The colonel shifted his weight in the chair to avoid the early morning sun, and gazed admiringly at Marge McGregor seated across the portable folding table from Donahue and his three senior command officers. The thought kept running through his mind that this little lady had to be some woman to be married to Mac McGregor. They'd just finished questioning her again about Mac's notes and her own recollections of the events taking place inside the Molokai-Surf since the terrorist takeover. Marge had not been able to add anything to what she'd told them the previous night.

"I've made arrangements for you to stay with my wife just outside of Honolulu. We'll have a chopper take you over this morning." The colonel smiled disarmingly, bracing himself for her reaction.

Marge sipped her coffee slowly, listening to the soft clucking calls of a gambel's quail from the *kiawe* thicket behind them. She set her cup down on the table, then spoke softly. "I'd rather stay here, if it's possible, close to Mac."

Donahue shrugged; he'd expected that answer from McGregor's wife. "We'll have to keep you out of sight."

"I understand," Marge said simply. "The media . . . it's hard to tell sometimes, whose side they're on."

Donahue smiled; this lady was bright. He nodded his agreement; she could stay.

Marge smiled her thanks. "Mac is such a sensitive and gentle man. I'm afraid he'll get hurt."

"Gentle!" Major Baldwin laughed. "Your husband was one of the most lethal . . ."

Colonel Donahue cut Baldwin off in midsentence. "What the major meant to say, Mrs. McGregor, is that your husband is a legend in the Marine Corps."

"My Mac, a legend?" Marge's face registered genuine surprise, close to shock. "What does that mean?"

"He's never told you? What he did?" It was Donahue's turn to look surprised.

Marge shook her head negatively, then her face brightened. "He did say once that he'd been in the marines." She paused, then quietly asked, "How much don't I know?"

"Well," the colonel ran his hand over his graying crewcut, "I don't know where to begin. I met Mac in Korea. We almost died together one night near Pusan, at a dark, sad place." The colonel shook away the memory. "Let's just say he taught me almost everything I know, but," he added in admiration, "obviously not everything he knew."

Major Fleming, arms as thick as a longshoreman's, leaned forward on the portable table. "In the Marines, your man was an event. He's a whole chapter in the curriculum at the war college." Marge noticed that the major's thick, bushy eyebrows had wiry, white hairs that stood out like weeds in a garden. "We probably shade his accomplishments with our imagination. But on Tarawa, he killed twenty-seven Japs after he'd been wounded . . . and his record on Okinawa speaks for itself."

Marge sat stunned, overwhelmed by the knowledge that Mac was remembered, almost revered, for having killed men. It was a side of her husband she'd never seen, known, or suspected. She tapped out a cigarette with trembling hands and Major Murray lit it for her.

"In Korea, killing was a job," Major Baldwin said. "You'd look at somebody like a piece of hamburger . . ."

Donahue cut off Baldwin with a withering glance. "Major, I don't think Mrs. McGregor is interested in combat stories or," he glared at Fleming, "kill records either." Turning back to Marge, he smiled. "Your husband was . . ." The colonel corrected himself, face slightly flustered. "Your husband is . . ." Donahue emphasized the present tense, "a fierce competitor."

Marge thought of their golf games, and her eyes twinkled and smiled.

"In action, Mac was here, there, and everywhere. Always the point man, facing nothing but trouble. He's traveled far and seen too much." The colonel paused again, doing his best not to be specific. "Every time, Mac came through. He's knowledgeable, creative, resourceful, resilient—somehow just tougher than the rest of us."

Again, Marge noticed a tone of admiration in the colonel's voice. She was having trouble understanding what was happening, what they were saying about her husband. "I'm confused. It just doesn't seem real."

"In this type of business, what is real often seems unreal. But Mac's got the experience and the intelligence, and he won't panic. He expects the unexpected, having been there before. He'll improvise, tough it out, and come out okay." The colonel sounded confident. "You must know he's stubborn and a loner."

Marge looked at Donahue questioningly. She knew Mac was set in his ways, but he was gregarious. On the other hand, he generally liked things his way. She leaned forward and tapped the ashes from her cigarette into a large coffee can half filled with sand.

"In the Marines," the colonel continued, "you're taught the importance of each man as an individual. But mostly, you're taught teamwork. People working together to accomplish goals. Then every once in a lifetime a unique man comes along who doesn't fit the mold. He breaks it. One who is excellent at teamwork, but as an individual overperforms and accomplishes unusual feats. Do you know what I mean?"

Marge wasn't quite sure. She gave a little facial shrug.

"Let me explain it differently." The colonel rubbed his head again. "You have seven men, each of whom can jump one foot off the ground. That won't win a high jump. You need one man who can jump seven feet. He'll win it for you." He smiled broadly. "Mac is the equivalent of an eight-foot jumper. I know, it's never been done before. That's the point. Quality creates its own image. Maybe God gave Mac this extra cross to bear because He knew he'd be strong enough to carry it."

It was later, walking away from the command tent, that Marge realized that she'd learned much more about Mac's Marine background and the man himself than she'd ever suspected. Although Colonel Donahue hadn't really said anything specific, somehow she felt much better. There was a shadow of a smile in the back of her eyes. They had told her that Mac knew how to handle himself in tough situations. This was all so new. Before this trip, tension had been driving with the brakes on. Suddenly she shuddered. She knew damn well Mac wasn't bomb proof.

The Marine officers watched Marge walk down the hill.

"Some lady," Major Murray commented.

The colonel nodded. He'd thought so, too. Now he knew why Mac had picked her—attractive, intelligent, soft on the outside, but with a hidden core of steel.

"You made McGregor sound like superman," Major Baldwin said.

"Reputations have a way of hanging on. Mac earned his." The colonel's face was grim now. "The guy really is a legend, and the legend lives."

"Maybe. Miracles do happen," Baldwin said, nodding his head toward the resort. "In there right now has to be a real exercise in survival. Mac's no longer in his thirties and he's on a solo. That man's been running through raindrops for a long time without getting wet."

"He'll come through." The colonel's teeth made an indentation in his lower lip. "Survivors are different. They see things others don't. To live through what Mac's been through, you have to be awfully good—and awfully lucky." Without thinking, the colonel raised his hand and touched the small Bible he always carried in his jacket pocket.

"Mahalo," Max Parker said as James Mason offered him a John Player Special. He looked at the hard black pack with interest before handing it back.

"I'd give anything for a *Times* crossword puzzle," the Londoner said. "My wife and I used to do them every morning at breakfast."

The heavyset man reached for a match. "I didn't know you were married."

"I'm not. It was love and war all in one marriage." The thin man chuckled. "A clever woman. I got a divorce. She got custody of my money."

Parker smiled wryly. Mason had a sense of humor, it just took a while. He'd found out himself that the first six months of marriage were the best. That's when his wife walked out. After that he'd learned that there was nothing meaner than a mean, spiteful woman.

"It took me some time to realize that it was our hostility that kept us together. Bickering was our line of communication, our rapport. I knew it couldn't continue. I don't think it was all my fault." The Englishman looked at Parker, as if seeking his agreement.

Parker noticed the look of sadness behind the other's thin smile. He lit his cigarette, then watched the flickering flame of the match for a long moment before snuffing out the match. Then he spoke.

"When our relationship cooled, it became one of mutual silence. We rarely talked." He exhaled a lungful of smoke. "After our divorce, I found out that my wife believed that marriage was give and take. What I didn't give her, she took."

Mason chuckled, stood up, took off his dressing gown, folded it neatly, placed it on the floor, then sat down, using the gown as a cushion.

"One day in our lives, remote controlled by a bunch of wild-eyed terrorists. It's a sticky wicket."

"One day of this is a long time. A week would seem like forever."

"It might be forever." The Englishman's eyes glanced at the plastic explosive package close to the other's feet.

"I can feel the sweat up my back." Parker put out his cigarette, then touched the back of his T-shirt. "If we don't do something, I'm afraid we're all gonna bomb out."

"Have any thoughts?"

"C-4 burns, doesn't it?"

"Yes, you can cook over it. Takes a jolt to explode. Usually an electrical charge to a detonator cap. These bastards are using primer cord, simpler and more reliable." The wiry man gestured at the thin rope snaking alongside them.

"Are the charges linked in series?" the bald agent asked.

"All set to go at once, micro-seconds apart." The Brit's lips formed a slight smile. "I doubt if we'll notice the difference."

"If we burned the cord through, would it block the electric charge?"

"Be better to cut it, primer cord smoulders and gives off an odor. Besides, it's interlaced in a grid. To do any good we'd have to disconnect it from the electrical source." Mason gestured to the box next to which Anahu was sitting, assault rifle in hand. "There's been a terrorist there every minute. I've been watching. They may have more than one detonator, also."

"Sometimes the impossible turns out not to be impossible," Parker muttered.

Mason laughed. "I was thinking that myself. A diversion perhaps. If there's one end of a string," he hesitated, "there has to be another."

It was more like being at the end of their rope, Parker realized. Seeing the irony, he tossed aside the thought. "We've got to do something," he finally said.

"The Marines will get us out," the Englishman said.

"You don't really believe that, do you?"

"Only fools never doubt." Mason rose, stretched and stared out the lanai door. Far out he could see small fish jumping for their lives. There were obviously terrorists out there, too. He sat back down and whispered in a low voice, "Last night at times, only one guard was on duty."

"That Marco, he's almost foaming at the mouth," the heavyset agent said. "A man of mercury, quick to anger."

The Englishman patted his rumpled blue silk pajamas, trying to smooth them. "That's not the only place he's foaming." He shook his head. "He certainly doesn't believe in putting all his eggs in one basket.

"His extracurricular activities may give us an opportunity." Parker ran his hand over his shiny bald head. "We could wait until there's only one terrorist in here and overpower him."

"What then?" The accent was clipped. "There must be a dozen terrorists in and out of here. No set schedule."

Parker swiveled his head around. "I don't know yet. Disconnect the electrical charge . . . get most of the hostages out of here away from the explosives . . . Most big ideas start small, I'll work on it."

"Let's hope so. They'd butcher the survivors. As you Americans say, 'we'd die with our shoes off.' "

Parker smiled. "That's 'boots on', old chap." He put his nose close to his T-shirt. "Boy, could I use a hot bath."

"One of the world's most civilized pleasures." The Englishman leaned back, savoring some memories of luxuriating in a huge bathtub at the Savoy. After a few minutes he sat back up. "At the right time we'll go for him." He'd put his doubts on hold. "My mother always told me, the meek will only inherit more abuse."

Parker nodded. He'd been watching the big black terrorist called Jumbo. He nudged Mason. Jumbo had just palmed a lump of plastic explosive in his rubber glove; now he put it in his pocket.

"That's odd," Mason clipped out. "Think he's going into business for himself?"

Parker didn't answer. He'd just noticed that Jumbo was wearing the same running shoes that Jorge had been wearing. Not only were they the same type, Nikes, but they had the same black smudge on the top of the right shoe.

The older terrorist called Carlos pulled off his mask and slumped into a lounge chair in the corner of the lobby, diagonally opposite Fire. "We're down to ten men." He spoke with little expression in his voice. Nine men and a damn woman, he thought to himself, rubbing his right hand over his bearded chin.

Fire nodded her head, staring closely at the terrorist's thin face, ragged whiskers, pronounced nose, and deep-set, penetrating eyes. All of the men considered her to be one of them and tried to treat her as an equal. They couldn't. At the right time she'd remind them with a vengeance. She was different—and better than any of them.

"Marco's already lost three of his team; Jorge, the Scorpion, and Angel. Mine's still intact." Carlos's voice was taunting.

"I need both Anahu and Michael here in the main building," Fire said, glancing out of the window at the sky which seemed to go on forever. Now she looked back at Carlos, who was picking his front teeth with his fingernail. "We'll have to move one of your men."

"Marco can have Moses, that skinny black. He's been running around like a crazy man looking for a pair of rubber gloves." Carlos shook his head. "It's that goddamn Jumbo."

"I feel like I'm running a turkey farm." Fire spoke lightly. "I'm surrounded by them."

Carlos grinned, wiping his finger on his trousers. He'd still have the two men he trusted the most. Ivan, the bearded Bulgarian, with ice water in his veins, and Milo, the tall, thin, swarthy-faced terrorist without a country. Both had worked with him before in the Middle East. Both were top professionals, dedicated fanatics. He'd been impressed by Anahu and Kimo, also cold-blooded killers. But both were Hawaiian and they were intensely loyal to Fire.

"We should get an answer soon from Washington." Fire spoke as much to herself as to Carlos.

"You know what it will be."

"Of course. They'll try to stall. Want to negotiate . . . offer us a plane to fly away."

Carlos nodded, the girl had a damn good mind. "The last thing they'll want to sacrifice is one of their precious nuclear bombs."

Fire laughed bitterly. "They need every one. There are only fifty thousand nuclear warheads in the world today."

"With an explosive yield of twenty billion tons of

TNT—over a million and a half times the yield of the atomic bomb dropped on Hiroshima." Carlos was pretty sure of his facts. The KGB and the DGI had both briefed him thoroughly.

"If we're not successful, Carlos, nuclear weapons will annihilate man, swallow all life, destroy civilization, end history." Fire's eyes sparkled as they sought the face of the older man. "Our cause is right. We must win."

"We've got the world's attention." Carlos grinned. "Now we have to keep them interested."

"How?" Fire bit her tongue. It was a stupid question to which she knew the answer. It showed a weakness.

Carlos's crooked grin broadened. "Start killing the hostages."

CHAPTER TWELVE

Colonel Donahue put down the radiophone and turned to face the three-man hostage negotiation team. "The President agrees, gentlemen. The answer is no. We cannot and will not give in to terrorism. He says it's a cancer eating away at civilization." He gestured toward Lieutenant Colonel McKenna. "Red, it's up to your team."

McKenna took a deep breath of the salt air mingled with the scent of eucalyptus and wild ginger, then spoke softly. "They've given us nothing to work with." He looked pleadingly at Donahue. "Can't we at least destroy some old bombs?"

Donahue shrugged, a pained expression on his face. "It's not my decision."

"If you're not going to give in to terrorists, Colonel, then you've got to deal with them." Bill Bailey spoke in his soft, buttery drawl. "We need a carrot."

"The terrorists' safety?" Donahue suggested.

"That won't work," said Corwin, "not if they're fanatics. It's a last card, anyway."

"We'll play it by ear," McKenna said simply. "There

are damn few options. Maybe the terrorists will suggest something." He motioned to Donahue, who nodded affirmatively. All four picked up phone sets. McKenna then dialed 522-3000. A male voice answered. "Unit One-HULA."

"This is Colonel McKenna, United States Marine Corps . . ."

There was silence on the other end of the phone, then a muffled shout. More silence, then a cold female voice came onto the phone. "HULA One."

"This is Colonel McKenna . . ."

"The hot-shit negotiator," the cold voice spat back. "I've heard about you."

McKenna swallowed his surprise.

"Your picture was just on the tube with two of your buddies. The specially trained hostage negotiation team that's going to charm away our guests." There was a cold laugh over the phone. "Colonel, the three of you can go fuck off."

McKenna looked at the others, and their shocked looks matched his. "We'd like . . ." he began.

"Good-bye, Colonel," Fire interrupted. "Put Donahue on the phone."

The senior Marine nodded to McKenna, waited a few moments, then said, "Colonel Donahue here."

"Last night I gave you a demand, Colonel. It was simple. We'll release one hostage for every nuclear warhead you destroy. One life for thousands. What's Uncle Kapu's answer?"

The big Marine officer took a deep breath. "We don't have it yet."

"Colonel, cut the shit." The voice was now charged with emotion. " 'NBC News' just had an interview with the Vice-President and the Secretary of Defense. They both said flatly that you imperialists will not destroy any nuclear bombs—for any reason.''

Donahue's eyes closed tight. He could feel the breeze from the trade winds coming steadily from the northeast on his eyelids.

'' 'CBS News' said they've just learned that the President has decided that, and I quote,'' the tone in Fire's voice was sarcastic, '' 'We cannot and will not give in to terrorism.' '' She paused. ''Colonel, you'd better get some new lines to Washington—or better yet, buy yourself a television set.''

Donahue could feel the knot in his stomach. What the terrorist had said left him stunned. The goddamned media knew the President's decision before he did. It was clear who was running the country. He opened his eyes, cleared his throat, then said, ''We'd like to meet with you.'' He could see McKenna, Corwin, and Bailey nodding in agreement.

''For what reason?''

''Well, assume we can persuade the government to destroy the nuclear weapons.'' Donahue paused; there was no reaction on the other end of the phone. ''How will you know?''

''Colonel, two of the seven storage bases the navy uses for nuclear warheads are in Hawaii. At Pearl Harbor and Waikele. HULA has agents at both places. Don't worry, we'll know.'' Fire laughed aloud. ''If everything else fails, Colonel, we'll turn on the T.V.''

''Do you need anything for the hostages?'' Donahue was trying desperately to keep the conversation alive.

''Colonel, their future is behind them. We have a saying in Hawaii. 'Aloha ino oe eia ihonei paha oe e make ai—May they receive mercy, because their death is close at hand. Ke ai manei Pele. The great goddess Pele comes devouring.' ''

Listening to the coldness of the voice and the message, Donahue's skin crawled. "Are you Pele?" he asked. It was a question from nowhere.

There was a sudden gasp of surprise on the other end of the phone, then, "They call me Fire."

Donahue and the men of the hostage negotiation team looked at one another. Pele and Fire. One and the same. What kind of a nut was this?

"Fire." At last Donahue could use the name of the terrorist McGregor had advised them was in charge of HULA One. "We must meet to talk."

"No we don't. You have our terms. There's nothing to negotiate. It's one for one . . . or Pele will devour the hostages . . . 216 of them. We believe in our cause, Colonel. Uncle Kapu is the baby killer—Hiroshima, Nagasaki, Vietnam. Remember?"

"Our team will be there at eleven this morning. Three unarmed men in a white car." Donahue's voice was crisp and factual.

"They'll be Pele's first victims."

"We've got to talk." Donahue's stomach twisted uneasily again.

"Colonel, no talk. We've told you what we want. That's it!" There was finality in the voice.

"We'll be there," the colonel said, with the same finality. McKenna gave him a thumbs-up sign.

The phone clicked dead.

Corwin exploded first. "The fucking media is ruining this country. They'll wind up killing the hostages. The media won't blame themselves. They'll blame us."

"It's unbelievable. They blew the negotiations before we even got started." McKenna's face was flushed with anger, knowing his team wouldn't get a second chance to make a first impression. He rattled the portable metal table with his closed fist.

"We have to get involved. If we don't, things are

going to get worse, much worse." Bailey ran his hand through his pewter-colored hair.

"We don't have a lot of time," Corwin said. "Got to buy some, somehow."

Donahue spoke sharply. "You've got 'til eleven. An hour and twenty minutes. I just set up a meeting for you. It's forced . . . you heard. But I felt it was necessary."

"It is. We're grateful." McKenna reached out his hand for Donahue's.

"She thinks she's Pele, the goddess of Fire. That could be helpful," Corwin said. "Colonel, where the hell did you get that inspiration? She was startled and tried to cover, but gave away her name."

"It came to me in a vision, like a man clutching at a burning straw." Donahue's mouth didn't smile. "It's the old maxim, 'never quit until you go another foot.' "

McKenna's face was grim. There was not much room to maneuver and none for error. "We'll just do our best. We'll improvise. Tell the truth, so our lies will count."

"Only those who dare truly live," Bailey said softly, almost to himself.

Donahue stood up. "It's a tough situation. For the hostages, survival is today. You'll have to play it off the wall. Just remember, gentlemen, in hostage negotiation there is no acceptable casualty rate." The others nodded and stood up. Donahue stopped them with his outstretched hands. "And now, if you believe in the power of prayer . . ." The four men bowed their heads. The strengthening breeze made ominous rippling, rushing sounds under the flaps of the tent.

The phone call came into the colonel's command post just fifteen minutes later. Donahue reached for the phone and recognized Fire's voice.

"Colonel, we've reconsidered. We'll meet with your team at eleven, but only under certain conditions."

"What are those?" Donahue felt elated, at least the terrorists were willing to meet.

"Our cause is just, Colonel. We want a chance to explain it to the world."

Donahue sat back and listened. McKenna had said that sooner or later the terrorists would want to publicize their cause. At least it was a start.

"We want television coverage, but limited to one hand-held camera and one microphone."

"A remote T.V. hookup will probably require some time. They'll need a remote truck," the colonel suggested.

"No trucks, Colonel. It doesn't have to be live coverage. One T.V. man, one camera, one microphone. That's all, a copy of the film to be given to all three networks. Newspapers can pick up from there."

"Any other conditions?"

"Only that this is our show. We get to talk. Your men can listen. There will be no negotiations."

"We'll be there," the colonel said.

"And no tricks, Colonel. Or everyone dies." Once again the phone clicked dead in Donahue's ear.

The lanky blonde in the full-length white satin gown leaned back from the backgammon board. Her sigh of disappointment was audible.

"That's twenty-four hundred dollars you owe me," the chunky man with the white wavy hair said with a slightly cockeyed grin. "I think you like to lose."

"Bullshit!" his wife hissed back. "El toro poo poo to you. You're the luckiest bastard alive. Set 'em up again, double or nothing!"

The man stared at his wife. Even under these conditions she looked as smart as a showroom model. Her gown hugged her curves and showed her off. The blonde had everything boyhood fantasies are made of—good looks and a good body. When he'd met her she'd been one of the beautiful sweater people going nonstop from midnight to dawn, in love with fun. Over the past ten years her face had matured and hardened, but even he had to admit she was still attractive. She was tough, maybe too tough, but then, it was well past the cocktail hour of her life. Her hair had volume, but was not wild or rebellious. It fit with the rest of her, an image of controlled luxury. The gold pendant around her neck looked real. It was. So were the dazzling diamonds, the sparkling sapphires, the radiant rubies, and the elegant emeralds back in their room. It was tough to satisfy her eighteen-carat mind. The most erotic thing in their marriage had been money.

Joey stared back at her husband. Without any liquor for the last forty hours, Larry had almost sobered. He was becoming alert, pleasant, interesting, intelligent—and frightening. The way she remembered him from a long while ago. He was still handsome, but now in his face she could see the lengthening shadow of the bottle and the ravages of a hard-lived life. Theirs had been a bittersweet marriage of spiced romance, scarlet memories, and creeping resentment. They'd verbally clawed at one another for so long they could no longer talk, except in vitriol.

"What's happened to us, Joey!" the white-haired man suddenly asked in a low, serious voice.

The question startled the blonde. She rolled the dice—six and five—and executed a lover's leap with one of her back men on the board. Her mind churned, fighting with the urge to spit hostility and arrogance at her husband. Why would he ask such a stupid question? The answer was obvious. His business required an incurable wandering eye. It wasn't another woman. It was beautiful young girls, hundreds of them. He dealt with young talent, twenty-four hours a day on a bicoastal basis. In his business, women over twenty were considered old horses.

At whatever hour her husband came home, there was always the unmistakable mixed odor all over him—liquor and teenagers. In his life, there were only two types of women, goddesses and doormats. The goddess would do anything for the right opportunity, the right part. Most of the doormats had *welcome* printed on them. Larry wasn't a middle-aged crazy chasing teenyboppers. They chased him. She swallowed her emotion and spoke quietly. "I thought you knew."

The white head shook negatively and the chunky shoulders shrugged. He rolled his dice, three and two, and exposed two of his men. "Passing fifty scares me," he said, his mind onto another thought.. "I remember when I was thirty. That was the oldest I ever felt. I vowed then I'd never grow old. That life would be fun and games. I've been playing hard ever since."

The blonde laughed lightly. That was as close to a confession as he'd ever come. "Look around, Larry. You may get your wish. None of us may get much older."

"I know it's an odd thought at an odd time." He swiveled his head, then grinned. "I'm on the down side of fifty. Maybe I'm losing my mind."

"It's always the second thing to go," Joey said with a touch of sarcasm in her voice. His virility had been drowned in alcohol.

"The world's gone mad. Goddamned murderers."
The chunky white-haired man looked at his wife again,
then in a low voice suggested. "Button the top two buttons. That young terrorist has been staring at your . . ."
He hesitated, then added, "cleavage."

"It's not easy being a sex symbol," Joey's smoky
voice whispered as she set down her dice cup and slowly
buttoned the top of her gown. She rolled again—another eleven—and moved the last man out of her home
board.

"Lucky broad," her husband said in a normal voice.
Then glancing around the room, he leaned forward and
whispered, "I'm tired of being bullied. Two days of this
shit are enough. I'm ready to make a move."

Joey's mouth opened slowly, but nothing emerged.
She was too stunned to speak. Deep down she'd always
suspected that under pressure Larry would prove to be
a born-again chicken. A real wimp. That face-to-face
with fear, he'd babble and fall apart. Instead, the man
was suddenly all macho.

"I'm not trying to impress you," he said flatly. "It's
no big deal. But even terrorists are people first and I
know how to reach people." He grinned. "It's my
business."

"Money?" she guessed, knowing he couldn't offer
the usual stable of young fillies.

"Money talks."

"Yeah, mine says 'good-bye.' " Joey smiled wryly.

He ignored her comment. "It never fails. The best
solution is often the most obvious."

"Sweetheart, don't do anything stupid. This is not
the Polo Lounge at the Beverly Hilton."

"Heroes are always hot, Joey. There comes a time
when people have to stand up for what they believe." In

the back of his head the bell had rung, and he could feel his blood rushing. For the first time in a long while Larry felt alive, in the center of something big.

She sat back, thinking. It might work. Larry was an achiever, a tough man to ignore, a winner—and he'd made a fortune wheeling and dealing. Business associates shook hands with him, then counted their fingers. He used his money lavishly as a substitute for manners and pedigree and generally got what he wanted. The look on his face said it all, as if he knew something that the rest of them didn't.

"How?" she asked softly.

He held his dice cup in both hands before him. "A wise man makes his own opportunities. See that big black over there?" He gestured toward Jumbo. "It's simple. He hates us. That's all there is to it. We're white and he's black. We're rich and he's poor." Larry grinned again. "It's because rich people are always in the right place at the right time. But that's not the way he looks at it. He's my man. I'm going to work on him, make him rich if he gets us out of here. I'm going to put him on the sugar cane train."

Joey stared at the big man in the terrorist mask, wearing rubber gloves, and asked softly, "How do you even know he's black?"

He smiled. "With a name like Jumbo?" Larry's face turned serious. "I've got a feeling in here." He tapped his chest. "Most of the hostages are going to die, you can count on that. I'm not ready for that yet. I've never done it before and the thought scares me." In Larry's mind reality was blending into melodrama and everything was fast becoming a scenario. He'd seen the plot before and knew the ending. "The Marines will make a move and the terrorists are going to deteriorate like unstable material in a test tube. When that happens, baby, boom! I want us out of here. Far enough away so we can ask, 'What was that?' ''

"You can't risk the lives of the other hostages," Joey whispered.

"Fuck the other hostages!" Larry's voice was almost a snarl. "We'll go it alone."

Joey nodded. That sounded like the old Larry. "Don't talk about it, do it," she hissed.

He looked at her and grinned again. Joey had balls. "I owe you," he said.

Joey smiled, a ray of sunlight played on her face. Maybe the trip to Hawaii hadn't been such a bad idea after all. Maybe it did offer a new start. "You don't owe me anything, except respect. Roll the damn dice. I'm going to cream you."

Mac could feel the tension growing among the terrorists. Ears open wide, he'd overheard enough to know that the Marines were sending a three-man negotiation team to the resort. Fire, Carlos, and Marco had been in the lobby area alternately watching news flashes about the takeover on television, talking, and laughing. Mac sensed that they had no interest in negotiating anything.

Anahu, the big Hawaiian, and Michael, the young blond terrorist, were on guard duty in the Koa Lounge. The hostages were quiet. The mood in the room had turned from doom and gloom to peaceful submission. The staff of the Molokai-Surf was coping remarkably well with the extremely difficult situation, and the hostages were being well fed and cared for. Mac had looked for Kona, but hadn't seen her. Apparently she was working hard behind the scenes, solving problems, acting as a buffer between the terrorists and their prisoners. From what he'd overheard from the hostages, the tall girl with the long black hair carried the sun on her shoulder. She'd now set up a system of rotating showers and clean clothes for the hostages and had reintroduced bridge, backgammon, and other games. Apparently, there was nothing bad in Kona, no malice, greed, or hate. Mac shook his head. What a difference from her sister, Fire.

In one corner of the room, Kona's staff was showing a selection of her films on endangered species. A group of maybe thirty or forty of the hostages had gathered in front of a large screen and, sitting on the floor, were watching with interest. The lights were dim, curtains drawn, the projector beamed, and the screen was filled with leaping dolphins, frolicking in the open sea. Their playful antics attracted the attention of the lookouts on the commercial tuna seiner cruising nearby.

"Dolphins," shouted the lookout in the forward tower.

Mac moved closer to the screen as the sonar operator focused his attention on the scope, adjusting it for range, understanding that for some unknown reason schools of sociable yellowfin tuna often traveled with dolphins. Now he made an adjustment for depth, knowing that the mammals swim near the surface so that they can breathe, while the tuna swim deeper, beneath the dolphins.

"The dolphins are carrying a large school of tuna," he said half aloud, pushing the alert button. Horns sounded. Within minutes, six waiting speedboats had been launched from davits while the seiner lowered a huge net, almost a mile long and three hundred feet deep, into the water. Following the dolphins on the surface, the fast boats raced ahead of the large fishing vessel, cutting off and rounding up the tuna, the net gradually encircling them. The dolphins were turned back, swimming in circles, the tuna being herded into a tight bunch beneath them. Slowly, with winches pulling in cables, the seiner pursed the bottom of the net until it closed.

On the surface, the dolphins watched with observant eyes. With their remarkable sensory capabilities, the dolphins knew they were trapped. Their chattering increased in frequency and volume. With a burst of speed and an arching leap, they could have easily cleared the top of the encircling seine. But not one tried to jump to freedom. Instead, the dolphins tried to swim through the net, entangling their snouts in the wire mesh. Their struggles to free themselves filled the screen. Not being able to swim backward, they were doomed. Slowly they suffocated, drowned and were still.

Now giant winches on the three-hundred-foot-long tuna fishing boat hauled the net up onto the sluiceway. The drawstring on the purse net opened and tons of fish tumbled out into a huge retaining vat. Four dolphins were still alive and were quickly seized and released overboard by the waiting fishermen. Seven dolphin were already dead, their bodies thrown overboard. The final sequence of the film showed the fins of huge sharks streaking toward the floating corpses.

Mac could hear the announcer saying, "During the last ten years, millions of dolphins, or porpoises as they're often called, have been killed by tuna fishermen. They've become an endangered species. The United States has required tuna fleets to use new nets designed to be less likely to trap dolphins, but these laws still don't apply to foreign fishing fleets that catch most of the world's tuna. In addition to the dolphin, the yellowfin and bluefin tuna are also fast becoming extinct . . ."

Mac turned away, his mind in turmoil. How could a group of young people concerned about the future welfare of whales, dolphins, and tuna be involved in the mass killing of innocent people? It didn't make sense. What was it he'd overheard Fire telling Kona? "You're just a dreamer, playing with whales, while I'm doing something important." He didn't remember the rest, but guessed that only Kona was really involved in saving whales and dolphins. Fire and her terrorist group had obviously used it as a cover for their operation. There was no question, Fire had used her sister, Kona.

It was a balmy morning with a strong breeze, but cold sweat seeped out of Mac's pores. A table had been set out on the patio in front of the main entrance of the resort. Chairs were now being placed around the table. A portable microphone was being attached to the resort's loudspeaker system. That was obviously where the meeting with the Marines would take place. From out of the slits in Jumbo's mask, Mac's eyes watched. The three leaders of the terrorists were just leaving the lobby. Fire had removed her mask, but both Carlos and Marco were wearing theirs.

Jumbo took a last sip of coffee and put his cup on the table. Glancing quickly around the room, he could see the lady in the muu-muu watching him. There was no question, sooner or later that determined old biddy was going to recognize him, leap to her feet, and shout, "Mac McGregor, what are you doing?" The Englishman in the rumpled blue silk pajamas and the big man in the boxer shorts had been watching him, too, but they had the eyes of pros. Mac could sense an occasional glance. That was all.

The big form of Jumbo moved toward the lobby, nodding to Anahu as he passed by. From the lobby he could see Fire talking with Marco and Carlos out on the front patio. The danger was acute. They were too close for comfort, but Mac knew he might not get a better chance. Taking a deep breath, he moved directly to the corner closet which was out of sight of the Koa Lounge, opened the door, stepped in, and closed the door behind him.

Clicking on a pencil-thin flashlight, he could see the portable Sam-7 missile launcher leaning against the wall. Next to it was a rack of missiles. Mac knelt and quickly removed a small piece of primer cord and a lump of plastic from his pocket. Pushing them together, he stuck the wad on the electrical contact on the rear of the missile. Even in the dim light it seemed too obvious. He peeled off the plastic and swore softly. He couldn't reach the electrical contact inside the missile launcher itself. It might not work, but then . . . just maybe. He rolled the wad of plastic into a thin string, put the small piece of primer cord in the center, and draped the center of the string down the barrel of the missile launcher, sticking both ends of the plastic string to the inside of the mouth of the launcher. It was out of sight, like a gooey cobweb.

Finished, expecting the worst, Mac held his breath as he opened the closet door. There was no one in the lobby. He breathed again, stepped out of the closet, and moved rapidly across the lobby area and back into the lounge. The tall black terrorist was talking to Anahu and spotted Jumbo as he entered the room.

"Hey, man, I got them," he shouted, holding up his hands covered in a pair of rubber gloves.

Jumbo gave him a high-five with his right rubber glove.

"What the hell are you two rubber glove freaks doing?" Anahu growled from his guard post.

Jumbo didn't reply but just kept walking through the lounge. At the door he turned and with the center finger of his right rubber glove gave Anahu an unmistakable sign. Then Jumbo was gone.

CHAPTER THIRTEEN

The Molokai-Surf was now in sight. The three officers of the hostage negotiation team in their dress whites, stacks of ribbons over their hearts, were seated in the back of the white Cadillac convertible. Corporal Reaves, their driver, had borrowed the white Cadillac from the Mayor of Kaunakakai. All four were unarmed. Trailing the Cadillac by about forty yards was a standard Marine jeep, containing a Marine driver and one television cameraman in a navy-blue windbreaker from the network affiliate KHOL, Honolulu, a hand-held camera, a microphone, and a recorder.

"We're fighting terrorism like blind men in a chimney," McKenna said, breaking the eerie silence.

"More like three blind mice," Corwin added.

"Mute ones, too," Bailey said. "As I understand the format for this meeting, we're not going to get to say anything, anyhow."

The two vehicles pulled to a halt behind the wreckage of the police cars. The charred bodies of the policemen were still on the pavement. McKenna instructed his driver to call in for a detail to remove the remains. "I'll clear it with the terrorists first and give you a signal," he said.

As the Marine officers and the television cameraman approached the resort, McKenna noticed that a very attractive redhead was seated at a table set out on the patio outside the front entrance. That had to be Fire. She was flanked by two terrorists wearing masks, one at each end of the table. Both were armed with AK-47s, which were pointed at the Marines. McKenna's mind ran through the terrorist descriptions given to him by Donahue, and assumed the two to be Marco and Carlos. He also noticed masked faces and gun muzzles in the upstairs corner windows overlooking both sides of the front terrace. The jeep driver set the microphone and the recorder on the table and retreated to his vehicle to wait. Fire gestured at the Marines to take the three seats across the table from her. "No names. No introductions. We're nameless," she snapped icily. "We know who you are. We've seen you on television."

Before McKenna sat down he looked at Fire and asked, "While we're here we'd like your agreement to remove the bodies." He pointed toward the policemen.

Fire glanced quickly at Marco and Carlos. Both nodded imperceptibly and Fire gave her agreement. McKenna waved to his driver and a few minutes later a cleanup detail of four corpsmen drove slowly down the hill toward the charred wreckage.

"Are you ready?" Fire asked the cameraman. Bob Banyan's head covered with dark wavy hair nodded. He turned on the camera, which panned over the table and then focused on Fire's face. Green eyes staring straight into the television lens, Fire began talking in a loud, clear voice. She looked intensely Hawaiian.

"Unit One of the Hawaiian Underground Liberation Army has taken over the Molokai-Surf and has cap-

tured 216 hostages. We have offered to trade one
hostage for each nuclear warhead the United States
destroys. One for one. HULA One has taken this dramatic action to call attention to the fact that the human
race is heading rapidly toward extinction. It is four
minutes before midnight on the doomsday clock. If the
world keeps arming with nuclear warheads, civilization
will not survive another ten years."

Fire paused, looked once at a pad of paper on the
table in front of her, then back into the camera, her
green eyes flashing.

"Do you know how big these bombs are? Do you
know what damage they'll do?" She paused again.
"The biggest bomb in the Second World War carried a
maximum load of eight tons of TNT. The atomic bomb
dropped on Hiroshima was equivalent to 13,000 tons of
TNT, all exploding at once. The hydrogen bomb can be
as big as twenty million tons—sixteen hundred times
more powerful than the original atomic bomb.

"One hydrogen bomb contains more explosive power
than all the bombs ever exploded in the entire history of
the human race. Yet that hydrogen bomb is small
enough to fit under this table." Fire rapped the table
with her hand.

"Just one twenty-megaton bomb exploded on Oahu
would dig a hole three-quarters of a mile wide and eight
hundred feet deep. Every person in that area, every
building, all the dirt and rock would be vaporized into
radioactive fallout which would be ejected into the
stratosphere as part of a mushroom cloud. Every person
within a twenty-mile radius would be either killed or
horribly wounded. Out to thirty miles in every direction
the heat of the blast would be so intense it would ignite
anything flammable. There would be tornadic winds of
up to five hundred miles per hour hurling people, cars,

and buildings like projectiles, smashing everything."

Fire paused. The three officers of the hostage negotiation team glanced at one another. Their eyes told
the story. Fire was making a very effective speech.
McKenna swallowed hard. They'd made a deal, they
had to let her continue with no rebuttal. There was no
choice.

"This one bomb would cause a huge radiation fire
storm covering three thousand square miles, sucking the
oxygen out of the air, replacing it with noxious gases.
Just one bomb would wipe out all life on Oahu. But,"
Fire pounded on the table, stood up, and gestured at the
camera, "the United States doesn't have just one nuclear warhead, it has 35,000 hydrogen bombs. Over
9,000 of them are big strategic warheads. Those 9,000
are enough to kill every Russian forty times. Yet Uncle
Kapu keeps building more."

McKenna noticed that Fire hadn't mentioned
Russia's 20,000 hydrogen bombs, or the fact that some
of their 7,000 strategic warheads were hundred-mega-
ton monsters that could obliterate America twenty times
over.

"We must scrap the nuclear arsenals," Fire continued. "In an all-out nuclear war, within thirty days
ninety percent of all American, English, European, and
Russian people would be dead or dying. The survivors
would be blind, starving, or diseased; any survivors
would envy the dead. But most importantly, a nuclear
war of any dimension would destroy the world's protective ozone layer. Most scientists believe that without
that protective layer all the people still living would in-
cur a lethal sunburn within an hour. In a nuclear war
there will be no survivors."

Fire paused again, then looked back into the camera.
The sun sparkled on her red hair. McKenna could feel

the fervor in her voice, the excitement and the energy. She was going to come across on television like a religious experience. He bit his lip hard enough to taste blood.

"HULA believes this situation requires action. We're not willing to sit around waiting for the end of life on earth. The end of four billion years of evolution. The unthinkable horror, charred bodies, pestilence, and mutated life forms of a senseless nuclear holocaust. It's lethal madness, suicide for the whole human race." Fire gestured, her arms swinging in an arc.

"The nuclear warheads must be scrapped. The game of Global Chicken must stop. Someplace there has to be a start. This is it. We'll give back one hostage for each nuclear warhead that the United States destroys. One life to save hundreds of thousands. Our action will signal the start of similar protests around the world until all nuclear weapons are gone from this earth." Fire stood up and pointed at McKenna. "And we're very serious, Colonel McKenna. We believe in our noble cause. HULA One is a suicide squad—all volunteers ready to die for the good of humanity. And if we die, all the hostages will die with us. Martyrs for humanity. It's your choice." Fire sat down abruptly.

McKenna stood up and reached for the microphone. Fire's hand grabbed it first, saying, "No negotiations, McKenna. Remember? Colonel Donahue agreed we could state our case. We've done that. There's no need to negotiate. It's one for one . . . or nothing."

Bob Banyan, panning his camera around the entrance area, suddenly muttered, "Oh shit." He was out of film. The hostage negotiation meeting was clearly over. McKenna, Corwin, and Bailey walked up the hill to the white Cadillac and got in the back seat. Their dejection was obvious. The television cameraman leapt into the jeep in an ebullient mood, knowing he'd captured excellent and exciting footage. Slowly the two cars drove away from the Molokai-Surf. In the rearview mirror, McKenna could see Carlos and Marco congratulating Fire on her performance.

The resort's loudspeaker had carried Fire's message to the hostages and the other terrorists. At Jumbo's post, Mac listened carefully to Fire's words. "Lethal madness. Suicide for the whole human race." He had to agree, it made him think about the unthinkable and he swallowed hard at his own thought. If you've seen one nuclear war, you've seen them all. One would exterminate the earth.

As far as Mac knew, everything she'd said about nuclear weapons was accurate, but it had nothing to do with the terrorists' actions. She'd used an old terrorist tactic. Include a nub of truth in the argument. Confuse and bewilder. Half of history is fiction anyhow, but which half?

There was nothing that justified holding innocent hostages and threatening to kill them. And Mac knew it was far more than a threat. Fire's group had already killed at least ten people. Now she had told the world that HULA One was a suicide squad. It would be tough to walk away from that boast. The terrorists were wild enough to do anything.

The symbols on their T-shirts were beginning to make sense. The small blue hula dancer had to represent their unit, HULA, the Hawaiian Underground Liberation Army. The blue whale probably stood for a larger organization of some type, possibly worldwide in scope.

Mac stood up and paced back and forth in the small room, occasionally stopping to stare out of the window. There was nothing moving. The Koa Lounge was a powder keg and the air was full of static electricity. All that was missing was one spark. Mac was expecting the worst.

Both the hostages and terrorists were becoming stressed out. There was always the danger that they'd become frightened and paranoid, especially under pressure. Paranoid people generally did irrational things. The terrorists had drawn a tough, thin line, one hostage for one nuclear warhead. Give in to that demand and crazies would take over half the world's hotels. Nuclear blackmail on a global scale. It was an impossible demand and they knew it. The danger was growing more acute with each passing hour. Something was going to snap.

Mac sat down and swiveled the chair around facing the window. Negotiations obviously hadn't worked. They'd probably put the cart before the carrot. Any further negotiations would be like throwing a car into reverse at sixty miles an hour. It just wouldn't mesh. He'd seen the hate glittering in Fire's eyes and the animal nature of Marco. Carlos was a professional, power-hungry terrorist. At any time, any one of the three might decide to do something spectacular to create excitement—and be recognized. All three were unpredictable—in another world. If he didn't know better, he'd swear they were on hallucinogenics. There was one thing that didn't make sense. Neither Fire, Marco, nor Carlos was suicidal. Deep down, Mac knew none of the three planned to die. They had to have an alternative plan. It was a gut feel—even if they killed the hostages, those three planned to escape.

Any mistake, even a small miscalculation, could be fatal to all the hostages, and that couldn't happen. Mac let out a deep sigh. It was time to speed up his plan. He chuckled to himself. What plan? He'd been reacting.

Now his ass would just have to be exposed a little further. If he died, only Marge would care. Maybe the office might send flowers. He wondered . . . what the hell was company policy on flowers for ex-employees who passed away? Maybe they'd lower the flag to half-mast during lunch hour.

In the Koa Lounge, the hostages had been stunned by Fire's speech. Several of the elderly wept when they heard her say, "And if we die, all the hostages will die with us. Martyrs for humanity. It's your choice." The collective groan was audible. A large group led by the heavyset lady in the muu-muu joined hands and prayed.

One man, an obvious New Yorker, spoke for the majority. "They should destroy the bombs. It's our democratic principles and freedom that wins minds, not weapons." Then he sat back and softly whispered to his wife, "After we're free they can always build some more. The number of warheads is not important, both sides have enough. What's important is the delivery system. You've got to get there first with the most."

"Don't forget the importance of antinuclear defense," his wife added. "We should be able to knock all the Russian missiles down with laser beams. Then we could tell them to stick it . . ."

"That's right, Sonia," the New Yorker said. His wife was a good listener, she'd learned a lot from him.

"Dammit," Connie said to the other two Avon ladies. "I feel like one of the dolphins we saw in that net, absolutely helpless."

We're in the middle of a giant crap game, and the dice are loaded." Bee Jay smiled weakly. "At least this time you two kept your powder dry. My back's killing me." She pushed the lower part of her back with her two hands. "We've been sitting on the floor too long."

"At least we can't fall off the floor," Connie said.

"And I'd have collapsed in a heap if I'd been standing when that fiery bitch said they'd exchange me for a nuclear warhead. I admit I'm a blonde bombshell, but . . ." She grinned weakly.

"I'm still shaking," Bee Jay said, holding out her trembling hands. "There's no chance that they'll destroy bombs. Our government's policy is peace through strength. The more bombs we have the safer we are. I happen to agree with that and wish to hell we had more. Dead is dead. What's the difference if you're killed with a nuclear bomb or a conventional one?"

"That policy may be a myth," the tall blonde, Evelyn, said. "And I've learned from my love life, it's dangerous to believe in myths. Nuclear bombs aren't like ordinary bombs. Enough may really be enough. I understand that hydrogen bombs have the energy of the stars. Those who merely look at an exploding bomb will have their eyes melted."

Bee Jay, the tall, attractive brunette, stood up, still rubbing her lower back.

"At least we've got a reason for dying. There has to be a justification. Otherwise I won't go. Martyrs for nuclear strength. It's got a certain ring to it."

"That's no ring, that's a knell—a death knell. When I die, I want it to be different," Evelyn said. "No weeping, no sermon, no tedious service, no harping on the sadness . . ."

"Just . . . boom!" Connie laughed.

"No, dammit," Evelyn said. "I'm going to have a concert of pop music—a full jazz group—and I'll be there to hear it."

"This is too heavy for me." Connie laughed brightly. "Maybe, just maybe, the government has a few extra bombs they can spare. It sure would be fun to fly the friendly skies . . ." she paused, "all the way home."

Evelyn stood up and suggested, "Let's talk about organic gardening, aluminum siding, glossy versus flat enamel. Anything to get our minds off of nuclear weapons."

The heavyset agent in the boxer trunks shook his head sadly. "Damn terrorists. That redheaded bitch will be on prime-time television around the world, diverting attention from their cowardly actions. They've already killed . . ."

James Mason interrupted. "I'm afraid she's hit a touchdown."

Parker grimaced; he knew what the Englishman meant. Fire had focused attention on the terrorists' demand. Why wouldn't the United States give up a few bombs to save the lives of innocent hostages? Everyone agreed nuclear weapons were evil. No sane government ever wanted to use them. The effects of a nuclear war would be catastrophic to the entire human race. Her televised speech would have people arguing about the use of nuclear weapons and the need for them, instead of condemning a criminal act of terrorism. Unfortunately, the argument gave a sense of respectability to HULA's actions.

"The problem is fundamental. It goes back to World War Two," Parker said, as much to himself as to Mason. "We allowed the Russians to take over East Germany, Poland, Czechoslovakia, Hungary, Bulgaria, Latvia, Estonia, Lithuania, Romania. In contrast, we gave up all the territories we'd taken over, then helped the Germans and Japanese rebuild. Through the United Nations we forced the British and French to give freedom to all their colonies. In all this time, the Russians haven't given up one inch of captured territory. All the citizens of those countries are really Russian slaves living in a communist world they hate. I blame Roosevelt,

Truman, and Eisenhower, all three, for not pushing the Russians back in 1945.''

"And Kennedy for not knocking down the Berlin wall!" Mason was smiling now.

"Right," Parker said. "Then we let the Russians get an advantage in conventional weapons by placing too much reliance on NATO allies, so that now the only defense for the free world is our arsenal of strategic nuclear warheads.''

Mason's smile had broadened into a grin. "And you'll, by God, save the world from communism—by destroying it completely if need be.''

"You know what I mean," Parker growled. "We've got to be stronger than the Russians or they'll hold the free world hostage. We have to negotiate from a position of strength. I wouldn't give up one damn nuclear warhead. I'd rather die first.''

Mason laughed aloud. "That girl has hit a touchdown and an extra point. That Hawaiian terrorist has got you defending nuclear weapons.''

Parker saw the humor in Mason's remarks and laughed wryly. Both stopped laughing a moment later when they saw Anahu rise from his sentry post, with assault rifle in hand, and start walking in their direction.

Mason leaned forward and spoke in a confidential tone. "The United States should agree to the terrorists' demand . . .''

Parker's face showed his shock.

Mason held up one finger. "With one condition . . .''

Parker swiveled his head around. Anahu had returned to his seat. "What's that?" he asked.

"That the Russians destroy a nuclear warhead also. One for one for one. Fair's fair. No one gets an advantage. It's forced nuclear disarmament. On a one-for-one basis. If the terrorists are really serious, they'd get what

they want and the world would live happily ever after."
Mason's accent was now pure clipped British.

Parker ran his hand over his bald head. "Mason,
you're a goddamned genius. That's brilliant."

"Not really." Mason smiled. "The terrorists would
have no interest. This is a KGB operation all the way."

Second Day—Afternoon

The fat man looked at Candy's face. "Scared?" he
asked.

"I guess we all have to be," Candy said, tenseness in
her voice. "Fire's into revenge. But," she sighed deeply,
returning Dan's look, "somehow, I feel at peace."

"You're *akamai*."

She smiled at the compliment. It meant smart, really
together. "*Mahalo nui*," she answered.

"No one tells a flower to bloom. You've just got it."
Dan's voice was soft and gentle. He held her hand as if
afraid he might crush it.

Candy hardly stirred, just nestled closer to the big
man contentedly and looked up at his face. "You
haven't told me very much about yourself."

The fat man laughed softly. She could feel his
stomach jiggle. "Well, I moved to New York when I
was nineteen. I got off the bus with two cardboard
boxes of clothes under my arms. I looked up at Radio
City Music Hall, put down my packages, and said, 'I'm
going to make it big, New York! Real big.' When I
looked down, my clothes were gone." He shook his
head at the memory. "Started out with nothin' but the
lint in my pocket."

The girl laughed, all tension gone, and squeezed his

hand. She liked him very much. He brought out the little girl in her and made her feel warm and needed. "Go on," she urged.

"At the time I considered myself a singer. I was loud, but out of tune, so I got a job as an elevator operator. Eighteen months later a push button replaced me." The fat stomach jiggled again. "For a while I drifted from failure to failure, struggling for crumbs, but always hopefully, even when there was little hope." He looked down at her face. Damn, but she was pretty. "Then I moved west and found myself. San Diego. Beautiful country. I love it and I've done pretty well."

"What do you do?" she asked.

"A lot of things, real estate mostly. I've got a few thousand acres—oranges and lemons, some cattle and horses."

Candy sat up abruptly, mouth open wide. "A few thousand what?"

The fat man laughed. "I thought you might be surprised. I'm lookin' forward to showin' my ranch to you."

The girl didn't answer, just glanced away to give herself time. Finally she turned and faced him. "You know my background, what I've been. No finer girl, only more expensive ones. Maybe you should pretend I never happened. Just erase me from your mind." Her finger touched the corner of her eye.

"Lady, I'm a damn good judge of livestock. I like what I see. You care. To me, that's important. I like people who care. I've been looking for you for a long time. In the meantime, I've been almost nibbled to death by ducks." The fat stomach jiggled again, but his face told her his comments were serious.

Candy studied his face, as if seeing it for the first

time. It had character. Somehow he reminded her of a fat, cuddly koala bear.

"You don't know everything. In time, you will. Last year I almost died. God gave me a second chance at life. Only He knows why." Dan's voice was so low she could barely hear it. "Many a life is wasted in empty reveries. Opportunities run by. You've got what I want. A touch of forever." He leaned over and kissed her.

Five minutes later his whisper broke their silence. "Fear is the reason people stay silent. I can't sit still and let people die. At the right moment, I'll make a move." He patted her shoulder. "You know, back a cat against a wall, he'll fight." The stomach jiggled. "Especially a fat cat."

She hugged his knee, knowing now that if they came out alive, she'd be more than happy to go to San Diego, ranch or no ranch. It would be fun to share the rest of her life with someone who cared. She'd bet her heart on him. First thing, she'd put him on a diet.

"Let me help," she suggested.

"Hang loose," he said. "Better, you just take it easy here. I know what I'm doin'."

Across the room, Chrome-dome Parker nudged James Mason of British Intelligence. "That fat man over there. The one with the pretty young blonde wrapped in a sheet. I'm sure I've met him before, someplace. I'm trying to place him. Reminds me of a former spook I knew. If so, he's smarter than he looks. A rich bastard."

"Good God," Mason said. "Aren't there any bloody tourists here?"

"We're all in this together. When I get a chance, I'm going to try to speak to him."

•   •   •

In the tent assigned to the hostage negotiation team, McKenna sat on the edge of his cot, reading a book on Hawaiian legends. Corwin and Bailey were each sitting on their own cot, talking.

"They call their shots, pick their targets," Bailey said. "You can't go through life looking around corners and behind trees."

"Or in all the hotel rooms," Corwin added. "Compared to terrorism, wars are simple."

"Controlling these nuts," Bailey sought the right words, "would be like trying to bottle a fog."

"They've got a media cause—one for one—planned to generate maximum coverage." Corwin rose from his cot. "Someday the world will realize that terrorist violence thrives on television."

Bailey stood up also. "If there were no T.V. coverage, these activities would shrivel up and die."

"Hey, you guys, listen to this." McKenna pointed to his book and read aloud.

> "Pele's eyes turned to glowing coals and her hair to a banner of flame. She stamped on the ground, opening a fissure from which lava burst forth."

"Sounds like someone we've met," Bailey said in a soft drawl.

"That's what I've been thinking," McKenna answered. "The more we know about Pele the more we may know how Fire will act."

Both Corwin and Bailey nodded, listening.

> "Throughout their history, Hawaiians have used stories of Pele to explain the volcanic activity in the islands."

McKenna's eyes were skimming now, picking out bits of information about Pele.

> "Sometimes Pele goes among mortals as an old crone, living in a deep pit lined with fire. Watch out for old ladies, one of them may be Pele. She has a white dog and drinks gin."

"Not our girl," Corwin said. "She's no old lady . . ."

"Get this one!" McKenna traced the sentence in the book with his finger as he read:

> "Sometimes Pele appears as a beautiful young woman with red hair, an *ehu* . . ."

"That's the one," Corwin said.

> "Demanding that a man sleep with her . . ."

Bailey's hand shot up. "Damn, a red-hot date."

> "When she's turned down she gets very angry, volcanoes rumble and erupt."

"I already volunteered," the fun-loving captain drawled.

> "Many Hawaiians still believe in Pele. According to local legend, she's now living in the firepit at Kilauea . . ."

McKenna snapped the book closed.

"The most active volcano on earth," Corwin said.

McKenna sat quietly. The foolish thought flashed through his mind that maybe Pele had moved to the Molokai-Surf.

Rick Waltz added up the score, scratched his bald head, and looked up triumphantly. "We're 15,000 points up," he said. "That's one hundred and fifty dollars."

"Our luck's about to change," Jerry said, cutting the cards for Joan's deal. "Let's make it two cents a point."

"You're on—it's only money," replied Rick, thinking that they'd never get to spend it anyway.

"Is this your first trip to Hawaii?" asked Carol, pushing her honey-blonde hair to one side before she reached for her cards.

"Yes, until this happened," Joan's pretty face clouded, "we thought Molokai was beautiful, a truly enchanting place."

"Your next visit, you must go to Kauai. It's our favorite. It has more trees, flowers, and birds than any of the other islands." Carol looked across at Jerry. "Maybe the four of us could go."

"What a great idea!" Joan's brown eyes sparkled.

Rick and Jerry exchanged glances. It was obvious that the girls expected to be rescued. There was no sense in dashing their hopes.

"We'll plan on it," Jerry said. "We could stay at Princeville on the northern coast. It has a magnificent golf course and overlooks Hanalei Bay and the beach where they filmed *South Pacific*. It's really spectacular."

Rick nodded his head in agreement.

Carol's face was almost radiant as she thought about the trip. "We'll take the helicopter trip up the Na Pali Coast. The cliffs plunge thousands of feet down into the foaming sea. Magnificent little beaches. If you like shells, you can pick up some beauties."

Joan asked Carol a question about Kauai and the two girls started planning the trip, their voices animated and excited. For a few minutes, the bridge game was forgotten.

Rick leaned back in his chair, looked around the room to spot the location of the terrorists. Hunching forward, he spoke in a whispered voice to Jerry. "What would happen if we rushed that big fellow?" His head nodded toward Anahu.

"He'd shoot us," the doctor's voice replied tonelessly. "Or worse. He'd push that plunger. We'd all disappear."

"Supposing we diverted his attention?"

"How?" The doctor's eyes narrowed.

"I'm into magic. In an amateur way . . ." Rick's voice sounded almost apologetic. His hands scooped up the cards that had been dealt and were lying face down on the table. He shuffled them expertly, fanned the cards out and offered them to Jerry.

"Take a card, any card."

Joan and Carol both stopped talking and turned to watch. The doctor selected a card, looked at it, then slid it back into the deck being held by Rick.

"Magic really happens in your mind," Rick said as he shuffled the deck again. "Your eyes see a lot of things that your mind doesn't notice. Take sleight of hand." Setting the deck on the card table with his left hand, he tapped the top of the deck with his right forefinger.

"Manipulation depends entirely on sleight of hand. Misdirection is the key to manipulation." Rick spoke confidently, continuing to tap the cards. "Carol has your card here." His left hand reached behind the blonde's head, returning with a card. He turned it over. "The eight of spades," he announced.

The doctor grinned. "Damn. That's right."

"How did you do that?" Carol asked.

"You were watching my right hand. I palmed Jerry's card in my left hand while I was shuffling. Looks like magic. It's simple misdirection. You get people to focus on a certain spot, while you do something on a different spot."

The doctor grinned again. "Hey, maybe that explains the bridge score."

Joan laughed softly. "Darling, isn't it true that the more logical the mind, the easier to fool?"

"That's right. This shows that both Jerry and Carol have logical minds."

"Well, I don't know what you and Jerry were whispering about," Joan looked sternly at Rick, "but forget it! The birdbrains who took over this hotel are not logical thinkers. They're crazy."

Rick and Jerry exchanged glances again. Rick laughed lightly. "Maybe we'd better just play bridge."

Mac eased himself carefully out of the chair in the corner of Jumbo's post. His back was singing to him. Hunching his shoulders brought a wince. Bending sideways, another. He closed his eyes in agony when he touched his toes, then straightened. "Mind over pain," he muttered half aloud. Forcing his muscles to exercise, he focused his thoughts elsewhere.

He'd asked the Marines to send in a man to replace Angel. They'd fucked it up by trying to send him in too early. He wondered what knucklehead was running the leatherneck operation? Probably a kid fresh out of Quantico. Would they follow through on his plan and send someone in tonight? He had to assume that they would. The path would have to be cleared. Moses was guarding Angel's post, and would have to be eliminated. That was a shame; the tall, skinny black was likable. Maybe he could incapacitate him, get the young terrorist out of the way for a few hours. Give him a prune juice fix. Mac's teeth clenched in pain when he raised his arms above his head.

So far things had worked well. He touched the beans in his pocket. He was still alive. A survivor. Parts of his body . . . well . . . that wasn't important. He knew he needed sleep. Odd, he didn't feel tired. His mind was totally alert. One false step and there'd be an eternity to sleep. He hadn't yet done anything especially heroic. The twinge of pain in his lower back belied his thoughts. Except the fight with Jumbo—that had taken guts. He had a lot of respect for that huge black. But once in, there was only one way out. Marge had saved his ass. Thinking of her, he wondered what she was doing. Damn, she was some woman. Her face was full of quiet beauty. The Hawaiians had a word for it—*nani*. He was a lucky man.

The decision on Moses could wait. He sat back down heavily in Jumbo's chair, rubbing his left shoulder. Time was running down, the situation becoming more dangerous every hour, for everyone. They were all waiting at heaven's gate.

CHAPTER FOURTEEN

In the White House situation room, a group of senior officials of the administration were gathered around the long conference table. John Becker, the Under Secretary of Defense, was talking.

"It's an asinine demand. We can't destroy any nuclear weapons."

Most of the older heads around the table nodded in agreement.

"What about the hostages?" asked Ted Jones, the bright young Secretary of Commerce.

Walter Hagen, the General of the Army, shrugged his massive shoulders. "Pawns of war," he said softly. "Wrong place, wrong time. We can't let their safety influence our nuclear strategy." His eyes focused on the portrait of George Washington over the mantel.

Brad Beaufort, the handsome, articulate White House liaison officer, stood up at an easel and pointed to a hastily drawn chart. "There's enormous pressure building up. The telephones are ringing off their hooks and the telegrams are pouring in. It looks like a flood.

Surprisingly, the reaction is better than three to one that we give in to the terrorist demands.''

"What?" came from three or four astonished faces around the table.

"Almost four to one," Beaufort said, looking around the table, knowing his words were shocking the senior officials, wondering how they could be so out of touch with public opinion. "People are showing a genuine concern. A real ground swell. It's not the hostage situation. People are using that as a justification for their deep feelings. They're just scared shitless about nuclear weapons." Beaufort paused. "It's simple. They don't want to be incinerated."

"Why couldn't we destroy some old atomic bombs? The first generation ones we've already agreed to replace," questioned Henry Cabot, the Deputy Secretary of State. "If I remember, there are at least five hundred of those."

"It's not the bombs, it's the goddamned principle. Do it once, where would it stop? You'd have leftist crazies taking over every hotel in the free world." General Joel Harnett, the normally soft-spoken staff director for the Joint Chiefs of Staff, was almost shouting.

"If we did decide to destroy nuclear warheads—you can't explode them—we'd have the same type of environmental problems as we have with runaway nuclear reactors." It was a worried-looking James Twitty, Secretary of the Interior, stating a fact.

"If we decide to do it, we can do it." General Hagen thrust out his bulldog chin. "Nuclear weapons are very precise pieces of machinery. We'd disarm them first of course. Then, for a convincing show, we could flatten them all with a bulldozer, nuclear cores and all. Probably put it on television for the terrorists and all their leftist friends to celebrate. We'd pack up the pieces for eternal storage.

"Can you do it safely?" asked Twitty.

"Of course," Hagen snapped. "There are currently three military nuclear disposal sites. The waste is stored as liquid sludge in giant carbon-steel tanks buried just beneath the ground."

"How long is the radioactive waste safe?" asked Twitty.

"A few decades," replied General Hagen.

"What happens then?" asked Twitty, the worried look back on his face.

The general hesitated, not really wanting to reply. His eyes went around the table. Everyone was staring at him, waiting for his answer.

"We replace the tanks when they wear out." The general swallowed uncomfortably. "But, we're working on a new system. We plan to combine the nuclear wastes with molten glass, which would be hardened into solid pellets resistant to leakage. These solid pellets would be stored in corrosion-resistant stainless steel canisters." The general glanced around the table as if for silent approval, then continued. "These canisters would be blanketed with an overpack of absorbent materials and the whole package buried deep underground in shafts cut into solid bedrock."

"How long would that system be safe?" asked the persistent Twitty.

"At least a thousand years. Probably much longer. It's safety overkill," the general replied, touching his folded handkerchief to his brow. "But you should understand, I'm opposed to destroying any of our bombs."

From the end of the table, the Vice-President of the United States, who had been silent throughout the discussion, suddenly rapped for attention. He spoke softly, but with authority, a slight smile forming in the corners of his mouth.

"Gentlemen, we may be looking at this from the wrong viewpoint. There are stirrings out there. They'll come together and grow. Both the Congress and the President are going to feel the heat. It's going to be intense. We've got to slow the growing momentum of the antinuclear movement. This hostage incident may have given us a golden opportunity to seize the initiative. This could be the biggest political issue in the next election. By putting pressure on the Russians for mutual nuclear disarmament we'll get on the side of the angels. Let's get the President on television as soon as possible. We'll take the high ground. He can lead the charge."

The Vice-President was smiling broadly now.

Joey, the lanky blonde, looked up from the backgammon board, watched the big body of Jumbo enter the lanai door, and followed his progress across the room. Her hand reached forward and touched her husband's, her smoky voice saying, "Hey baby, your big black buddy is back."

Larry's heart skipped once, then beat faster. He inhaled deeply to calm himself, and touched his hand to his wavy white hair. "Give him a few minutes to settle in, then I'll make my move," he whispered back, rolling the white dice and blotting one of Joey's exposed pieces. Larry grinned. "That'll teach you to expose your ass. I'll jump you every time."

The lanky blonde grinned back. "Get us out of here, baby, and you can jump me any time. We'll love the

world away, like Bogey and Bacall.'' Her leg snaked out
under the table, bare foot caressing her husband's leg.

"For Crissakes, Joey . . ."

"Do you know, darling . . ." She stared at his used
face covered with a two-day stubble of salt and pepper
beard. "This is the most time we've spent together in
years." She glanced around and laughed lightly. "I
want you to know if anything happens, I've enjoyed it."
Her big hazel eyes sparkled at her husband.

Larry stared back at his wife. For some time now,
they'd been strangers passing in time, like ships in the
night. He'd been a lousy husband. Their water bed had
become a dead sea. Maybe it wasn't too late to make
waves again.

It was almost twenty minutes later when Larry rose
from his chair and crossed to the corner where Jumbo
was standing, drinking a cup of coffee. Mac had been
mentally checking the hostages to see who might help
when the crunch came. It was about time to make contact.

"Mind if I join you?" Larry asked, interrupting
Mac's thoughts.

Jumbo's rubber gloves gestured toward the coffeepot. Larry poured himself a cup, took a sip, then turned
back toward Jumbo. "This is a hell of a mess!"

Jumbo said nothing.

"I've seen the future and it terrifies me," Larry said.

Jumbo sipped his coffee. He couldn't disagree.

"I've always liked blacks," Larry lied, his voice trailing off. It was a stupid statement and he knew it. The
second he'd said it, he wished he hadn't.

Jumbo's face mask was impassive. Some blacks were
good, some bad, he thought. Just like whites.

"My wife has a heart problem," Larry lied again.

"We'd like to get out of here. It's worth a lot of money to me."

Under any circumstances, Mac knew he would have disliked Larry. He was short, feisty, and abrasive, with a certain obnoxious quality that rode on the surface—totally self-centered, buying his way through life. Like a lot of little guys, he probably hated big ones. Jumbo's shoulders shrugged.

Larry swallowed hard. The big black treated conversation like a contagious social disease. Who would know what was going on in his head? "Don't you talk, man?"

Jumbo nodded negatively. "I listen," he growled.

"I'll give you five thousand dollars, cash, if you get me . . ."

"Crawl off!" Mac said angrily. The creep was interested only in saving his own skin. The chunky guy didn't give a shit about anyone else. He'd barter his soul.

"Ten thousand." Larry raised the ante, and his voice. Money wasn't talking, it was stuttering. Suddenly he felt like a magician with only one trick and he'd reached into the hat and come up empty. The rabbit was gone.

Out of the corner of his mask, Mac could see Anahu watching the two of them. It wouldn't do to raise the suspicions of that big Hawaiian. Mac put down his coffee cup.

"Fifteen thou." Larry was pleading now.

Jumbo's punch traveled only eighteen inches. It looked professional, but stopped short of being serious. Larry turned white and fell back into a chair, then passed out.

Mac glanced at the New Yorker. That was one marshmallow who'd lived the soft life. Heading for the lanai, passing Anahu, Jumbo slowed and snarled, "That creep said he doesn't like Hawaiians. If he says it again, cleanse his soul—kill 'em.''

Anahu stared at the back of Jumbo as he went out the sliding glass doors. That big black was one strange dude.

Brad Beaufort, the White House liaison officer, released a press announcement at nine P.M., EST, to all three television networks.

> "The terrorist takeover of the Molokai-Surf resort and the terrorist demands for unilateral destruction of vital nuclear warheads is designed to make Russia look like a peacemaker and to make the United States look like the seekers of war. That is completely contrary to fact. Our government has consistently maintained that we are willing to consider substantial reductions in nuclear warheads if the Soviet Union will do likewise.
>
> "The President will address this subject in detail in his press conference which has been advanced one week and rescheduled for eleven A.M. EST, tomorrow morning."

"Is he willing to go along with the terrorists' demands and obtain the hostages' release on a one-for-one basis?" asked John Churchman, of "NBC News."

Beaufort flashed his usual brilliant smile and held out his arms. "John, the President is considering that option carefully. We'll let the President answer that one himself, tomorrow morning."

By early afternoon, a television set with a large screen had been installed in Colonel Donahue's command post. Corporal Willoughby, the colonel's personal aide, had been assigned to monitor the channels and tape anything pertaining to the terrorist takeover.

The first showing of Fire's speech came on a two-minute news special on station KGMB at two o'clock. There was ninety seconds of fiery excerpts and a few words of factual commentary. Similar news briefs were delivered on station KHOL starting at two-thirty. All were repeated at half-hour intervals. By midafternoon, Hawaiian stations reported they were being deluged with phone calls that were running three to one in favor of the terrorist proposal to destroy nuclear weapons in order to free the hostages. One young Molokai girl was quoted as saying, "Let's get rid of the nukes. We don't want to go to heaven. We already live in paradise."

Donahue was slumped in his chair, mouth dry, tongue flicking over his lips. He accepted an iced cola and sipped it slowly. "Goddamned mental moths. They're all attracted by the candle of television."

"The tube is like a full moon. It brings out the weirdos," Major Fleming muttered.

"Nobody loves the bomb. It's nucleorosis—a new disease," Major Murray said, a trace of sorrow in his voice. "It may be more contagious than herpes."

"It seems to be spreading about as fast." Fleming shook his head of white hair. "That pretty terrorist has got us by the short hairs, manipulating the whole country."

"We stepped on a pressure booby trap. Can't move. If we step off, the fuckin' thing will explode." Baldwin punched his big fist into his palm. "We've got them right where they want us."

"It's the goddamned T.V." Donahue spoke angrily. "Stirring up mass reaction. They don't say anything about the hostages. It's all about reducing nuclear weapons. A fucking crusade. They're putting that red-headed bitch on a white charger . . ." The colonel's voice trailed off.

It was two minutes after four in the afternoon when Corporal Willoughby signaled Donahue. The Marine officers quickly gathered in front of the television screen and watched Brad Beaufort deliver his announcement that the President was going to discuss the hostage situation and the terrorist demands the following morning.

Donahue checked his Timex, then smiled at the others. "That P.R. guy is smooth . . . probably eats silk for breakfast. He's just bought us fourteen hours. Our friends won't do anything drastic until they hear what the President has to say. Eleven A.M. in Washington, D.C. It'll be six in the morning here. Sunrise."

"You know the President won't destroy any nuclear warheads," Murray said matter-of-factly.

Donahue nodded, looked around the tent, and motioned Willoughby out. As soon as the corporal had left, the colonel leaned forward and spoke in a low voice. "We'll make our move while the President is talking on T.V."

Baldwin looked at Fleming and winked. Both of their faces lit up.

"I'm going in there tonight," Donahue said.

"What!" came from Murray.

"Mac and I worked pretty well together in Korea. It's time to give the old bastard a hand."

From a spot just outside the front entrance, Fire watched the bright yellow Cessna circle the resort. The bold blue letters KHOL stood out on the fuselage of the plane. A television camera pointed out an open window, revealing the mission. She ran her fingers through her bouquet of curly red hair, then checked her watch. The plane had been circling for almost twenty minutes. The pilot was getting bolder, moving closer on each circle, flying low over the outer buildings. Now he was buzzing the main building.

On the last circle, a blue Piper Cherokee had joined the Cessna. There were no markings on the plane. Probably station KGMB, thought Fire. Media attention was important, but enough was enough. Next time it might be the Marines. She signaled to Carlos. A warning shot might be appropriate. At least it would make the television footage more exciting, hold viewer interest. The public loved violence.

Carlos passed on the signal to Milo inside the lobby. Moments later the tall terrorist with the swarthy face came out of the lobby carrying the SAM-7 missile launcher and a rack of three missiles. While he was maneuvering into position about fifty yards up the road from the entrance, Carlos sighted his AK-47 in front of the Cherokee and fired several shots. They went unnoticed.

Buzz Muth, the pilot of the yellow Cessna, spotted the activity at the front entrance of the Molokai-Surf and swung the twin-engined plane in closer, television camera zooming in on the action. Not to be outdone by the rival television station, Ace Esselen, the pilot of the blue Piper, turned tight inside and under the Cessna, giving his cameraman a better shot of the entrance and partially blocking the view of the KHOL camera. "Up yours, Buzzer Boy," the veteran pilot shouted over the roar of the engine.

On the ground, Carlos's face turned angry. Fucking idiots, playing games. He'd give them a taste of the ultimate game, death. The scope of his AK-47 moved just in front of the blue Piper, which was banking steeply just above him. Squeezing off a sustained burst, he could see the bullets slam home. Little bits of metal sprayed off the plane, a sudden puff of smoke came out of the engine, then bright orange flames, followed by a thin trail of dark smoke. The plane veered off in a gentle dive, disappearing behind a grove of trees on the other side of the road. The terrorists heard the loud sound of an explosion and saw a ball of fire, then a plume of ugly, oily black smoke.

Milo watched Carlos shoot down the Piper Cherokee, then slammed a missile into the SAM launcher. God-damn, there was a string of used chewing gum in the barrel. No time to bitch now. He'd chew someone out later. Hefting the missile launcher to his shoulder, he aimed the scope. The bright yellow Cessna was in his sights . . . a dead pigeon. He squeezed the trigger and in the next instant lost his head. The missile tube exploded with a loud roar, spattering little bits and pieces of Milo in all directions.

Fire blinked her eyes shut, Carlos clenched his teeth, Marco forced his little boy smile. The damn Cubans had sent them a defective missile. It had to be. The launcher had worked perfectly before, and Milo had been a good, reliable terrorist, devoted to the cause.

Overhead, Muth pushed the throttles forward and nosed the Cessna down behind a line of trees, then out over the Kaiwi Channel, zooming just above the white-capped waves, heading for Oahu. He thought of Ace Esselen and swallowed the lump in his throat. It could have just as easily been his plane. Just hadn't been his time to go. Muth turned his head and looked over his shoulder. The cameraman gave him a victory sign. He knew they had captured great television footage, both of the Piper going down and a major explosion in front of the resort.

Now the pilot turned to his other two passengers. "Did you learn anything?"

Captain Bailey looked at Major Corwin. Both of the Marine officers nodded at the same time. Those terrorists were nuts. They even shot down planes that were filming their activities for television.

CHAPTER FIFTEEN

In Angel's old outpost, Moses had his transistor turned to rock music. He was facing out, feet on the window-sill, body twitching in time with the music, rubber gloves tapping out the tune. His AK-47 was on the floor alongside him. The big body of Jumbo moved up silently behind the tall, thin black, a piece of rubber tubing looped between the gloved hands.

Mac's eyes blinked, the gloves hesitated, the shoulders gave a shrug, and the piece of tubing went into the pocket of Jumbo's coveralls. A big hand reached out and tapped Moses on the shoulder. The thought ran through Mac's mind that he was getting soft, the killer instinct gone.

"Hi, man," the black said, without even turning around. "Sit down and listen. They're flyin'." His body moved with the music until the song ended, then switching off the transistor he turned his chair to face Jumbo. "Love that music," he said. "Give me five."

Jumbo slapped his rubber glove against Moses'. "How yah doin'?"

The tall, thin black gave a triumphant thumbs-up

238

sign. "No leprosy," he said, a twinkle in his voice. "Rock fever, maybe."

"It's gettin' close to crunch time. How good are you in a fight?" Mac asked.

Moses gestured. "Gimme a broken bottle or a knife, I go crazy, but my sundae punch is Carvel—all marshmallow and whipped cream."

Mac laughed. "My best days are memories, too."

They sat in silence for a while and watched three black-footed albatross fly in line past the window. Moses spoke first.

"Those gooney birds are bad luck. What's goin' to happen?"

"Sooner or later the Marines will move in. Fire will blow up the hostages." Jumbo's shoulders drooped. "Fire, Marco, and Carlos will probably escape. The rest of us will be blown away."

"I figure it the same," Moses said quietly. "I don't trust either of those spics."

"Me neither," Mac said. "A spic is a whitey turned inside out."

Moses laughed heartily, banging the table with his right rubber fist. "I don't hate minorities." He chuckled again. "I just don't like to mix with those suckers."

"What the fuck we doin' here?" Jumbo asked.

"Up in Harlem it seemed like a good idea," Moses answered. "I was in trouble with the wrong people. Thought I might find myself at the bottom of a river, sipping sewage. Hawaii offered a new start, the good life. All that soul shit."

"It may be time to bail," Mac said softly, testing the water.

"I busted out of Attica once." Moses laughed. "This might be tougher." His right glove rubbed his bloodshot eye. "Damn red dust, it's everywhere."

"If . . ." Jumbo's mask swiveled around, "I got a plan . . . you got an interest?"

Moses nodded slowly. "Sometimes to win, you gotta keep from losin'. Life is bettah than death. I don't like nukes, but I draw the line at dyin'."

The big body of Jumbo rose and gave Moses a high-five. "I'll be back later, after dark."

As he moved down the stairs, Mac could hear the rock music start again. He was not only getting soft, but stupid as well. Maybe senility had set in. Even Houdini never put himself in such an impossible situation. All he needed now was an imaginative plan for a triumphant escape—a plan to lead Moses to the Promised Land. Mac smiled a little smile. Things were ass-backward. Besides, he didn't have a plan. Legend had it that ancient Molokai was inhabited by dwarfs called *Menehunes* who came out at night and did amazing things. Where were the little bastards when he needed them?

Dan Hanson lit a cigarette and stared moodily through the lanai door toward the glistening sea. Gulls strutted on the edge of the cliff, started, and flew up, wheeling in the air, then diving to skim the breakers. Far out in the channel a flippered giant surfaced to breathe, emitting a steamy sigh.

The fat man saw everything through a dark indigo haze, mind staggering from one thought to another. Once again, the blue Piper was trailing light wisps of smoke and orange flame, then the vision disappeared in an acrid, oily, black cloud. His round face was tight and hard, eyes glinting with intensity. He rubbed the bruise on his face angrily.

Max Parker watched the big figure silhouetted against the coppery sky. Nodding to Mason, he rose, stretched, and walked slowly toward the fat man.

"Don't I know you?"

Raising his eyes, Hanson looked blankly at the heavyset, bald man. Parker noticed the eyes were hard as gemstones, no sign of recognition in them.

The agent smiled wryly and knelt down beside Hanson. "Bitter memories die hard."

The fat man didn't answer, but he nodded slowly.

"Time is running out."

The round head bobbed again.

"I've heard them talking." Parker glanced around. "This is the first of a series. Next week other HULA units will take over Mauna Kea on Hawaii, Princeville on Kauai, and the Kahala on Oahu. Resorts all over the world will be seized."

Hanson closed his eyes and inhaled audibly before he spoke. "There are a lot of crazy people everywhere."

"A coordinated action on a worldwide basis. The same demand, one for one."

"It's more than a little scary."

Parker leaned forward and spoke in a low voice. "We'll have to take them. The Marines won't be able to get in . . ."

"What are you—a mercenary?"

The agent smiled thinly. "Family, like you."

The fat man winced inwardly, but his face stayed impassive. "You got the wrong man," he said quietly. Long ago that part of his life had been put behind him.

"They wouldn't be talking if they expected any of us to get out of here alive."

"On this earth we're all terminal."

Parker grimaced. "We're close to the edge, not many options left. Somebody has to do something. Are you with us?"

"What's your plan?"

"We thought we'd jump the big Hawaiian."

The fat man laughed mirthlessly. "You may as well hit them with a fistful of wet noodles. They'd blow up everyone from their control post in the lobby. A real die-in."

Parker's face reddened.

"Miracles are like the *nene* bird—they're pretty rare, hard to come by." Hanson's voice was toneless. "My crystal ball is cloudy. When you get a plan, you know where to find me."

The fat man stood and walked toward Candy, who was curled up catlike, sleeping. Seeing her, his face softened.

Anahu had been watching the two big men. His broad shoulders stiffened and a scowl came over his dark face.

It was almost three-thirty in the afternoon when Anahu and Ivan moved the larger of the two television sets into the Koa Lounge and set it up on the small raised stage. Most of the hostages gathered around and found seats on the floor from which they could watch the film of Fire's speech being televised, as well as view other news specials on the takeover.

Station KHOL followed Fire's speech with a twenty-eight minute movie, "The Final Epidemic," in which doctors and scientists explained in harrowing detail what would happen in the event of a nuclear war. The hostages sat in stunned silence, their faces reflecting horror, confusion, and uncertainty. The breeze moving through the open door rustled the louvres, causing a shimmering dance of sunlight on the floor.

The lady in the muu-muu, with the face like a carp, turned to the elderly lady sitting next to her and broke the strained silence. "It would be awful."

"Absolutely horrible," the old lady said, her thin face pinched and strained, her voice heavy with emotion. "Think of the millions of burned and mutilated bodies, and no facilities to treat them."

"If it comes, I hope the first bomb hits me square on the head," the lady in the muu-muu replied. "I'd rather not know . . ."

The three Avon ladies watched the movie together. Connie's sigh was almost an explosive whistle ending with, "Good God!" She lit her last Vantage, inhaled a mouthful of smoke, and coughed violently.

"I always thought they were building the bombs to protect us, not destroy us," Betty Jane said, her face ashen, hands trembling.

Evelyn didn't say anything, her knuckles pressed to her mouth.

Connie coughed again, tears welling in her eyes. "The world would become a global gas oven."

Sitting nearby, Max Parker leaned closer to James Mason and whispered, "The days of the jolly little wars are over. Boy, were you right. Fire's got the world's attention focused on nuclear bombs and not on the Molokai-Surf." The heavyset agent shook his head as if in disbelief. "Even the hostages are talking about nuclear war and not their own freedom."

The wiry Englishman in the rumpled silk pajamas smiled. "That redheaded Svengali has pulled a mirror reversal. She's placed the burden of proof on the innocent."

Parker's glance showed he didn't fully understand.

"Everyone's against nuclear war, even the hostages. Therefore, why shouldn't the United States destroy a warhead to free a hostage? By being prisoners we're serving a good cause." The look on the Englishman's face showed his admiration for Fire's performance. "Taken to its extreme, there are probably a lot of people around the world saying, 'Don't free the hostages unless they destroy the nuclear bombs.' That's some trick.''

"The media is fueling the fire that's going to consume us," Parker said, a touch of anger in his voice.

Mason nodded his agreement.

Kona and her staff moved through the room offering tea and cookies. The tall good-looking girl with the golden skin and the long black hair made her way slowly, trying to reassure the hostages.

The Waltzes were still sitting with Jerry, the doctor, and his partner in everything except marriage, Carol.

"This game is for keeps," the doctor said. "We don't have another planet to play with. The world's nuclear overkill makes common sense blush."

Carol wrinkled her nose. "This place is becoming a morgue. It's that damn television spreading fear about nuclear war. We've got enough problems of our own."

Both Rick and Joan looked at the girl, then at one another. The doctor's assistant was right. Rick grinned. "Good girl. Keep your eyebrows up."

Joan smiled and added, "The terrorists are bluffing. Another day and they'll probably ask for a plane out of here."

Kona poured tea for the four of them, then leaned over and spoke quietly. "I don't think so. Fire is my sister. I'm afraid that HULA is totally committed. It's a cause for which they're all ready to die. Escape for them is not an option."

As the pretty manager of the resort moved off, Rick looked at Joan and both looked at the other couple staring back at them. The constant in all of their eyes now was fear.

Jeanne Black, United States delegate to the United Nations, parked her silver Cadillac Seville in the under-

ground garage and walked quickly to the bank of elevators. Impatiently, she jabbed at the up button. Moments
later she emerged in a marble and glass corridor on the
third floor, and moved rapidly toward a small, private
meeting room. A fireboat spraying water in the East
River caught her momentary attention out the window.

Igor Zaturof, the delegate from the Soviet Union, was
waiting. He rose heavily from a chair as she entered,
held out a large, clammy hand, and smiled a greeting.

"It was very nice of you to meet with me on such
short notice," Ms. Black said, closing the door.

The Russian shook his head sadly. "As I told you on
the phone, the takeover of the Molokai-Surf was a total
surprise to my government."

"Some of our people say it's your action," Ms. Black
said coldly.

"*Nyet*. We've never even heard of HULA," the Russian said, just as coldly.

Jeanne Black stared at Igor Zaturof's face. As usual,
it showed a total lack of emotion. It could have been
chiseled out of Siberian granite.

"The terrorists are using Russian weapons," Ms.
Black said flatly.

Zaturof shrugged, the shoulders of his gray suit flapping like the wings of a dead bird. "We help our
friends. They help their friends. It's a long chain. You
do the same."

"You've heard the terrorist demands?"

The Russian smiled. "One for one. An interesting
concept."

"You know we can't destroy nuclear warheads on a
unilateral basis," Ms. Black said.

"Why not?" Zaturof asked. "You've got more than
we have."

"We do not, and you know it," Ms. Black snapped.

"You've got more than enough."

"So do you."

The Russian smiled again. He had guessed the reason for the meeting, and knew the attractive, stylish American was uncomfortable. It showed in her face.

"We thought your government might see this as an opportunity," Jeanne Black hesitated, clearing her throat, "to reduce worldwide tensions, actually reduce nuclear armaments on a one-for-one basis."

The Russian stared at his American counterpart, a frown on his forehead, as if not understanding the thought.

"Let's assume we agree with the terrorist demands. We destroy one nuclear warhead for each hostage released—and you do likewise."

"What?" The Russian feigned a look of surprise.

"The world's major powers, the United States and the Soviet Union, reducing nuclear warheads on a one-for-one basis." A flicker of a smile crossed Jeanne Black's face. "We thought that was an interesting concept."

"Why would we want to do that?" the Russian asked, a real frown now furrowing his forehead.

"Your premier has said that your country is interested in a meaningful reduction in nuclear weapons, if a fair and equitable basis can be found. This plan would be meaningful, fair, and equitable." Ms. Black looked at Zaturof's blank expression, sighed deeply, then said, "For Crissakes, Igor, at least it would be a start."

The Russian diplomat held up his large hands. "I think we both know the answer. But if your government insists, I'll pass on your request."

"We'd appreciate that very much, Igor. This request comes from the President himself. Time is very important."

The Russian nodded, then muttered a few pleasantries and good-byes. He watched the American delegate walk down the corridor to the elevators. Never negotiate from weakness, he thought. There was no way his government would agree to destroy nuclear warheads to free American hostages. Terrorists never took any hostages in Russia. He laughed, cracking his knuckles. That wasn't allowed.

Bill Alexander brought the two trays of food into the tent and set them on the table. A shaft of sunlight sliced through the tent opening, made bright patterns on the floor, and lit up the three geraniums in a water glass on one of the trays.

The Marine adjutant smiled and gestured at the flowers. "Cranes bills. They grow wild here."

Marge opened her eyes through a soft-focus haze, swung her feet off the cot, and stood up, suppressing a yawn. "Thank you, Captain. I'm afraid I've slept away most of the day."

"I think you needed a little nap." He started to say something about the sedatives the corpsman had given her, then decided against it.

The captain pulled up two folding canvas-back chairs. "I thought you'd like company while you ate. It's not hotel cuisine, but . . ."

"It will do fine." Marge's stomach had been poking at her. Stifling another yawn, her face colored. "Excuse me. What happened?"

"We just learned that the President is going to speak on television tomorrow morning. Nothing will happen until then."

"I'm glad," she said. "I'm sure the President will see that the hostages are released. People are more important than bombs. He's a sensible man. Nuclear war,

that's real Russian roulette.'' Her eyes looked at the
captain for the first time. He was on the chunky side,
with powerful, sloping shoulders and the hint of a
paunch struggling against his belt. His face was round
and pink, with twinkling eyes and a pleasant smile.

Alexander swallowed. McGregor's wife was hooked
on hope. He wasn't going to discourage her, so he said
nothing.

The flaps to the tent were tied back, and through the
opened doorway they could see the sun rapidly moving
toward the horizon, the fluffy clouds orange in the sky.
The coconut palms on the ridge nodded in the freshen-
ing breeze.

"I wish Mac could see this sky, it's so magnificent,''
Marge exclaimed, standing and walking to the doorway.
"Sharing with him makes special times twice as beauti-
ful."

Alexander stared at her silhouette against the sunset.
McGregor's wife was simply elegant because she was
elegantly simple. Mac was in her heart, and living there,
he'd be safe.

Marge jumped back as a dragonfly flew past her face.
She turned and walked back into the tent.

The captain smiled before he spoke. "Two good
omens. Hawaiians believe that dragonflies are good
luck, and so is rain. You've seen the dragonfly, and it
should rain before midnight. Now all you need is a rainbow. That's a guarantee of good luck.''

Marge sat in her chair and started talking about her
life with Mac.

Donahue's aide listened. He'd learned early that a
good listener is not only popular, but after a while,
knows a lot. It was a characteristic that had served him
well. Listening to her talk, he was convinced that
women really did support half the sky.

It was almost an hour later when the captain suggested to Marge that she take the two pills on her tray. "The doctor said they'd make you relax."

In a few minutes, she was sound asleep on her cot. The captain removed the trays and closed the flap on her tent, heading for Donahue's command post.

In ocean suite seven, Mac climbed out of the bathtub and toweled himself dry. He dressed quickly, then with the makeup kit that Marge had left him darkened the areas around his eyes, mouth, and wrists. Pulling the mask over his head and slipping on his gloves, he checked the reflection in the mirror. Once again Mac was Jumbo. He sniffed and shook Jumbo's head. The camouflage outfit sure as hell smelled like Jumbo.

He checked his watch. There were only a few hours left before the Marines were supposed to send in a man. He wasn't sure they were going to do it, but had to assume that they would. It was time to deliver on his promise to Moses. Besides, if a Marine didn't come in, then he was going to have to go out and talk to them. They needed to coordinate a plan of operation. Things were moving toward a climax. The action would speed up now. Whether a Marine came in or he went out, Moses had to go. The post he guarded covered the route in and out. But Mac didn't want to kill the tall, thin black, he just wanted to take him out of action until the terrorist operation was over. He'd probably have to lie to Moses, but that was better than killing him.

The day was going fast. Out over the channel behind Diamond Head the sunset was still a nightly spectacular. Watching, Mac's thoughts were of Marge, wishing he could have shared the sight with her, knowing she would have enjoyed it, believing that every sunset held the promise of a new dream. The sky was filled with fluffy

orange cotton balls threatening to make rain. The wind
had picked up and was now moaning through the trees.
Mac opened a small can of tunafish and ate it. Leaving
his suite, with a coil of rope and a folded-up mattress
cover under his arm, he walked rapidly toward the
ocean, tossing the empty can into the sea, heading for
the large ironwood tree at the edge of the cliff.

Fifteen minutes later, Jumbo clumped up the stairs to
the outpost on the northeastern corner of the resort.
Moses was waiting. The music was soft jazz, Ben
Aranov on piano, Bob Jackson on drums, his brother
Chip on bass, Jerry Dodgion on alto-sax, and Vicky
Delicious as vocalist. Leaning against the door, Moses
had a streetcorner look, with a shoulder slouch and a
soft shrug that acknowledged the presence of the bigger
man. His bloodshot eyes looked past Jumbo, almost
into another dimension, watching the music. It gave
Mac an eerie feeling. Moses looked dusted.

"Hey, man, you okay?" Jumbo asked.

Moses nodded. "That's some group. Beautiful! I get
high on jazz—ride moonbeams out and back—don't
need no drugs."

The tune over, Moses snapped off the transistor,
pushed down the antenna rod, and inserted the small
radio into its soft case, which clipped onto his belt.
"I'm packed and ready. What's the plan?"

"It's here today, gone to Maui."

Moses laughed. "I like the sound of that." Looking
closely at Jumbo's eye slits, he suddenly said, "Your
leprosy, it don't look no bettah. Still all purple."

"It's bett-ah," Jumbo said, beckoning Moses to the
window. Left glove on Moses' shoulder. Mac was
struck by the sudden thought that the tall, thin black
was built like a stick, a praying mantis. Jumbo's right
glove pointed to the strip of disturbed earth barely visi-

ble in the dim light. "Land mines. Can't get through there."

"No way," Moses said, eyes staring at the earth.

"On the other side are the Marines. We'd be caught, sure as hell."

Moses shook his head negatively. "No way. I'll stay heah, be back in the slammer. Death would be easier, just like blowing out a candle, one last breath, poof, and gone."

"What were you up for?" Jumbo asked.

"Rape." Moses looked down at his feet, then back at Jumbo. "Learned early on black girls in the ghetto. Then I branched out, the suburbs . . . housewives . . . twelve convictions." Moses said it matter-of-factly. There was neither pride nor remorse in his voice.

Mac swallowed hard. That changed things. He couldn't help a rapist. "That stinks," he said angrily.

"That was long ago. I was a kid. Life wasn't easy in the ghetto. Every mistake could be fatal," Moses said, drawing a deep breath. "Then I learned that God's lookin'. Man without Jesus, you ain't got a prayer." The thin black's eyes squinted through the eye slits in his mask. "Got an old lady now. The baby was on time. The weddin' was late." Moses laughed, then quickly the laugh dissipated as he realized he was laughing alone. "What's the plan?"

"We've got to hurry," Jumbo said. "Follow me." He turned and started down the stairs. Walking rapidly, Mac could hear Moses behind him.

"Where ya goin'?" he gasped. Mac noticed that Moses was panting even going downhill.

"Trust me, brother," Mac replied, knowing that on the street trust was everything. You either had it or you didn't.

Reaching the top of the cliff overlooking the ocean,

Jumbo stopped. A coil of strong rope had been looped over a sturdy branch of the mature ironwood tree. A mattress cover was folded at the base of the tree.

"There's a small motorboat down there on the beach." Jumbo's arm gestured. It was the truth, but not the whole truth. The bottom of the boat was missing.

"So?" Moses asked.

"I lowah you down, then lowah myself. It's off to Maui."

"No way, brother," Moses said. "I can't stand heights. I might fall down dead and I know the good-hands people won't find me down there." The thin man stared out over the cliff, afraid to get close to the edge. All he could see were whitecaps whipped up by the strong wind on a black sea. Moses moaned, feeling like a blind man in a dark room looking for a black cat that wasn't there. It was a total negative feedback.

"It'll be easy." Jumbo's big hand rested on Moses' shoulder. "It's your life. Nobody else but me cares, man."

"It's not happening!" Moses' voice rose to a shout. "It's comin' up a cloud."

"Don't argue, man." Jumbo moved behind Moses and slipped the large noose at the end of the rope down over Moses' head then up under his arms.

"You're not putting me out on a limb!" Moses' struggles were feeble, born of fear rather than anger. Suddenly, his struggles stopped. Clasping his hands together in front of him, he raised his head and closed his eyes. "Lord, I've been a great sinner. I don't deserve to go to no heaven. Let me stay heah."

"Trust me, brother," Mac shouted as he pulled on the free end of the rope, lifting Moses' body two feet off the ground. Mac now looped the rope around a fork in the tree and tied it temporarily. In one quick motion

Mac held Moses' feet together while the mattress cover
was slid up over Moses' legs. "Put your arms down. I'm
savin' your ass," he hissed in Moses' ear. "Stop
worryin'. No one can kill you one moment before God
permits." The mattress cover went up over the black's
head and was zipped up, the zipper hooked to a small
wire Mac had previously attached, leaving a small air
hole at the top through which Moses could breathe. The
thin terrorist was in over his head. There was no way
out.

Pulling on the rope, Mac maneuvered the bundle out
over the cliff and lowered it about twenty feet down the
cliff, just out of sight, tying the rope securely to the fork
of the ironwood tree. "Hang loose, man. I'll be back,"
he shouted.

Mac peered over the cliff. Moses was out of the way,
perfectly safe, bagged and ready for delivery to the
Marines. From the inside of the mattress cover, mixing
with the whistling wind, Mac could hear the sounds of
Moses' transistor radio. Out of the opening at the top
Mac could see the thin antenna rod. Moses would be
suspended in time, high on jazz, riding moonbeams.

CHAPTER SIXTEEN

Second Day—Nighttime

The hostages had been served dinner and most were watching a rerun of "Hawaii Five-O" on television. Carlos's man, Ivan, was on guard duty, sitting with his hand next to the switch connected to the explosive charges. During the first commercial break, a local news announcer, Janet Kamahe, interrupted with a special news flash.

> "Good evening. KHOL special reporter, Lloyd Reynolds, on the scene at the Molokai-Surf, has reported that the Marines under command of Colonel Donahue have now killed three terrorists and have captured another one. Reynolds reports that nine of the HULA One terrorist group are still holding 216 hostages who have been wired to C-4 plastic explosive packages.

"Early this morning Reynolds actually witnessed the escape of one of the hostages, a
short, middle-aged woman with a bandanna tied
over her head, who drove out of the resort in a
golf cart accompanied by two terrorists—one
dead and one still alive, bound hand and foot
and screaming in pain. The Marines apparently
have established contact with an ex-Marine who
is operating inside the resort. This man and his
wife were guests who evaded capture when the
Molokai-Surf was taken over by the terrorists."

Ms. Kanahe looked up into the camera from the news
bulletin she was reading and in a low, confidential voice
told the television audience:

"Station KHOL knows the name of this ex-
Marine who has infiltrated the terrorist organization inside the resort and his wife who has
escaped alive, but in order to protect their safety
we are withholding the information at this time.
We will interrupt our regular programming for
any further news bulletins."

The lady in the wrinkled muu-muu suddenly smiled
and turned her head to look for the big terrorist. Of
course, now she knew why he looked so familiar. It was
that rude man she'd met at the cocktail party on the
lanai.

The three Avon ladies glanced at one another, a look
of shock the common bond on their faces. Evelyn
mouthed the words, "The McGregors—Mac and
Marge." Connie bit her lip, Betty Jane closed her eyes.
My God, if they knew the terrorists must know, too.
They had to warn Mac McGregor.

Chrome-dome Parker nudged James Mason. "The
big guy with the Nike shoes and the rubber gloves—
Jumbo." Mason nodded, a pained expression on his

face. "He's a dead man, now." Just a few minutes before, they'd seen him over in the area where they normally sat, with a small paper bag in his hands. Parker turned his head slightly, eyes searching. Jumbo wasn't there. He was gone.

It was ten minutes later, after Parker and Mason had returned to their blankets on the floor and sat down, that the big man felt the uncomfortable lump. His hand reached under the blanket and pulled out a small paper bag. Inside was a pair of Vise-Grip pliers with a sharp cutting edge.

"Jumbo left us a present," he whispered.

The Englishman's face registered no emotion, but his left eyebrow arched imperceptibly.

"Wire cutters."

"Snip through primer cord?"

"Like ripe cheese." Parker slipped the paper bag to Mason, who put it in the pocket of his dressing gown.

"Timing would be important. Anahu checks the grid about every eight hours."

"After midnight," Parker whispered, glancing across the room at Dan Hanson. "I'll try to get word to our fat friend."

Mason nodded. "I'll deep-six the pliers." Stretching, the wiry, thin man rose and walked slowly toward the men's room. Ivan's eyes followed him.

In the lobby, Marco and Anahu were watching the smaller television set. Anahu had his hand next to the second switch connected to the C-4 charges. Carlos was patrolling the two outposts on the southern side of the resort. Fire was asleep. Hearing the news bulletin, both Marco and Anahu sat bolt upright.

"I'll wake Fire and tell her," Anahu said, excitement in his voice.

Marco laughed. "That's bullshit. Television never

gets anything right. The Marines killed Jorge and the Scorpion. They did that before Fire made her announcement. They haven't killed anyone since. I, personally, blew up that fucker, Angel. The Marines haven't captured anyone." He looked at the big Hawaiian and smiled his little boy smile. "It's simple. No one else is missing."

Anahu frowned. "I still think we should tell Fire."

Marco checked his watch and sat back in his chair, putting his feet up on the coffee table. "Fire will be up in less than two hours. You can tell her then. I'm going to check my outposts as soon as Carlos gets back. You'd better stick close here. That Bulgarian doesn't understand much English." He nodded toward Ivan.

It was almost twenty minutes later that Carlos stomped into the lobby, shaking the first raindrops from his jacket. Marco was dozing in his chair. He opened one eye. The eye closed again and he lapsed into quiet breathing.

"It's going to be a wet night," Carlos said to Anahu.

The big Hawaiian nodded. The wind had swung around and was blowing from the southwest. A kona wind usually meant rain. As soon as Carlos had sat down, Anahu told him about the special news flash— they had an ex-Marine in their group.

Carlos glanced at Marco, head back, feet up, eyes closed. "Does Fire know?" he asked.

Marco stirred, shaking his head negatively. "No need."

Carlos nodded in understanding. The fiery bitch was nothing but a goddamn woman. He picked at his front teeth with his fingernail, then slammed down his hand on the coffee table. "It's that big nigger. Those rubber gloves. I'll kill 'em."

Marco swung his feet off the coffee table and sat up,

blue eyes wide and cold. "No you won't," he spat out. "If it's Jumbo, he's my man."

"You'll need help," Carlos said, eyes mocking the younger terrorist.

"Fuck you, chicken lips," Marco snarled. "The guy can't know we suspect anything. I'll unmask him. If it's not Jumbo, he's dead." He picked up his AK-47 and stood up. "I'll tattoo him." His little boy smile was firmly in place.

Colonel Donahue was meeting with his senior field officers and the hostage negotiation team when they heard the announcement on television about the Marines having a man inside the resort. The air inside the command tent was instantly filled with short, pithy curses about the media, slowly calming to frustration and anger.

"Some son-of-a-bitch leaked this information. They'll kill McGregor for sure. I'd like to get my hands on that . . ." The colonel pushed away the last of his chicken salad sandwich, swallowed his coffee, and rose from his chair. Grabbing his weapons belt from a hook on the side of his vehicle, he strapped it on over his dark green jumpsuit, then began smearing his face and hands with combat blackening.

"That settles it. This situation won't stay stable long. I'm going in. McGregor needs help now, not in the hereafter." The colonel turned to face the head of the hostage negotiation team. "McKenna, I want your group in place, talking to the terrorists at least a half-hour before the President's speech. Promise that redheaded bitch anything—just keep her talking."

McKenna nodded, grim faced. He knew the plan.

Putting on his helmet, Donahue turned to Murray. "Cover their every movement with sharpshooters. Set up a crossfire. But don't shoot until the President finishes talking. Then," he gestured to the officer, "pick off every fucking terrorist you see."

"Luke," Donahue put his hand on Major Baldwin's broad shoulder, "you're in charge. The President finishes, move in, hit them hard—full force. No firing toward the lounge. Mac and I will be in there with the hostages."

Baldwin looked at him levelly. He knew what to do. Reaching for the colonel's hand, he said simply, "The Lord be with you."

Donahue smiled, his white teeth in stark contrast to his blackened face. He touched the small Bible in the left breast pocket of his combat jacket. "The Lord may be waiting for us to do something," he said, picking up his assault rifle, turning, and starting toward the rise separating the Marine command tent from the Molokai-Surf. He sucked in his stomach. It was do-it-yourself time.

Major Murray spoke first. "I still think he's wrong to go in there. His command is here. The old man is stubborn, headstrong and," Murray's shoulders squared, "brave."

Fleming's eyes were on the back of the colonel. "He's got a right to be wrong. A leader has to have the right to make his own mistakes. This isn't war. Dealing with terrorists takes experience, guts and a helluva lot of luck. He and McGregor together may just pull it off."

Baldwin's eyes narrowed. "The colonel's right. They don't teach it at Quantico, and you can't learn it from a book. Knowing when to make your move and when to lay back. It's instinct." The rawboned major watched the colonel until he went over the top of the rise out of sight, then his eyes moved back to the others in the tent. "It's one of the penalties of leadership. Every once in a while you have to get your ass out front and lead."

"That man's got a heart that goes along with his pride and guts!" Unseen by the others, Fleming crossed himself.

Mac reached Jumbo's outpost just in time to see the pinpoint flash of light aimed at him. A Marine was coming in. Mac blinked his shielded SabreLite, saw the answering blink, then through the nightscope watched the Marine's progress on foot down the thirteenth fairway. The man moved with a distinctive lope, covering ground with the fluid grace of a tight end. He was a big man. Mac's eyes narrowed. There was something familiar in the way the man moved. Mac shook his head and looked again. Images of Korea and a dark place near Pusan flashed through his mind. The memory was still fresh, like an open wound. No, that had been long ago. It couldn't be. Old furnace-face would be a senior bird colonel by now, with his own command. Only young leathernecks went out on patrol behind enemy lines.

In the dark sky great heavy clouds were massing, and the rain had begun falling lightly. Moving rapidly, Donahue felt as if he were going up a one-way street the wrong way. Mind tense, nerves on edge, adrenaline pumping, imagination working overtime, expecting the worst without warning, cradling the automatic rifle in his weatherbeaten hands, the colonel crossed the thirteenth tee and swung up the cart path headed toward the twelfth green. His breathing eased. No one had fired at him. McGregor must have neutralized the terrorist guarding the other outpost. Old Mac was reliable.

Crouching low, Donahue moved across the green and down the slope, heading diagonally between the green and the big bunker on his right. He would be out of the line of fire from Angel's old station now. Mac's outpost covered this area. Donahue swallowed the thought in his throat—unless the terrorists had been shifted around. No, he'd gotten the answering flash from the corner room near the ocean. McGregor was still there.

Seeing the line of freshly disturbed earth ahead, the colonel felt a new trickle of fear, an old and familiar sensation. Sucking up his courage, he crouched lower and moved on, each step expecting an explosion which he'd never get to hear.

Mac stared with disbelief. The big Marine was built like his old buddy, Donahue. Moving with sure instinct, he snaked through the path that Mac had cleared. There was no doubt the Marine was a heavyweight, a tough guy to ignore. The man moved like Preach. Mac chuckled at the memories. They'd called him Preacher because the big man had the voice of a southern reverend and always carried a small Bible with him. Claimed it was his bulletproof vest. The name stuck because Preach was always using the Lord's name.

It couldn't be him, but the lovable bastard had always been a hands-on guy, coming up with the unexpected, a maverick original, a bird colonel out on the point! Mac grinned. A strong bird needed a lot of room to fly.

Less than two minutes later Colonel Donahue, assault rifle at the ready, moved silently up the stairs toward the corner room. Mac waited patiently. Outside the doorway Donahue moved to one side in a crouched position, and hand on grenade, whispered, "Mac McGregor, I presume?"

Mac recognized the raw Tennessee voice instantly. "Preacher, what the hell are you doing here?" Pulling off his mask, he leapt from the chair. The two old friends clasped hands in the center of the room, both grinning broadly.

"Everybody's got to be someplace. It seemed the right thing to do," the colonel said softly. "Goddamn.

Just like old times. You never could handle anything yourself."

Mac laughed aloud. The years had been kind to Donahue, but his face was now rugged as parchment. "I've got to admit I'm glad to see you. They cared enough to send the very best."

Donahue laughed back. "Well, maybe the second best. The very best was already in here." McGregor looked fit, but the old fart was bald as a billiard ball. His face hadn't changed at all. Now his age fit it.

Suddenly the laugh on Donahue's face was replaced by a serious look. "They know about you." He ran a finger across his throat. "'The goddamn T.V."

The smile left Mac's face. "I know, I heard."

"They'll come looking for you."

"Probably Marco."

"He'll come alone?"

Mac nodded. "I'm sure they don't know I know they know."

Donahue's eyes narrowed. "Maybe we should let him find you."

Mac grinned. "I was thinking the same thing. But," his eyes caught Donahue's, "Marco's mine."

The grin back on Donahue's face said it all. He was still a vicious bastard. When the going got gruesome, the colonel wouldn't blink an eye.

Sitting at a small table in front of a television set at the Bloody Duck bar in the Pau Hana Inn in Kaunakakai, the tanned young man with the blonde, wavy hair, in the yellow Adidas shirt inhaled deeply to calm himself. He felt hyper again, blood pounding through his veins. His exclusive news report had been given prime time coverage under his own byline, "KHOL Special Reporter—

Lloyd Reynolds.'' He smiled broadly. It had probably gone out on all three networks. One more scoop and they'd hire him permanently.

The bar was crowded. The regular customers, the *paniolos*—real Hawaiian cowboys in their faded blue jeans and aloha shirts—local wahines in their bright print dresses, and a few plantation workers mixed with a sprinkling of tourists and a crush of reporters, photographers, cameramen, and technicians covering the terrorist takeover. Most of the media people had no intention of getting any closer to the Molokai-Surf. To them the bar at the Pau Hana was the front line. Their dateline was Molokai and the best terrorist stories were being generated at the bar. The Bloody Duck was the liveliest spot on the island.

The room that buzzed with the rich and melodious sounds of pidgin and Hawaiian English quieted during the special news bulletin. Now it buzzed again, at an even higher level. The overhead fans stirred the conversation and moved the heavy moisture-laden air.

Lloyd Reynolds turned to the young man in the navy-blue windbreaker sitting with him at the small table and flashed a smile. ''You and me, Banyan, we scooped the pool.''

The fellow with the dark wavy hair and the bland pudding face stared back at Reynolds with his coal black eyes and felt nauseated. For the last four years he'd been KHOL's roving cameraman. He'd always operated alone, solo. Until this evening, when Reynolds had knocked on his motel door, he'd never seen or heard of the baby-faced reporter. It had been instant dislike. Now, seeing the special news report, he was ashamed of KHOL. It was not their kind of reporting, risking a man's life, just for a story. It was sensational yellow journalism, updated for television. Reynolds was a moral cripple, a night crawler with evil in his face and nervous, brooding eyes.

"Nice guys never finish nice," the reporter said matter-of-factly, with a little smirk on his face. "Unless you put yourself on center stage, you can't be great."

Bob Banyan grimaced and took another swallow of his *okolehao*. The damn glass kept refilling itself with that skull-popping, rumlike concoction. Tonight he felt like an empty suit, a half track. Fatigue was taking over; his mind was drifting, lurching from one thought to another. It couldn't be the drinks. He'd only had three or four, and drinking was his specialty, the thing he did best. It was that goddamned baby-faced flake staring at him, cigarette dangling insolently from his lips. The guy was probably gay. If he made one pass, it would be a pleasure to kick the *mahu* in the balls.

He should never have told Reynolds that he was going back to the Molokai-Surf with the marine negotiation team. He'd seen the green flash of jealousy in the blond's eyes. He had to get back to his room and get his head in shape. McKenna was supposed to call him with the details. "I've got to be going," he said.

"Suck 'em up," Reynolds said, a hint of a smile in the corner of his mouth, but there was no humor in it.

Banyan gulped the *okolehao*, anxious to get away from the probing eyes. He never noticed the white powder that Reynolds had dropped into the drink while he'd been watching the news special. He whipped his head back and forth to shake off the blue haze descending on his thoughts. He was rapidly swimming out of focus, dissolving in a puddle of panic.

He saw a giant gecko scamper across the table, jump down, and run up on the small stage where a hula girl with tantalizing hips was swaying to the music of a feathered gourd. His eyes undressed the beautiful young wahine, took her apart, and slowly reassembled her. The wriggling, naked body was replaced by a magnificent golden eye that filled his entire field of vision. The eye kept winking at him in time with the music.

Lloyd snapped his fingers to attract the attention of the waitress. "Add ten percent and charge it to room 12. Mr. Banyan doesn't feel well." He took hold of the arm of the windbreaker, pulling the other man to his feet and leading him out of the bar.

In room twelve, Reynolds pushed the cameraman onto the double bed and undressed him. He gave a satisfied chuckle. The windbreaker and blue jeans were a size large, but they'd do fine. From Banyan's wallet, Lloyd appropriated his license, press card, and KHOL identification. Now he checked the contents of the room. The camera case and equipment were on the closet floor. He opened the case and took out the portable Panasonic and breathed easier. It was simple to operate. On the top of the dresser he found the pass to cross through the Marine lines.

Reynolds undressed down to his undershorts and walked into the bathroom, carrying a small package and Banyan's hair dryer. For almost a minute he stared into the mirror, then opened a package of black hair dye that he'd bought that afternoon at Kappa's Drugstore, mixing it in the bowl of the sink. Slowly, with a washcloth, he patted the solution onto his head. Finished, he dried his hair with the blower, watching his actions closely in the mirror. His build was similar to Banyan's. The odds were that no one would check closely. The hair color was the key. The face in the mirror winked at him. With the dark hair, he looked more mature.

Back in the bedroom he stared at Banyan's lily-white buttocks. Maybe he'd teach the bastard a lesson. Grabbing the other's feet, he rolled the body over. The coal-black eyes stared unwinkingly back at him. Smiling wryly, he prodded the cameraman with the hot hair dryer. Banyan's body flopped like a fish, the whites of his eyes turning red. "Crazy!" Lloyd muttered, and poked him again.

The phone on the dresser rang and Reynolds picked it up.

"Bob Banyan?" the voice on the other end asked.

"Speaking."

"Colonel McKenna here. If you're still game, my driver will pick you up at five tomorrow morning."

"In front of my motel?"

"Yes."

"I'll be ready."

"Thanks, and good night.

"Good night, sir."

Reynolds checked his watch. He had only six hours to sleep. Turning back to the bed, a look of disgust crossed his face. Some people just couldn't tolerate drugs. They went down the chemical dumper. Sitting on the bed, he set the alarm on Banyan's travel clock and turned out the light. Rolling over, his hands touched the body alongside. Shit, he didn't have time for games. With his legs he pushed Banyan slowly to the edge of the bed and in a singsong voice said, "Humpty Dumpty sat on a wall . . ." With one last nudge, the body toppled over and crashed to the floor. Reynolds laughed wildly. Humpty Dumpty was pushed—everybody knew that.

The cameraman would be out for at least twelve hours, probably longer. His mind would be muddled for days, and he'd have no memory of what had happened. Tomorrow was going to be Reynolds's big day. He'd scoop everyone and have it all on film. His fortune was made. Rolling back, he curled into a fetal position and closed his eyes.

The big frame of Jumbo slouched in the swivel chair, back to the door, head bent over resting on the night-scope pointed out the window overlooking the golf course.

Marco moved noiselessly up the stairs and down the hall, hesitating at the door to the corner room, eyes adjusting, sensing the presence of another, then seeing the silhouette of Jumbo outlined against the window. The boyish grin was on Marco's face. The big man didn't suspect anything. Now he moved toward the big bulk in the chair, Kalashnikov pointed at his back.

"Turn around, Jumbo!" Marco's command was a snarl.

The big form of Jumbo didn't move.

"Turn around, you slimy gyrene!" Marco bit down hard on his anger.

The big frame stayed still.

The quiet of the room was shattered by the burst of rapid fire from Marco's assault rifle. The bullets slammed into Jumbo's back, tearing a hole in the big camouflage jacket, blowing the mask off the broad shoulders, revealing the sheets and towels stuffed inside.

"I'll be a son-of-a-beeeech!" The words ended in a horribly inhuman squeal as a thin cord snaked around Marco's neck, blocking the carotid arteries, silencing his screech, dimming his thoughts, wiping away the little boy smile, bulging the cobalt blue eyes, ending his life.

Mac dropped Marco's body to the floor. Donahue stepped out of the darkened corner, M-16 still pointed at Marco.

"You haven't lost your touch," the big Marine colonel said, admiration in his voice. "You're still world class."

Mac stood, head bowed, mouth grim, eyes staring at the lifeless form. "Death is always sacred," he said softly. "Even for a scum like this one."

Donahue swung his rifle to cover the stairs. "We'd better move," he whispered. "The gunfire might attract others."

Mac nodded. They glided down the stairway like two shadows on the wall. The shadows hesitated at the doorway.

The night was turning nasty, the rain coming down hard now, the wind rising. Donahue slipped on his Marine poncho, and from a small pack produced another one for Mac. "For the duration, I guess you're back in the Marines," he said with a smile.

"It's been a while," Mac said, putting on the poncho. "Even my tattoos are faded." Suddenly he stiffened. "Jesus, we'd better haul up Moses. The poor bastard could drown in this."

Fire heard the burst of rapid fire, and swung her body off the bed. Even in the blur of waking she recognized the distinctive whine of the Kalashnikov. One of her group was shooting. But in the distance, at Jumbo's outpost. There had been no return fire from the Marines. She headed for the lobby. Damn, she couldn't even take a nap. If she sat on the toilet, the phone would ring.

Anahu saw Fire coming and met her at the front entrance. In a low voice he explained what had happened.

"Why didn't you wake me?" she asked, voice rising, shaking the rain from her curly hair.

Anahu shrugged, a sheepish look on his face. Carlos wiped his finger on his trousers, ran his tongue over his crooked teeth, and said, "Relax, Red. Everything's under control. Blue-eyes just blew taps for an old ex-Marine.''

Fire looked out at the tropical rain. ''It's closing in,'' she said. ''I think we should pull our men in from the outposts, cover the perimeter of the lounge, close in. The hostages are the key. If we play them tight, the Marines won't dare attack.''

Carlos's deep-set eyes stared at the tall girl. She had a good military mind. ''You said 'think.' Is that an order?'' he asked, running the back of his hand under his pronounced nose.

''Yes,'' Fire snapped, choking off her irritation. The grizzled terrorist was still jealous that she was in command. It was eating him like acid.

Carlos picked up his walkie-talkie and gave the new orders to Ivan and Kimo. ''Move back, set the booby-traps.'' Michael was in the Koa Lounge. Fire, Anahu, and he were in the lobby. He couldn't raise either Moses or Marco. Moses was probably listening to his damn radio and Marco was on the move. When Marco got back, he could fuckin' well tell Moses himself.

Mac led Donahue along the top of the cliff, the heavy tropical rain driven by half a gale from the southwest stinging their faces, blinding their vision, making talk almost impossible. They reached the ironwood tree. Mac breathed a sigh of relief. The rope was still tied to the tree, timber-hitch securely in place.

Donahue moved close to Mac, a puzzled look on his face.

Mac gestured. The colonel put down his assault rifle and together they pulled on the rope. Slowly the bundle containing Moses moved up the side of the cliff. They swung the soggy, lumpy mattress cover up over the rock

ledge at the top and set it gently on the ground. Mac
could see movement in the bag, but the antenna had
been pulled in. The radio was off, the bag silent. Donahue recovered his rifle as Mac's knife slit the top of the
mattress cover. A pair of rubber gloves emerged, then
Moses wriggled his lanky frame out of the body bag. He
came out like a caged animal, on all fours. Rolling to his
knees, the tall, thin black man had difficulty standing
on his shaking legs. Pushing himself erect, he reached
his hand into his pocket.

For one moment Donahue saw a knife that wasn't
there. The barrel of his M-16 swung to touch the back of
Moses' head. It was then that Moses realized that his
rescuers were dressed in Marine ponchos. Both men
heard his mournful swearing.

With a signal to move out, Mac led the way. Moses
followed, and the colonel brought up the rear. An idea
was forming in Mac's head, but they needed to get inside where he could talk it over with Donahue. With the
wind at his back, he headed for Moses' old outpost.

Inside, the rain drummed on the roof and slashed
against the windows. The two big men took off their
ponchos. Soaked to the skin, Moses took off all of his
clothes. Mac tossed him a towel, and the tall, thin man
dried himself thoroughly. Moses pointed to his small
satchel in the corner, and Mac picked out clean underwear, jeans, and T-shirt. While Moses put them on,
Mac wrung out his terrorist outfit, mask and all, and
hung it to dry over the bathtub.

"Thought I was goin' down the dumper," Moses
said, sitting in a chair, face still drained of normal color.
"I was swingin' like a pendulum in that wind, hangin'
by a spider thread. Love the open spaces, but that
Jumbo hung me out. I'll kill that big black prick."

Moses' mind was rambling, mouth repeating thoughts aloud.

Mac moved a chair and sat facing Moses. The thin man stared at the big man's face, then pointed. "Damn, man, you got purple marks 'round your eyes." A light of understanding broke on Moses' face, and his mouth gaped open. "You're . . ."

"Jumbo," Mac said quietly.

"A whitey?"

Mac nodded.

"You damned near killed me. What are you? A fuckin' nut?" Moses' mouth was sullen, both eyes now bloodshot and intense.

"I saved your ass. You're alive, aren't you?"

"Haven't been this happy since parole day," Moses growled. "All that leprosy horseshit. Soul brothers. In the next life, I'm gonna be white. You grow up in Harlem."

Mac grinned. "Sounds fair."

A scowl and a smile competed for a place on the black's face. The scowl won. He sat like a stone, drained, empty, betrayed. The Marines had him. It was back to prison. That was worse than death. Eyes searching the room, he saw his AK-47 still in the corner.

Donahue's eyes caught Mac's, and his lateral head movement said, "Let's talk." They moved to one side of the room. Moses stayed seated on his chair.

"What are you up to?" the colonel asked, eyes still riveted on the terrorist.

"We need Moses." Mac spoke in a voice loud enough for the tall, thin man to hear. "If he helps us save the hostages, Preach, you could get him a pardon."

"Don't pump sunshine up his ass," the big Marine warned. "I'll do my best, but don't make promises I can't keep. A promise never made can't be broken.''

"Two hundred and sixteen lives ought to be worth a pardon—and a new identity here in Hawaii.''

Moses' ears were straining. A pardon and a new identity. But this was the same guy who'd hung him over the cliff. His old man had told him, you don't learn anything the second time you get kicked by a mule.

"Moses can get into the lounge. He's one of them. He can distract Anahu, let us get to the plunger, disarm it.''

"Trust him?'' Donahue's eyes went wide. "He'll lie to live.''

"Colonel, Moses has found the Lord. He told me so. He's a believer, just like you.'' Mac tapped the small Bible in Donahue's jacket. "He's got the Lord in his pocket, too.''

Donahue looked closely at Mac's eyes and had trouble reading them.

"The Bible tells us Moses killed a man and ran away. God forgave him, used him. Should it be different now? This Moses has paid his dues. If he helps save the hostages, he should get a chance at a new life. For him, the alternatives aren't too good. Back in the States, he'll wind up in a trash compactor. The terrorists had his cement shoes already fitted with dynamite caps.''

Moses was tempted. But he'd learned the hard way not to trust anyone. Live for opportunities, when you see one, grab it. His eyes moved from the assault rifle to the two Marines and back to the Kalashnikov. It was a close decision. As fast as he moved, he wasn't fast enough. The colonel's rifle butt caught him behind the ear, just as his long, thin hands touched the gun. He crumpled to the floor.

Mac trussed him up and put a gag in his mouth. "I had to give him a chance,'' Mac said. "It's too bad. The son-of-a-bitch could have helped.'' He picked up the

AK-47, removing the banana-shaped clip and tossing it to Donahue. "Oh, yeah, Preach. I took the bullets out when we first came in."

The big Marine shook his close-cropped head and almost smiled. "Don't do that again. You tease an old man's brain too much, it turns mean."

Mac moved Moses into one corner, then stared out the window. The rain seemed to be letting up.

"Without Marco and Moses, they're down to six," Mac said quietly. "Six sadists—a dirty bunch."

"They'll have to pull back." Donahue gestured. "A tight little circle around the hostages."

Mac nodded his agreement. "They don't have enough men left to man the outposts."

"We could bring in a squad or two."

Mac nodded again. It was time.

The colonel moved to the window and blinked his light. From the top of the rise came an answering wink of light. Donahue flashed back a prearranged signal.

Peering through the nightscope, Mac could see the movement now. They came in single file. Crouching, running, crouching, then running again, following the trail Donahue had used. He counted twelve of them. He could tell from the way they moved that they were professionals.

Four of the Marines entered the room. Mac could smell the pride. Swiveling the chair around, he stared at them. It was like looking into a forty-year-old mirror. God, they were young. Trim, lean, fit teenagers with shiny dog tags and sparkle in their eyes, fresh from the pugil-stick pits at Parris Island. He suddenly felt shriveled up, ancient. Standing up, all of his bones hurt. He sighed wistfully.

Two Marines carried Moses out of the room. He could hear Donahue talking in a low voice to a young lieutenant in the hallway just outside the room. "Keep your men out of sight. Spread out. Take the perimeter buildings. No noise, no gunfire. Don't risk the lives of the hostages."

Donahue came back into the room, picked up his light, and flashed another signal out the window. Mac knew Preacher was ordering more Marines into the complex. It was sound military strategy, but Mac felt uneasy. Things were going to get ugly. They were moving into sudden death time. It had to be played minute by minute. One mistake, and it was all over. The hostages would never be freed by strength. It had to be by guile. They didn't need numbers, they needed smarts.

When Donahue turned away from the window, Mac suggested, "We've got to get in close. We need two volunteers. A guy Marco's size with bright blue eyes and a tall, thin, jivey black. Two men who will fit into the terrorist outfits we've got."

The big Marine sat down, reached into his pocket, and fished out a pack of Marlboros. He offered one to McGregor and took one himself. Mac saw the battered lighter and smiled. It brought back memories of times they'd survived using only their wits and cunning. The colonel's eyes looked off into the distance, as if thinking similar thoughts. His eyes crinkled at the edges, the furrows in his brow smoothed away.

"Major Fleming's on his way in. He'll take over here. I thought the two of us might do some scouting in closer to the lounge."

Mac blew a perfect smoke ring, barely visible in the dim light.

"By the time we get back, Fleming will have our two volunteers dressed and ready." The colonel stood up.

Mac finished his cigarette and snuffed it out in the ashtray. "Don't forget the rubber gloves on Moses."

"Why the hell was that cat wearing rubber gloves?" Donahue asked.

Mac touched the lucky beans in his pocket, glanced at the small bulge in the colonel's breast pocket and smiled. "I guess some people are superstitious. Let's just say he wore them to ward off evil spirits."

Lieutenant Colonel Red McKenna hung up the radio-phone, a look of concern on his face.

"I told Fire we're going to arrive first thing in the morning to watch the President's speech with her . . ."

Captain Bailey half closed his eyes, his face wrinkled with apprehension.

Major Corwin sat on the edge of his cot, scratching the back of his neck nervously.

"I told the terrorist bitch that the President wanted us there, that he's going to go along with her demands, and we have to work out the details." McKenna rubbed his bad knee. It always hurt when he lied.

Bailey and Corwin looked at one another. Bailey spoke first. "She knew you were lying."

McKenna shrugged. "Who knows?"

"She told you to fuck off, didn't she?" Jim Corwin asked.

The tall redhead shook his head negatively. "No. It was blunter than that. She said if we drove up to the Molokai-Surf, she'd kill all three of us."

Bailey and Corwin both closed their eyes. McKenna scuffed his foot angrily in the red mud. They fell into a brief silence, in each of their thoughts their worst fears becoming monsters.

"We've got our orders," McKenna said.

Bailey nodded. "Maybe she's lying, too."

"We go in, like we planned." Corwin made it unanimous.

CHAPTER SEVENTEEN

Third Day—Midnight to Dawn

Donahue and McGregor were putting on their ponchos when they heard a small explosion from the other side of the resort. The colonel swore. Both men knew instantly, having heard the sound many times before, the unmistakable whump of a booby trap.

A breathless runner burst into the room confirming their thoughts. "Sergeant Harris, sir. He just bought it. Their nightscope had a trip wire on it."

"Pass the word. Don't touch anything. And get a medic over there." Donahue's face was grim.

The runner moved out in search of a body bag.

"Goddamn! It's one of the first things they're supposed to learn, Mac. They never do. Harris was one of the best."

Mac shook his head sadly. "We also lost the element of surprise. They know you're in here now."

The colonel's face showed he knew it.

In the lobby, Fire and Carlos both heard the explosion and exchanged glances. She noticed that the crooked grin was on the chameleon's face. He spoke out of the corner of his mouth. "The Marines are moving closer."

"Fuck the Marines, we've got the hostages," Fire snapped.

Carlos's grin left his face. "They've probably got Marco and Moses."

Fifteen minutes later, the two big men in ponchos crouched in the shelter of a huge umbrella-shaped heliotrope plant, their backs to the driving rain. Donahue, chewing on one of the leaves, plucked another and offered it to Mac. "Try one, they're good. Tastes like parsley."

Mac shook his head, spraying water from side to side. He thought momentarily of their golden retriever back home, wading out of the river, then shaking himself dry, spraying water all over Marge while the two of them laughed. Bending forward, he adjusted the portable nightscope.

"What do you see?" the colonel asked.

"They've set up two gun emplacements on the lanai, guarding the entrance to the lounge. There's a terrorist manning each one."

Donahue swore softly.

"They've probably done the same in the front lobby. One man just inside the door out of the rain." Mac wiped the water from his face.

"Any other way in?"

"There's a service entrance on the side of the building. It leads to the kitchen area which connects to the lounge. But I've never been back there. Don't know the layout."

The colonel picked another leaf and began chewing thoughtfully. "We talked this morning to several of the locals who used to work in the kitchen. The storerooms are in the basement. Stairway and conveyer belt up to the kitchen. Heavy metal doors to the outside. Double doors on the inside, top and bottom. Locks and bolts and an alarm system."

"I thought there was no theft in Hawaii."

"It's getting as bad as the mainland."

"Knowing this group, they've probably booby trapped any door they're not using."

Donahue winced, lips tightening as if in pain as he thought of Harris.

"I'd forget the unknown. It's too risky. We've got to go through the lanai and the front entrance." Mac glanced at the colonel and forced a smile. "Just like the tourists."

"Let me take a look."

McGregor moved aside and Donahue peered through the nightscope. He swore again. "We'll have to take those two first."

Mac said nothing. It wasn't going to be easy—without any noise and without alerting the terrorists inside. The wind and the heavy rain would help. But they'd all be on pins and needles now.

The big Marine officer folded up the nightscope, then stood up. "Let's go back inside where it's dry."

As they were leaving, Mac picked a leaf and took a small bite. It wasn't bad, it did taste like parsley. He blinked his eyes, hoping the leaf was loaded with caffeine.

Donahue led the way back to the corner outpost and introduced Mac to Major Fleming. The inside perimeter just out of sight of the main lounge was now crowded with Marines in full battle dress. It looked like they were getting ready for an all-out assault, a fire fight.

"I've got the two men you asked for. They're ready. What's the plan?" the major asked eagerly.

The major was too anxious, Mac thought, staring at the big man's bushy eyebrows, smiling wearily, saying nothing.

Donahue interrupted the silence. "I'm anxious to get your thoughts, Mac. Where can we find a quiet spot?"

"How about some coffee? My place, ocean suite seven."

After the second cup of black coffee and his third cigarette, Mac started talking. "There are six terrorists left. Two of them are guarding the lanai. If we can take those two out they'll have only four left."

"It only takes one to push the plunger," the colonel said grimly.

Mac nodded, then looked around at the others, seeing only shapes in the darkness. "Neither Fire nor Carlos will be on outside guard duty. Anahu is Fire's right hand man. He does what she says. He'll be the one to throw the switch, so that big bastard will be on guard duty in the lounge. Simple elimination leaves Ivan, the bearded one, he's iron curtain, I'm sure; Kimo, another Hawaiian cutthroat; and Michael, the big blond. Two of these three will be on the lanai."

"Why are their identities so important?" The major's voice reflected his impatience.

"It's critical for the final action. Take those two out and you have four left. Fire, Carlos, Anahu, and Mr. X. We know where Anahu will be."

"We're planning to make our move during the President's speech," Donahue interrupted.

Mac nodded again. "Both Fire and Carlos will want to hear whether he'll go along with their demand. We all assume he won't."

"We know he won't," Fleming said flatly.

Mac stood up and poured another cup of coffee, the small red light on the coffeemaker the only light in the room.

"The minute he says no the hostages are dead."

"They'll really blow the place?" the major asked, his shaggy white eyebrows climbing high onto his forehead.

"Absolutely. No question in my mind," Mac answered grimly, sitting back down.

"The terrorists, too?" Donahue asked.

Brow wrinkling, Mac rubbed his head before answering. "That's different. I don't think either Fire or Carlos plan to go with them. They're not the suicidal type, but they'll waste the others. If they try to escape, it could buy us some time."

"They can't get out. We've got them surrounded," Fleming said.

"They could take a few hostages with them."

"My God, our three-man negotiation team will be in there, too," Donahue said, remembering his orders.

"Armed?" Mac asked.

"No."

"Hidden weapons?"

"Nothing. It's against their code." The colonel shrugged his big shoulders, as if in apology.

A strong gust of wind rattled the sliding glass doors, and Mac's head turned toward them. The rain was slanting in under the overhang now, pelting against the glass in a steady drumbeat. So Fire and Carlos would have a vehicle if they wanted to use it, and three special hostages. It really didn't matter. By then it should be all over. One way or the other.

"Visibility outside is about zero. I think we could risk some light." Donahue clicked on the small table lamp alongside the couch. The sudden glare caused all three to blink.

Fleming glanced nervously at his watch. It was one-twenty A.M. and they still didn't have a plan. He could feel his neck and shoulder muscles tightening. He popped a Rolaid into his mouth.

Mac leaned forward. "The final action depends on timing. Anahu at one switch, Mr. X at the other. Fire and Carlos roaming loose. We've got to keep their attention on the President for as long as possible."

Donahue flipped out a cigarette, lit it, and passed it across the coffee table to Mac, lit one for himself and inhaled deeply. "Take out the two at the control centers. It's a race for the buttons."

Mac nodded.

"Have to take them both . . ."

"At exactly the same instant."

The colonel inhaled again. "We'll need a signal."

"Clear as a bell."

"I'll take one. You the other?"

Mac suddenly grinned broadly. "Our own one for one plan."

Donahue grinned back, flexed his fingers and stood up. "Goddamn arthritis."

"We're all getting old," Mac said sadly.

Donahue glanced at his watch and reached for his poncho. "I'm going out to the command post and call Washington." His light blue eyes were twinkling. "I've always wanted to wake up the President."

Major Fleming's jaw was clenched. He still didn't understand the plan and the colonel was leaving. He reached into his pocket for another Rolaid.

Mac clicked off the light as Donahue opened the outside door. When the door closed, he clicked it back on and turned toward Fleming. "Major, why don't you get those two young men—Moses and Marco—in here? I think it's time we get going."

It was a few minutes before three in the morning when James Mason nudged Max Parker. The agent opened his eyes slowly and followed Mason's gesture. Anahu was leaving the main lounge. Only Ivan was left on guard. Most of the hostages were asleep. The wind-driven rain slashed against the windows.

Parker took a few minutes to collect his thoughts. The big Hawaiian terrorist was probably going to take a three or four hour nap. That seemed to be the pattern. If he and the Brit were ever going to make a move, this was probably as good a chance as they'd ever get. The President's speech was first thing in the morning. If he said the wrong things, it could get very ugly. Everything could blow sky high. Parker knew that Mason's thoughts had to be similar. Catching the Englishman's glance, he nodded his agreement.

About ten minutes later, Mason rose, stretched, smoothed a few of the rumples from his blue silk pajamas, slipped on his dressing gown and moved toward the men's room. Ivan's eyes followed the thin, wiry man until he disappeared inside the door.

Parker waited almost a full minute, then stood up, adjusting his boxer shorts. He yawned audibly, attracting Ivan's attention, then moved slowly towards the chair where the terrorist was sitting, the plunger connected to the plastic-explosives resting between his knees. The agent's mind ran through the simple plan. As soon as Mason came out of the men's room, Parker would stagger and fall to the floor, clutching his chest, diverting Ivan's attention. Mason would cut the primer cords between the plunger and the first explosive pack-

ages. Then, if the switch were activated the C-4 charges
wouldn't explode. Parker crossed two of his fingers.
Ivan watched the big man moving toward him, AK-47
pointed directly at the center of Parker's T-shirt.

Inside the men's room, Mason moved to the left-hand
booth. Closing the door, he raised the toilet seat and relieved himself. First things first, he thought. Finished,
he put down the seat, then removed the white ceramic
top of the water tank behind the toilet and set the top on
the seat. Peering down into the bluish colored water in
the tank, he couldn't see the paper bag containing the
Vise-Grip pliers. Rolling up his right sleeve, he reached
his hand into the water under the float, feeling for the
bag. His hand closed on the bag and felt the pliers. In
the murky water, Mason never saw the thin trip wire
that had been attached to the bag. He lifted the bag.

The sharp explosion dissolved the water tank, shattered the toilet bowl, and blew away most of James
Mason's head.

Fifteen feet in front of the Russian terrorist, Max
Parker heard the explosion. His eyes, focused on Ivan's
face, blinked once before Ivan shot him dead.

The rest of the hostages woke in terror. There were
screams and shouts and then a mournful quiet, interrupted by the occasional sound of sobbing. Anahu and
Carlos burst into the room from the lobby, assault rifles
at the ready. Kimo and Michael came in from the lanai.
Ivan told them what had happened. After checking the
men's room and the dead bodies, the terrorists moved
up and down the grid of primer cord, checking to make
sure that none of it had been cut or disconnected and
that the plastic explosive was still in place. Satisfied, the
terrorists dragged the lifeless bodies of Max Parker and
James Mason across the corner of the lounge, through
the lobby and out the front entrance, leaving a thin red

trail behind them. Placing the two corpses underneath the veranda overhang, they threw a blanket over each one. With the toe of his boot Anahu kicked the corners of the blankets under the bodies.

Finished, the big Hawaiian glanced out at the driving rain. The wind was shifting. It would probably clear by dawn. He wiped his bloody hands on his pants, then spoke aloud, as much to himself as to the others. "I told Fire that booby trap would work. It was just a question of who left those pliers there." He paused and a grim look crossed his face. "I hoped it was that fat guy, the one with Candy."

"You're jealous," grinned Kimo.

"Up yours," replied Anahu. "Get back to your posts."

Dan Hanson heard the explosion and watched Parker's death with a sickening hollow feeling at the bottom of his stomach. It was a bitter and empty end for two brave men. Candy woke with a start, and Dan held her close and turned her head away as they dragged the two bodies past. It was almost half an hour later that he whispered, "It's almost time." He could feel her body stiffen. "I've got to make my move."

Candy gasped aloud, and Dan's hand covered her mouth. Rising on one knee, he turned his head and stared into the barrel of a Kalashnikov held by the snarling Anahu.

"We'll tie up everyone," the big Hawaiian said to Ivan. "And we'll start with these two."

Candy's gasp was almost one of joy. Dan wasn't going anywhere.

Mac was impressed. The young, tall, thin, black Marine called Socrates was perfect, a jivey ham, heavy into jazz, another Moses. Eric, the boy with the swarthy, handsome face and the blue eyes, would pass as Marco. His eyes weren't cobalt color, nor hard and cruel, and the mean streak wasn't there, but he'd do. Both terrorist outfits fit fine, except for the tennis shoes that had been worn by Marco. In the darkness and the rain Eric's combat boots would have to do.

"This isn't going to be easy," Mac said for the tenth time. "They'll be watching you all the way. Kalashnikovs pointed right at your chests. Your rifles won't do you any good. I've taken the bullets out so you won't be tempted to use them. They've got their backs to the wall and they're crouched behind a low barricade. Best I can make out bags of sugar and cases of canned goods, piled about three feet high. I'll be with you, but . . ." Mac looked at the two boys closely. To think he was once that young. "You'll each have to take your own man."

Mac turned to the big major. "Cover us, but no firing. There are 216 hostages in there. If this works, it's a thirty-second operation. If not, forget us. Are the two karate experts ready?"

The white-haired Marine officer nodded.

"Are you sure these goddamned Tasers will work?" Mac picked up one of the two flashlight-sized weapons on the table.

Fleming's big hand picked up the other one. Mac noticed the Marine's thick arms. "It delivers a shot of 50,000 volts."

"And it doesn't kill?"

"No. There aren't any amperes."

Mac shook his head. Science was beyond him. "Any noise?"

"None."

"Okay." Mac gestured to the two young Marines dressed as terrorists and pointed toward the bathroom. "Take your nervous pee, then we'll move out. Just in case, keep your knives handy.'' His hand dropped to the one on his belt.

Moving single file, the small group was almost in sight of the lanai when they heard the explosion inside the lounge and the burst from the Kalashnikov.

"They're getting edgy," Mac said testily, recognizing the sound of another booby trap from inside the lounge. He couldn't fathom that. At Mac's hand signal, the group split up. "Their attention may be diverted. Let's move. *Wiki-wiki*. Watch out for trip wires.''

Three figures approached the steps to the lanai in a close vee formation. Mac was in the center, flanked by the two Marines dressed as terrorists, Moses on his left, Marco on his right. Mac's hands were behind him, as if tied. Moses' AK-47 was pointed at Mac's head. From the steps Mac could see the outline of two terrorists against the background light of the lounge. They were coming from inside, out onto the terrace, and were just sliding the door closed behind them. Mac recognized the build of one of them.

"That's Kimo on your side," he whispered to Moses.

They started across the lanai. Mac's elbow nudged Moses.

"Hey Kimo, man," the tall, thin, black shouted in a jivey voice. "We caught the son-of-a-beech."

The two terrorists hesitated, both still standing outside their barricades, assault rifles swinging up, pointing at Mac.

"Don't shoot 'em, man. Fire wants to talk to 'em." Socrates sounded exactly like Moses.

They were within ten feet now. With his left hand, Marco pushed Mac forward. The big man stumbled awkwardly. Both of the terrorists swung their AK-47s to cover him. In that moment, Marco and Moses pushed the buttons on their flashlight-shaped Taser guns. Two

little darts connected to thin wires shot out of each. Two
hit Kimo, two hit Michael. Both terrorists slumped to
the deck like wilting flowers, totally immobilized, their
AK-47s clattering harmlessly alongside them.

Within a minute the Marines had carried their prisoners off the lanai, and the two Marine hand-to-hand
experts wearing Kimo's and Michael's terrorist masks
had settled in behind the barricades guarding the lanai
entrance. Each was armed with a terrorist's AK-47, a
knife, and a thin wire. They had strict orders not to fire
under any circumstances, but to garrote any terrorist
who came out of the lounge.

Back in ocean suite seven, Major Fleming and
McGregor were both smiling broadly. "We were
lucky," Mac said. "With that rain, the lounge windows
are steamed up. No one inside can see out. It's inky
black."

"With that wind, they couldn't hear anything,
either," the major said.

Moses and Marco came out of the bathroom. Mac
grinned at them. "Act one was a smash. If you do as
well in act two, you're both headed for a medal. Why
don't you rest up in the suite next door? We've got the
grand finale in a couple of hours."

Both of the young Marines smiled their thanks and
moved toward the door.

Mac reached out and tousled Socrates's short, kinky
hair as he walked past. "And you, Moses, you've got a
hell of an acting career ahead of you."

The boy turned, an embarrassed look on his face, an
expression of hope in his eyes. "Do you really think
so?" he asked.

"Of course. Old men never lie," Mac replied.

The buzzer sounded in Jeanne Black's penthouse at one

minute after eight A.M. EST. The doorman announced
the caller, and a few minutes later the private elevator
door opened. The servants had been dismissed, so the
U.N. delegate met the elevator herself.

"Igor, it was nice of you to come."

Zaturof extended his large, clammy hand and smiled.
"When you told me caviar for breakfast, how could I
refuse?"

Jeanne led the way into the dining room. The Russian's eyes surveyed the penthouse filled with an attractive mixture of English and French antiques, oriental
rugs, exquisite decorations, and paintings. On the living
room wall he noticed a Renoir and a Matisse, and felt a
stab of resentment against the capitalist system which
allowed such material acquisitions. Even the thick
dossier the KGB had provided on Jeanne Black and her
husband had not prepared him for the luxurious fur-
nishings.

A lavish breakfast had been laid out on hot plates on
the Hepplewhite sideboard. The Chippendale table was
set elegantly for two, a bouquet of yellow rosebuds in
the center. Jeanne indicated a chair to her guest and slid
into the other one. "How do you like your coffee?" she
asked.

"Black, thank you," he answered, staring out of the
window at a magnificent view of Central Park, with the
Hudson River and the George Washington Bridge in
the distance.

"Help yourself, whenever you're ready." She smiled
and gestured toward the sideboard. "The President is
speaking at eleven. He was hoping . . ."

Zaturof shrugged and sipped his coffee. His sallow
face, normally devoid of any emotion, looked sad.

"One for one. We'll go along if you will," Jeanne
Black suggested hopefully.

Zaturof slid back his chair, rose, and moved to the sideboard. He took a small portion of scrambled eggs and a large helping of caviar. Sitting back down, he looked at the attractive woman, her face soft and radiant in the morning light. "I love beluga. It comes from the Caspian where they catch the *huso huso*. Southern Russia, that's my home, you know."

The American smiled, sipped her coffee, and said nothing. Two hundred and sixteen hostages were about to be blown up. Unless she could pull off a miracle—make a deal with the devil—and he was talking about fish eggs!

The Russian took a bite of toast heavy with caviar. "My government regrets . . ."

Jeanne Black's face fell.

He finished chewing, swallowed, and wiped his mouth with the corner of his napkin. "We can't go along with your request."

"But why?"

"It would give your country unilateral advantages."

"But how? If we agree to destroy nuclear weapons on a one-for-one basis?"

"It would disrupt the existing balance of forces."

They fell into a silence, looking at one another. She sipping coffee, he taking large bites of caviar, washing them down with coffee. After a few minutes, Zaturof went back to the sideboard. Jeanne poured them both more coffee.

"Your warheads are larger. Is that your concern? You'd be destroying more throw power?" The American's face was harder now, more professional.

"Our strategic arsenals are about even."

"Nonsense. You have tremendous advantages, especially with your new generation of land-based missiles with multiple warheads." Jeanne's eyes flashed anger.

"You have three hundred super-heavy SS-18s. They're accurate and incredibly powerful. We have no counterpart."

Zaturof scowled. "The Soviet superiority is nonexistent. Washington stresses the differences in structure of our nuclear armaments." He shrugged again. "That's not important. We're a peaceful nation. It is your government that's pursuing an openly hostile policy, rearming. Your aggressive arms buildup could compel the Soviet Union to react."

The American delegate laughed. "Igor, you're priceless. We don't need a U.N. speech. There are no recorders here. No microdot transmitters. Just the two of us."

The Russian glanced around the room, then laughingly asked, "Do you mind if I finish the caviar?"

"Please do." She wondered how one man could possibly eat a half-pound of caviar by himself. It would shoot her food budget for the week. She waited for him to sit back down, then started to talk from her own deep feelings.

"Think of the enormity of the stakes—one giant step for mankind. This nuclear thing is getting too big for all of us. Your side. Our side. The rest of the world. We'll all go up in flames. We don't need cosmetic agreements. We need actual arms reductions, cutbacks in the nuclear arsenals. One for one. It would be a start."

The Russian stopped eating. He could sense the change in her tone. The conviction in her voice. Jeanne Black was scared that the world was going to be incinerated. Despite their great differences in ideology, he had the same fear. It was just a matter of who pushed the button first and when.

"Off the record?" he asked.

Jeanne Black nodded.

"Actually, my government was intrigued with the proposal. One for one. Start small. Hopefully keep going. But there just wasn't enough time to work out the details. First we'd have to freeze nuclear weapons at the current level. Your government's against a freeze. But that's an essential first step or we won't go along. What's the sense of destroying weapons if you're still building others?" His eyes looked questioningly at the American, and could see the tiny shrug of her shoulders. "Then we could set guidelines on what will be destroyed. After that, we'd consider reducing nuclear warheads on a one-for-one basis."

Jeanne Black's eyes were staring, wide open. Zaturof sounded almost human. Their thinking wasn't too far apart. Maybe there was still hope.

"If we could agree now, we could save the lives of the hostages."

The Russian diplomat finished eating, wiped his mouth with the napkin, and tossed it alongside his plate.

"An agreement under pressure would only encourage terrorism. Next week the crazies around the world would take over hundreds of resorts. My country doesn't have a problem with terrorists and we certainly don't want to encourage it in the Western world." He smiled across the table.

Bullshit, thought Jeanne Black. The Russians instigated most of the world's terrorism. They were probably behind the takeover of the Molokai-Surf. This sounded like the Zaturof she knew.

They said their polite, diplomatic good-byes. As he was stepping onto the elevator, she asked him, "Igor, I wonder what would have happened if your government had said yes today?"

Zaturof didn't reply. His eyes looked away as the doors closed. He wondered, too.

• • •

It was almost four in the morning when Donahue came through the front door of ocean suite seven. Mac and Fleming were sitting in chairs. Mac had his feet up, and was dozing; the major was fidgeting.

"I hear you took two prisoners," Donahue said. "Saw them on their way out, as I was coming back in."

"Smooth as silk," the major replied, shaking his head in admiration. "I got to watch."

Donahue grinned, knowing how McGregor used to operate.

Mac's left eye opened. "Did you reach the Big Man?"

"You wouldn't believe the red tape, but I finally got to speak to him. Told one of his aides that I'd blow up the hostages myself if he didn't put me through."

"What did the old boy say?"

"Said there should be more direct communication with his men in the field."

Mac grunted. "Political bullshit. Probably doesn't know you're a liberal."

"I've matured. I'm a conservative now," the colonel growled. "The President got the message. He promised to hold the terrorists' attention 'til the end of his speech."

Both of Mac's eyes opened. "And a signal?"

"The one we agreed on."

Mac's mouth twitched.

"By the way, he wished us luck."

"We'll need it," Mac muttered, closing his eyes.

Donahue beckoned to Fleming and whispered, "Old men need a lot of sleep." Quietly the two slipped out the front door.

Mac's soft snores were the only sound in the room.

• • •

In the early hours of the morning the winds had shifted to the northeast, blowing the heavy rain away. The sky, still confused with intermittent drizzle, showed promise of clearing rapidly. An early morning mist was drifting in from the sea, wispy fingers probing the hollows. In the east the dark sky was growing lighter. It was the half-hour before dawn.

With headlights on, top up, and windshield wipers going, the white Cadillac convertible cleared the rise at the top of the hill and started down the long, straight road to the Molokai-Surf, the white flag of truce flying from the radio antenna. Colonel Red McKenna drove slowly, Bailey and Corwin sat quietly in the back seat, each with his own thoughts. The tires made whirring sounds on the wet asphalt. Trailing the Cadillac by about forty yards was a standard Marine jeep, with a Marine driver and a television cameraman wearing a navy-blue windbreaker with the hood pulled up over his dark, wavy hair.

"Can you imagine. That kid Banyan insisted on coming along with us?" Bailey said.

"That cameraman's got a lot of guts," Corwin answered. Glancing at the captain, he almost smiled. In the early morning light, Bailey was a dead ringer for Buddy Hackett.

"I'd feel better if we were armed," McKenna commented over his shoulder.

The other two nodded slightly, automatically adjusting their white armbands over their khaki uniforms.

The white Cadillac slowed and then stopped about one hundred yards short of the entrance. The jeep pulled up behind it. McKenna turned off the lights and the windshield wipers, opened the front door on the driver's side and got out, saying, "We'll walk from here. They'll be looking for tricks."

The other two officers of the Marine hostage negotiation team slid out of the car, closed the doors, and together the three of them walked slowly down the road toward the front entrance, their feet splashing in the occasional rain puddle. Each had his hands raised slightly above his shoulders, empty palms forward.

Trailing behind and slightly to one side was the television cameraman. Reynolds switched on the camera, focused on the backs of the Marine officers and the front of the Molokai-Surf. The film began to roll.

They were within twenty yards of the front entrance when McKenna signaled for them to stop. There was no warning. It came at them from out of nowhere. Three bursts of rapid machine-gun fire from three different directions.

Captain Bill Bailey felt a stabbing pain in his chest and knew no more.

Lieutenant Colonel Red McKenna involuntarily reached for his damaged knee. It felt like all the screws were popping out through the flesh. He crumpled to the ground and was still.

Two hollow-nosed 7.62mm bullets slammed into Major Jim Corwin's forehead, emerging out the back of his head, carrying with them most of his computerlike brain.

The firing stopped as quickly as it had begun. Three Marine officers lay dead in a large pool of blood at the entrance to the Molokai-Surf. The mist mixed with the blood, and little red rivulets ran off the side of the road. The ocean breeze carried away the strong smell of death.

For long moments, Lloyd Reynolds stood alone in the road, frozen in fear, camera jerking from side to side. Slowly, his knees gave way and he sank to the ground. Then three Kalashnikovs fired as one. Reynolds's body was ripped apart, spattered. The camera, pointed at the swirling mist above, continued to roll.

The Marine jeep roared into action and raced up the road, away from the Molokai-Surf. The driver was the only survivor.

From the lobby area came a shrill, female laugh.

CHAPTER EIGHTEEN

Third Day—Morning

In ocean suite seven the last briefing ended at five forty-five A.M. The faces of the Marines were blackened and grim, the mood tense and angry. They had all heard the bursts of the machine guns at the front entrance. Their lookouts had described the gruesome scene by radio-phone. The command post had passed the bad news along to Washington.

Donahue put his hand on his old friend's shoulder. "Mac, you sure you want to do this?"

Mac nodded.

"The major will take your place. We get paid . . ."

"I've come this far," Mac interrupted. "Besides, I know the layout and the terrorists. Let's get it over with."

Donahue slipped on his helmet and picked up his M-16. "We stay with the plan."

Major Fleming gave a thumbs-up sign. "We'll be right behind you." His mouth was tight. So far he'd seen more action in a prayer meeting.

Donahue's face clouded. "Not too close. Just in case. Wait for the signal."

Four men headed out into the thick *manoa* mist, moving single file toward the Koa Lounge. At the huge poinciana tree they stopped briefly.

"Good luck, Mac."

"*Semper fi*, Preach."

The colonel and Eric, the stocky young Marine wearing Marco's mask, took the path toward the lobby entrance. Mac and Socrates, the tall, thin, black wearing Moses' mask and rubber gloves, headed for the lanai.

Dan Hanson strained against his bonds. Like the other hostages, he was tied hand and foot, Vietnamese style, all linked together with nylon cord. The fat man's stomach churned, his mouth grim. The terrorists had just finished connecting additional charges of plastic explosive. There was little doubt, they were getting ready to blow the place. Anahu was seated in the guard position, eyes moving around the room, the plunger connected to the explosives between his knees. Cradling an AK-47, Ivan roamed among the rows of prisoners, an ominous, threatening presence.

Across the room, Rick Waltz leaned sideways, kissed his wife's cheek and tasted the salt of her tears. Their night had passed in a blur, ending with the violent explosion and rifle fire that had killed two of the hostages. Their day had begun in terror. Through the lobby door the Waltz's had seen the three Marine officers carrying a white flag and the network cameraman gunned down in cold blood. The air was thick with cordite and the sickly, sweet smell of death. Heavy mist swirled past the windows.

A grim silence had settled over the Koa Lounge, interrupted only by the occasional sobbing of some of the hostages. It was a sea of downcast, weary faces and bloodshot eyes. The three Avon ladies looked at one another. Connie tried to smile and failed. This was the hour they all feared. The hour everyone knew was coming. The President was appearing on television to answer the terrorist demands. One for one. A hostage for a nuclear warhead. Would he give in? Was a compromise possible? Their lives were the chips on the table. A nervous excitement thick as smog settled over the group. As best they could, the hostages turned their heads toward the small stage, their faces lined with fear, their eyes focused on the large television screen.

In the lobby, Fire and Carlos turned their chairs to watch the small set. Ivan entered the lobby and sat down next to the second switch connected to the explosives, assault rifle across his lap, right hand still on the trigger, left hand resting lightly on the switch. The microphone connected to the resort loudspeaker system had been set in front of the television. The words rang out loud and clear.

"From the East Room of the White House, the President of the United States."

On the screen, the President stood behind the lectern with the official seal, face grim and taut. He nodded imperceptibly.

> "Good morning, ladies and gentlemen. You are all aware of the tragedy unfolding right now on the island of Molokai in Hawaii, where a group of armed terrorists called HULA One have taken over control of the Molokai-Surf resort, seized 216 guests and employees, and are

holding them for ransom. The terrorists have
announced that they will free one hostage for
each nuclear warhead that we destroy.

"It is with heavy heart that I advise you that
just a few minutes ago I received word that this
morning the terrorists murdered three unarmed
Marine officers and a television cameraman.
These brave men, under a white flag of truce,
were shot down while approaching the hotel entrance to negotiate with the HULA One leaders
for the release of their prisoners."

The President looked up from his notes, speaking
directly into the camera, his face heavy with sadness,
voice angry.

"It is difficult to reason with people who
make a demand and then kill those who try to
discuss that demand with them. It's impossible
to deal rationally with irrational animals."

At the word *animals*, there was a collective groan
from the hostages. Rick Waltz closed his eyes. The
President couldn't have said anything worse.

Oh shit, thought Hanson, breathing hard. They were
all dead now.

On the lanai, Mac whispered to the two Marines who
had replaced Kimo and Michael. "On the signal, come
in low and fast." The two terrorist masks nodded
solemnly.

To the side of the lobby entrance, from the shelter of
a clump of poinsettia bushes, Donahue could see the
bodies of McKenna, Corwin, Bailey, and the television
cameraman. He spit out the bitter taste rising in his
throat.

Carlos looked at Fire and flashed a crooked smile.
"He's got us pegged, baby."

Fire's face flushed. Standing, she began to pace up

and down in front of the television, shouting at it angrily, "You're the animal, baby killer, you and your nuke bombs, playing wipe out."

The President pointed into the camera, like an Uncle Sam poster, directly at his unseen audience.

> "The leader of HULA One is an attractive young Hawaiian girl with a most unusual name. I have an important personal message . . . a pledge . . . that I will give to her, but not until the end of my talk."

Fire stared at the screen and sat down.

The corners of Donahue's mouth twitched. Thank God. They were following his plan. The President would have Fire's attention.

Glancing at his notes, the President continued.

> "Our hearts go out to these innocent hostages and their families. We want to see them freed. But the United States can never allow itself to give in to terrorist demands, especially those which would weaken the defense of our country and the entire free world. If we gave in just once, there would be no end to terrorist blackmail on a worldwide scale.
>
> "In my lifetime I have seen the world plunged blindly into global war that inflicted untold suffering upon millions of innocent people. I share the determination of today's young people that such a tragedy, which would be rendered even more terrible by the monstrous inhumane weapons in the world's nuclear arsenals, must never happen again. There would be no winners in a nuclear war. Everyone would be a loser.
>
> "I'll take second to none in my concern over the threat of nuclear war. To those who protest against nuclear war, I can only say I'm with

you. I pledge to do my utmost to prevent such a war. No one feels more than I the need for peace.

"I want to assure the terrorists as well as all Americans that it is our intention to reduce our store of nuclear weapons dramatically, assuring lasting peace and security. We are willing to do this on a one-for-one basis with the Soviet Union. We are willing to start as soon as the Soviet Union agrees to join with us in reducing its store of nuclear warheads and the proper guidelines and safeguards can be established. But we cannot do so unilaterally or under pressure from terrorist threats. The Soviet Union must join with us in nuclear weapon reductions so that neither country has a nuclear advantage. If we were to destroy any of our nuclear warheads without a corresponding reduction in the Soviet atomic arsenal, it would deprive the Soviet Union of an incentive to join in a meaningful reduction.

"As it stands today, the Russians have a definite margin of superiority over the United States in nuclear weapons. They have an ability to absorb our retaliatory blow and hit us again. Before we destroy any of our warheads, we must be sure that Russia will do likewise. We cannot put our country at risk and open the window of vulnerability for all of the people of the free world."

The President paused and took a sip of water.

Carlos stood up, the crooked grin back on his face. "They've turned us down. We blow up the hostages." He pulled on his mask, picked up his rifle and headed for the lounge.

"I'm in command here. I'll give the order," Fire shouted. Goddamn faceless hothead. She wanted to hear the President's personal message to her. They still had plenty of time, and all of the hostages.

"That's why I've called for negotiations leading to major arms reductions, including a substantial reduction in the number of nuclear warheads, from about 7,500 to 5,000 each . . ."

Evelyn whispered to Connie, in a frightened voice, "What difference would that make? There are enough nuclear bombs now to wipe out a million cities the size of Hiroshima. We'll all be fallout. The world will be nothing but mindless dust."

"Once Russia agrees to this reduction and an equality of nuclear strength exists, we would like to reduce the number of nuclear weapons further . . . on a one-for-one basis with the Soviet Union. Our ultimate goal is to eliminate nuclear weapons totally. To this end, we are proposing that both major powers agree to stop production of any additional nuclear warheads, immediately.

"We want an agreement that reduces the risk of war, lowers the level of armaments, and enhances global security. We can accept no less. America's national security policy is based on enduring principles. Our leaders and our allies have long understood that the objective of our defense efforts has always been to deter conflict and reduce the risk of war, conventional or nuclear.

"I invite the Soviet Union to join with us now to substantially reduce nuclear weapons and make an important breakthrough for lasting peace on earth. I believe all the people on earth want to return to a level of civilized behavior. They want peace . . . and so do I."

Carlos waved to Anahu and ducked into the men's room. It was time to put his own survival plan into action. He was no martyr. He'd become a legend among terrorists not by dying, but by surviving.

Fire stood up. It was the same old bullshit. We'll reduce our bombs if they reduce theirs. No one would take the first step. Carlos was right. It was time to give the order. Time to teach the world a lesson. Don't fuck with Fire. "I'll be back," she said to Ivan. The Bulgarian nodded.

Pulling on her mask, picking up her Kalashnikov, she walked into the lounge. Anahu saw the tall terrorist and smiled. She moved both hands sharply downward, the clear signal to blow up the hostages. The big Hawaiian's face paled. She repeated the signal. He nodded his understanding and checked his watch. Fire knew she had exactly two minutes. Moving rapidly, she headed toward the door at the far side of the lounge, the one leading to the kitchen.

Lying prone just outside the lanai doors, Mac took off his helmet and touched Socrates on the shoulder. Big white eyes looked out of the terrorist mask at the older man. A high-pitched, jivey voice whispered, "Man, I sure hope you're as good as they say you are." The tall, thin black bit his tongue. He'd almost said, "old man." Moses took a deep breath and stood up.

The lanai doors slid open and Moses sauntered into the room, unarmed, transistor radio tuned to rock, rubber gloves in plain sight keeping time to the music. Anahu saw Moses and an evil grin spread over his face. The rubber-glove freak had come back just in time. Too bad Jumbo wasn't with him.

In the lobby, Ivan heard the footsteps outside the front entrance. Instinctively his hands lifted his assault rifle. As Marco came through the door, it was pointed at his chest.

The lady in the muu-muu glanced at Moses, then saw a big man with a bald head and a blackened face snaking his way along the floor, M-16 in front of him,

elbows and forearms driving him forward. Her mouth
flew open in astonishment. The scream that started low
in her stomach caught in her throat.

The loudspeaker droned above everything.

> "The issue is the very survival of the earth
> and the realization of God's vision for it.
> Nuclear war would represent the height of ar-
> rogance, divesting the Creator of His creation.
> My faith is grounded in the Bible. The example
> of Jesus Christ must be our guide as we steer the
> nation through these treacherous waters, on-
> ward to the shores of hope."

A piercing soprano voice ravaged the air. "There's an
old, rugged cross, and it stands on a hill . . ." The hymn
was coming out of the fat lady with the face of the carp.

Startled, Anahu swung his rifle in her direction.
Two elderly Baptists joined in at the top of their voices.
". . . The emblem of suffering and shame."

"Shut up so we can hear the President," shouted the
obvious New Yorker.

A chorus of hostages picked up the hymn.

Moses moved closer to Anahu, clapping his rubber
gloves together. The Hawaiian's eyes followed the tall,
skinny black.

The big man with the bald head and the blackened
face rose up on one knee.

Anahu glanced at his watch. Fifteen seconds to go.
He started counting to himself. Fourteen . . . thirteen
. . . He put down his rifle, both hands reaching for the
plunger.

In the lobby, Ivan sensed that something was wrong.
Marco didn't look right. The bearded terrorist's eyes
moved downward. The Cuban was wearing Marine
combat boots! Ivan's finger tightened on the trigger.

On the television screen, the President pointed again.

> "And now for my personal message to the leader of HULA One, Fire . . ."

At the order from the Commander-in-Chief himself, Mac shot Anahu out of his chair.

Marco dove for the floor as Ivan fired, and Donahue blew away the Bulgarian terrorist's head.

Hostage screams drowned out the President's pledge, as Moses leapt onto Anahu's chair, arms extended under the explosive plunger so that it couldn't be activated. On hands and knees, arm burning in pain, blood dripping on the floor, Marco crawled forward and pulled the wires from the other switch.

Out of the corner of his eye, Mac saw a Marine coming through the door from the men's room. Neither Donahue nor Marco had come through the lobby yet. His eyes opened wide. The Marine was moving forward, aiming his assault rifle with the distinctive banana-shaped clip at Moses. Mac fired a burst from his M-16 and blew a hole in the Marine's chest.

The hostages screamed again.

Entering the lounge, Donahue spotted Mac and shouted across the room, "Carlos?"

Mac drew a finger across his throat, then pointed to the dead Marine on the floor. Donahue's teeth showed white against his blackened face.

Mac mouthed the words, "The girl . . . Fire?"

Donahue shrugged his big shoulders and nodded negatively. Mac's eyes continued searching the room. Marines in full battle gear were now pouring into the lounge, assault rifles at the ready, searching for any remaining terrorists. The hostages were now screaming excitedly, deep despair having given way to hysterical elation.

Moving quickly to the lanai door, Mac slid it open and stepped out. Through slots between huge cumulus clouds, the morning sun was bathing the top of Diamond Head across the channel, the bright yellow glow moving steadily down the mountain, spreading across the land. A double rainbow arched high over the channel. A promise of better things to come, Mac thought, as he moved across the lanai to the top of the cliff. Standing close to a clump of bougainvillea bushes, he glanced down. The surf, still angry from the night's storm, was crashing in a mountainous foam and a continuous roar against the rocks below.

Suddenly, Mac felt the barrel of a rifle in the center of his back and a whispered, "Drop it!" It was the hard voice of Fire coming from the bushes. Mac's M-16 clattered on the rocky ground, bounced once, and skittered over the edge. It hit the side of the jagged cliff, then plunged into the foam below.

"Walk slowly." Fire's gun prodded him back toward the lanai. "Don't do anything foolish." The voice was a hiss.

Mac moved slowly. He could see Donahue just coming out of the lanai door, crouching low, head moving back and forth, searching. And from the corner of his eye, Mac could see Marines moving around both sides of the main building. Mac's teeth were clenched, waiting for the bullets to slam into his back and tear him apart.

"Turn around," the voice commanded.

Mac took a deep breath and turned. Fire had not followed him. She was standing on the edge of the cliff, her assault rifle pointed at his stomach, the bush shielding her from Donahue's sight. She had taken off her terrorist outfit and was dressed in jeans and a T-shirt. There was a scarlet gash down her right arm where she'd scratched it on the thorns in the bushes.

"Aloha, Mac McGregor," she said, a sadistic smile splitting her face.

Mac's eyes narrowed, focusing on Fire's face. He saw death staring back. The thought flashed through his mind, at least he could watch his own execution. The sound of a heart thumping loudly drowned out the other noises.

Suddenly, in one fluid motion, Fire dropped her assault rifle and turned to face the ocean. The tall girl stood motionless on the very edge of the emerald cliff. The shimmering rays of the morning sun glistened on her golden skin. Flecks of fire sparkled in her dark red hair. Her leg muscles tensed and she dove into the frothing, angry sea below.

Mac rushed forward to the edge of the cliff. He could barely see the rocks below for the spray and foam surging over them. It was a white maelstrom. The rolling breakers, thirty feet high, were smashing into the wall of the cliff. Donahue had come up alongside him. "Good Christ," the colonel said, almost in awe. "She killed herself!"

"I thought she was going to kill me."

"A ghost just walked over your grave," Donahue said, putting his hand on his friend's shoulder.

Mac stared down. There was no sign of Fire. No one could live in that crashing sea. It was all over, and, somehow, he felt sad. Mac turned toward Donahue. The big Marine grabbed Mac and gave him a bear hug. "We did it, old man. We did it!"

"Look out, Preach!" Mac yelled. "We'll go over the goddamned cliff."

                    •   •   •

With all the terrorists now either killed or captured, Mac and Donahue walked back into the main lounge. Teams of Marines were moving through the lines of hostages, cutting them loose from their bonds. Other Marines were removing the C-4 plastic explosive packages and rolling up the primer cord. As soon as the explosives had been removed from the building, waves of reporters, television interviewers, and cameramen swarmed into the lounge.

As the hostages were freed, they milled about laughing, shouting, weeping openly, unable to believe that their long ordeal was over.

"Free at last. Thank God, we're free at last!" shouted Bee Jay, jumping up and down, alternately hugging Connie and Evelyn.

"It's the Friendly Skies for me," laughed Evelyn. "All the way home to our little corner of the world. I'm never going to leave Colorado again."

"Stand back, stand back," a medic was shouting. "Stretcher coming through, make room for the stretcher."

Face pale, eyes closed, an elderly man with thinning white hair, strapped to the stretcher, was quickly moved out the front entrance and put into a Marine ambulance. His weeping, frail wife was helped in the vehicle with him, and the ambulance drove away.

The lady with the carp face and wrinkled muu-muu stood pale and trembling, and stared with wide, unblinking eyes. Mac saw her, moved quickly to her side, then with his hand under her arm, helped her into a chair.

"Thank you," she said, color returning to her face, eyes focusing on the big baldheaded man.

"My thanks to you." Mac smiled. "That was a brave

thing you did. You saved my life." He leaned over and kissed the lady on the cheek. "You're a beautiful person."

Calmer now, the lady smiled at Mac. She'd obviously misjudged the man. He wasn't rude at all. Actually, he was quite charming. She stood up. It was time for a long, hot bath.

Dan Hanson had his arm protectively around Candy. They were standing talking with Jerry and his girlfriend, Carol.

"I learned one thing in the last few days," the handsome doctor said, rubbing the stubble on his face. "Life is short. It's time I got mine straightened out." He put his arm around Carol's waist.

Carol looked up, cameramen were taking pictures, and Jerry wasn't hiding in his anxiety closet. He was looking full face into a television camera and smiling broadly.

"I think you're going to be on the evening news," she whispered.

"Frankly, darling, I don't give a damn." He squeezed Carol tightly as she snuggled closer to him.

Dan nodded his understanding. "Candy and I already decided. The past died this morning." He smiled down at the pretty blonde. "Our future is ahead of us."

Joey, the lanky blonde, looked at her husband slumped in a chair, a despondent look on his face. "You should be happy, not sad," she said.

"I made an ass out of myself. When I get a chance, I'm going to apologize to McGregor."

"I don't think that's necessary," Joey said, her big hazel eyes staring at her husband's face. She liked what she saw. "You tried to bribe Jumbo, and he's dead." She leaned over and kissed Larry. "Cheer up. You're

turning into a nice guy. I think I'm falling in love
again.''

Things were quieting down, when there was a sudden
commotion near the kitchen door and Kona walked
through a group of cheering hostages. Several of the
Marines whistled. Television cameras whirred. In a
long-sleeved, white silk blouse and black pants, the tall,
golden-skinned girl with an orchid in her long black hair
looked radiantly beautiful. Everywhere she walked, the
freed hostages thanked her for her kindness and care
while they were prisoners.

"Please have patience," she said, her brilliant smile
flashing. "The staff will have your rooms cleaned and
made up as soon as possible. Dinner will be at eight.
Our desk will help you make travel arrangements.''

Major Baldwin watched the resort manager in awe.
He tapped Murray on the shoulder. "Watch that girl.
She's doing her best to unscramble an omelet.''

Colonel Donahue introduced himself to Kona, then
spoke softly, "I'm sorry about your sister.''

Kona blinked her green eyes. "Thanks," she said
simply. Then touching the colonel's arm, she added,
"We never did see eye to eye. She was . . .'' Kona hesitated as if searching for the right words ". . . a bitch.''

Marge came back with the ambulance. Dashing into
the lounge, she saw Mac talking to a group of reporters
and cameramen and ran toward her husband, face glowing. Instinctively, Mac sensed her presence, turned and
opened his arms, just as she ran into them. With Mac
holding her tightly and kissing her, Marge didn't even
realize that her feet were off the floor.

"Happy birthday, darling," he said, kissing her
again, then setting her down.

'I couldn't think of a better present,'' she said, voice
cracking, tears splashing down her face.

"You look beautiful," Mac said softly.

"So do you," she whispered back, touching his blackened face with both hands.

"Let's get out of here," he said, taking Marge's hand. They edged toward the lanai door.

Third Day—Afternoon

It was a beautiful day in Molokai. The sun shone brightly, and fluffy, white popcorn clouds drifted over the turquoise sky. A slight breeze blew in from the ocean.

The Marines, after removing the dead, had finished checking all of the rooms for booby traps and weapons and had cleared the mines from around the complex. By afternoon, they were cleaning up, and helicopters were ferrying back and forth to Oahu, moving men and equipment out.

Colonel Donahue and Major Fleming stood on the brink of the formidable cliff and stared over the edge. The sea was calming. Down below they could see fascinating tidal pools among the volcanic boulders jutting out into the ocean.

"Haven't found Fire's body yet," Fleming reported, shielding his eyes from the glare.

"The surf probably took it out," Donahue said, his boot kicking a rock loose, his eyes watching it shatter on the ledge below.

As they walked away from the cliff, Fleming sighed wistfully. "This is some resort. You'd ride many a day by mule to find a better view. You can almost see for a week and a half."

In ocean suite seven, Mac was sound asleep. Marge sat by the bed watching him, a novel on her lap. She felt so lucky. All but two of the hostages had come out alive, thanks to him. Her husband was such a compassionate man. They'd built a beautiful dream together. It was still intact. She closed her eyes and thanked God. The sun made little windows on the wall. The windows stretched and lengthened. It was almost six o'clock when she leaned forward, kissed him, and whispered, "Love, like bread, has to be made fresh every day."

Mac's eyes flickered open, and there was a smile at the corner of his lips. "Would my birthday girl like rye, pumpernickel, or French?"

The sun melted as one red flame in the west, dripping into the sea. The happy hour had started and the guests began trickling out to the lanai, most in a festive, sunset mood, all talking about the miracle of their escape. The champagne was on the house . . . Domaine Chandon. It drank beautifully. Kona and her staff had arranged a sumptuous buffet dinner under the stars. The hostages and the Marine officers were all guests of honor.

The McGregors arrived late to a chorus of cheers and a ripple of applause. Marge was wearing her best black and gold caftan. They joined Donahue and his staff at the center table, the colonel held the chair for Marge, then introduced Mac to Murray, Baldwin, and Alexander.

"How the hell did she do all this?" Mac asked, glancing in Kona's direction, admiration in his voice.

Donahue shrugged his big shoulders. He'd wondered the same thing.

"How's that boy, Eric?"

"We flew him out. A shattered arm. He'll be all right."

"Both he and Socrates deserve a medal," Mac said.

"I'll see to it," Donahue promised.

"Thanks. They had a lot of guts to put their trust in an old museum-piece like me."

Donahue grinned. "When you shot that Marine, it was an instant decision. How'd you know it was Carlos?"

"He didn't look right," Mac growled.

Donahue sipped his champagne slowly, watching Mac's face.

"His gun was an AK-47. His shoes Cuban loafers." Mac didn't think he'd add that he'd seen Carlos without his mask. He'd recognized the son-of-a-bitch, scar and all. After all, he had to maintain a little mystique.

"The Marine outfit must have been part of his escape plan."

Mac nodded. "His passport out. But he cut it too close."

Mac stopped talking as Kona leaned over the table and suggested that they start the line at the buffet. He inhaled deeply. She smelled of white ginger.

It was after dessert that Kona stood up and with a small microphone called for attention. She looked beautiful in a long-sleeved white blouse and matching slacks. People stopped talking. There was a bittersweet look on her face. "As manager of the Molokai-Surf, I want to apologize to all of you for the pain and suffering you went through during the last three tragic days. I cannot begin to explain my sister's actions . . ."

The beautiful Hawaiian girl pushed back her long, black hair, voice cracking with emotion.

"For her I pray that the secret of life is death. As an ugly caterpillar turns into a beautiful *Kamehameha* butterfly, may death for her also be a transition from evil to good. I am *kamaaina*, born here and raised within a stone's throw of this resort. This place is deep in my heart."

Donahue leaned over to Mac and whispered, "Emotional wounds leave the deepest scars."

Mac nodded, thinking about what Kona said. He'd always hoped death would be a transition, but to what?

"Rock Resorts has asked me to tell you that through today there will be no charge for your stay here." Kona's smile was tentative. "Further, each one of you will be entitled to one free week, room and meals, at any of the fine Rock Resorts. That's our one-for-one plan."

There was cheering and applause from all of the tables and a shout from one in the furthermost corner. "Let's hear it for Kona. Hip, hip . . ."

The answering "hooray" was almost deafening.

At their table, Evelyn whispered to Connie and Bee Jay, "I'm taking the free offer only if they've got a resort in Colorado." The other two laughed.

Kona stepped back to the microphone, smiling broadly now. "To Colonel Donahue and the Marines, our sincere thanks for what you did in rescuing all of us." Kona raised her glass.

The cheers were again deafening. Donahue and his officers stood briefly and waved.

"To Mac and Marge McGregor, our heartfelt thanks. What you did as guests was unbelievable. The Marine officers have told us that if it hadn't been for you, none of us here would be alive tonight." Kona paused to more cheers. "If you ever want anything, just ask." She smiled. "For Marge McGregor, today is a very special day. Will you please all join me in singing 'Happy Birthday'?"

All of the guests stood and sang, then applauded. At

the finish, there was a hint of moisture in Marge's eyes. After everyone had settled back in their seats, coffee and after-dinner drinks were served. It was a brandy and Tia Maria night.

After the dinner began breaking up, the guests milled around, personally thanking the marines and the McGregors for rescuing them.

"Let's get out of here, Preach," Mac whispered to Donahue. "Stop by our place for a nightcap."

The small group sat on the lanai at ocean suite seven, drinking brandy. At the shoreline, the blackness seemed to stretch off into infinity. Above, the heavens were speckled with stars.

Donahue summed up their admiration for Mac. "The last few days you sure left some deep tracks." He grinned. "A day in your life is a career for most."

"There was a lot of luck involved." Mac reached into his pocket and fingered his heart-shaped lucky beans. Thank God he'd found four. If each one brought a day of good luck, there was still one to go.

The colonel laughed lightly. "I learned early in this business, you make your own luck."

"I found out I'm getting old," Mac said ruefully. "Jumbo damned near killed me. If it hadn't been for Marge . . ." His voice trailed off.

"Must have been a helluva fight," Baldwin said enthusiastically. "I wish I'd seen it."

Mac shuddered in the cool night air.

Fleming reached forward and poured another dollop of brandy into his glass. "Yeah. Who would've thought terrorists would strike here, in Molokai?"

"I'm afraid you haven't heard the last of HULA," Mac said.

Mac took a sip of brandy. "This group was HULA

One. Unit One of the Hawaiian Underground Liberation Army. Why number the units, unless there are
others. Unit Two, Three, who knows how many?''

"My God," exclaimed Baldwin, the lines on his face
deepening.

Mac leaned forward. "HULA was part of the
WHALE. I don't know exactly what that stands for,
but it's a worldwide group. They probably have set up
small cells all over the Western world. You may be in
for an epidemic of resort takeovers."

This time it was Donahue's turn to shudder.

Marge brought out the coffee and poured them each a
cup. They drank it, watching the midnight moon light
up the channel.

The Marines rose to go. They all gave Marge a birthday kiss and shook hands with Mac.

"You've mellowed with age," the colonel said.

"So have you, Preach," Mac replied, a warm smile
on his face.

"Thanks again, for everything. We'll see you off
tomorrow."

The two old friends clasped hands.

After everyone had left, the McGregors sat on the lanai,
holding hands, watching the moon drift across the sky.

With his feet up, totally relaxed for the first time in
days, Mac thought about the young terrorists. What a
waste. Why did they have to seize innocent hostages and
threaten to kill them? The answer was obvious, they
wanted broad media exposure to put public pressure on
the government. Their cause—the reduction of nuclear
warheads—actually had a lot of merit. But nothing
justified the seizure and killing of innocent people.
There had to be a better way. There was no question
that the two superpowers had to cut out their nuclear

nonsense. The game of global chicken was already out of hand and getting worse every day.

Both sides had to reduce the number of hydrogen warheads drastically. There was only one world for everyone. It wouldn't take very much to blow it! Just one miscalculation, one mistake. He sighed. Now that he had more time, maybe it would be a project he could get his teeth into. Doing something for the kids, and their kids. The thought appealed to him. When he got home, he'd check it out.

Mac leaned over and kissed Marge's cheek.

"*Okole maluna*," she whispered.

As they stood up to go inside, Marge noticed it first. There was a rainbow around the moon.

PART THREE

ALOHA

CHAPTER NINETEEN

Hawaiian Air's flight nine to Oahu pulled away from the gate of Hoolehua Airport and taxied slowly toward the runway. Marge McGregor took one last look out the window. Colonel Donahue and his command officers were still waving. Kona stood to one side with the large sign that her staff had made out of orchids, reading Aloha. Marge smiled. Kona had told her that Hawaiians never said good-bye. It was always aloha. The send-off had been an island spectacular, the farewells tearful.

Donahue stood quietly near the gate, looking over the waist-high, wire-mesh fence, mind absorbing the startling information that Dan Hanson had given him just before boarding the plane. The agent killed by the terrorists had told the fat man that other units of HULA were planning to take over the resorts of Princeville, Mauna Kea, and Kahala with the same demand, one for one. Hanson didn't remember when, but knew it was soon. The colonel's eyes looked up. When one door closes, another opens. They'd be ready and waiting for the next terrorist move. They'd wipe out HULA. Crack them right down the middle. Maybe Parker and Mason hadn't died in vain.

The Marines had pulled this one off, thanks to McGregor. Without him, HULA's takeover of the Molokai-Surf would have been a bloody disaster. Old Mac had added to his legend. When he died, they'd have to bronze the old bastard. A smile crossed Donahue's face. He'd been tempted to tell McGregor about HULA's plans, but had decided against it. The old man would have wanted to stay.

As the plane taxied, Marge could no longer see the gate area. Turning her face away from the window, her eyes moved around the interior of the plane, which was filled with tired, but happy faces. The same faces that just thirty hours earlier had reflected abject terror and despair. She nodded to the three Avon ladies, smiled at the heavyset lady with the face of a carp, and felt a pleasant glow seeing the fat man holding hands with Candy.

As the plane made its last turn and pulled onto the end of the runway, Marge's eyes settled on Mac seated alongside her, eyes closed, brow furrowed, as if in deep thought. She placed her hand over his and squeezed gently. In that instant, Mac's eyes opened, his hands unsnapped his safety belt, and rising from his seat, he bolted up the aisle. The stewardess, strapped in her bulkhead seat, reached for the microphone, shouting, "All passengers stay in your seats. We're about to take off."

Mac's fists were already pounding at the door of the cockpit, his voice shouting. Engines, which were almost at full power, were slowly throttled back. Mac was now in heated discussion with the stewardess, who was trying to persuade him to return to his seat. The door to the pilot's compartment opened slowly, a pistol pointed at

Mac. Hands above his head, he explained his actions to the flight crew.

Slowly, the plane started to turn off the runway, back onto the taxiway. With an embarrassed look on his face, Mac walked back to his seat, as the stewardess explained to the passengers, "I'm sorry, ladies and gentlemen, but we have to return to the gate area for a few minutes. One of our passengers has forgotten something very important."

The announcement was met with a collective groan. As Mac slumped down into his seat, Marge glanced at him, a questioning look on her face. Her heart skipped when she saw Mac's answering wink.

At the gate area, all eyes had been on the plane poised for takeoff at the end of the runway. Now the plane was turning and heading back toward the gate.

"I wonder what's wrong?" Donahue asked, as much to himself as to the others near him.

No one answered. They all wondered.

Four minutes later, the airplane was back at the gate. The portable stairway for the passengers was rolled up to the front area of the plane. The door opened, and Mac and Marge McGregor stepped out into the bright sunlight and walked down the steps. Mac headed directly toward Donahue, a smile on his face. "I forgot something," he said.

The colonel's face had a puzzled look.

Mac turned toward Kona. The beautiful girl with an orchid in her long, black lustrous hair smiled her welcome, a puzzled look also in her green eyes.

"You told me if I ever wanted anything . . ."

Kona nodded, the bright smile still on her face.

Mac stepped closer. "Perhaps to remember you and all of your kindness," he looked into her eyes, "a lock of your hair."

Kona's mouth flew open as Mac's hand snaked out and touched her hair, and then, with one fluid, upward motion, pulled off a long, black wig. Underneath was a tight bouquet of curly red hair, suddenly sparkling in the bright sunshine. Underneath Kona's long, black hair was Fire.

"You shithead," the tall girl snarled, green eyes flashing. "I should've killed you."

Mac grinned. "Probably. But you needed me alive. Someone had to see you dive off the cliff to a watery grave. If I hadn't seen it, everyone would still be searching for you."

Colonel Donahue's mouth was open, muttering, "I'll be a son-of-a-bitch."

Mac gestured to Fleming and Baldwin. Each of the majors grabbed one of Fire's arms, holding her firmly between them.

"It was almost a perfect escape. Very clever and well-planned. In the side of the cliff, under the water in one of the tidal pools, there must be a tunnel—an old lava tube—that comes up on dry land. A risky dive, one that must have taken a lot of practice. Even for a water-baby . . ."

Mac pointed at Fire. "You never had a sister. You invented Kona and a fake background, then got her a job at the Molokai-Surf. It was an elaborate role. You lived Kona's short life for her. In her off-hours, you could be yourself, Fire."

Mac looked around at the astonished faces. "During the takeover of the hotel, Kona was a saint, Fire a tyrant. But no one ever saw the two of you together. Just once I heard you arguing in the kitchen." Mac looked at Fire. "That was clever, very clever. It threw me off."

Fire snarled again. "I suspected Jorge. The argument

was for his benefit." Her lips curled into a hateful grin. "I was right. I should have killed you then."

"The Scorpion almost did," Mac said.

"No one knew. Not Carlos, not Marco, no one." Fire's eyes flashed in defiance. "The plan was perfect."

"Almost," Mac said.

The two majors led Fire toward one of the command vehicles.

"What made you suspect?" Donahue asked Mac.

Mac touched his forefinger to his head. "Instinct." Then, smiling broadly, "You've got my number, Preach. Now I know you'll call me as soon as I get home." Laughing, he took Marge's arm. "Come on, darling, we're holding up a lot of people."

Mac and Marge re-entered the plane to a round of cheers, the pilot having explained over the intercom what had happened outside.

It was later, on the flight from Honolulu to San Francisco, while they were having coffee after dinner, that Mac told Marge the reasons he suspected Kona might be Fire.

"It was a gamble. But, Fire was a killer, dedicated to her cause, yet she let me go free. Think about that. I was her main tormentor, she hated me, yet she didn't kill me. It didn't make sense. Fire had to have a reason, a purpose. It just took me a while to figure it out. She let me live to provide her cover. By telling everyone that Fire had killed herself, I provided the chance for her escape. No one would look any further. The sea had claimed Fire, no one would question Kona. After time, Kona could slip away and become Fire again."

The stewardess saw Mac finish his coffee and poured a refill.

"Yesterday, on the lanai, I noticed that Fire had scratched her arm. It wasn't serious, but it was obvious.

Yesterday evening, Kona, the girl with the golden skin, was wearing a long-sleeved blouse. Again this morning. It was out of character. She was hiding the scratch.''

Marge took a small sip of her coffee and looked at Mac in wonder. His face was alive with enthusiasm. If anything, he looked years younger than he had the week before on the trip out to Hawaii.

''I thought about the two sisters a lot. Both with Hollywood faces and figures. In looks, identical except for their hair, one long and black, the other short and red. The more I thought, the more I wondered. The bodies and faces were too similar. Change the hair and,'' Mac laughed, ''Kona becomes Fire.''

''But they were both in there together.'' There was an unasked question in Marge's voice. ''Kona was everywhere, helping.''

''Kona, the angel, just too good to be true. In all that time,'' Mac continued, ''I never saw them together.'' He chuckled. ''I guess no one ever did. Kona would appear, help the hostages, then disappear into the kitchen, and later Fire would appear in the lobby. After the fake argument I heard between them, I thought Kona was avoiding Fire.''

Mac leaned over and took the remains of Marge's chocolate cake, swallowing it in one bite. ''Bad for your diet, dear.'' Licking his fingers, he continued. ''They even smelled the same, white ginger. It's a haunting fragrance. All along, I had a strong gut feeling that Fire didn't plan to die when the hostages were executed. To escape, she had to have a plan. She dove off the cliff. I finally decided that the high dive was part of her escape plan. It had to be timed perfectly. She hadn't counted on the rough weather, but once under the waves it wouldn't make any difference, if she didn't have to surface. That meant an underground cave and a lava tube.

Molokai's honeycombed with them.

Marge looked at her husband's face again, smiling in admiration.

"Fire grew up there. Knew every foot of the place. Swam like a fish. It would take a lot of guts to dive off that cliff into a small pool among the rocks, but I never doubted her courage, or her determination. Just before she dove, with her rifle pointed at me, Fire said, 'Aloha, Mac McGregor.' How did Fire know my name? She had never met me. But Kona had." Mac took a sip of his coffee. "Just suppose Fire survived the dive. Where was she hiding? It could have been anyplace. But every time I thought of Fire, I smelled white ginger, and saw Kona's face, and her long, black hair.

"When we first turned back, I was going to ask Donahue to check out Fire and Kona's backgrounds to see if they really were sisters. When we got off the plane, I decided I had to see for myself. It was a risk. But Kona was just so beautiful, I had to ask her for a lock of her hair."

They finished their coffee in silence. The stewardess took away their trays, and Mac adjusted his chair for a nap. His hand reached out for Marge's, then he spoke again. "Maybe, in a few months, we'll go back to the Molokai-Surf."

Marge squeezed his hand. "I'd love to."

"It's really a great place. I'm thinking of starting a collection of lucky beans."

Marge laughed.

Mac leaned closer, whispering, "Maybe this retirement won't be so bad after all. So far, it hasn't been too boring."

Marge looked at Mac. He was grinning from ear to ear.

LAWRENCE SANDERS

"America's Mr. Bestseller"

___THE FIRST DEADLY SIN	08169-9 — $4.50
___THE MARLOW CHRONICLES	07463-3 — $3.50
___THE PASSION OF MOLLY T.	07960-0 — $4.50
___THE PLEASURES OF HELEN	07695-4 — $3.50
___THE SECOND DEADLY SIN	07155-3 — $3.95
___THE SIXTH COMMANDMENT	08012-9 — $3.95
___THE TANGENT FACTOR	07156-1 — $3.50
___THE TANGENT OBJECTIVE	07281-9 — $3.50
___THE TENTH COMMANDMENT	08096-X — $3.95
___THE TOMORROW FILE	07641-5 — $3.95
___THE THIRD DEADLY SIN	07172-3 — $3.95
___THE ANDERSON TAPES	07503-6 — $3.50
___THE CASE OF LUCY BENDING	07640-7 — $3.95

Prices may be slightly higher in Canada.

Available at your local bookstore or return this form to:

 BERKLEY
Book Mailing Service
P.O. Box 690, Rockville Centre, NY 11571

Please send me the titles checked above. I enclose _____. Include 75¢ for postage and handling if one book is ordered; 25¢ per book for two or more not to exceed $1.75. California, Illinois, New York and Tennessee residents please add sales tax.

NAME_____

ADDRESS_____

CITY_____STATE/ZIP_____

(allow six weeks for delivery)   22

Bestselling Books from Berkley — action-packed for a great read

___	$3.95 07657-1	**DAI-SHO** Marc Olden
___	$3.50 07324-6	**DAU** Ed Dodge
___	$3.95 08002-1	**DUNE** Frank Herbert
___	$3.95 08158-3	**RED SQUARE** Edward Topol and Fridrikh Neznansky
___	$3.95 07019-0	**THE SEDUCTION OF PETER S.** Lawrence Sanders
___	$4.50 07652-0	**DYNASTY: THE NEW YORK YANKEES 1949 — 1964** Peter Golenbock
___	$3.95 07197-9	**THE WORLD WAR II QUIZ AND FACT BOOK** Timothy B. Benford
___	$2.95 06391-7	**JOURNEY INTO FEAR** Eric Ambler
___	$2.95 07060-3	**THE KHUFRA RUN** Jack Higgins writing as James Graham
___	$3.50 06424-7	**SCARFACE** Paul Monette
___	$3.50 07372-6	**THE BILLION DOLLAR BRAIN** Len Deighton
___	$4.50 07664-4	**INFAMY: PEARL HARBOR AND ITS AFTERMATH** John Toland
___	$3.50 06534-0	**THE KILLING ZONE: MY LIFE IN THE VIETNAM WAR** Frederick Downs

Prices may be slightly higher in Canada.

Available at your local bookstore or return this form to:

B **BERKLEY**
Book Mailing Service
P.O. Box 690, Rockville Centre, NY 11571

Please send me the titles checked above. I enclose _____. Include 75¢ for postage and handling if one book is ordered; 25¢ per book for two or more not to exceed $1.75. California, Illinois, New York and Tennessee residents please add sales tax.

NAME _____

ADDRESS _____

CITY _____ STATE/ZIP _____

(Allow six weeks for delivery.)   **BB**